$ 30,99

THE LOVE NOTE

THE LOVE NOTE

JOANNA DAVIDSON POLITANO

THORNDIKE PRESS
A part of Gale, a Cengage Company

LIBRARY OF CONGRESS CIP DATA ON FILE.
CATALOGUING IN PUBLICATION FOR THIS BOOK
IS AVAILABLE FROM THE LIBRARY OF CONGRESS.

ISBN-13: 978-1-4328-8623-3 (hardcover alk. paper)

Published in 2021 by arrangement with Revell Books, a division of Baker Publishing Group

Printed in Mexico
Print Number: 01   Print Year: 2021

This is for the #POstables —
especially Amy, Joy, and Crissy.
You are all a joy to know.

ONE

There are two ways to truly know a person — one is to begin a friendship with them. The other is to end it.

~A scientist's observations on love

Brighton, England, 1865

It always came to this, didn't it? Amid the glittering swirl of music and gowns, I looked up into the handsome face of Lord Cumberland and forced a smile as if nothing at all were about to happen.

He leaned close. "It's time we spoke privately."

No. No, not privately. I looked up, willing it not to be so, but his face was sober. Determined. *Decided.*

And things had been going so well between us.

I tried to swallow. Tried and failed. The grand affair swelled around me, sparkling beneath the crystal chandeliers. The vibrant

7

music, the swish of gowns and shoes, faded into the background as our eyes met over the cup of cider he handed me with a lingering touch, and I couldn't look away. Good gracious, how I wanted to, but his gaze was relentless. Searching. Full of anticipation. Of course, to make matters worse, he was terribly handsome in that dark and reckless sort of way. Bows continued to hum over violin strings, shoes beating a rhythm on the wood floor, as if life weren't shifting dramatically in this shadowed corner by the drink table.

Cumberland glanced toward my father, the great Dr. Phineas Duvall, who was spouting his opinions to a senator and two solicitors across the grand parlor, then back to me with a self-satisfied smile. Unfortunately, the coast was clear. "Suppose we stroll out to the balcony?"

I was going to be sick. I forced a brilliant smile. "Oh, come now, I've hardly danced."

His brows knit. "Are there other men with whom you were hoping to dance?"

"Of course not." Too quick. Too eager. My voice had pitched higher than old widow Tarskin's roof. I took his arm, looking straight ahead at the dreaded balcony where words would be exchanged and futures altered.

Staring down the barrel of my fourth marriage proposal left me cold and shaky. I had no remedy in our little clinic for what I now faced, no antidote to reverse it.

An evening breeze slipped through the curtains from the balcony and cooled my face. "You'd have me catch my death, would you?" I kept my tone light and swept toward the waiter carrying a tray of tarts. I turned back to make another cheeky comment, but Lord Cumberland's eyes were brimming with the unasked question.

"Just for a moment." He moved close and I felt his breath. "I promise to keep you warm."

My arms prickled inside my long gloves. His voice felt invasive. Intimate. I glanced around for Father, but he had stepped out, likely to discuss the never-ending research for his new clinic. How I wish I could trade that discussion for the one being thrust upon me.

Cumberland leaned down, his hand cupping my elbow. "Come now, you know I'm a gentleman."

But I *didn't* know. How could I? With chaperoned outings and puddle-deep conversations, we were strangers. Yet he was about to suggest we share a home, our lives, ourselves, for good. Oh, heavens.

What was *wrong* with me, anyway? Hadn't men and women been stepping into such a promise for centuries? Willingly, no less.

With an impulsive smile, I grabbed his hand. "Come. I've not given you your dance yet."

His look darkened. "There's no need —"

"Of course there is." I could be relentless too. "I promised you, didn't I? And I never make a promise I don't intend to keep. Ever." I let my gaze linger, but his expression didn't register understanding. Only frustration at the interruption to his plans.

With a set jaw, he swept me into the dance, and the familiar rhythm pulled us along.

His voice was terse. Acidic. "I suppose this is the most privacy you will afford me tonight, so I'll simply have to pose my question here."

"What could two friends have to say to one another that couldn't be said on a dance floor?" He'd been *such* a good friend too. Quite diverting.

He spun me close in the waltz. "You know I want more, Miss Duvall." His mint-laced breath washed over my face. Deeper meaning darkened his eyes.

Innocent. Look innocent. Smile. "Nothing is greater than friendship."

10

"Willa —"

"Especially when I'm so busy helping Father. He has more patients than he can tend, and plans for a most brilliant clinic."

"You wouldn't have to do that anymore. I'm offering you a fine home in Manchester."

Offering four walls, closing in around me.

"I'm trying to rescue you from all this. You don't deserve what's been heaped upon you."

Rescue me from a rich and glorious life, working beside a most beloved father? Rescue me from saving lives, from pouring myself out for the broken and desperately needy? And he was right — I had done nothing to deserve the beauty and richness of my life.

His arms framed me in a way that was strong and guiding, yet restrictive. "Please. I can give you everything you desire."

But no one seemed to recognize what that was — least of all the men who proposed.

My heart sifted through tender memories from earlier this day. A new child entering the world. A man whose foot had been spared by my work and a girl whose life had been saved. I had saved a life. A whole *life*. How could anyone think I'd wish that taken away from me? We twirled faster and harder, my heart thudding the rhythm.

I recalled the girl's mum clinging to that dear child, sobbing in messy relief. Even now I had a lump in my throat thinking about it. I wasn't ready to stop having days like this. Not for any man in the world. I lifted my chin and looked directly into his handsome face. "I'm sorry, but I cannot accept your offer."

He blinked. "You are refusing me?"

"Most apologetically, but firmly." I was probably the only girl who would. Myles Cumberland was a squire's son, well-educated and handsome to boot.

His neat mustache twitched. "After all the time we've spent together, I demand a reason."

"As for the time together, my reason is simply that I enjoyed your company as another human being. As for the refusal . . . I cannot say." How desperately I wished to, for the truth burned my tongue, but I restrained myself. There lay the problem with every failed courtship I'd ever experienced — the men had expected to lay claim to all I was, minus my brain. Female intelligence was an unwelcome intruder in every romance. But why? *Why?*

The music crescendoed and his voice grew

loud. Urgent. "I must request that you tell me."

I racked my brain, but found it overrun with patient data, clinical trials, and the periodic table, of all things. "We are not suited. Oil and water. Sodium and nitrogen."

He frowned. "Sodium and . . . ?"

"Nitrogen is stable, and sodium would never react with it. In fact, sodium is stored —"

"In the queen's English, please."

I sighed. "There's no combustion, no change to either element. They're a terrible combination." His eyes narrowed, and I pushed myself to land closer to the truth. "I do not have feelings for you that a wife should possess for her husband."

"Perhaps I can change your mind."

Not unless you can change yourself. I cut my thoughts short before they tumbled out of my mouth. "I'm sorry, but my answer is firm. I cannot marry you."

He glared with the threat of argument in his eye.

Louder. Firmer. I collided into his arms as he stopped. "Myles, I do *not* love you."

I froze in the sudden awareness that the music had ended — before I'd made my bold pronouncement. Chittering laughter and whispers filled the silence, and heat spidered up my face.

He stepped back and cleared his throat, voice low and private. "Well, now. It must be true, for you've ensured there are a hundred witnesses to verify your blatant lack of affection."

"Myles, please don't —"

"Good evening, Miss Duvall." He bowed deeply. "Good evening, and goodbye."

I escaped home and up to my attic room with a sickened heart, a biting conscience, and a burgundy-colored stain on my gown where I'd collided with someone's drink. Fanny, our only maid, loosened the fastenings of my gown, then I dismissed her in a fit of agitation and pulled off the heavy gown myself. I had yet to face Father, who had buried himself deep in conversation at the reception. Hopefully the carriage had already returned for him so he wouldn't be stranded long. I let down my hair, the great untamable mass of curls, and finished undressing.

Down to my chemise and stays, I donned a soft wrapper and shoved aside the notebooks and medical journals cluttering my desk. A little framed portrait smiled up at me and I leaned close to it. "Mama, I said no again." I touched her face, forever preserved in the sepia-colored daguerreotype. It was a strange, rather starkly empty world when one's mother was no longer in it, but here in this private attic dormer room, I felt traces of her. "I said no this morning to a doctor who tried to brush aside my concerns, and I saved a girl's life. Then I said no to a man who wished to marry me . . . and I believe I saved my own." I laid my cheek on the desk, tracing her gentle eyes. "Are you terribly disappointed?"

Her warm smile made it impossible to think she would be.

Yet the truth remained. I had a problem. Spinsterhood was setting in like a malignant disease, and I had an adverse reaction to the only remedy — marriage. I pulled out my lined notebook and fitted the last nib to my pen. It was time to address the illness, look for patterns, and determine an acceptable treatment.

The inevitable result of any friendship with the opposite gender seems to be, unequivocally, romance and matrimony — or a complete break. Therefore, the solution is that I must either give myself over to such a fate or end all friendships with the entire male population.

I recalled the bouncing lanterns of Lord Cumberland's retreating carriage. Perhaps a lack of men in my life wouldn't be terrible.

How anyone can find a remedy of any sort in —

The nib popped off my pen and went flying, rolling into the dark crevice on the left side of the desk. I attacked the little space with a hat pin, threading the nib out, and something crinkled as the nib inched out. I prodded deeper. A lovely vellum envelope appeared, still folded and sealed with wax, the corners softened by years. How long had it been there? I looked over the unmarked missive with delight, only hesitating a moment before breaking the seal and feasting on the lines meant for someone else.

Dear one,

I have no business writing to you, and I'm not certain I'll even have the courage to deliver this, but I must open my overfull heart and let it spill onto the page. I have no right to care for you, but it simply wasn't a choice. You inspired in me a passion both bright and deep when

I wasn't looking, and I cannot help but feel you are a sort of clever thief. As I've watched your nature unfold, it leaves me breathless with wonder and profound respect for who you are, and involuntarily craving more of you.

Lest you think my affections misplaced, let me remind you that I've known you long enough to see it all. I've seen the strength and kindness you believe go unnoticed, watched when you thought no one was looking, and observed what exists below the surface. I know your strengths, and I know most of your weaknesses too — know them and appreciate them as part of the person I have come to admire deeply, the one who has now utterly and unexpectedly captured my heart after all this time. I marvel at the way you are, those strengths and weaknesses woven so deftly together, driving you through life with such passion and sometimes holding you back until I simply want to wrap my arms around you and whisper everything I've tried to say in this letter.

I even know that secret you hoped to keep from everyone. Yes, I know all of it, and I choose you in spite of — or maybe because of — all those things. I choose

17

those unbelievable strengths, those weaknesses you try to hide — every bit of it because it's all you, and I choose you. Every day, every moment, I choose you.

You needn't feel any obligation concerning me. My deepest wish is simply to openhandedly offer up to you these words of affection, that you might walk through your day knowing someone loves you and finds you remarkable. Dearest, if only you could see yourself from where I stand — how brave and unstoppable you would become. I want that for you, more than I want a return for my affection.

If this letter finds you favorably disposed toward me, I'll be happy beyond all comprehension. If I hear nothing from you, I will cut all ties to Crestwicke and go far away, for I cannot bear to remain. Even then I would not forget you. Every time I smell forget-me-nots, I will think of you . . . and remember.

Warmly, your most affectionate
and ardent admirer

I drank it all in, the painfully authentic words wrapping themselves around my heart, and I could not look away. I'd made the right decision each time I'd said no, because every romance I'd ever encountered was nothing compared to the passion and devotion in this single page. What a farce they all seemed in comparison.

I fitted nib to pen and wrote again.

My adverse response to the cure of spinsterhood may indicate a problem with the treatment rather than the patient. The missing ingredient in the tonics I've been offered is authenticity. A thick coating of that, and I should be able to swallow any marriage without breaking out in hives.

Alas, most of the men with that virtue have already become someone else's antidote to spinsterhood . . .

I pushed aside my notes and tucked my legs up to my chest, returning to that wonderful letter, both giddy and enchanted with my find. I had a healthy obsession with love stories, after all — as long as they were not mine. I read it again, and a surge of energy bore through me, like a calling. What had happened to its writer, and why had it never been delivered?

When I came to the name "Crestwicke," an idea took shape, like a silent whisper answering my morning prayer for direction.

I blinked at its brilliance and wondered if I had the audacity to see it through.

Low voices below distracted me. A door slammed. When footfall pounded on the stairs, the rail creaking under the force of Father's grasp, I had an instinctive urge to flee. I shoved the letter into a drawer and rose, fumbling in my wardrobe for a simple front-button frock.

Trinkets rattled on the hall table as Father pounded toward my room.

Bang, bang. His fist rattled the door. "Willa!"

I stiffened. "I need to dress."

He shuffled in the hall as he always did when presented with such awkward declarations. He used to pass me off to Mother at this point, God rest her. "Things went well with your suitor?"

I buried my face in a clean dress and cringed, then slipped the simple thing over my stays. "I should say not." *Please don't ask, please don't ask.*

More shuffling. "So. He did not propose yet."

I braced myself, awash in prickly heat. My silence answered his question.

He growled and banged the door with his fist again. "What are you *thinking*? Four proposals, Willa. *Four!*"

My nervous fingers fiddled with the buttons as I tried to fit them into the holes that seemed to have suddenly shrunk. "What of it?"

"That's four fine men who entered our home with hopes for a future with you and left empty-handed." Then he asked the question I dreaded. *"Why?"*

I leaned against the metal bed rail. "Oh Papa, we weren't suited." When faced with the men who offered to share their various homes, freedom always seemed sweeter and ripe with possibilities in comparison.

"Aaargh. At least come up with a new excuse! Some man pours his heart out and asks for your hand, and the only word in your foolish little head is *no*?"

"My soul cringes at the idea of marrying any of them, Father. Please understand."

He exhaled, and I could imagine him looking heavenward as if begging the Almighty for patience. "What am I expected to do with you? You are breaking hearts, girl."

"You overestimate their affection for me, Father." The only reason they'd offered for me at all, I was convinced, is because I'd kept my hands busy and my lips closed in their presence. They noticed my vigorous efficiency about Father's clinic, my prudent nursing nature, and they thought how well those skills would be applied in their own homes. Yet there was so much about me they didn't know — or care to know.

How is your dear aunt these days? She's well, thank you, but she has a touch of the stiffness. Did you enjoy the jaunt into town? I hear the queen has ordered new curtains for the third largest parlor in Osborne House. That's all my courtships had ever amounted to, and every fiber of my being craved to be worth more.

Explaining this to Father would be useless, for he had chosen my own dear mother on their second meeting, and they had been inseparable. Embarrassingly so, at times.

His second wife, my honored stepmother, had wheedled her way into our home after two years of "assisting the widowed doctor," and theirs was a functional relationship. "It's good to have someone," he'd said when announcing his engagement, and my ten-year-old self had wondered why I was not a "someone." Despite the countless hours I had spent assisting in his research, caring for his patients, all I poured into his dream to open Brighton's first hot springs clinic, marriage was the only solution he saw to his problems — and mine, apparently.

22

Yet I shivered every time I thought of all the people dying in London's hospitals, and I knew *that* was the problem I wanted to solve. I crossed to the door, leaning my back against it. "Let me make a go of it, won't you? I could take nursing positions, earn my own tuition for university." I had one life to spend, and I wanted to use it on those who truly needed me. I would be different than all those busy, overworked doctors in hospitals, and I would save people.

"All the funds in the world won't help if they all refuse you admission."

"One. Only *one* school rejected my application. But Durham will consider a woman eventually, I'm sure of it. They're progressive, I've heard. And next week is the general election — anything could happen, if Darby's government doesn't gain majority in the house."

A growl rumbled deep in his chest. "What'll you do if nothing changes? Become a spinster?"

"There are worse things a body could be." I rested my fingertips on the paneled door. *I saved a life today, Father. Fought for a little girl and won. She's with her mother now because of me. Because of what you taught me. Aren't you proud?*

"You'll be forever shuffling about my

23

house, eating at my table when you're thirty. When will you grow up and make something of yourself?"

I stepped back and perched on the edge of my bed, the burden of my very existence weighing me to the quilted cover. How did he do that? They were mere words, but everything the man said had the ability to pierce deep and remain lodged in my heart, my world forming around them.

"Cumberland has offered you security, comfort, and ease."

None of which I wanted. I closed my eyes, willing this man who had raised me to understand. I'd spent years of my life buried in reports and clinical studies, poring over design ideas for the very modern and sterile hot springs clinic Father meant to open. I'd given up socials and plays, trips to town and all novels, to devote myself to perfecting his dream — *our* dream. A contrast to London's "death halls," it was needed. *I* was needed — and not as a manager of some man's home. "I'd never make a suitable wife, Father. I'm not cut out for it. I'm meant to heal and serve and study medicine. Like you."

His voice had a gruff edge to it. "It's time you find your own way. Not mine. You're four and twenty, and you need a home of your own." He sighed. "It's that infernal Blackwell woman, isn't it?"

I clenched my fist at the mention of her sacred name — one that was now recorded in the General Medical Council's Medical Register. It was the first female name there, which opened up the possibility for a second. "Won't you let me —"

"No."

"Not even a small —"

"What part of no isn't clear?" He spun, mumbling down the hall.

"Papa, wait. What if I promise . . ." I gulped. The boot clomps paused. "Promise to consider marriage if it doesn't work?" That's how drastically I believed in my passion. I staked my freedom on it.

A shuffle. "Without argument?"

"I have an idea." Rising, I walked back to my little teakwood writing desk and dipped the pen tip.

I, Willa Duvall of Brighton, do solemnly vow and promise to return and entertain more proposals in the event that I am not able to successfully complete one long-term nursing assignment. However, if I am successful, I will be allowed to pursue a medical education and never be forced to marry.

25

I whipped it off my desk and shoved it under the door with a swish. Grumbling reached my ears from the other side. I pictured the great Dr. Phineas Duvall lowering those dark thundercloud eyebrows and whipping the pen from behind his ear to sign. I heard intense scribbling against the door as I picked at the hem of my sleeve, then the note was shoved back under the door. *Swish.*

I, Willa Duvall of Brighton, do solemnly vow and promise to return and ~~entertain more proposals~~ **immediately marry the man of my father's choosing** in the event that I am not able to successfully complete one long-term nursing assignment **within one month's time.**

I frowned at the change, then added one of my own.

Nursing situation to be chosen by Willa without complaint from her father.

Swish. It was shoved again, and I waited. More scribbles. I chewed my fingernails — when did I *ever* do that?

The day I considered signing my independence away, apparently. I reached for the knob to fling open the door and retract the deal, but it was too late. *Swish*. The contract came back.

Signed.

I lifted it with shaky fingers and read it several times without truly digesting it all. I stood on the edge of a precipice. Soon I'd be a full-fledged medical student — or a wife.

Checking to ensure my hastily donned frock covered everything necessary, I opened the door and stared at Father, taking in the long gray frown of his mustache, arms folded over his broad chest as if letting nothing penetrate his heart.

I'd seen the list of his patients requesting a nurse, but I didn't even have to think about which name I'd choose. I lifted my chin, thoughts of that beautiful letter making me bold. "I choose Golda Gresham at Crestwicke."

"Crestwicke?" He paled, a red vein protruding on his forehead, then those stormcloud eyebrows lowered.

Crestwicke Manor stood on the salty coast outside of Brighton, a rambling old Tudor structure of dark wood and shadowed mysteries — much like my lovely desk that had come from it. Its walls contained one

Golda Gresham, in need of a nurse, as well as the writer of that enchanting letter.

Father's powerful gaze that could wither full-grown men on the hospital board was now directed at me. "*Gresham's* Crestwicke?" A growl vibrated his chest. "Out of the question."

I simply pointed a steady finger at the last line. He was allowed no arguments. If he insisted on choosing my husband, I was owed that.

His eyes flashed. "No, no, no, *no!*" He kicked the wall, rattling the little bottles on my dresser.

Footsteps hurried up the stairs, and Thelma's generous, pudgy face with too-close eyes appeared on the landing behind Father, shadowed by the lamp she carried. Compared to my beautiful mother, she was, like her position here, merely serviceable. "Phineas?"

Father handed her the paper we'd signed. The very gown about my ribs seemed to constrict as I stood before them, waiting for her appraisal.

"She chose Crestwicke." Father growled and slapped the paper with the back of his hand. *"Crestwicke."*

She looked up at both of us with raised eyebrows, her face like the lump of dough she kneaded every evening. I held my breath. Sometimes life hinges on a few words, and these were the ones that would pivot mine: "Crestwicke it is, then."

My breath gushed out.

His eyes widened. "You can't be serious, woman."

"There are some things, Phineas, that you eventually must let her decide for herself." She sent Father a look heavy with meaning.

When the door closed behind them, I dug out that wonderful letter and read it four more times, losing myself in the poetry of its lines. How beautiful it was. How romantic. Languishing for years in a dark crack of my old desk, this letter had waited for the right person to find it — one who would become enchanted by its contents and do something with it. I, the spinster scientist who had just rejected yet another suitor, was the keeper of this letter, and nothing could be more fitting. Normally I heal people's bodies for a living. Now I hoped to heal hearts as well.

Downstairs, I touched my stepmother on the arm as she kneaded dough with the strength of a cart horse. We had a maid-of-all-work, but bread was her specialty and she insisted on torturing herself this way. "Thank you, Thelma."

She turned, wiping her forehead with the back of her floury hand, and gave a single nod. Her eyes searched mine as if wishing to connect to something there. "I know what it is to love someone deeply. Every girl ought to have that chance."

I studied this woman with whom I'd shared a house for many years and wondered at the soft heart that beat within her sturdy chest. "Father?"

She turned away and kneaded harder, her bent neck mottled with rosy color. "He's a fine man, that Phineas Duvall. A fine, fine man."

I was speechless.

"You'd best win yourself a husband at Crestwicke or you'll come back to find one waiting for you." She cut through the dough with a long knife, then brandished the tool in my direction with narrowed eyes. "And whatever you do, keep that tongue in your head. Hear me? *In your head!*" She swatted my cheek with her floury hand for good measure.

"Words have always been my secret weapon."

She glanced at me, a tiny sparkle in her eyes. "Aye, and you have a quiver full of them."

I smiled as I backed away, thinking of the

powerful words in that letter. Maybe being in the presence of such a raw and beautiful love story, of helping two souls find their end of the rainbow in each other, would finally inspire my own.

Because secretly, very secretly, much as I feared it, I did wish to fall in love. I just hadn't any idea who . . . or how to still be who I was.

I pictured Crestwicke Manor, that proud old country house hunched on the coast watching decades of shipwrecks and sunsets and lovers on the beach. Somewhere in those vast ivy-covered walls lived a person who was about to have the happiest surprise ever.

As long as it wasn't too late.

TWO

Perhaps I'd be more inclined to fall in love
if it didn't require a fall.

~A scientist's observations on love

A still, white face looked down at me from high up in the ivy-covered mansion as my hired carriage crunched up the lane the following Tuesday. My heart seized. *I'm coming for you. Just you wait. Help is on the way, Golda Gresham, and it'll change everything.* Clutching my hat to my head against the sea breeze, I closed my eyes and inhaled the briny air of Crestwicke Manor and felt alive.

Yes. Yes, this was my purpose. I tightened my wrap against the cool spring air. Let them all pity and scorn me, threatening me with years of solitude. Loneliness and regret had no place in the life of a woman who was so needed. Why wait on marriage when there was considerable life in the journey? Even if that trek lasted my whole life, the path would be rich and beautiful.

I slid the note into my apron pocket, ready for the time I'd have a chance to compare the handwriting to papers about the house. I held my hand against it. *Help is on the way for you too — whoever you are.* Then I stood at the edge of my new adventure, looking up at the manor house that regarded me with an imperial air as only a Gresham could.

I paid my driver and climbed the windswept steps, a shiver overtaking me. Five years it had been since my last visit here with Father, but the place was still just as heavy with carefully guarded secrets and veiled reality. In childhood, I'd called that "haunted."

A tall liveried servant welcomed me at the door, and I explained my errand.

"Welcome to Crestwicke, miss."

He extended a hand to receive my straw traveling hat and then my valise and carpetbag. I declined surrendering my medical bag, which gave me confidence as I clutched it.

Soon I was being ushered into the deeply private home of the Gresham family. I'd seldom been inside, I realized now. The stallions and the beach had always captured my girlish attention when Father had come to call on Mr. Gresham, and the rambling old house had scared me a little.

The butler set my hat on the side table and my bags on the floor, and scurried off with my card, leaving me in the foyer that was as silent as a forest at dawn. I cast long glances around this unsettling place that was so much dimmer inside than out. Musty old sorrows clung to the thick carpet and papered walls, the glow of candles neglecting the unexplored corners. It could be so beautiful, if it were allowed to be. The ancient windows seemed to groan with the weight of drapes that might be drawn back, allowing light to warm their leaded glass surfaces. Healing and restoration awaited this household, and I was itching to begin.

On second glance, my eyes locked onto an ancient face watching from a balcony above in the mezzanine. Her eerie stare jolted me.

"It's you, is it? There you are, there you are. Back at last."

"Yes." I struggled with what else to say. Perhaps she didn't even know who I was. I certainly didn't recognize her.

A smile drew her face into folds. "Thrilling and filling. So it begins, little Miss Duvall."

Cold spidered up my spine as she spoke

my name. She had the air of a defunct old cannon from which one had no idea what to expect, or whether or not it would be safe. "What do you mean?"

She cackled. "As if you don't know. Stupendelicious!"

"I've come as —"

"I know why you've come." The words dropped heavily from her lips.

I blushed to the roots of my hair, as if the woman could see through my apron pocket to the letter that had driven me to Crestwicke. The butler returned and beckoned me. Removing myself gladly from the odd encounter, I followed the man who introduced himself as Parker.

"In here, miss." The man knocked and the door swung open to reveal none other than the heir of the estate in a dark suit and stunning green cravat — Burke Gresham.

The man's bold smile beamed down at the butler. "Ah, Parker. What a pleasant diversion. Has the post arrived?"

Burke Gresham's commanding presence struck me with full force, lighting something in me. Perhaps it was only the lingering apprehension left by the encounter with the odd woman, but from what I remembered of him, no one could go toe to toe with me quite as well.

"Yes, sir." The butler held out the mail on a salver. "But so has something else." He stepped aside when the mail was collected and gestured me forward.

I had the fleeting notion that Burke might be the letter writer, for he was unmatched in both passion and frankness. Yet there was a softness to the letter I didn't sense in him.

"Good day, Mr. Gresham." I graced him with my most winning smile and a curtsey. "I've come to assist your mother as her nurse."

Golden eyebrows arched over the man's face. "You may return the way you came." His posture brooked no argument as he backed into the room again, flipping through the envelopes. "My sincerest apologies, but we are not in need of a nurse. Good day." The door closed on the end of his sentence.

I blinked at the dark paneled wood so unexpectedly shut in my face. Shock rippled as I turned back toward the foyer with a hard, angry pivot. But returning home, the contract . . . shock curled into dread. Fear.

In a moment of lightheaded panic, I saw a sleek stallion through the narrow window ahead, a horse bucking wildly against his harness. A tall, brawny man lunged to grab the bridle and wrangle him back down.

A creature in bonds who was meant to be free. If I returned, that was my fate, as well. Yet what could I do? Closed doors behind me, dead ends ahead — and an unfinished love story in my pocket.

My hand curled around it. No. I would not be forced. I would not concede before I'd even begun to fight. I'd been brushed aside my whole life, and becoming a doctor would change that. The only way to achieve that goal was to succeed right now.

Squaring my shoulders, I forced back the swirling panic and spun toward the study. I rapped hard and the door opened. Burke Gresham's cravat had been loosened as if he were about to retire with his feet up in the smoking lounge. He stopped opening his mail and cocked an eyebrow. "You don't accept refusals lying down, do you?" His pointed stare seemed to demand an explanation as to why I was wasting his valuable time.

"Your mother sent for a nurse weeks ago, and I've come to fulfill her request."

"This isn't the sort of case you believe it to be. I'm saving you a world of trouble by sending you on your way, believe me." He turned away, silver letter opener slicing through another envelope.

"I'm well-versed in practical medicine and

have a wide scope of experience. More so than most nurses, thanks to my father." He frowned, but I pressed on, fighting an impending sense of meekness. "I've trained at Miss Abernathy's in Kent, assisted under Miss Florence Nightingale in Crimea. I've made the highest marks . . ."

His gaze flicked past me to the clock in the hall. He was not amused. My thoughts disintegrated as sand slipping through the hourglass, and I scrambled to catch the last grains.

"I've studied the newest methods of care, and we have —"

"Argh!" He hurled the letter opener onto his desk and clutched his palm, as it oozed with dark red blood.

As he fumbled about for a handkerchief, I stepped forward and flipped a clean wrap from my bag, pressing it to the gash, then dabbing the injury with iodine. "You really ought to cleanse that weapon before you go brandishing it about."

A pointed stare of annoyance hardened his features. "I had no intention of using it on my hand. Now will you kindly take your leave?"

"Mr. Gresham." I wrapped his injury and spoke with quiet calm, as if he did not have the power to change the direction of my life.

"One day you will be in her place, and I pray your children will embrace you with all your infirmities and needs rather than casting you into some lonely room of the house." I couldn't erase the memory of that white face in the upper window.

Something flickered deep within his green eyes. Regret, maybe guilt. His jaw flinched.

"If you'll only allow me to help, I think you'll be pleasantly surprised with my care." I tied the bandage and stood back, arms folded.

He flexed his fingers. "This will be more complex than binding cuts. Are you aware of the type of woman you've come to serve?"

"I've seen her from afar." I stoppered my iodine bottle and replaced it in my bag as he attempted to usher me out.

"She's a challenge on her best day, and now . . . well, she's become downright impossible. Too impossible for the likes of you." He stepped back, preparing to shut me out once again. "Good day, Miss Duvall."

I jammed my boot against the closing door. "I happen to specialize in impossible." I met his gaze, daring him to challenge me. I sensed a foothold in the silence that followed. "Please, at least let me try. I'm known for turning patients around in quick order, convincing them to cooperate better than any doctor."

His jaw flinched and he studied me. "Is that right? Complete cooperation?"

"And for being utterly forthright and plainspoken in every way, which can only be an asset to you both."

"I see." Burke pursed his full lips, head angled. "Very well, Miss Duvall, we'll let you try." He tucked his good hand under my elbow. "Come with me. But don't bother to unpack."

I inhaled with a smile, and a lovely cedar and black tea aroma greeted me as we turned down a long passage, the homey scent smoothing the edges of my tension. I parted from Burke to collect my carpetbag as we passed the door but paused at the sight of something now tucked into the ribbon of my hat — lacy pink petals.

My smile flickered. *Gabe was here!*

I held a satin petal to my lips and smiled at the memory of the charmingly awkward horse trainer fumbling the name of the little flower — *"Ammenome." "No, anemone."* Years ago, he was the only adult to let me follow him about, to tolerate me prattling on in my girlish way. Where was he now? I'd ask him about the letter. Gabe Gresham, brother to Burke yet so vastly different, knew more than anyone suspected because he so seldom spoke but heard everything.

"Right this way, Miss Duvall." Burke beckoned me down a narrow hall that seemed to disappear into a bleak eternity.

In the gallery, I glanced up at the balcony where the ancient woman of mystery had looked down upon me. "Who is the woman I met earlier?"

Burke turned with a question darkening his brow.

"I saw her observing from a balcony, with a lace cap and —"

"Ah, her." Burke stood beside me in the gallery, arms clasped behind his back. "That's only Crazy Maisie, our ancient aunt, who roams about muttering nonsense. You mustn't mind her." He waved me on, and we ascended the stairs.

"You'll find your patient takes tea at half past three, two sugars and the red-and-gold filigree cup. She loves red, by the way, and if you don't care for the color, you'd best develop a speedy appreciation for it. Expect to rise early and stay up late, as she detests sleep, as well as anyone who falls prey to it longer than her. Though you will find her 'resting her eyes' throughout the day to make up for it. She has written several volumes of verse, for which you should demonstrate great appreciation. She'll want to break the happy news of their authorship to you herself, so naturally it'll come as a complete surprise."

"Naturally."

"She fancies herself another Longfellow, with all her verses."

"Longfellow, the poet?"

"No one is superior, in her mind, to that revered man of poetry. Now, she's never one to make light of her ailments, real and imagined, and you will be expected to do likewise."

I pinched my lips shut, heeding Step-mother's advice — *keep that tongue in your head!*

We climbed the stairs, and I stared into the painted faces of all three Gresham children, my childhood playmates, and my mind wandered pleasantly, drawing warm memories to the surface. First Burke, then solemn Gabe, and delightful Celeste. We turned down a long, carpeted hall, and there, deep in the shadows of the gallery overlook, hovered a hauntingly beautiful girl with dark hair spilling down her back, large violet eyes watching us from her hiding spot. *Her.*

She was far too young, but my chest ached with certainty. Somehow she had to be the letter writer — or at least connected to the whole thing. No one else in this entire family could be. They were far too modern and busy to birth such deep and poetic thoughts, much less write them down. Yet this young woman held untold depths behind her lovely face, as if she'd witnessed centuries of families and wars and deaths. She'd been observing us in the gallery, that much was clear. What I didn't know was why — or who on earth she was.

Her gaze was hard. Accusatory. Especially when it was directed at me.

Burke sailed past the shadowed corner where the ghostly girl lingered, sweeping us along down the hall. "You'll stay in the little room off of your patient's bedchamber. I assume that will be acceptable."

"Quite."

"Any questions?"

Only about a million, but just one I dared voice. "This might seem odd, but I'd like to know who owned the little writing desk that now sits in my room at home. It was sent to Father in gratitude about two years ago for work he did here."

He frowned. "The little teakwood affair with carved ivy?"

I nodded, unable to even swallow as I awaited his reply. *That girl. It's hers. What's*

43

her name?

"Why, that didn't belong to anyone, really. It sat in the morning room, and everyone in the family did their correspondence there."

We turned a corner and desperation dogged me. I just wanted a glimpse, a little taste of her story. Something to let me know if she matched the letter. "One other question. You've taken in a girl, it seems. Is she a ward, or a cousin?"

His polite smile faded, and he stared at me as if I were mad. "A girl? There's been no girl about the manor since Celeste was small."

The answer jarred me into silence for the remaining few seconds we had alone together, for we'd already reached the closed double doors.

THREE

The words that fill a house seep into the pores of the walls, creating the atmosphere in which you carry out your life. I will choose only a man who speaks vivid color and life into my home.
~A scientist's observations on love

He ushered me into an outdated but tasteful sitting room, with drapes shielding it from the blessing of sunshine. Only a dying fire lit the long room, glowing over the impeccable old furniture that smelled of turpentine.

Then I spotted Golda Gresham, stately and poised as she leaned forward in her striped chair, gripping the carved arms. Age had caught up to this woman no older than my own parents as if she'd never even tried to outrun it, and a hardness had settled into fine parentheses around her mouth. The fire crackled and popped behind her, throwing

45

garish shadows over her unwelcoming face, and the red teacup sat on the table beside her.

Burke addressed her. "You've finally managed to summon a nurse, it would seem. May I present to you Willa Duvall, daughter of Doctor Phineas Duvall. Miss Duvall, your new patient."

Golda Gresham rose in all her red and gold glory, and I could not look away, any more than if she were Queen Victoria herself. Slow, measured treads brought her to the center of the dark room that seemed to hold its breath at what she might say. "So. Some poor little thing has finally braved the position."

She had the same commanding presence as her gregarious son, yet with a fraction of the volume — which somehow made it even more effective. "I rather expected a woman of some experience." She looked me over as an antique broker from Christie's might, assessing every flaw that detracted from a piece's value and cataloging her finds.

A chill passed over me and a dusty old memory crept to the surface. I had, at ten years old, dipped into a philosophical discussion on romance with Burke's younger siblings, Celeste and Gabe, as I faced the reality of walking my own father down the aisle for his second wedding.

"How would I know anything about love? There's not an ounce of it at Crestwicke." Celeste, who was normally one of the few Greshams with any sense, said this to me from atop her tall black horse. *"You'll see when you hang about the house someday. They're simply too busy for it."*

"No one carves out time for such a thing — that's why it's called 'falling in love.' You simply fall, right into it." I smacked my leg. *"One can't help it. Don't you agree, Gabe?"*

Her brother Gabe dipped his gaze, and I could see from his profile that I'd earned one of his rare smiles. *"Sounds dangerous."*

"Oh, it is. Wonderfully so. But it's nothing a person can help, any more than falling out of a barn loft."

"Crestwicke doesn't have those sorts of people," Celeste mused. *"The people here all remain on solid ground, I'm afraid."*

"I pity all of you if that's true." I looked up at the great ivy-covered house on the cliffs sprayed with the sea below and felt a sudden release from lifelong envy. Marriage was only an acceptable fate if love was involved. No amount of wealth could make up for the lack of it.

Celeste sighed, looking up at the grand old estate. *"When one is rich, one cannot afford*

47

to marry for love."

Yet the somber house swelled with deep, authentic love pulsing just beneath the surface, romance buried in shadows, kept away from practical eyes and sharp tongues. I could feel it. Someone had fallen in love the way Alice fell into that rabbit hole. I *would* find them, and the letter *would* be delivered — it was merely a matter of time.

I touched the apron pocket that held the letter. How I wanted a taste of such love myself, like a girl holding out her tongue for the delicate swirling snowflakes. Perhaps that taste would come from a distance, as I reunited the couple. What a delight if it was meant for the woman now poised before me, with a lost love in her past that had folded her so tightly into what she was now — and the letter would unfurl it all.

"You will begin your duties immediately?"

"Of course. I sent word of my arrival, but perhaps it hasn't come yet." I set my valise down to tug my gloves off by each fingertip. "I'll begin with a thorough examination, then I'll ask a few questions about your symptoms and . . ." I fell silent at her look of patronizing amusement, head tipped just so. She twined her lace-covered fingers and waited.

A cat. That's what she reminded me of. I

48

could picture her tail flicking back and forth as she watched me, her every movement weighted with grace. Even her eyes, stunning blue slits that were drawn up in a lovely slant at the corners, watched me with feline detachment.

I'd never been much of a cat lover. My nature more closely resembled a dog, with my bounding eagerness, fierce loyalty, and habit of crashing headlong into things.

She sipped her tea, gaze always on me over the gold rim of the cup. "Why is it you believe you're here, Miss Duvall?"

And now she was playing with me, batting me about and watching to see what I'd do.

"To monitor your chronic health concerns and ensure —"

"Burke, have you told her nothing?"

His low voice came from behind. "I didn't want to take the pleasure away from you."

She lifted a red volume from the table beside her, fingering it tenderly, then handed it to me as if it were a scepter. "I need your assistance to perform . . . these."

My eagerness ground to a swift halt. "Perform?" Perhaps she had misunderstood my profession.

"It's her throat, you see." Burke crossed his arms, eyes snapping with mischief. "There's something the matter with it when

49

she attempts to sing. It tightens on the high notes, gives out on the long notes, general fits of coughing and then a bit of swooning. She needs a nurse to attend her as she practices to help her overcome these . . . ailments."

I raised my eyebrows, uncertain how to take the direction of this conversation. I glanced toward the closed doors. Where was Gabe, anyway? He knew I was here, but he hadn't shown himself yet. Oh how I needed his quiet smile to defuse the tension, to explain in commonsense terms what was happening in this increasingly odd situation.

Burke settled a condescending smile on his mother. "Come, show Miss Duvall the problem and we'll see what can be done about it."

She straightened, a tower of silk poplin and lace, and glared at him. After a reverent pause, she breathed deeply, chin raised as if looking up to a heavenly sphere from which she would draw her music, and released a somber melody that stretched out, reedy and thin. Soon she became lost in it, seeming to forget we were there. Her cheeks grew flushed and her low voice wavered over the tones.

Her singing wasn't intolerable, at least to

my untrained ear, but neither was it pleasant like the full-bodied voices of opera or even pleasant like a second-rate parlor singer. It rose to higher notes, grating on my senses, then shattered at its peak when her voice broke. With a few delicate coughs, she cleared her throat and looked about for tea.

My official diagnosis was swift and complete: an over-abundance of time and wealth complicated by an utter lack of skill and vainglorious delusions. I shoved those ungracious thoughts aside with a gnawing guilt, and a great deal of unease about my future here.

Burke leaned toward me. "Well now, Miss Duvall, you did promise honesty in all matters. I eagerly await your assessment." *Now* he looked amused. His lips curled into a wicked smile. Apparently no one had openly discussed the fact that she simply wasn't a singer, but that shouldn't surprise me. It was the Gresham way of doing things — every unpleasant thing was either ignored or paid out of existence.

"Well?"

I looked away, my instincts at odds with each other. I had promised this family my forthrightness, yet I felt the dire need to tread carefully and protect my new position. I took a breath and settled on another virtue in which I prided myself — thoroughness. One never pronounced a judgment before performing an examination. I turned to the patient. "Open, please." That should buy me a few moments to think, anyway.

She cleared her throat and opened her mouth. I pulled a small mirrored instrument from my bag and held a light up to it, peering into her throat. Then I massaged the outside. There didn't seem to be polyps, or anything truly preventing a prime vocal range. Not every throat, it would seem, was meant to create music. With Stepmother's warning weaving through my thoughts, I pondered and smoothed out every word before releasing it. "It appears the larynx has become inflamed, possibly from strain, which might cause it to tighten around the vocal cords, minimizing its ability to project. With the natural thickening of the vocal flap that comes with maturation —"

"Miss Duvall, are you calling me old?" Her stare held. "I'm not asking you to prepare me for a London stage — merely a few parlors among our acquaintances. Surely I'm capable of that much." She turned her unblinking gaze on me, daring me to contradict her.

I opened my cotton-dry mouth and closed

it again. There was simply no way to be both honest and diplomatic in this moment.

Her eyes glinted like sun against gunmetal. "You cannot expect to be impressed when I haven't a proper warm-up or accompaniment."

Yes, a piano *would* drown out her voice a bit. "I suppose I ought to hear an official rehearsal then." I forced a smile, to which she offered only a deepened glare.

"So you shall."

I released my breath. I was staying — for the moment, at least.

"Right, then." Burke's voice was jarring. "I'll leave you to settle in to your new position, and I'll send the porter after your trunks. I assume they're still in the drive?"

I nodded numbly, and the wretched man bowed and slipped out, closing me into this opulent old chamber with its owner.

So this is what my grand dreams had come to. I had wrested my fate from the hands of no less than four men — five, counting Father — and spent years studying medicine, all so that I could squeeze talent out of this woman like water from a rock and be her glorified pillow when she fainted. Simply lovely.

I looked up and she was still studying me. "Miss Duvall, there is one other reason I've asked you here."

"Oh?" My heart ricocheted. This could be a good turn, one that made everything fall into a sensible order, or it could be bad. Quite bad.

"I assume you are able to remain discreet."

"Of course."

She looked away. "I've brought you here for my protection. You see, they are trying to be rid of me."

My jaw went slack. My utter astonishment was now complete. Experienced as I was, this position was completely out of the scope of my abilities in so many ways.

I stepped carefully out onto the proffered limb. "And who might wish to harm you?"

She frowned, gaze narrowing on me. "You think me paranoid."

"It's possible that you have imagined —"

Her delicate nostrils flared, eyes shooting a warning. "I don't care for you, Miss Duvall." The quietly arresting statement, hardly audible, stabbed me. Yet I had spoken the truth, and I could not regret that.

"Please understand, Mrs. Gresham, it is certainly not a reflection of you or your sterling character, nor of your intelligence."

"Your attempts at flattery fall flat."

My heart began to wither as I gathered the direction this particular assignment was heading, but I forced poise into my spine. "I shall work to improve your opinion of me."

"Don't." She eyed me with open contempt. "It'll only tire you. Simply prepare yourself to stand between me and those who have decided my existence is hindering what they want."

I glanced at my medical bag still slouched by the door where I'd left it as the waters of doubt rose higher. "Why hire a nurse? I'm not a guardian."

"My death is not what they're after, Miss Duvall. At least, not my physical death. Come, sit."

I did. "Perhaps I'm not the most —"

A scrape and a thump sounded below, drawing our gazes to the weakly glowing hearth. A hard look silenced me, then she pointed one slender finger at the fireplace.

"She's up to something, you can be sure of that." It was the voice of Burke Gresham, climbing up the chimney from some distant room below. "She's never allowed a nurse to attend her before, much less requested one, and I've half a mind to force the issue and find out her plan before she gains the upper hand."

Celeste's tight voice sounded next. "And how will you manage that, Burke? No sanatorium will take her based on her exaggerated swooning spells and fictitious complaints."

"An asylum, then."

My throat cinched. I'd been inside such places, and a few moments as a visitor was suffocating. Years as a patient would be unbearable. As much as I despised all institutions, none were worse than asylums.

"She's mad, Cec. I'm telling you, she needs to be sent away, and the business left to me. One wild decision from her could sink us. Foolish woman, always scheming."

Yet not deserving of inhumane captivity. Animals were treated better than residents in those clammy places that echoed with wild cries. I couldn't let this happen. *Where was Gabe?* He would set this to rights, but he was conspicuously missing from the gathering of Gresham siblings below.

"You know Father would never commit her, and Dr. Tillman has already refused to recommend her. How ever would you . . ."

More shuffling. "There is a way. We could be done with her before Father even returns from London, but it has to be handled right."

"But now that a nurse is here —"

"That won't last. You know that. She'll make her miserable and that poor woman will be gone before two shakes. Then our way will be clear."

"How will you convince anyone she's mad? Do you truly believe it yourself?"

Footsteps sounded and the voices faded as they moved away. "Do you know anyone else like her? It's unnatural. Suppose she happened to make a . . ."

Then the voices were gone.

My patient lifted a demur smile in the shadows. "And there you have it, my loving family." She sipped her tea and returned it with a gentle clink to the saucer. "Do you still think me paranoid?"

"You don't belong in an asylum, I know that much." Another thing I knew — my position was a dangerous one, a tenuous tug-of-war between my patient and her grown children, a delicate balance of remaining in this woman's good graces *and* theirs.

And me, with more truth than sense.

"I'm delighted you think so. Now you must, as a certified nurse, convince everyone else of that. They cannot send me away if you declare me fit."

"I'll say what's true." It was the only promise I could make, and I desperately hoped it was enough. Her silence stifled my confidence, stabbing it with memories of

Mother's precious life slipping through my hands so long ago. The harder I had clung, the more she wilted. Then she was gone, even while I held her tight in my childish arms.

That familiar panic swirled up in me now.

My patient looked out the window as she sipped her tea, unmoved by the lightning cutting through the dull gray sky. Low rumbles followed. "It seems a storm is approaching." Another cube of sugar, then a stir. "I do hope you are prepared."

I wasn't.

Several silent moments passed, then Golda turned back to me, summing me up again. "Why is it you've never married, Miss Duvall? Have you found no respectable man willing to take you on?"

This again. Always this. "I've not found a man *I* wish to take on. I've great plans for my future, and much I want to accomplish. There isn't a single man of my acquaintance who might do anything but hinder those plans."

She leaned back in her Queen Anne chair, looking past me with a vague smile. "Well now, there's Gabe."

Gabe? Sometimes it seemed the world had a binary vision — they saw people in pairs and felt compelled to match everyone

58

who wasn't wed. It had been this way when we'd last parted — I'd suggested Gabe and I write letters, and somehow that meant I was proposing marriage. My face burned at the way that had left our once-dear friendship. Was the entire world given to playing cupid and pairing people at random? Quiet and brotherly Gabe was no love match, and all we had in common was our unmarried state. Apparently, that was enough. "I beg your pardon, but there couldn't be a more ill-fitting match." I stood, flustered, and began pouring tea just to give my hands something to do.

Golda's eyes flashed a venomous shade of green and blue. Her body stiffened, displeasure radiating from her white face. My breath strangled me as footsteps thudded on the rug. I looked up as a tall, distinguished man strode into the room, followed by the faint scent of cinnamon.

My breath caught. I was dizzy. Suddenly tea was spilling everywhere, warming the front of my dress and splashing onto my shoes. I sprang back and righted the pot. *There's Gabe,* she had said, and she'd quite literally meant, *There is Gabe.* For there he was, nicely filling out his trim suit, wild curls slicked into wavy submission, warm gentleness radiating from his face.

59

FOUR

Two opposites often make a terrible combination that leads to explosive results. Worse yet is the combination of truth and poor timing.
~A scientist's observations on love

Gabe Gresham knelt beside me to help, blotting at the floor with awkward jerks of his broad shoulders. His nearness unsettled me and the air was thick with my foolish words. What was I supposed to say now?

Golda rang a tiny bell to summon the maid, and the sound echoed through my skull. "Gabe, don't touch that. I've sent for someone."

Oh, how terrible. How wretched.

At close range, I could see his comely face had settled into lines of deep maturity and untold strength, but it still wore the freshness of youth — as well as unveiled traces of hurt. There was no wondering if he'd heard my blunder. I looked down as heat climbed my neck and needled my face. Golda rang the bell a second time, with more force.

When I looked his way again, Gabe's face warmed with a sad smile of instant forgiveness. What had I been thinking? I was here to fix, not destroy. And no one deserved kindness more than Gabe Gresham.

I tried to catch his eye again and whisper an apology, but as usual, he kept his somber gaze down on his work. Mrs. Gresham, however, had absolutely no qualms about staring openly, and the heat of her gaze warmed through the top of my head.

I rose and peeled off my damp apron, mind whirring, and Gabe took it along with the other ruined linens. I had the distant sense of loss as I handed the apron to him, as if I was forgetting something, but my scattered brain couldn't land on what it was. Then Essie, the nervous little upstairs maid, hurried in to help, and I concentrated on not withering under the weight of my embarrassment.

"Heavens, child, where have you been?"

Essie cringed, bobbing two or three curtsies. "Sorry, ma'am. In the kitchen, ma'am."

"What's the rule?"

"The bell takes precedence."

Golda glared at the maid, as if burning her instruction into the poor girl's skull.

A few moments of silence passed as Essie knelt to clean, and Gabe strode to the window and peered around the faded drapes. "Sir Reginald will be a racer, Mother. His agility is unmatched and he's practically built of muscle." The words came out in his low, soothing voice and the tension disintegrated. What he did to skittish horses also worked on humans, apparently, with that deep voice working its way into the fibers of my tense muscles and loosening them. It seemed to do the same to his mother.

"Oh?" A sudden lightness came over Golda like a curtain parted over a sunny window.

"He's bound for the derby next year, and he'll make quite a fine showing."

The curtain parted farther as a smile touched her lips. "I knew from the moment I saw him he held such promise. What a magnificent creature."

How odd it was that the first benevolent words from the woman's mouth since I'd arrived . . . were about a horse.

Golda Gresham rearranged the little tea items on the table so that the napkin was perfectly centered between her beloved red cup and its saucer. "What about Saxon? How is he handling?"

"Better, but aggressive since the new stallion has come. They could never share a pasture."

"Ah, but he's a gorgeous creature. Simply stunning." Her eyes shone. "Is he ready to . . ." Her voice trailed as she looked to me, as if suddenly remembering I was overhearing this business discussion. "Perhaps a new pot of tea would be nice, Miss Duvall, with something in it to soothe my headache."

I hesitated. "Should a nurse not remain with her patient?"

She leaned near, taking hold of my arm, and spoke in a dangerously low voice. "Let us be clear, Miss Duvall. I do not enjoy your company, nor do I need a nursemaid following me about. You know the purpose of your employment here, and I'll thank you to leave me to the solace of my own company when I request it."

Jaw tense, I bobbed a curtsey and turned to go with Essie. In the hall, the maid began to tremble and she blinked back threatening tears. "Sorry, miss. I'm such a ninny. Always afraid of being sacked."

I gave a shaky laugh. "Not a bit of it. You should have heard my blunder." I unearthed the embarrassing moment I'd worked to bury in the last few moments.

She threw me a pitying smile. "Don't take it to heart, miss. That Mr. Gresham is a good sort. A fine gentleman and quick to forgive. He may not be the most commanding one in the house, but he has a strong heart and a fine nature. No one better, in fact."

The man in question appeared in the doorway with the pile of tea-stained linens and handed them to Essie, who blushed profusely. His smile was tender as he considered her. "You're a peach, Essie." He lifted her hand and kissed it with gentlemanly warmth, then he disappeared down the hall.

Essie and I hurried down the servant's stairs with the linens, breathless to the bottom. The poor girl's face flamed as we reached the kitchen.

"Now that we're out of earshot, tell me, Essie — how have you been keeping yourself? I want to hear all about your adventures in love and mischief."

She laughed heartily, her charming overbite apparent. "Not much to tell, Miss Duvall. No love for me, no mischief."

I readied a fresh teacup and saucer as the fire warmed the water. "What came of the gent you spoke of when I was here before?

Come, tell me everything."

She paused, her eyes clouding as if I'd poked some sleeping giant within. Her face mottled red again. "There's no gent."

I pinched my lips together as regret soured my mouth. Of course there wasn't — five years had passed and she was alone. "Forgive me. I thought there was someone who had caught your eye."

She stoked the stove fire again and slammed the door. "It hardly matters if I've never caught his, now does it?"

I was suddenly aware, looking into the shining eyes of this young woman, of a fever pitch of desperation she wore when discussing men, and it softened me. "There's nothing magical about romantic attention, you know. Truly. Sometimes it's quite burdensome, if it comes from the wrong man."

Her eager eyes told me she'd welcome this burden — from nearly any man. "I thought I'd met the right one, but he up and left Crestwicke some years ago."

"Oh." My heart drooped, but then a realization seized me and I lifted my gaze, blinking. "He departed? He's gone, and neither of you spoke of your affection?" My words came tripping out in my excitement.

She threw me a look, but my hope only grew.

Perhaps there was a reason the letter didn't seem to fit any of the Greshams. "Say, didn't he used to bring you little blue flowers?"

She shrugged. "Someone did, maybe him, but those forget-me-nots are as common as grass at Crestwicke, miss. Just look out the window."

Rolling fields spread across the yard, their grassy slopes lavishly dotted with the little blue blooms. Heavy clusters of them stood at the threshold of the cliffs, as if gathered to look over the water.

"Perhaps you ought to have the courage to say something to this man of yours." I caught up her hands in mine. "Think of it, Essie. Think of how romantic it would be to find out he's felt the same way all this time. Imagine what it could be like between you."

A dreamy look clouded her face. "Aye, it would be the first stroke of luck in me sorry life. I'd best not do it though, miss. She wouldn't like it." She jerked her head toward the stairs and Golda Gresham.

I pinched back a smile, assailed with a sudden burst of plans and ideas. Just then the kettle whistled and she snatched it off the fire.

First, the tea.

I carried it all up to the sitting room

through shadows that stretched up the dark walls and set it on the little side table. She watched from the reddish gloom until my skin prickled and I became overly aware of myself under her gaze. "Come here, Miss Duvall."

I obeyed.

"That adorable little speech you made about not needing a man — I assume you meant it."

"Of course."

"Good." She smiled. "I'd hate to think that someone at Crestwicke might cause you to stumble from your lofty ideals. There is no one here to tempt you in that manner, is there?"

I shifted in the dimness.

"Pray, allow me to provide you with an answer. There is no one at Crestwicke, servant or son, who is a fitting match for you, is that clear? It'd be a shame for you to be sent home in disgrace, with your name tarnished across the medical community."

My heart pounded, chest tight. I curtsied and escaped to my room to change, but I couldn't shake the tenor of underlying romance lurking in the shadows of this house. It was there, pulsing and sweeping through like a ghost, even if everyone attempted to stifle and deny it.

Until now, at least. I dug to the bottom of my valise and traveling bag for the letter, but it was not among my things. Unease tickled my skin. I dumped out the bag and checked every crevice, then glanced toward the closed door between my room and Golda's. She wouldn't invade my belongings, would she? I clutched the empty bag, searching around the room.

As I tied on a fresh apron, my gaze landed on my washstand, and a small paper propped there. I rose and went to collect the scrap with a single line scrawled: *Meet me at the ruins if you can get away. Dusk.* Well then, that would explain the lecture just now, if she'd seen this. I stuffed the paper deep into my valise, but the message had imprinted itself on my mind. I wasn't sure what would be worse — snubbing Gabe on top of what I'd done or being caught alone with him at dusk.

FIVE

If I marry, I shall choose someone because of their quirks — not in spite of them.
~A scientist's observations on love

Queen of the linens, that's what I am. Alone in the servant's hall, upstairs maid Essie Bellows dropped the soiled tea linens onto the table, her movements fueled by frustration. *Filthy rich and they don't even hire a wash girl. "Essie can do it," they always say. "It's no trouble for her."*

She flipped out each linen as if beating back the rising despair and cast a look toward the door where the lovely Miss Duvall had gone. There was a woman whose life was brimming with possibilities and love just around the corner, if only she'd step down out of the clouds long enough to notice it. Any number of men likely wanted her. A pretty little laugh, bewitching face, a slender waist, and oh, her energy! A burst

69

of sunshine and heart permeated the air around that one, with dimples to boot.

And all Essie had was this position at Crestwicke. Chapped hands, sore muscles, looks of disdain — those were her lot. Stiffening against jealousy, Essie sped up her work, flipping harder, shoving faster. A sudden wave of loneliness, dark and consuming, pummeled her, and she collapsed onto the bench, dropping her face into the tea-soaked towels.

Loneliness was not silent — it was loud and painful, like a whirring noise that crept up on you and wouldn't leave you alone. She'd existed for so many years in a state of placid acceptance, until she'd met *him.* Interest led to hope, and hope to dreaming, and dreaming to pure and utter longing. He'd been so kind to her that she'd fooled herself into believing him interested too, but the passage of time had dulled that hope. Until Miss Duvall had brought it all up again, she'd convinced herself she'd completely forgotten about Charley Mason.

But the familiar pain of rejection rose like a buoy.

She lay there for several moments, giving in to it, which left her weak and desperate. It always went this way, when there were weddings or babies or walks in the park behind happy couples. Anything, really, that paraded in front of her what she didn't have. Round and round she went in her busy, never-ending days followed by nights of exhausted slumber, and time passed her by without a hint of love. It was easy to be happy for those who had found love and family, but it didn't lessen the ache carving a hole in her own gut. Not even a little.

The tears came then, hot and pitiful, wetting the pile of laundry. What a sorry mess she was. If she planned to wash the linens anyway, could she wipe her nose with them?

A door banged deep in the house and she jerked up, a stray paper plastered to her moist face. Grimacing, she batted the fool thing away, but then she caught sight of it. What was this? Peeling off the beautifully embossed vellum paper with red edging, she stared at it. Flipping it back and forth and seeing no label, she opened the thing. Lovely, slanted letters met her gaze, and she skimmed for a few smaller words she might sound out. "A-D-M-I-R-E-R. Admirer."

Admirer? A short laugh burst out despite her drying tears. An admirer — *her?*

Wryly amused, she skimmed to the end . . . *someone truly loves you and believes you remarkable.* Re-mar-kable. What was that? She frowned. A dire need to know what someone believed her to be drove her through the kitchen and out into the hall in search of the one Crestwicke servant who could read better than her.

She found him near the front doors. "Parker. Parker, come look at this, will you?" She tapped his arm, and the towering butler spun, his face displaying shock.

"Essie. My, what a fright. You're looking . . . ah, well. Are you well?"

"Aren't I always? Here." She flipped out the paper toward him. "What's this word here?"

He followed her point. " 'Weaknesses.' "

She grimaced. "Someone's written to tell me I have flaws? Heavens, I tell myself that enough as it is."

"This is, um, *your* note, then? Someone's written it for you?"

"What do you take me for, a snoop? You think I'd go around reading other people's letters? Here now, what's this word?"

" 'Remarkable.' It means someone finds you unusual and . . . well, rather extraordinary." He cleared his throat, shifting his weight. "There now, you see? It's not just about your flaws."

"What about this — what does this mean? *happy beyond all comp . . . compre . . .*"

" 'Comprehension.' Well, there he's saying

72

that he'd be delighted beyond what a person could understand if you're favorably disposed . . . that is, if you return his feelings." Another shift. "Do you?"

"What about this?" She pointed out an especially long word.

" 'Involuntarily.' It means, against his will."

"So he doesn't *want* to desire me. Well now, isn't that flattering."

"It simply means he cannot help himself. That your nature is so appealing to him, even if it isn't convenient to feel such an attachment, and he . . ." Parker cleared his throat. "He's simply drawn to you because of who you are."

Essie closed her eyes, holding her breath, then exhaling and smiling up at him. "Thank you, Parker. You're a peach."

The words caught in her mouth, clicking a memory in her brain. *Essie, you're a peach.* She blinked, then looked up at the stairs where Gabe had disappeared after saying those very words . . . and handing her the linens with the letter. Well, glory be — it was from Gabe Gresham! With a smile and a final pat to Parker's arm, she dashed off to do the beds and ponder the miracle that had entered her quiet life.

She stole glances at the page while she

worked, and the gentle words warmed their way into the quiet places of her soul. She made her way through it again, skipping some of the harder words. By the third time, her tired eyes were eating up those lines with a hunger she'd never known. *I've seen the strength and kindness you believe go unnoticed, watched when you thought no one was looking, and observed what exists below the surface.*

No one ever noticed her — no one. She'd lived and worked by the passage "And whatsoever ye do, do it heartily, as to the Lord," knowing the Almighty saw what no other did. Yet was it possible that someone . . . ?

She looked down with wonder at the chapped hand Gabe Gresham had kissed. *I have no business writing to you . . .* Was it possible a gentleman had come to care for a maid? Had he, years ago, left those flowers for her? The scandalous nature of such an idea prickled all over. She might have dismissed the notion except for one little sentence that had planted itself firmly in her head: *I even know that secret you hoped to keep from everyone.*

She had known for some time that someone had found out about her mother, but it was never clear who. A hand went to her throat. Awareness seized her. *Someone's been to pay her bail, miss. I'm not allowed to say who.* It would have been someone with the means to pay it — someone with money.

Heart pounding in her plain little chest, she spread the clean linens across the bed and looked at herself in the long looking glass across the way. She'd mostly hurried past mirrors and kept her nose in her work, using only the warped looking glass in her room for morning toilette, but now she allowed herself a lingering glance. The longer she stared, the more the words invaded her solidly built self-doubt and cracked it apart. *Dearest, if only you could see yourself from where I stand.*

She touched her rounded cheeks where the freckles had begun to fade — when had that happened? — and her flame-red hair had tempered down to a burnished copper color that was quite fetching. She wasn't terrible to look at, when taken at a glance. She'd never noticed how comely her figure was, how pleasant and affable her face.

But he had.

She felt dizzy. Was he toying with her, hoping for a dalliance? But no, this letter spoke of a deeper affection than that. Unless Gabe Gresham was only the deliverer . . .

Rising to her feet, she tucked a stray curl

75

into her cap, secreted the precious missive in her pocket, and swept up the linens. As she carried them to the laundry, the load of her life felt considerably lighter.

Tossing the sheets into the tub, she climbed up to the little chamber where Miss Duvall was to stay, whipping linens off the bed with stunning alacrity, always feeling the eyes of her secret admirer on her — he might be anywhere about the house. She finished preparing the room in record time, then curiosity finally overwhelmed her work ethic. She ran up the stairs and burst into the attic gables, breathless from the climb, and the object of her search turned on her stool in the window, paintbrush in hand.

"Why, Essie, whatever is the matter?"

"Miss Clara, I've had a letter."

The young woman turned fully away from her painting, beautiful even with her dark hair tied back by a cloth. "News from home?"

"Oh no, nothing of the sort. It's a good letter. A *very* good one." She handed it to the young lady who had become more friend and sister than mistress.

Clara scanned the page in silence, her eyebrows arching. "I should say so. Who sent it?"

"I haven't any idea. I was hoping you

might help me find out."

She brushed stray hairs off her face and glanced out the gable window. "Let me think on it. May I take it with me? I want to see if it matches any handwriting about the house."

"You'll give it back, though?" Essie stared at the letter in Clara's fingers that were tinted by oil paints.

"Hopefully with a man attached to it." She winked and spun back toward her work in progress — a portrait.

Essie moved to stand behind her. "Looks real nice, Miss Clara."

"It's just a wash now, but it'll look like the real person when I fill in the details."

"Can I bring you anything, ma'am? A fresh cherry tart or maybe a lemonade?"

"I couldn't eat a thing now, Essie. I'm in the throes of creativity and I must give in to it."

With another nod and bobbed curtsey, Essie moved back toward the steep stairway, taking two last glances at the precious sheet of paper now lying partially open on a nearby stool.

There it was. It existed. Someone very specific had written down those feelings and secreted them to her. In a few days, perhaps even a few hours, she would know who.

Six

Childhood has an expiration date, after which a woman retires into marriage for lack of other options.
~A scientist's observations on love

Huddled over John Snow's *Infectious Diseases and Germ Theory* in the dimming light that evening, I marked passages about microscopic pathogens on medical instruments and forced myself to concentrate. I glanced up at my patient, who silently stabbed at her cross-stitch project in an ornate striped chair by the hearth. When Gabe appeared in the yard below striding toward the stables, all concentration disintegrated. Moments later, his stallion burst from the doors and galloped toward the hill. I felt a tug on my heart.

Meet me at the ruins.

It was nearly dusk. I took a sidelong glance at Golda. Her lips were pinched as she worked, her eyes alert. Yet as the sun spread its orange glow across the sky, her head lolled against her shoulder, eyes fluttered closed — one of her famous "eye restings."

"Go on then, get some tea and get settled. I'll sit with her a while." Essie appeared behind me and I breathed a sigh of relief. "She'll be out for at least an hour."

But it wasn't tea or settling I wanted. Outside, fresh air washed my skin and great bursts of water sprayed the cliffs. The yard was alive with night music from unseen critters, and the shadow of a distant horseman stretched long across the hill before me, a familiar rider tall and agile astride his mount.

I climbed the steep foot path and moist air dotted my face, cooling my skin and refreshing my soul. Even as I neared the ruined tower, I could feel the impact of its atmosphere.

I'd never forget the first time I'd seen it. Father had dragged me on his rounds again, unable to stay put in the crypt of his memories still so fresh with Mama's voice, and we'd landed at Crestwicke Manor to call on Mr. Gresham. I remember Father's black medical bag and shirtwaist, the only part of him at my eye level, and I didn't lift my gaze in those days. He'd swung that bag out of the carriage, patted me on the head, and strode off to attend his patient while his very brokenhearted daughter slipped once again into isolation.

Children don't grieve in the same way as adults, he'd told one of his sisters at the funeral. They simply didn't understand the depth of loss or the implications of it. That was true, for I had no way to express the flat metallic pain that rested against my chest, squashing my motherless heart in a way that seemed would last forever.

I remember scrambling up this same hill then, in a desperate attempt to be near Mum, or to God. Either would have been fine. I tore my stockings and caught my satin bow on nearly every twig, but I finally reached the peak.

I knew instinctively when I found the old abandoned tower at the top that a magnificent presence resided there. It wasn't a frightening one, like a specter, but one grand enough to thicken the very air of the place. I crawled onto a crumbling ledge inside the ruins and lay there, feeling strangely comforted, pretending Mum would come to find me when it grew dark. She didn't, of course, but neither did Father. It was Gabe who'd come and rescued me from isolation, and now I had returned to this old tower on the hill to face that same boy.

I reached the top a bit winded and caught a glimpse of Gabe's shadowed profile, still astride his horse as they looked over the cliffs together. He'd always been an ageless soul with a wealth of unspoken thoughts, and a solid, older brother aura that he wore on broad shoulders with grace. How perfectly his nature matched this ruin we both loved.

I walked into the center of the old tower, and it muffled all outside sounds. I'd forgotten what it was like to be here, the grassy land lifting me in its palm toward heaven so I might bask in the warmth of God's nearness.

Gabe spun and dismounted when he saw me, wearing the same look of settled contentment I felt as he approached. Sparks of light flickered in his dark eyes. I released a breath and looked around the quiet space where even the air stilled. "Why does it feel as though he's here more than most other places?"

"There's less to crowd him out."

I was struck with the sudden urge — no, the *need* — to visit often and realign my heart when the world seemed to crowd my thoughts. I sighed and turned to my companion. "Gabe, I need to apologize —"

"Shh. None of that, now." He took my hand with a playful smile and led me to the cliff's edge. The enchantment of the place caught me up in its spell again — the sea below, the stars freckling the sky above, and wildflowers perfuming the air. Gabe sat on the grassy ledge, arms folded across his bent knees, and stared down to the rippled sand. "They've been moving about for days and I've no idea how long they'll stay in the area."

I lay on my belly and inched toward the edge, straining to see the beach below. Gabe's breath was a calm, steady rhythm beside me, and the silence stretched pleasantly. *This is easy.* The thought struck me before I had time to stop it. Marriage could be pleasant — not exciting, but tolerable — with a friend like this. I studied his rugged profile, his endlessly welcoming face.

But then a great rolling thunder of hooves started in the east and pounded down the beach. A cloud of sand billowed out, then they were there — dozens of powerful bodies flying over the packed sand, manes flying and heads high.

The sight elated my heart and sparked my desire for freedom again. I simply *had* to succeed at Crestwicke. I was born to practice medicine, to take Father's brilliant research and make it blossom beyond his life. I was not like other girls, seeking shelter under some man's roof — I secretly craved a taste of deeply authentic love, but I also wanted the stars and open sky.

My heart thundered against the limestone I lay on, along with the pounding hooves below. There is a magnificence to wild things, a beauty that resonated with me deeply.

When the thundering receded, Gabe's low voice rumbled beside me. "I didn't know you were coming to Crestwicke."

"It was a hasty decision. And I wasn't certain . . ." *how to act around you. How you would receive me. What it would be like between us.*

Five years after the ill-fated day, I still felt the awkward ending of my last visit. I'd merely asked if we could write letters — *letters* — and when word got out, the scandal had swelled almost as if I'd suggested we slip off and elope at Gretna Green. I always seemed to do that — enjoying a friendship and delighting in the company of another human while being totally unaware that anyone else saw it as romance. I'd argued loudly with them about my intentions,

83

decrying any notion of romance between us, but we hadn't returned since.

I sat up to cover the silence as my pathetic sentence faded away, but he picked up the thread. A smile warmed his face. "Don't give it a thought. We'll always be friends. Nothing more, and certainly not less." He threw a stone down the rock face. "No one else around here will take these little jaunts. I'm always glad when you come."

At least I had one trait on my side. "You are doing well?"

He gave a single nod, staring over his bent knees down at the beach. Gulls called out. "You seem unhappy."

And there we were again, back to being friends, easy in each other's company as if we'd always weaved seamlessly in and out of each other's lives. "Not terribly. In the moment, anyway, I have freedom."

"You say that as if someone has threatened it."

I looked down and split a grass blade. "Only every man who has traipsed through the cottage asking for my hand."

"It sounds like a small cavalry came to your door."

"There were only four." My flippant voice masked the immense trouble those "only four" had brought to my life.

He merely watched me, his narrowed eyes seeing much more than I'd choose to tell. "And you will have none of them?"

I pinched my lips. "Truth be told, I cannot bear the idea of marrying any of the men who have offered their hand."

"Hmm."

"I find independence much more alluring. Besides, I have work to do." I sat up, suddenly energized. "Gabe, we're so close — *so* close — to opening a clinic in Brighton. One that's safe and sterile, with fresh air and ventilation, a place where patients can truly heal."

He frowned. "Another Brighton mineral bath for the wealthy?"

"At first, perhaps." Then my face warmed as I told him what I'd not yet dared voice to anyone. "One day I want it to be for the common folk — the ones dying in those dirty, infection-ridden hospitals all over England. When Father passes it on to me, that's what I'll make of it — a refuge for healing, inside and out, and real care. Dignity. I simply *must* become a doctor and finish this work. Life is too meaningful, too important, to spend it on the wrong thing."

"Hmm."

I smiled at the way each *hmm* from Gabe had a different meaning, distinct and clear.

85

This one had been full of approval, perhaps a tinge of admiration.

It was so different with Gabe than with any other man of my acquaintance, for we knew each other as two books whose pages were worn from heavy reading, their lines memorized and recalled in a moment. Knowing him was not exciting and romantic, as marriage should be, but there was a sweetness to it, a weighted sense of peace, that brought never-ending contentment.

"It seems you have quite a path carved out for yourself. Have you asked God what he thinks of it all?"

"If doors open, I'll assume he's inviting me to walk through them."

He eyed me. "Or he's giving you a choice. And a choice is nothing but an invitation to have a talk with him."

I pondered this, then turned to Gabe. "What about you? Do you still spend your days in the stable, or has some woman managed to tame you?"

A wide, open silence followed, making me aware of the distant hiss of tide over sand. Gabe looked out at the water and strained to see something far beyond our little scene on the hilltop. The expression on his face was one I dared not intrude upon, so I waited, studying his profile against the darker parts of sunset.

It struck me suddenly that Gabe, steady and ageless Gabe, had a love story. By the distant look on his face, the woman he loved was nowhere within a ten-mile radius of Crestwicke.

Wind ruffled the hair on the back of his head. "No wife."

Was there pain in that admission? Feeling as though I'd intruded, I threw out a light-hearted smile. "There's nothing so special about marriage, anyway. You'll find your wild horses far easier to manage."

Out came the easy smile that was slight but powerful, carving pleasant creases in each cheek. "I have to find one who thinks me a tolerable pairing first."

I turned away from the quiet humor in his expression as my foolish words from earlier were echoed back to me. "Well, now you know the great secret of my spinsterhood. I cannot manage to keep my tongue in my head, and that is why I do not have a husband."

"I thought you were the one rejecting them. Besides, speaking your mind is a rare asset in a person. A blessing."

Guilt twisted even tighter. "A blessed curse is what it is. I owe you every apology ever invented for what I said before, and you owe me a lecture."

"I never lecture. Lessons are best learned firsthand, not second."

"You should yell at me. It'd give me a great deal of relief, and I have it coming."

"I never yell, either. Especially at a lady."

"But it's *me*. You can tell me anything."

He looked down again as another wild horse wandered onto the beach, snuffing about in the sand. "I speak up when I've something worth saying."

Something worth saying. I studied the profile of this rugged man, the one who had rescued me from the dark valley of invisibility and loneliness years ago. It was he who convinced me to study medicine and work with Father, although I couldn't remember just then, as I stared at him in the burning red sunset, how he'd done it exactly.

He'd simply harnessed his few words with amazing strength and sent them sailing directly into my soul. It was as if God had wrapped his directions up in my friend's voice so I'd be sure to hear them. There was always something of God in Gabe's words, it seemed — eternal truth leaked out when he opened his mouth. I gave him a light shove. "Perhaps you ought to speak up more often. The world would be the richer for it."

"The Almighty has blessed you with a fine voice. Not me."

"Just because you haven't used a skill doesn't mean it isn't there." I stood, brushing off my skirt. "Come now, you'll start with me."

He simply faced the beach below, letting the wind muss his dark hair. "I couldn't yell at you, Willa."

I smiled and danced backward toward the cliff's drop-off, bracing my feet on the worn sandstone and laughed into the night air, throwing out my arms. "Care to place a bob on it?"

He swung his gaze toward me and did a double take, then sprang up. "No, stop!" He practically flew toward me, tripping over himself. *"Willa!"*

He pounced and grabbed my skirt, yanking me away from the edge. I laughed as we tumbled onto the grass, my giggles a staccato echo against the crash of waves below.

He rolled away and pushed up, panic showing white and tense across his face. "What were you *doing*?"

"Winning." I gave a wicked smile and held out one hand. "My shilling, please."

He stared at it, then took hold of my hand to pull me up instead. I expected his good-natured grumbling and a brief, awkward lecture. Instead, he only held onto my hand, staring into my face as if he could see through to the little gears turning within, understanding their mechanics in a way few others could. Including me.

I sobered. "Truly, I am sorry for what I said before. I can't abide people making a match out of me, and it just came out."

He waved off the apology. "No harm done. Part of me wonders if she did it on purpose, to test you. She knows we were close years ago."

I tugged his hand. "And still are." This earned a tender smile. "Why does she disapprove of me so, anyway?"

"She has a match for everyone, and you are not mine. She's chosen to pair me with Caroline Tremaine, the daughter of our longtime friends."

"I see. What do *you* think of that match?" I tried to imagine the woman his mother would choose for him.

That same faraway look came into his features. "A fine woman. Quite beautiful and accomplished." He dropped his gaze to his boots and pinched his shoulders into a shrug. "I doubt she'd have me."

That simple statement squeezed my heart. "Have you tried? At least asked her for a dance? You could sweep her off her feet without saying a word."

"That only works if we happen upon one another at an event with dancing. I don't dance, and I don't attend social functions unless forced."

I could imagine him attempting to speak to some lovely flower of a woman, stumbling as if his brain couldn't locate the words. It happened when something mattered to him, and that particular issue threatened, I was afraid, to leave this wonderful man unattached forever. Unless . . .

I narrowed my eyes and assessed him. "Gabe, have you any special attachment to forget-me-nots?" A letter would be the perfect way for a man like Gabe to approach a lady.

"What are they?"

"A flower. A rather beautiful one."

"Like the ammenomie? That's the only one I know."

I paused and braced myself against the urge to giggle. "They're similar, I suppose." *Stop it. Don't laugh. Enough poking this man for one day.*

There was a slight pause. "You want to laugh, don't you?"

"I never said a thing."

"Go ahead, have your laugh." He shot me a playful look, eyes narrowed in fun.

"Amenomie."

A laugh burst out, and I clapped a hand over my mouth. "I'm sorry, Gabe. I think no less of you, but I cannot help it."

He lifted his face that was not devoid of amusement. "Amenomie. Annennemonie. How do you say it, anyway? Amenenom-enomie."

I laughed wholeheartedly, falling backward in the grass. "Oh Gabe, I tried so hard."

His smile only grew. "It's why I leave them for you. It pleases me to know I can make you laugh on my whim."

I smiled up at him towering over me. He was always able to accomplish a great deal without saying a thing.

"Come, I'll walk you back." He helped me up and pointed down the hill. "Unless you wish to take the tunnel."

I glanced at the spot where a heavy wooden door near the ground covered the entrance of a priest tunnel that had allowed many men of the cloth to escape persecution. It had always fascinated me, but just now being in the presence of my dear friend pleased me more. "I think I'll walk back with you. We can part on the side of the house, before we're seen."

With a nod, he took hold of his horse's bridle and placed the other hand lightly on my back. It felt good to once again have a close friend — an older brother looking out for me.

As we neared the well-lit house, I couldn't shake the notion that he'd written the love letter. Perhaps he'd forgotten the flower's name. "I don't suppose you're in the habit of writing a lady letters."

His brow furrowed as he paused near the ivy-covered wall. "What sort of letters?"

Oh, you know, simply the most beautiful piece of poetry dripping with love and affection ever penned. "I came across a note that was unsigned, perhaps quite old, and I'd like to return it to its owner."

"What was in it?"

"I never said I read it."

He gave a pointed look.

"Fine, then. It was quite lovely and irresistible, and the writing was of the most beautiful sort."

"And it mentioned those flowers."

"And Crestwicke." I shifted. "Well?"

"I think you know the answer. I've never written a letter to anyone outside of business matters. Love is meant to be spoken aloud."

"Have you any idea who might have written it, then?"

He was silent for several seconds, then a

shrug. "Aunt Maisie might know. She knows everything about Crestwicke."

I frowned, remembering the odd woman in the balcony with the circular answers. "Truly — her?"

He studied me for a moment, disappointment evident on his brow. "Do you know how many countries that woman has visited? Seven. How much her cleverness has amassed for Gresham Stallions? Nearly double its value. Her life may seem small in scope now, but she's lived well. She speaks her mind, notices much, accomplishes a great deal. And like you, she's never needed a husband to do it."

I cringed. "I suppose I judge too quickly."

Then he turned to me in the shadows of his family's great home. "Will you stay long?"

"I hope so." I stopped short of telling him about the contract with Father. I couldn't bear to see silent disapproval in his eyes again, and I was fairly certain I would. "At least while your mother needs me."

"Actually, *I* need you." It was stated simply.

"Oh?"

"I could use an accomplice where my mother is concerned." He raised his eyebrows. "Keen for a mission?"

94

My heart wavered. "Well, that is my job, isn't it — helping her?" Although I had a sinking feeling he had something more than nursing in mind. Something far more complicated.

"Partners?" He held out his hand and I took it. "I'm glad you're here. I know I can count on you."

I gave a weak smile.

"Here's to a few more adventures, then." He bowed and backed into the thickening shadows toward his horse.

Inside, I took a candle from a little table in the foyer and went to my patient.

"She's still sleeping," Essie whispered from her chair in the corner.

I roused the woman and, along with her ladies' maid, readied her for bed, but the pull of the lost letter was strong. I glanced around my room again, but it didn't appear. I couldn't bear the thought of it being mislaid among the scraps and litter of this household — or worse yet, discovered and read by the wrong person.

If I'd left it anywhere, it must be the library, for that's where I'd gone to find those medical journals earlier. I sat with Golda and perfumed her pillow, rubbed her head, and read aloud in low tones until her breathing evened. Then I slipped down to

95

the tall circular room delightfully lined with books. Setting my candle on a table, I leafed quickly through papers scattered on the desk, then pulled a few books I'd looked at off the shelves and paged through. *Please be here.*

Just as I was about to give up, I was flipping through a book and my eyes focused on the same fanciful handwriting I'd seen in the letter. The sight of it struck me. It was an inscription in the front cover that read "Property of G. Aberdeen." Inside, several papers bore the same writing — market lists, from the looks of it, and short business-like notes and half-sentence reminders. I frowned at the inscription, reading it several times. *Aberdeen.*

There it was, the identity of the writer. Shivering in a sudden chill sweeping in from the window, I stared at the writing in the candlelight.

Footfall nearby startled me, and I dropped the book to my side, backing away, but I saw no one — at first. The dim light threw a garish glow across an ancient, speckled face high up on the circular stairs.

"Pray, what do you think you're doing?" The aged woman I'd seen before loomed above me, passing judgment from the high courts.

"Visiting the library."

"You're windblown."

"I've been taking in a little fresh air."

"Without a wrap?" Doubt shadowed her face. Leaning heavily on the railing, the shrunken woman descended the last few steps and came to stand before me. Two sharp eyes rested atop an overlarge nose, and her lips were pinched over bare gums. She looked older than the foothills, and just as craggy. "Or perhaps my nephew provided his coat when you were together."

I gripped the book in my hands, then forced myself to set it on the table, feeling as though I were back on that cliff's edge, with only my toes gripping solid ground.

Her whiskered chin trembled. "He *is* why you've come back, isn't he?"

"There was absolutely nothing untoward occurring, I assure you. No romance exists in my life." I tasted those words on my lips, making my peace with them.

She turned and squinted as if she had only one good eye, a frown of disapproval curling her lips. "So, then. You won't have him, won't have the others who've asked for your hand. One is left wondering just who *is* good enough to catch your fancy."

My neck heated to think of all she'd heard

about me. "I've no desire at present to marry."

"You wish to become a knitting, gossiping little spinster, a permanent fixture at your father's table, a burden to your family? You want to be —"

"Like you." It tumbled out before I could stop it.

Shock cascaded over her spotted features, her lashless lids blinking.

"I wish to be like you." With only a small glimpse into her life, I wanted it. Craved it. "You've done a great deal with your life, made important decisions and helped those you loved, all without marrying. I want an independent life too."

The shrunken old woman stepped slowly from the shadows, angling herself against her cane as she studied me. At close range, a thousand years of wisdom seemed trapped behind her faded eyes, her lined face a road map of adventures. Her eyes looked me over, then her mouth twitched. A smile wobbled on her face, followed by a great rumble of laughter deep in her chest. She waved me off and turned away. "Oh no you don't, child. You haven't the stomach for it." She hobbled back into the shadows.

"Wait."

She turned, her lined face expectant.

"Would you happen to know . . ." I forced myself not to glance at the open book on the table. "That is, can you tell me who is named Aberdeen?"

She blinked, unmoving. "Aberdeen." She spoke the name slowly, as if tasting it again for the first time in many years. "One single day at this house and you've managed to unearth the great secret of Crestwicke Manor. I'll not be the one to share his story, Miss Duvall. The tale of Grayson Aberdeen is best left alone."

I bowed my head in acceptance, but a smile tickled the edges of my lips. Even if she was unwilling to tell it, there was a story behind this secret love, and whoever wrote the letter. I had been right all along — the letter I'd found in that desk was a piece of something much larger, a story more epic than mere romance. And piece by piece, it was about to be uncovered.

SEVEN

There's nothing so precious as secret love. It's tucked close to the heart, protected from the scrutiny of the world, ready to be presented like a rare gift when the moment is right.

~A scientist's observations on love

Gabe Gresham preferred the shadows. He felt most comfortable there, where he could observe life without being seen. He leaned back in the stiff parlor chair hidden under the balcony and let the tea warm his insides. When soft footsteps approached, he stiffened, barely daring to breathe.

It was her, at last. Willa Duvall moved through the silent hallways like a wraith, her boots soft against carpet. He had idled here for another glimpse of her before he returned to his own cottage at the edge of the property. He simply couldn't wrap his mind around what she'd become. She paused in the gallery, looking about at the tall paintings, and he watched for her dimples. It had become a game, trying to draw them out. They appeared now as she pursed her lips, making him wish desperately to kiss her one day. He'd give half his savings for a single sweet taste of those laughing, quick-witted lips. She turned toward the stairs, and her candle warmed the shadows of this murky old space as she climbed, taking her glow with her.

Willa Duvall had flitted in and out of his life for years, and though most people made him uncomfortable, he was inexplicably drawn to her flame. A startling collection of opposites, childhood Willa had captured his attention with her little-girl voice speaking grown-up thoughts, the bold recklessness paired with loyalty, the long hair that loved to be unruly, while under it resided a meticulously logical mind.

Through the death of her mother and her father's remarriage, such strength, such passion was evident in her heart, pouring out with every sharply intelligent word. It surprised him every time he looked at her tiny frame that it could contain such depth of thought, such largeness of life. Now that she was grown, it had multiplied and it overflowed through her smile, her sparkling face, that huge, wholehearted laugh.

He'd observed her with amused interest for years, but nothing — *nothing* — had prepared him for the return of grown-up Willa. The sight of her had hit him like a steam engine he couldn't sidestep.

It had become his habit over the years as he lay struggling to fall asleep to picture those elusive dimples tucked just beside her pert little mouth when he earned her smile. It began there, and then it reached her eyes — oh, those *eyes*! They glowed warm and bright, piercing the sullen darkness of his room. She both calmed and excited him, enjoying him like no one else did, yet still nudging him out of his cocoon of quiet and privacy. Her presence unsettled and compelled him at the same time.

He adored every minute of it — adored *her.*

It all began the moment she had punched one of the local boys and followed it up with a string of impassioned threats that only a naïve young girl could make. The boy ran off wailing about his broken nose, which in truth she'd only bloodied.

Then she marched into the stable where Gabe had hidden himself to lick the wounds of his pride. She perched up on the stacked bales of hay, swinging her legs. "What a wretched fool he was. There's nothing the matter with your voice. At least there isn't a whine in it like his." She wrinkled her freckled nose.

He scowled and turned away from this scrap of a girl who thought she needed to rescue him. Thankfully she didn't pepper him with questions and force him to talk like everyone else. That's how they'd set out to cure his quietness, a deep flaw in their eyes, but that only made it worse. In those moments, it felt his hands would forever be clammy, his ears always ringing with the echo of his stuck voice, as if someone had stolen his box of words and he had nothing from which to draw when he opened his mouth.

She scrambled to stand on the hay bales, arms out to balance. "I hope he runs home to tell his mother so he has to answer for his crimes. What a sorry excuse for an heir. I suppose it's evil to wish him pain though, isn't it?" She spun around and looked down at him quite suddenly. "I'll wish him justice, then. There, that seems fair of me, doesn't it?" She flailed. "Oh!"

On instinct, he lurched forward as she tumbled, her bony limbs jabbing his chest as she landed. He grimaced at the pain, but it evened the score of his pride.

She scrambled up, brushing off straw. "Thank you kindly."

He blinked down at her, wondering if she'd done it on purpose, sensing even as a child that he'd needed to be in the position of rescuer rather than rescued.

She looked up at him with that frank, open little face as he steadied her on the ground. "He's probably only jealous of how strong you are. I saw you rein in that wild horse in the corral, and he probably did too." She picked straw from her hair, then went to lay beside his abandoned spot on the lower bales. He sat beside her, intrigued. "Pity for him, his only strength is his ability to spot weakness and poke at it. You needn't say anything to me if you don't want. Your silence is far nicer than his voice."

Besides that, she had enough to say for the both of them. It tickled him, this little sprite of a thing who filled his constant silence with chatter. Nothing she said was memorized or repeated, and all of it was slightly unsettling. In a good way. "He didn't mean any harm."

"There, you see? You speak perfectly well."

He shrugged. Only with her, in this aura of cheerful chatter that was free of expectations. It didn't matter if he couldn't get his words out with her, so he suddenly found he could.

And it was delightful.

She never did face punishment for the bloodied nose, for when the simpering little heir had dragged his governess back to the stables and pointed out his attacker, the disgruntled woman had boxed her charge's ears — for lying.

He looked forward to Dr. Duvall's visits because he always brought his adventurous sprite of a girl. Then on one trip Gabe heard it whispered that the girl's mother had died, and help flowed the other direction. It ebbed back and forth like that between them, even though they saw each other so seldom, a bond forming as they leaned on one another.

Helping her left him feeling unbelievably strong and able, yet helplessly captivated by her too. Such an odd mix it was, but powerful.

Gabe found himself hungry for her company and greedily stealing as much of it as possible whenever she was there, for it was the one bright spot in his otherwise bleak days. He spoke to few others and was close to no one, but she'd managed to break through. Whenever she rode up to Crestwicke with her father to attend some member of the family, Gabe basked in her bright personality, coming alive and feeling normal for a precious few hours.

She had an uncanny ability to both talk and listen, thus drawing out his reluctant voice, and eventually teaching him how to slow down and ease his thoughts out rather than allowing a collision of the chaotic overflow in his head. She'd talk until her playful little voice replaced the silence of his existence.

And he cherished it like one starved.

Then she'd returned, a fully grown woman, with poise and dimples and laughing eyes . . .

Whap.

He jerked, tea sloshing over his thighs, and glanced around in the dark.

"You missed your chance." Aunt Maisie stepped out of the shadows behind his chair with a rolled-up serial, her ancient mouth drawn tight. "Out alone with you, and she comes back without a romantic notion in her head. I can only imagine what *didn't* happen out there."

"You'd be right."

"Only you, Gabe Gresham, could muck up a moonlit walk. Why, you practically have all the work done for you, if you'd only put in a hair's breadth of effort. Did you tell her anything about the feelings written all over

106

your face?"

He slunk down in the chair. No point in denying anything to Maisie, even though he couldn't lay his own finger on the nebulous thoughts swirling around. "Words have never come easy for me."

"They come easy as flowing water for her. Simply turn on the spigot with a few questions and let her go."

Maybe he didn't want to hear what she'd say. He firmed his jaw, looking up at the landing where her slender little figure had stood. Her presence here seemed a delicate thing, and he didn't want to risk losing it. Yet perhaps . . . perhaps he'd finally tell her the truth about himself. The big truth. Even as a good friend, she deserved that much.

If he could work up the courage.

He blotted his trousers with a linen napkin Maisie dropped in his lap before hobbling off and wondered if he ever would. Meanwhile he'd handle the great ache of desire as he did everything else — in silence.

EIGHT

Settling breeds resentment, and that is a lifelong punishment I will not cast on any of the men who have yet asked for my hand.

~A scientist's observations on love

I had several important missions at Crestwicke — treating a patient, finding a missing love letter, reuniting lost loves, planning for medical school . . . but my days were mostly spent conducting singing lessons. *Singing lessons.*

Heaven help us.

"No, no, relax your shoulders, body limber, lift your chest." I pressed my patient's shoulders back and demonstrated. By Friday, my third full day at the manor, I had become fully absorbed in inventing all manner of ways to improve my patient's lung function and throat, but little was changed. *This cannot be what you have in mind, Lord.*

Yet I sense a purpose in it all, a reason I've come . . .

Golda braced herself on the back of a chair in the opulent music room. She closed her eyes as if to summon heavenly talent, but the same reedy sound came from her lips. I cringed as her melody rose, tightening to a pitch far higher than her voice was ever meant to go.

Here it was, the end of my eardrums.

I turned to fetch my bag, just to give myself an excuse to face the other way. When I lifted the latch and stretched the bag open, there in plain view lay three lovely purple flowers, their faces shining innocently up at me atop my instruments. My heart pounded as I fought back the giggles that rose like buoys in my chest. But then I saw a curled paper underneath them and flattened it to find a snippet of Robert Nicoll's poem, with one small change:

If winter fields be cauld and bare —
If winter skies be blae —
The mair we need thy bonnie face.

But so it is; and when away
For dreary months you be,
The joy of meeting pays for all,
Sweet, wild Ammenomie!

With those lines, all was lost. Laughter spurted out, and Golda spun with a look of horror, her exercise cut short.

I snapped the bag closed as heat climbed my neck in a suffocating manner. "I beg your pardon, my lady."

The dangerous sparkle didn't leave her eyes. "What, pray tell, is in your bag?"

"Shall we try again?" I rose and walked to her with my most charming smile. "There, now. Try to think of your arms as heavy sandbags, relaxed down at your sides. Keep your shoulders down."

I held them in place and Golda released one long note that gradually strengthened as she drew it out, like pulling taffy.

In the passing days of failed attempts and frustration, my mind was often stilled by the casual whisper of chilly air, the shadows in the corridors, the veiled expressions of everyone I encountered, and I felt it there like a ghost. Secret love, authentic romance, hovered somewhere in this house, just waiting to surface in broad daylight. It always felt just out of reach, like a luscious, delicate flower I could not quite see for all the smog in the air. I closed my eyes in those moments and imagined where the letter might be, what its writer might be doing that very minute.

Golda Gresham's hovering note finally snapped to a close. I reached out to steady my patient as she faltered, her voice hitching and body trembling, but she batted me away. "Enough, enough. This is ridiculous."

She turned, but I wasn't ready to give up yet. "Breathe up instead of out. Try that and see if your lungs last longer."

She took a tall breath, lifting her chest and releasing a single long note, but a violent coughing spasm cut it short. I rushed to find a tonic, tumbling my little flowers out of the bag. She wilted into a nearby chair and closed her eyes, forehead propped on her fingertips. She sat up as I administered a spoonful.

I dabbed lavender water on her temples while her lids fluttered. "Perhaps you should rest."

Her eyes flashed open, cat-like poise solidifying again. "How dare you patronize me. I know my limits." Her bright gaze landed on my bag, and the flowers that had fallen out.

I clutched the bottle, toes curling in my boots.

A knock on the door pivoted her attention.

"You have a visitor, Mother." Celeste glided into the room as I scooped the flowers into my bag and snapped it shut. "The housekeeper couldn't find you. Are you — oh!" Her gaze landed on me with keen appraisal, and a touch of gladness. "Why, Miss Duvall. *You* are the new nurse?"

"Tell our guest I'm not at home." Golda turned away.

"Yes, of course." She stared at me.

I looked over my old acquaintance, the only daughter of the Gresham household, and realized there were levels to spinsterhood. By all appearances, she was several rungs beyond me. Narrow features were framed by hair scraped back into pins, her figure squarish and comfortable. She might have made a fine headmistress, or perhaps a nun. Direct and efficient, she seemed far more suited to instructing than mothering. I remembered her as warm and imaginative, but that girl had been tight-laced into the modest, practical woman before me.

"How nice that you have a nurse to look after you, Mother. I know how you —"

"Indeed."

"She'll be wonderful company, and I —"

"Quite." Golda Gresham straightened, and I was struck with the sudden awareness that she did not care for her daughter.

"You seem strained. Shall we take a turn about the gardens? It will do you good."

The woman's hard stare turned her direction. "Haven't you a society meeting tonight? I thought that was Fridays."

"Mary had to postpone. Her husband is home for the weekend and he doesn't approve of our goings-on."

"I rather thought that'd fuel your fire, offending a man."

Celeste adjusted the little fringed pillow behind her mother. "We've nothing against men, of course. We simply want our own rights."

"Rights." Golda sat back. "No God-fearing woman demands such things."

"No God-fearing man would hinder them, though, would he?"

Golda's voice was soft. Dangerous. "How nice that she has one to care what she does, and try to keep some sense in her head."

The subtle rebuke had me gripping the table edge.

Celeste tipped her head and offered a simple smile. "Not every woman needs one. There's so much to be done at the women's league that I haven't time for much else. Do you know, we've decided to auction off the quilts we've made? I was thinking of asking Cook to make pies to add as well. Wouldn't that be splendid?"

Golda's eyes narrowed. "I hope to *high*

heaven that no one ever connects your foolish pastime with this family."

"Not to worry, then." Celeste's airy voice sailed around her mother's insults, and I couldn't help but stare at her with admiration. "I'll simply keep the pies anonymous if you wish. Miss Duvall should come, and Caroline Tremaine. I'll ask her."

I cleared my throat. "I'm afraid I have duties here, and —"

A dry cough took hold of Golda. "Both of you, take your chittering voices away, if you please." She leaned her forehead on her fingertips and closed her eyes as the cough subsided. A deeply troubled sigh followed. "Miss Duvall, something for my infernal cough, please."

Celeste took my arm and we moved to the far end of the long room, where I dug through my bag for a throat tincture.

She spoke privately. "I'm glad you've come. Parker told me how Burke tried to send you home, and I'd forgotten how delightfully feisty you are. It's nice to have a woman in the house who uses her own mind, even if it differs so from my own. Perhaps together we can put the men of this household in their place now and again. Now, tell me all your news."

The last five years spun through my brain

in dizzying color. "I've been to nursing school, I work with Father, and plan to one day —"

"No no, not that, silly. The *other* news." She lowered her voice on this last bit, eyes glittering. "I heard you've rejected multiple men. Am I to assume you're one of us?"

I'd heard rumors of Celeste and other highborn women who'd linked arms in some political movement. The Kensington Street Women's League, they called themselves. The word *unnatural* had floated about, as well as *suffragette* and *gender rebellion*. Yet I had no powerful feelings on the rights of women in England — only on my own. "I do believe marriage would stand in the way of both our ambitions, so on that matter we are alike, I suppose."

"You're set against marrying then, are you?" Her bird-like eyes were eager and probing.

"Staunchly so — the wrong ones, anyway. And I'm weary of being matched with every wrong one between here and Newcastle."

"So are most of us at Crestwicke." She winked and jerked her head toward her mother.

I blinked, recalling her heated speech on my first night. "She, a matchmaker?"

"More of a calculated chess player. She's

115

been working on dear Gabe of late, and his childhood sweetheart across the way. What a stunning match that would be, and a valuable connection to a wealthy family. She'd do Gabe a world of good too, drawing him out into society."

I studied the Bayer cough tonic label and squeezed a dropperful of the medicine into a fresh cup of tea as I pondered the fate of that letter writer and his beloved. "I suppose such a chess player might also maneuver to divide couples as well as bring them together, no?" Perhaps that's why the letter had been hidden rather than delivered.

She flushed, her mouth pinching into a rosy oval as her gaze fell. "I'm afraid so."

I paused, noting her reaction. "One of yours?"

"Long ago. Oh, it was nothing, really. If a man cannot stand up to Golda Gresham, he won't last long as part of the family, now, will he?"

I clenched my lips shut, burning with anger for her.

"Oh heavens, don't look that way. I'm not the only one. Why, even Essie's young man was sent away, although I don't believe she knows why."

I huffed. "Does everyone in the house go along with these schemes, arranging their

116

lives and marriages as she deems fit?"

"If they know what's good for them. She makes everyone see reason, sooner or later."

I looked long at Celeste. "That man of yours. Was his name —"

"Miss Duvall, have you any plans to actually carry out your duties?" Golda Gresham's voice jerked me back to my task.

I stirred the mixture and hurried over. "Here you are, Mrs. Gresham. My apologies, I haven't seen Celeste in so long, there was a great deal to discuss."

She raised her eyebrows. "Pray, what about? I hope she hasn't convinced you to cast your lot in with those women. You'd think she'd spend time cultivating qualities that might *attract* a man, rather than running them all off."

I lowered my voice, embarrassed for Celeste. "She has many virtues a man might value and she's quite accomplished. She attracted a suitor once, did she not?"

"A French scoundrel." She spat the last word. "A man of no account."

I peeked over my shoulder, but Celeste had vanished.

I settled back before my patient. "Mrs. Gresham, I don't suppose you remember anyone named Aberdeen, do you?" It didn't *sound* French, but perhaps . . .

She narrowed her gaze and sipped her tea. "Wherever did you come upon that name? You're a first-rate snoop, you are, and only a mediocre nurse."

I studied her face, and everything it veiled. Anger glowed in her eyes, but this mediocre nurse smelled fear too. "I came upon the name in passing, in relation to this house."

She blinked several times, lowered her tea. "He was a servant who left Crestwicke years ago for town." A forced smile of gentility. "I'm afraid your curiosity has led you to a rather dull end." She watched me with rapt attention, pressing her lips together, then wetting them with her tongue, and I realized how important my response was to her. Yes, she was afraid.

My gaze nearly burrowed into her head, so desperate was I to peel back that perfectly coiffed hair and glimpse her knowledge on this man.

"Those servants, a rather dodgy sort at times. Here today, gone tomorrow." Her gaze remained steady as she spoke.

A knock on the door cut in, and Parker entered to announce that their rejected guest had persisted. "Shall I bring him 'round, madam? Mr. Burke insists you see him."

"Very well, then."

Before I could ponder further, a well-dressed gent approached with long strides, black bag in hand. Dr. *Tillman*? I held back a groan. I knew the man well — but wished I didn't. Father's former protégé had been all science and no heart — an intolerable sort of physician. Worst of all, he'd patronized Father after a time.

"Good day to you, Mrs. Gresham, Miss Duvall." He set his bag on the table and smiled at the lady of the house while I willed myself not to roll my eyes. "How are you this morning?"

She straightened. "Why are you here again? I'm not your patient, nor do I wish to be."

"No, but your husband is. Therefore, I'm duty-bound to concern myself with the health of his entire family."

"And a larger share of his pocketbook."

He offered a grim smile and opened his bag. "I hear you've hired a nurse to aid with your voice. I hope you are not unwell. Have you any recurring symptoms?"

"None but you."

I coughed my tea back into my cup, choking on my restrained laughter. There it was at last, a ray of kinship with this woman.

Undeterred, he fished something from his well-oiled leather bag. "I have something

119

I'd like you to try."

Golda Gresham rose, a pillar of disdain. "I know what you're about, and you can take your leave before you say anything more."

"You haven't even given them a chance yet." He lifted a blue stoppered bottle from his bag. "Tillman's tablets will redeem your good health and have you singing like a bird in no time. Only two pounds a bottle."

"I never waste a pound, much less two."

His gaze was steady. "What if they truly help you feel better?"

"Or I could simply hire a new physician for my husband. Now wouldn't *that* make me feel grand." Her smile curled into her cheeks.

"Mrs. Gresham, I wish you would seriously consider —"

"Leaving this house." I hurried over to escort him out. "That's what *you* will consider, anyway. She has no need for your magic beans."

I glimpsed a flicker of approval from my patient.

"Just a moment, Miss Duvall." He folded his arms over his chest as if to brace against me, anger hardening his features. I hadn't meant to make an enemy of him, but clearly I had. In seconds. "If you refuse to let her

120

even consider the tablets, then tell me —
has she improved since you've come to stay?
Her lung capacity, her throat?"

I flashed a look up at the odious man
before me, then at my waiting patient who
sat very straight in her chair, a cat with
perked ears.

"I assume you've already worked together
on the obvious things. What difference have
you seen in her voice?"

Strangled by the waiting silence, by both
pairs of eyes on me, I searched for the right
words, for I knew they'd get back to my
father. I was walking through a field of
buried explosives, and I had no protection.
"I do believe that Mrs. Gresham sounds
better today than she ever has before."

"Is that so?" I wished I could slap the
smile right off his face. "Perhaps she should
perform her verses before a crowd. Yes, I
believe she should."

Charged with fury and dread, I propelled
that man toward the door and lowered my
voice to a harsh whisper. "You despicable
man. My father would in no way condone
such underhanded behavior. Both the magic
elixir you're trying to foist on her and that
horrible display just now."

He sobered. "My apologies, Miss Duvall.
I meant no harm."

"Take yourself away from here and leave my patient to me. And never even implicate an association between your name and my honored father's."

Golda had slid onto the piano bench behind us, her fingers idly plunking keys.

His gaze was steady, intentional. "I rather hoped my name might be intimately associated with Phineas Duvall for a long time to come . . . through marriage."

Every muscle tensed. "Marriage generally requires permission from the bride, which you'll find nearly impossible to obtain."

"I see. I was given to understand . . . that is, he mentioned an agreement between you . . ."

I convulsed, sudden illness sweeping over me. "He told you about that, did he?" Weak. I felt weak. My knees were pudding. I looked up at him, full in the face of where my failure would land me. My skin tingled and something swelled in my throat.

He looked down, bag in hand. "I'm the one he's picked, it would seem. If you find you must, though — marry, I mean — I'm not the worst option available. He's always envisioned us together, and I've come to see the wisdom in it. Perhaps . . . give it a thought?" A half smile warmed his face. "I'd never force you, of course, but do give it consideration. Think what we could do together, a doctor and his little nurse."

I cringed. How desperately I needed those precious letters beside my name — not M-R-S but M.D. I felt the need for it in my marrow.

"I know you care about helping people as much as I do." His face grew soft. "You're really a wonderful helper, you know. Done wonders for that father of yours, even when he should be put out to pasture. How perfect would it be to work side by side, as medical partners, but also as husband and wife?"

"You'd best go." Or I'd end his silly infatuation by becoming sick all over his patent leather shoes.

He turned, but paused in the hall. "Consider it, will you? Whatever it is you have against me, please, Willa, don't let it stand in the way."

By all means, one should never let a complete lack of affection stand in the way of marriage. "I should see to my patient." I turned away as dread rolled in my belly.

Shoving aside my panicked thoughts as the doctor departed, I turned again to Golda Gresham and crossed the room to her. I'd not failed yet. "A little better now?"

She looked up from her idle tune, a smile

of distant amusement playing with the edges of her lips. "A performance. I had no idea I was ready, but what you said . . . Perhaps it's time." She ran her fingertips along the keys and closed her eyes. "Yes, it's time to give the world a taste of my heart and soul, and let them enjoy what I've created. Imagine it!"

I did.

NINE

I cannot decide if marriage would be a waste of the only life I have . . . or if avoiding it would be.
~A scientist's observations on love

When darkness settled over the estate, I couldn't sleep. My mind raced, worry clouded my rest. *God, what do you intend in all this? What exactly did you have in mind for me?* Truth and kindness, both traits of God, seemed to be in stark opposition in this position, and I couldn't seem to balance them. I rose and dressed, sliding my hands absently down the front of my cotton uniform where apron pockets should be, and suddenly I knew.

Pockets! That's where I'd put that letter. I pounced on my bag and pulled out both uniform aprons, digging through the pockets. No letter. I touched a faint stain on one, remembering that first night and . . .

The laundry. Would the letter be a sodden mess at the bottom of the washtub? Or would it have been mixed up in the linens? Finding it now might be futile, but I had to try. Some beating heart had bled those feelings onto the page.

And I had lost the wretched thing.

Flinging a wrapper around me, I slipped downstairs, candle in hand, to attack the laundry. I shook out every linen napkin and bedsheet, inspected the cramped little shelves, washbasin, and hand-wringer, but I found nothing. I heaved a sigh that nearly put out my candle and poured myself a calming cup of tea in the servant's hall. With cup and candle in hand, I moved back toward the stairs.

Yet when I slipped past the library, sounds of shuffling slowed my progress. "Hello! Who's there?"

I jumped, pulse thudding erratically.

"Hello, hello. Who's come to see me?"

I glanced around, heart pounding, and stepped into the library if only to assuage my curiosity. Finally I spotted the old woman in layers of gauzy white peering down at me from the second-story balcony. She blinked. "Oh, it's you."

Lifting her plumage, she hobbled down the steps.

I put a hand on my chest, willing my heart to calm, and moved to help her descend the final steps. "You gave me a fright, Miss . . ." I realized then I'd never been formally introduced, and the only name I knew was "Maisie."

"Just aunt. Aunt Maisie." She paused at the bottom and took my hand. "I despise being reminded I am not 'Mrs.' every time someone says my name. And heaven forbid you call me anything with the word 'crazy' in it."

I forced a wobbly smile. "Aunt Maisie, then."

She looked me over with a mild stare. "I do like you, Miss Duvall."

I blew out a breath. Her frank approval released something in me that had been knotted up since arriving.

"You've done a lovely job with Golda."

"Thank you, but honestly I've done very little." I set the candle down. "I've begun learning what I can about her condition, but I am mostly discovering I'm completely unqualified for this."

"You've come to the right place for help." Her bright little eyes watched me.

I breathed in the aroma of old books and ink. "I have enjoyed this place. Why are you here so late?"

"Why, this is my quarters. If you look right up there, that arched door leads to my chamber. I seldom sleep anymore, and I need some old friends to keep me company." She ran a hand tenderly along the spines, leaning a weathered cheek on them. With a sigh, she released them and hobbled to a chair. "So where did you find the letter?"

Shock split through me. "The . . . letter?" She couldn't know about the one from the desk.

"Yes, of course. The one you were telling young Gabe about."

A rush of spiteful energy threatened to spill out of my mouth. "That was a private conversation. You were eavesdropping?"

"Eeeeavesdrop." She drew it out with a pleased smile as if licking honey from her lips. "Eavesdrop, yes. I must have that one." Without a hint of apology, she shuffled to a little table in an alcove and flipped open a massive book, dipping her pen, and scribbling something. *Eavesdrop,* apparently.

I cleared my throat, forcing myself past the irritation. "What's in your book?"

She returned without answering and perched on a chair, head tilted on her hand as she studied me. "Now tell me, what has you speaking with such contempt?"

128

"A mere desire for privacy in my conversations."

"Not to me, Miss Duvall. To yourself. You cannot succeed if you are telling yourself you won't." She folded her arms across her bosom. "Now tell me, how did such a pretty young lady come by all those ugly words?"

The bare truth of her statement shifted my thoughts. "I suppose I never thought about it."

"Well, you should."

All right then, think about it. Words shape reality, after all, right? *I* will *be a doctor. There's no reason for me to fail. Dr. Duvall. Dr. Willa Duvall. At your service, Dr. Willa Duvall, first woman to be educated at Durham University's School of Medicine. How may I help you?* They tasted good to my heart.

"I forget words all the time, so I capture them. Bottle them for later use."

"I beg your pardon?"

"My book. You asked about my book. I collect words so I won't lose them all into the black hole of feeblemindedness. When words are all you have, it suddenly makes you want to keep as many as you can so you can use them when you have need."

I had heard the whispered comment *"Not all there"* concerning this woman, but as I lived and breathed, if she wasn't all there, she was somewhere far higher and better. She reminded me of an aged fairy that flitted about, never truly having to land her feet in the real world. Not anymore, at least. That was the beauty of age, it seemed, if there was any.

I considered this unusual woman. Words, then. Perhaps I could entice her to spill a few. "I'd imagine you know all the secrets of Crestwicke, yes?"

"Only the ones worth knowing." She puffed out her meager chest. "Even yours."

She flattened me with the turn in conversation. "What do you know of mine?"

She watched me carefully. "That you don't understand love yet, but you're here looking. Thank heavens, you're looking."

My ears turned painfully hot. "I wouldn't call it 'looking.'" More like longing without the hope of actually finding. "I've no need of love." I stared at her. "Just like you."

My statement struck her as it had the last time, melting the challenge from her face. "Not needing and not having are two entirely different matters, mind you." She held out one crooked finger. "Let me tell you something, Miss Duvall. Few people have the great — and I do mean *great* — fortune of falling in love. No one should ever turn her back on it."

"By 'no one' you mean me, I presume?" I couldn't keep the sarcasm from my voice.

She leaned forward, as if willing her wisdom into me through her narrowed eyes. "I *know* you have the hunger in you — I can see it glowing in those eyes of yours. Perhaps it feels safest to quench it, to pretend it isn't important because you fear you'll never find your happy ending, but let me tell you, Miss Duvall, that hunger may be the most important force in your life."

My face heated.

"Lean into it, strengthen it, fan that desire into flames and never let it go out. Allow yourself to feel that ache fully, driving you on until you've found the sort of true, authentic love that few truly have. I've been on that journey and it was the most incredible one I've ever taken in my long life."

Returning her gaze with equal intensity, I turned a daring corner. "I'm going to guess, then, that his name . . . was Grayson Aberdeen." I cast out the lovely name like a lure, reeling her in with a sparkling smile.

She stared, a glint in her eye. "Still trying to untangle that puzzle, are you? What on earth has driven a young lass like yourself into so sad a story? You should be busy forming your own tale. Not chasing someone else's."

"I've stumbled upon part of this man's love story, a letter he wrote, and I dearly wish to know the rest."

Her thinly drawn eyebrows arched into her lace cap. "What exactly was in that letter?"

"Things meant only for the recipient — whom I hope to find." I dared her with a look to admit she knew who it was.

Her eyes flashed, gaze fixed on me. The clock ticked away several seconds before she answered. "T'won't do any good now, you know. It's too late. No matter what's in it, that letter is best forgotten."

"Perhaps you're right." I rose and made for the door. "I suppose it's no good you reading it at this point, is it? I'll just keep it to myself and —"

"Hold on, now."

I paused with a coy grin but painted my face with innocence when I turned. "Yes?"

Her features contorted in a grimace. "I suppose an even exchange would be agreeable."

"Marvelous idea." I hurried back to the chair I'd abandoned. "Why don't you start, since you have the beginning?" And since I seemed to have misplaced my piece.

"Very well, then." She settled back and her eyes widened with the faraway look of one about to embark upon an epic tale. "It started, as most good stories do, with a handsome young man who fell deeply, madly, passionately in love."

I settled in with a sigh, curling up in the chair and cradling the warm teacup with both hands. How beautiful that I knew the middle portion of this story, and if I heard the beginning, perhaps I could change the ending.

"They were not terribly young when they met, already nineteen and twenty, but they hadn't any idea of things. In fact, the object of Grayson Aberdeen's affection nearly overlooked him. She had no notion of marrying, especially not him."

I narrowed my gaze at the story that began to sound familiar.

"But he was persistent and certain, and —"

"I suppose the boy trained horses and the girl worked in medicine, and there was a meddling aunt who believed the pair should be matched."

She smacked the arm of my chair. *Whack.* "Hush, now. I'm telling it."

"A story will not convince me to upend my life."

"Do you want to hear the Aberdeen story, or don't you? It's all true, and it isn't about

133

you a'tall."

I sighed, eyeing her with suspicion. "Very well, then."

"Their love wasn't suitable, but they couldn't help themselves. Both families had such traditional ideas about class and marriage, but the pair sensed how rare it was to find love in any sphere. They were each so different from the people they normally encountered, yet there was something similar — no, the same — between them and they recognized it instantly.

"Now then, there was no earthly reason their union should occur, no advantage other than love itself, and that alone made it special." Her watery gaze lifted to the tall window beyond us that sparkled with moonlight. "Those are the stories that deserve a happy ending, but rarely seem to get one."

I could scarcely breathe. "Which was wealthy and which was poor?"

As if in a trance, she continued right over my question. "The girl who caught Grayson's eye, Rose Ellis, had a deep love for people, a loyal and good heart. She was wildly beautiful, and as fate would have it, she eventually fell deeply in love with Grayson Aberdeen, who was bold and dashing but so very unsettled. It was like fireworks — beautiful sparks of energy and delight when it was good, and a blazing fire when it was not. There, you see? It's nothing like your story. Nothing at all."

I pinched back a smile.

"He met her quite by accident one day in the gardens as she was pilfering some prize flowers to make a rose crown for her beloved godmother, who'd taken ill."

"Forget-me-nots, by chance?"

"Roses."

"So they were *his* flowers she was filching, I assume?"

Her face scrunched. "Are you going to let me tell it? No, they were *not* his flowers. What man has flowers?" She grumbled, eyeing me. "So then, he came upon her settled among the tall grass, her long hair in a glossy black waterfall down her back, and he immediately became enchanted with her."

Black. Long black hair. *The ghost girl!* At times my instincts were uncanny. I tipped forward with eagerness to drink in every drop of the story she was serving.

"It wasn't love at first sight, mind you, but a definite enchantment settled around the man's heart that first day, never to be removed. He peered over her shoulder at her sketchbook. She was an artist and a writer, she told him, and she illustrated her

135

stories in charcoal. Her mind filled in the colors her papa refused to buy for her. So of course, upon their next meeting in the field beyond the garden — for he returned every day until he saw her again — he came bearing silver tins full of fresh pigment. Oh, but she was ecstatic, and more than a little drawn to the young rogue who flirted and brought her paints. 'Will you teach me to paint too?' said that grown-up imp. He was determined, you see, to win her heart however he could."

I sighed, slipping into the dreamy scene she painted. Perhaps that's what I needed — a man to bring me a gift of medical equipment or perhaps a new bag. Only then would I know he truly appreciated my chosen profession . . . and me. My mind wandered, thick with tiredness that pulled at the edges. My eyes were suddenly dry and weary. "So did she teach him to paint?"

"She gave it her best, but he wasn't a quick hand. Poor lad wasn't one for sitting still, so he'd often dash the paint across the canvas in anger and walk away while she laughed him off. But he always came back to see his little Rose. They didn't talk of everyday things, but of art and love and things they found beautiful."

The soft voice was lulling. Almost magi-

136

cal. What a lovely story. Perhaps someday I'd have such a love, with sweet days passed together in fields of flowers. I could picture a man standing behind me to watch as I painted, then we'd look out over the water . . .

My eyes blinked open. How had they closed? *When* had they closed?

Aunt Maisie was smiling at me. "You're exhausted. Traveling to Crestwicke, days of rigorous demands, and now a sleepless night."

"But who was he? You didn't finish the story."

"Well, if you slept through the ending, that isn't my fault, now is it?" Her lips tucked around her gums again as she smiled. "You will come back though, won't you? Come back and hear the rest of it?" Eagerness curled her body forward.

"Will you tell me all of it?"

"Eventually. You'll have to visit enough times to hear it all."

"At least tell me this — did they find a way to be together?"

She sat back a little, content with my response. "They did."

So the letter writer had found his happily ever after already. I couldn't help but feel a tad disappointed that I'd had no hand in it.

"What a wonderful ending."

Her narrow eyebrows raised. "I never said it was the ending. Did I say that? I didn't say that. You'll have to come back and hear more. You promised to come back."

"But they married, did they not?"

She fidgeted. "In a manner of speaking. Well, yes and no. But it didn't end there. The good ones never do. There is far more to come, and you simply must come back to hear it." The woman stood and fluffed her many layers. "Another time, though. Go and take yourself to bed."

"Where is he now? Grayson Aberdeen, that is."

"Your questions have no end, do they?" She grimaced. "Ask them all, and there'll be nothing left to hear next time."

I looked over the woman most deemed useless and found utter delight in her presence. "Last one, I promise. For tonight, anyway. Please tell me, Aunt Maisie. Where is Grayson Aberdeen? I need to find him."

She leaned forward until I could see the thin hairs on her upper lip. "You'll never find him, Miss Duvall. It isn't worth looking."

"He's at Crestwicke, isn't he?"

She merely raised her eyebrows. "Do you know anyone here by that name?"

"He's changed it, then. Who is he?"

She shook her head. "Grayson Aberdeen would never change his name. Too much a part of him. Of his legacy. No, that man will be Grayson Aberdeen until his death."

I lifted my candle, now dripping large tears of wax down its thickening sides, and strode into the hall. Realizing I'd forgotten my teacup, I turned back to the library, but the sight of Aunt Maisie stopped me in the doorway. She stood facing the darkened window, aged back hunched, her frail body so small in the center of that old library. How odd that of all the interesting thoughts and wisdom in her lace-capped head, the advice she'd dragged out to the front was giving one's self over to falling in love — even though she was alone. *I've been on that journey and it was the most incredible one I've ever taken in my long life.*

Yet it had ended, as had Grayson's and so many others. I'd reminded myself of that many times over the years, whenever I faced a flicker of longing, a temptation away from my goals. At least a medical degree would be forever — once I became a doctor, no one could take it from me. It would be *who I was.*

I turned back to the stairs through the dark hall, but a noise ahead stopped me,

139

and I stared into the shadows. Grayson was at Crestwicke, wasn't he? Hiding, perhaps. That'd be why I hadn't run across him . . . yet. I held my candle aloft, but everything beyond its glow was black. "Hello?" I swallowed back the urge to add the name Grayson Aberdeen, fearful of what that might summon. "Is someone there?"

Only my own voice ricocheted about. What a terribly sad house this was, within beautiful walls. It echoed with something terrible, something only magnified by the somber moan of wind forcing its way through the cracks along the windows and groaning high up in the rafters.

Moving swiftly through the passageways and toward the stairs, I jumped when a clock bonged in some distant room, and there on the landing stood the dark-haired ghost girl, a long, thick plait down one shoulder as a hall light flickered just behind her. "Oh, it's you." She descended to meet me, stepping into the little circle of my candle's light, and I saw her clear as day — she was no ghost. "I heard people about. Who were you speaking with?" She spoke with a delicate, lovely voice, yet it was tight and clipped with tension.

"Just an acquaintance."

Pink washed over her high cheekbones.

My, but she was lovely. She looked older than a child, though, when seen up close. Maybe eighteen or nineteen years of age. "Burke?"

"Aunt Maisie, actually."

Something crucial released in her face and her expression smoothed.

"You needn't hate me, you know. We've never even spoken. Though I've been wondering who you are."

Sparks returned to her eyes. "I saw the way you looked at him on your first day here. Burke doesn't care for you, though. An old spinster like you doesn't know how to catch a man's attention."

My shoulders tensed. Yet the longer I studied that angry little face with its pure contours and wide eyes, pity swarmed my heart. "You fancy him your suitor, do you?"

Those deep violet eyes flashed, slicing me with a look. "No, I *fancy him* my husband."

I blinked, stumbling to reorder everything I thought I knew. No wonder Burke had been confused when I'd asked about a girl at Crestwicke — truly, there was none, for it was a married woman standing before me. "Forgive me. I was never told of the marriage. I had no idea you were —"

"It was a quiet ceremony. Burke didn't wish to have a large affair."

"Yes, of course."

"If you'll pardon me, Miss Duvall, Burke will be wondering what's become of his wife."

"O-of course." I fumbled the two simple words as she turned, braid hanging between her two jutted shoulder blades, and left. She moved with purpose into the deep shadows of Crestwicke, and I knew. I knew as I watched the poise and slenderness of her retreating back, that there was so much more to her story.

TEN

Choose wisely whom you allow to share your home, for you will slowly become what he or she believes you are, an image chiseled out word by word, day by day.
~A scientist's observations on love

Clara Gresham chided herself all the way up the grand staircase as she climbed by feel, hand gliding along the well-oiled railing. Her suspicions were silly. Burke was likely buried in work, not sneaking off for dalliances with the new nurse. He'd warned her when they married that work consumed him, and it had proved truer every month of their life together. She paused outside their chamber for a moment, leaning on the door and allowing the cool dark to swallow her thoughts. She brushed her hand against Essie's love letter in her pocket, willing herself to stop longing.

Suddenly the door fell away and she

stumbled into Burke. She looked up into his chiseled face, the one that had drawn her away from her childhood home. She'd gone willingly enough then. To be always in the presence of such a formidable man, to claim him as hers, would be nothing short of heaven, she'd thought. What girl didn't dream of having such a man to call her husband?

Yet now, only hope kept her there. She'd been outrunning her misgivings all this time, stuffing them down, but they'd caught up with her. That simple love letter — given to the maid, of all people — filled the cracks reality had made in her heart and enlarged them, making her fully aware of how much was lacking in her marriage to the great Burke Gresham.

Burke's frown was magnified by the shadows. "Where were you?" How readily that frown came, especially around her. She'd never have guessed their union would turn into this.

"I couldn't sleep." Especially with him still not abed. She puffed up her meager courage and lifted her gaze. "Where were you?"

His sharp warning glare was the only answer. It was an offense, she knew, to poke at him with questions to which she should already know the answers, if she trusted the man she married. And mostly, she did. Yet it seemed impossible for a woman who had married so well to not have doubts now and again.

Ducking past him, she slipped into their chamber and tightened the robe about herself.

"I've given you the grandest suite you've ever had in your life, but you hardly ever use it. I suppose you were up in that attic again, buried in your paints."

"I wasn't painting."

"But you were wandering alone by yourself at night. What will it take to entice you to act a lady?"

"You needn't treat me this way. I'm not a child, Burke."

"Then stop behaving as one. I need a wife, Clara. One who can walk among nobility with poise, stand beside me as an equal."

His words assaulted her as tiny pellets to her heart that stung but did not kill.

"I purchased that book of manners for you. I suppose it was a waste, just like all the costly gowns with paint smears on the sleeve. It's as if you don't care a whit for the beautiful things you have. Do you? Do you care at all?"

Her very soul curled in on itself as her body remained in the room but her mind separated itself from what her life had become. She should have changed the wretched frock. Instead she'd let passion send her hurtling up the stairs when inspiration struck, heedless of what she wore, and she'd ruined it. She hated to know how much these gowns cost, but he always made sure she did.

"Tell me how to make this work, Clara. How can my wife and the opulent life I've brought her to exist together? Tell me what needs to be done and I'll do it. Shall I hire a tutor? Would that help you remember the social graces that always seem to elude you?"

"I'll try to remember." She turned away, humiliated. She wasn't certain exactly where the failure was, in herself or in the marriage, but she felt it keenly. Hurt welled up in her, its abundance spilling warm and wet from her eyes and falling down her cheeks.

Burke saw, and growled. He always saw. "Why are you crying again?"

She cowered into her settee, which made him growl louder.

"For pity's sake, Clara, stop doing that. Have I ever struck you?" He paced. *"Have I?"*

She forced herself to straighten and turn

back to him. "No."

"You were so eager to take on this life when we were courting." He gripped the chair back, face intense.

A glimmer of hope sparked in her chest at the earnest way he looked at her. It was as if he was fighting a battle within himself concerning her, and perhaps everything was about to change. He'd come to himself again, adoring his little Clara and delighting in her amusing ways.

"It brought me such joy to think of giving you everything you'd always wanted, showering you with the beautiful gowns you used to gaze upon in the windows of Harrods, but you barely seem to care."

"I *do* care." Indeed, she was the problem. She was such a child. Irresponsible and rash, flitting about her lovely life without concern for what others did for her. Though she'd been a Harrington, she lacked the deportment that went along with that old family name, their natural dignity wiped out by a single generation of poverty. She'd have to try harder, especially since it was important to him. "Truly, I do."

His gaze oozed with doubt.

Turning, lashes fluttering away tears, her hand crumpled against the letter still in her pocket. That terrible, troublesome, utterly beautiful letter. She'd meant to look through the study for handwriting samples, but she couldn't help feel a personal connection to this note now.

How she longed for — ached for — what the letter offered. Burke had been that way once, hadn't he? Everything she did had been splendid and charming. He'd even been the one to purchase her paints and set up the attic studio, where he soon after proposed to her.

Slipping the note onto her desk, for she could not bear to be reminded of the fool thing every time she moved, she turned and looked at her husband's back outlined by candle glow as he stared out the window.

Without another word — for what could she say in the face of her obvious lacks? — Clara slipped beneath the sheets and curled around her hurt. She did not even bother to remove her robe. Though they were man and wife, she could not bear to be vulnerable in any way just then. She tucked her hand under her pillow and caught sight of a blue-green dash of paint still on the inside of her wrist.

She touched it, remembering the first time Burke had kissed her. It had been a sacred action, much like a crown being placed on her head. "You mustn't feel you need to hide yourself from me, Clara," he'd said when she tried to conceal a similar paint smear.

At that point, a whole twenty-six months past, she'd been young enough to believe him.

One day things would be better. They had to be, for she belonged to God even more than Burke, and no one was more able than God to right every wrong in the lives of his children.

It wasn't until morning that everything changed. Burke Gresham woke to a cold bed and flung his arm across the rumpled sheets. Head pounding, he pushed himself upright and stared into the harsh glow slicing through a crack in the drapes. The lovely little form beside him was gone. Not that he was surprised.

With a groan, he planted his feet on the morning-chilled floor and splashed his face with water from the pitcher, willing the ache in his head to recede. Feeling for a towel, he knocked books from a chair and papers from a desk. Finally his hand connected with a cloth and he blotted his face and blinked, looking down over the mess. It was a bit like his life at this moment.

He stooped to shuffle the chaos together,

and that's when he saw it. The letter was edged with crimson, and it begged to be pursued further. She'd slipped it from her pocket to the desk last night when he'd turned his back, but he'd watched her in the window's reflection. He lifted the little missive from the invitations and clippings on the floor and flipped it open, catching a brief and sickening glance at the opening. *Dear one,* it began.

Dear one?

He dropped it like hot coal. Firming his jaw, Burke swept the entire pile together, letter and all, and deposited it back on the unkempt little desk. She was his wife, letter or not. It was better not to know.

He rose and fresh pain assaulted his head, sending him cowering away from the bright window and into the desk chair. Why did she have to be so wretchedly closed off these days? It was as if she'd pretended to be this woman of poise and raw talent, a true lady simply fallen on hard times, so that she might catch the attention of Crestwicke's heir. Once she'd wedded him, the light had slowly dimmed to reveal a simple, absent-minded child-creature who was nothing like the woman he'd chosen. That letter might explain what had changed. He had a desperate urge to read it.

But he wouldn't lower himself to snooping. He had plenty of work set out for the day, especially with traders coming through within the fortnight. Everything in the logbooks, every pedigree paper and purchase record, must be perfect if he was to make an advantageous trade. Straightening, he moved toward the door and touched the handle. There he stopped, that simple opening ringing in his head. *Dear one.*

This was useless. He'd never get the wretched thing out of his mind until he read it and saw for himself it was simply a misunderstanding. He crossed to the desk and yanked out the note amid a flurry of papers, reading it with growing dread from start to finish — twice. Then his hand shook. He controlled this estate, a house full of staff, even several investments, but his marriage and wife eluded his firm grasp.

He read it a third time and anger boiled within. With an incensed growl, he jammed the note in his pocket and marched out the door. What a fool he'd been to ignore the signposts. Distant and withdrawn, Clara had disappeared into the attic more and more until she'd begun missing meals and outings. Family events. Chances to be alone with him.

Now he had a clear view of the wedge that

had formed between them.

Disbelief feathered in him at the notion that his wife had a secret love. She was pretty, no doubt about it, but what about her might drive a man to such desperation, to take such great risks with his reputation and hers? It was her old family name that had drawn his mother to suggest her, and her sweetly unsullied beauty that had drawn him, but besides those traits she was sadly reserved and unremarkable. A nice little addition to the house and his life, but nothing to inspire the raw passion on that dreadful page.

His anger burned, desperate for release, and he channeled it into every physical movement as he banged out the door and up the stairs. "Clara?" Who was the man, anyway? Likely some nobody little artist who wasted as much time as she did on useless frivolity, abandoning family and responsibility. That was the only sort with whom she'd truly connect.

The man was obviously important to her, for he'd seen the way she gazed at his note when she'd slipped it onto the desk. He pictured the woman he'd chosen to marry with a wave of fresh pain. Why on earth did she need another man, anyway? What about Burke was not enough? Was he not even able to keep a simple shop girl happy? There *had* to be an explanation.

Bang, bang. The attic door rattled against his fist, but no one answered.

Wait. What was he doing? Was this not *his* family's estate? He shoved the door open, stumbling into a raftered space hazy with floating dust. Wide-open silence greeted him, and the messy clutter that seemed to naturally trail behind his wife. Brushes, overturned cups, broken pencils, and un-stretched canvas littered the fringes of the room.

No Clara.

He glanced around at the sum total of the work she poured herself into. Her painting had been a nice little benefit at first, some-thing to keep her from becoming a cloying, demanding wife, yet he had to admit, he'd always thought it a rather pointless en-deavor. Replicating a horse or a flower, the foaming ocean, when one could simply step outside and see them, made little sense to him. All this effort, time, and expense for what — a wall hanging? It baffled him that she threw herself into it, heart and soul, as if it would bring in a living or save a life.

He moved deeper into the room, shoving things aside with the toe of his boot. Com-pleted paintings stood propped against the far wall, and he gazed upon each, shaking his head. How did this steal so much of her attention? They were wasters of her time and heart, for it seemed she spent all she had of both up here.

He lifted a small square picture of a man's face and held it close, looking for some hint of who he might be, some connection to the letter. A picture of an unknown stone chapel had received much of her careful attention, down to the shading of the ivy climbing its side. He'd never even seen this place, nor the man in the other painting. Most of the others were a view out an unfamiliar window.

Burke's frown deepened. How foreign she was to him, this woman he'd married. She had such odd things, pictures that held the faces of other men, and letters that started with *Dear one.*

The pain of betrayal assaulted him again fast and hard, stabbing at his usual composure. How could she? How *dare* she? It was abominable. Wretched! Why would she even do it? *Why?* The question burned inside, his soul a furnace of anger. A primal noise rumbled in his chest and exploded out in a terrible growl. He spun, kicking paintings and easels with the force of his pain.

He fell back onto a crate and dropped his

face into his hands, chest heaving, and that's when he saw it. There in the dormer window was the image of a beastly man in hard, angular lines with blazing eyes. It was *him.*

He peeked again at the window, looking at the face she saw every day, the face from which she so often cowered, as she did last night. He spun away and covered his eyes, trying to exit the memory. It was, after all, no excuse for the letter he'd found. She was his *wife* — she'd vowed to honor and obey him, forsaking all others. There was no addendum to that promise, no loophole. Besides, they'd been mere words he'd launched at her. Only words.

Rising, he tore down the stairs and into the study, his sanctuary full of meaningful, logical work where there was always one right answer, a clear-cut expectation. With a firm jaw and resolute mind, he took one last look at the letter written to his wife by some other man, let it flutter down toward the cold hearth, and turned his back on it.

This was not over, but at least he didn't have to look at the thing again.

Eleven

Words sink into the parts of our hearts that no physical weapon can go. And it's those standing nearest to us who can thrust their swords the deepest.
~A scientist's observations on love

I caught Essie in the parlor Saturday morning, cloak and bag in hand, as she attempted to steal out a side door. She spun when I touched her shoulder and her face was mottled, eyes red. "Essie, what's happened? Is it your family?"

She shook her head, erratic curls bobbing. "I'm not cut out to be in service, miss. I make mistakes. I *am* a mistake."

Stricken, I grabbed her arm. "What nonsense, Essie. Tell me what's happened."

"I've gone and broken something again."

"Nothing that can't be —"

"Her red teacup."

"Oh." I pulled back and looked over the

156

doomed girl's face. "You've not told her yet?"

"Why should I? She's going to sack me. She tells me so all the time. Might as well start the leaving before she makes me."

"Do you have somewhere to go?"

"I've a friend in Cheapside who says he can find me work." By the dip and hard angle of her face, it was obvious what sort of work she meant. "It's decent pay for a sacked maid with no references, and he says there are men who favor red hair."

I tightened my grip on her arms. "Oh Essie, you *cannot* do that."

"Well, I can't do much else now, can I?" She stiffened, chin jutting. "Alls I've ever done is this, since I was ten, and if I can't do it anymore . . . Well, any job is better than the workhouse, ain't it? At least I'll have a chance."

"You *can* do this work. Surely you see that. There's more to service than a lack of mistakes. You're amiable and prudent, with a fine heart — exactly what a maid should be. Hasn't anyone ever told you these things?"

She sniffed, eyes downcast. "Someone did tell me once that I had a great deal of strength and kindness. I rather liked hearing that, and I suppose kindness is a fitting

157

virtue for a maid."

"There, you see? Won't you stay and give it a try? I'll even talk to Mrs. Gresham for you. You're a wonderful housemaid who sometimes makes honest mistakes. There's no need to throw away all that good. Especially when someone else sees you that way too."

She fidgeted. "He told me if I could see myself as he does, I'd be brave and unstoppable, and . . . well, I only wish I could be."

"Brave and . . ." Dread crawled through my veins. I knew those words. "Who is it, Essie? Who's said all this to you?"

She pursed her lips. "I don't rightly know, miss. It was in a letter, and he wasn't brave enough to sign it. He passed it to me in the linens one day."

I looked at that freckled face, the lines under her eyes, and the wayward hair — and I pictured her clinging to that letter while she hung over the washbasin.

"It's only because things like this aren't allowed to happen at Crestwicke, miss. You needn't worry over his character. He's only taking care that we're not caught."

"Might I see this letter?"

"I gave it to Miss Clara. She promised to help me figure out who sent it."

"Who's Clara?"

158

"Why, it's Mr. Burke's wife, miss. Haven't you met her? Such a sweet little thing."

I held back an inner groan. Of *course* it was her. The ghost-girl who was not a girl or a ghost, the one who hated me. I swallowed back the rising panic and took Essie's hands. "Promise me you'll stay, and there'll be no more talk of the friend in Cheapside. You belong here, pouring your heart into service as you've always done, with or without mistakes. Let me worry about the teacup." I hadn't any idea what to do, but I couldn't ever resist fixing a situation, whatever it took. It was the doctor in me.

She studied me, then gave a nod. "All right, then. I do so want to find out who's written those lovely things." She smiled. "I want to tell him what he's done for me. I'm quite low sometimes, but I cannot help feeling he knows something I don't. That makes me hope, and hoping makes me a fresh, shiny new woman."

I forced a smile and squeezed her arms again.

She heaved a sigh. "I suppose I should start with the linens in Miss Clara's room, and perhaps steal that letter back for a moment. I'll show it to you."

She disappeared then, leaving me alone in the chilled parlor where Essie was to have stoked the dying embers. I rubbed my hands together and moved to stoke the hearth as best I could, but stopped, struck by the pale face of Clara Gresham watching me from the opposite double doors. When our eyes met, she floated toward me with her usual ghost-like movement and held out a letter. "It isn't the one you're looking for, but this has come for you. It was delivered to my room by mistake with some other correspondence."

I recognized Father's bold scrawl across the envelope and tucked it into my apron pocket. "Thank you."

"That was kind, what you said to her. Very kind."

I released tension I hadn't even known was there. "She deserves every kindness. Essie is a good sort."

She studied me, as if assessing my motive. "That letter of Essie's — you know something about it, don't you?"

"I can't be certain unless I see it again. Would you mind —"

"Impossible." Her lids lowered, and she glanced to the side. "I've misplaced it. Or someone's taken it, I cannot tell. Don't tell Essie until I find it — she'll be terribly crushed."

My tense heart twisted further. "Of course."

I helped my patient open up her day, bringing her correspondence and listening to the lively planning of her performance. My brain galloped with worry, here and there, but I came to no brilliant solutions on anything.

Finally when the early afternoon sun drove Golda to her damask lounge chair and her eyes fluttered closed, I moved to the window and looked down over the yard to the stables and saw man and horse in their delicate dance. Gabe stood tall and still in the corral before a sleek and glorious creature of deep walnut color, palm up and waiting. It was amazing, really, watching him approach the great beast with both gentleness and supreme control, even while the skittish animal leaped away to circle the corral over and over.

The horse took a few quick sniffs of the upturned palm, then Gabe moved closer and smoothed his hand down the length of its neck to the shoulders. It was like an invitation, warm and gentle, that drew the horse in spite of his fear. The horse flinched and jerked away, its massive muscles quivering, and Gabe approached again, palm turned up. I nearly felt the gentle, calming caress this time as his hand moved along the great beast's neck and down to his shoulders and back, his quivering muscles easing at the touch. Perhaps that's why we got on so well — I was just as skittish and he had the same impact on me.

Turning back to glance at my patient, I wondered at the way even Golda seemed drawn to him, comforted by his mere presence when she tolerated no one else. Watching her sleep, I sighed and pulled out Father's letter, breaking the seal and slipping out the contents. It was a letter as well as three notices of local betrothals from a newspaper, a recipe my stepmother had clipped, and a notice of a poetry night with Longfellow in Brighton. I pondered this last one — perhaps I should tell my patient her favorite poet was in England. I unfolded Father's letter, skimming through. The paragraphs about his new clinic made me homesick.

I've begun speaking with investors about building. I have a few on board, but most see it as little more than another small-scale hospital. I only hope my work outlives me, so people realize from it exactly what is lacking in London hospitals.

A few more paragraphs, then he wandered awkwardly into advice on love.

You will find joy in marriage, Willa, even if it isn't what you hoped for. Belonging to a person, and having someone who belongs to you, has a surprising sweetness and comfort in maturing years. I pray you'll find such comfort, daughter. No medical career has arms to hold you in the dark nights.

If you should happen to return unsuccessful, do not deal too harshly with yourself. Your old father — and Dr. Tillman — will welcome you back with ready arms, prepared to make a soft landing for you here.

What he'd meant as a comfort lingered like a threat, driving me to succeed — both with my position and with the love letter that had brought me here. I glanced again to the window, and Gabe stood now with his face beside the great creature's, a cautious mutual trust forming between them. Not many could convince a wild stallion to allow them close, but it took the right man, a gentle touch, and a great deal of patience. *This, Father. This is how a man should woo a woman. Gentle, patient, humble.* Suddenly it

163

occurred to me why I'd naturally tied that letter to Gabe — their approach was the same. How rare, how valuable, was that writer and the love offered to some unknown person.

"A love letter?" Golda's voice made me jump.

Stomach clenched, I shoved the missive in my pocket. "News from home. From Father."

When the dressmaker came for a fitting of the performance gown, Golda shooed me out and I went in search of Aunt Maisie. It was time to find that letter while I still had my position here, and deliver it. If anyone had *taken* the missing letter from Clara's room, it would be her. Rightfully, it might be hers anyway.

I found her before a cold hearth in a little sitting room near the front of the house, a handkerchief draped over her upturned face as she slept. With a knock she stirred, the handkerchief floating to her lap. She glanced about, then settled her gaze on me with a smile. "You've come to hear more."

"No, actually —"

"No matter. You've *come.*"

I moved a chair closer to her and helped her sit up. "Aunt Maisie, I must confess something. I've misplaced Grayson Aberdeen's letter, and now it's leaked into the household."

She blinked. "Leaked?"

"You haven't . . . taken it back, have you?"

"I only wish I had. Tell me, who's found it, and what has happened?"

With a sigh, I clutched my knees and summarized the letter, Essie believing it was hers, and what had become of it. "I was hoping you'd found it among Clara's things and —"

"What do you take me for, a common snoop?" She bounced in her seat on that last word.

"Of course not. I just thought perhaps you saw it and picked it up. I've no idea where it is now, or how to get it back."

"I believe I know. Clara was the last to have it, you say?" She sighed. "It'll be Burke who found it. Burke, who was slinking around the foyer, asking the poor butler to keep account of his wife's comings and goings, and especially to notify him if she received any letters. Now what on earth would make a man say such a thing?"

I wilted against the chair, hand to my forehead. "A love letter among his wife's things. Oh, Aunt Maisie, what shall we do? We must get it back, but how do we untangle the damage it's already done? Burke

165

thinks his wife . . . and Essie. I couldn't bear to tell her the letter isn't hers. Not after . . ." I told her in hurried sentences about the broken teacup and Essie's dilemma, despairing over the scaffolding being built throughout this house and the mess it would soon leave behind when it fell.

Her prim little smile gave me hope. "Don't trouble yourself over that silly red cup. She'll have it come teatime."

"But that's a mere half hour from now. Where on earth will we find another?"

She straightened. "Why, in my little alcove of course, in a box under my bed where I keep the rest of the set. There were a dozen, you know."

"Why, Aunt Maisie, you're brilliant!"

"You think that poor little parlor maid is the first one to break the sainted red cup? I've eight left." She winked.

I laughed out loud, squeezing her hands and beaming my warm thoughts in a smile. "You were the perfect one to come to with this trouble." I helped her stand, balancing her with a gentle hand. "Now, if only you could help me solve the riddle of this performance too. She's being fitted for her costume now."

She grunted as she shuffled forward.

"That would be *your* mess, Miss Duvall. I'll be no help in convincing them of anything. Precious few care what an old woman thinks."

The informal planning meeting happened accidentally the following Monday evening, after Golda had sent me off with a few assignments in preparation while she had a soak in her white porcelain tub. I'd gone to find Celeste, but it was Gabe who found me, and I rushed toward him. "Oh Gabe, I need your help terribly."

"Of course. But first, there's someone I want you to meet." He pulled me into the music room.

He pointed toward a cameo-like woman draped in blue silk with luscious blonde curls twisted over her shoulder, and the truth jolted me. This must be her, the fabled match. In a breath, she was before me, looking me over with flashing eyes as Gabe made the introductions. "Caroline wished to meet you."

"So this is Willa Duvall." Caroline Tremaine offered a smile, her eyebrows arched. "I have to admit, she isn't what I pictured." The woman spoke with such calm, as one who had nothing to prove.

I curtsied, highly aware of my plain uniform beside her robins-egg blue gown edged with fine lace. "A pleasure to meet you, Miss Tremaine. I've heard only good about you."

Her laugh was quick and sure, highlighting a well-placed beauty mark on her cheek. Even her flaws made her pretty. "What a dear little thing she is. I cannot believe we've never met in all your other visits to Crestwicke."

"Thankfully we've remedied that. I've looked forward to making your acquaintance."

"And I you." She smiled. "I'm certain you know all the stories about our dear Gabe."

The word *our* rankled in an odd manner.

Gabe frowned. "Not *all.*"

She merely raised those perfect eyebrows with a knowing smile.

I licked my lips and looked upon Gabe's familiar face, wondering what untold stories lay buried there. What did I not know? A small, sharp sense of betrayal snaked through me, even though I tried to brush it aside. He owed me nothing.

Except now I was intensely curious.

"Oh Miss Tremaine!" Celeste sailed toward us and clutched the woman's hands. "Parker told me you were here. Won't you show me that piece on the piano again?"

"Of course." She glanced once more at Gabe and hurried with Celeste to the instrument that stood at an angle in the sunny windows.

I turned to Gabe. "So that is Caroline Tremaine, the perfect match."

"It is."

"I've no idea why you say she wouldn't have you. Speaking strictly on a scientific level, the slight angle of her body in your direction suggests she feels some measure of attraction to you. I saw her touch your arm, signifying familiarity."

"Hmm."

"Would she at least be accepting of your work with stallions?"

"Her father breeds racehorses for the elite of London society."

"Oh." I licked my lips. "I suppose she'd tolerate it, then."

"She's the best rider I've ever seen. Fluid and agile atop the wildest creature. She has an uncanny ability with them."

Just like Gabe. "And your combined businesses . . ."

"The result would be incredible. We've considered a merge at some point."

As had Golda, I was sure. No wonder she didn't want her stallion-breaking anomaly wasted on a mere nurse from Brighton.

"Now, what about that help you needed?"

"Well, it seems your mother wishes to hold a performance. And that's simply —" I exhaled. How did I put into words the truth of the situation?

"Truly, a performance?" His eyes lit, then he smiled, seeing my unveiled distress. "Not to worry. You'll not be left to plan it alone." He leaned forward, giving my arm a squeeze. "I knew I could count on you." His face brimmed with delight and something else — relief?

I stepped back, speechless. Horrified. What did one say to that? *Temper your excitement. Your mother actually sings like a strangled bird halfway down a cat's throat.* I opened my mouth, hoping it would fill with brilliant words, but instead the door opened and Burke strode in.

His steps slowed as he saw us standing close and one eyebrow cocked up. "Well, now. I do hope I'm not interrupting anything."

"Not at all." Gabe looked bright and alive. I was dying inside. "We were just beginning to discuss plans for Mother's performance."

Burke's eyes snapped with open amusement, his lips twitching into a wry smile as he strode into the room. "Really?" He stretched the syllables out far longer than necessary. "A performance, is it? You must have had a profound impact on her, Miss Duvall, and you are to be congratulated."

"Oh no, I —"

"Come, don't be modest. We must honor you at this little soiree, perhaps announce you as the genius behind her singing. We'll bring you up front for applause and let everyone see you."

The piano music stopped, and all of them were listening. If only I could shrink into myself. "Truly, that isn't necessary." All I wanted was to understand what God wanted of me in all this, and a list of instructions clear as an apothecary's mixing.

"No, it's brilliant." Gabe tipped his head with such a dear smile of encouragement. "You deserve every bit of praise. You always manage to fix what's broken."

Except I hadn't. Her voice was still quite broken.

"You could make it a dinner, a formal affair." Caroline approached from the piano. "How many do you imagine would fit in the parlor, if the chairs were arranged in rows?"

I blinked. Dinner? *Rows?*

Burke grinned at me. "Why not rent a hall? No need to leave anyone out."

Oh no. Oh heavens, no. I had to stop this

mess. It was like a runaway carriage without a horse. Or a brake.

"Maybe a harvest soiree in the fall." Gabe turned to me with a face so wretchedly hopeful. "Do you think she'd be willing?"

I looked to the others hanging about the fringes, the staff scurrying back and forth with dinner trays. I could see the truth just beyond the surface of all their faces, the abundant awareness of what this performance would be, yet no one said anything against it. "Perhaps we should wait and see what —"

Burke crossed his arms. "Didn't you say she requested it? Best ask her soon, while she's still of a mind to do it."

Gabe's face melted further into gladness. "I shall ask her the first moment I see her."

The truth echoed in my throbbing head. This was terrible. Wretched. The reactions of her friends would devastate her. Everything would crash down if no one put a stop to it now.

"Oh yes, do." Caroline stepped beside him.

"She's ready for company, miss." A maid approached with the demure comment, and Caroline seized on it.

"Let's convince her right now." She took Gabe's arm and led him to the door.

The others turned to follow and one word burst from my lips: *"No!"* They paused and all eyes were on me in an instant. The moment of truth had come. Isn't that what I'd promised at the outset — honesty? It was time to administer a large dose of it. "Please. We must all acknowledge the truth of this matter." All I could see was her pale face, that delicate poise, receiving the laughing reactions of her friends, who'd think it all a farce. A grand joke.

"Won't you tell us what that is, Miss Duvall?" Burke stepped forward, eyes narrowing in his distinguished face.

They all quieted, faces turned toward me as if awaiting a prognosis. Good heavens, I was the child announcing the emperor's nakedness.

"The truth is, the state of her larynx is such that . . . her vocal cords and her lungs have not been properly strengthened to produce auditory tones pleasing to the ear, and the entire vocal system . . . well, it is not congruent with tonal quality . . ."

"What are you trying to say, nurse?" Burke placed a hint of irony on that last word.

"The truth is, well . . . her voice. She cannot sing."

After a moment of silence, Caroline Tremaine shrugged. "Why not let her have her little amusements? Let us host her performance and clap loudly enough that she'll feel the whole room is applauding."

Burke crossed his arms. "You're suggesting we pretend her singing is as glorious as she wishes it was?" Gone was the wicked amusement that had colored his features. "Clap loud enough to drown out the stunned silence of the rest of the audience? Invent compliments to feed her inflated pride?"

"You needn't pretend." Clara's soft voice came low and smooth as she stepped from the shadows. "When you truly love someone, you find what's good about them and say it. It's all a matter of where you focus."

Tension thickened the air.

Caroline waved them all off. "Come now, a few harmless white lies, some sweet pleasantries —"

"Lie to save her precious feelings?" Burke tensed. "Don't we do enough of that around here?"

I gripped the back of a chair. The woman was intelligent enough to glean the truth. "Please, let us figure out how —"

"I won't do it." Celeste shot from her chair, silencing them all. Her shoulders trembled, the coldness in her stark face chilling. Had

the atmosphere of this place finally soaked into her as well? "You'll never make me lavish praise on that vain peacock of a woman, not even for a moment. She's controlling. Arrogant. Self-important. Utterly domineering. Mean-spirited and brutish. Worse than any man and only half as intelligent."

"You don't mean it, Celeste." Gabe's quiet voice failed, for once, to turn the situation. Servants paused to listen discreetly.

"I *do* mean it. Look what that woman's done to the household." Celeste shook, face pale and eyes wide, as she stood before her family, spitting out feelings as if they'd been pressurized for years. "She's stuffed Burke into a society marriage, made his wife feel like a leech. She has poor Essie so afraid she's tripping over herself, and she's chased Father from his own home. Can't you all feel the poison she oozes into this house? It's killing us all, and if she isn't happy here, then so be it. Let her leave. But I will not fluff her feathers this way after all she's done to Crestwicke. Do *you* like her? Or you?" She pointed to Clara, then to Essie. "Does anyone here like Golda Gresham at all?"

The silence seemed to echo off the papered walls, strong enough to curl it at the ends. Gazes lowered.

Burke's voice broke the silence. "Well

175

now, Miss Duvall, you've done what you promised and brought out the truth. Congratulations."

A distant tinkling crash somewhere above jarred the tension. The truth struck me hard and fast. Golda was above us. The fireplace. She could hear. She'd heard everything.

I bolted up the stairs, chest burning as I burst through the double doors of her suite. *No, no, no, no. Please, Father.*

She lay wilted on the rug like a fallen dove, a broken teacup on the hearth. Two gold slippers protruded from the hem of her massive skirt, and she looked white as death.

Apoplexy?

I dropped to my knees, felt for a pulse. Weak. *Please wake up, please wake up.* If those words spoken below were the last ones she heard on this earth . . .

The old nightmare swept over me in cool, bold strokes as I dug through my bag. Our quiet cottage, the clock thunking out the seconds, Mother's blood oozing onto my hand where she'd struck her head. She'd fallen down the stairs, onto that vase. That truly ugly, awful vase. I clutched her there on the kitchen floor, but she wilted, slowly escaping breath by breath, leaving me behind.

No, Mama. I don't know how to stop it. I don't know.

Golda's slender body now lay wilted in my arms, heavy and helpless. This . . . this is exactly why I'd become a doctor, so it would never happen again. So I'd always know what to do when heaven began beckoning to a soul too early. I leaned over the mother of my best friend with a bottle of smelling salts and prayed he wasn't about to experience the same wrenching pain I still couldn't forget.

TWELVE

When watching one's tongue in a relationship, there's a difference, I think, between
using kind words and safe ones. The first
seeks to protect their love's heart, the
other only their own.
~A scientist's observations on love

After many long moments, Golda Gresham
came back into the world with a delicate
shudder and blinked up at me. Gabe rushed
in, his body tense.

"She's fainted," I said.

"I can see that." His voice had a hard edge.

I set aside the smelling salts and closed
my bag. "I mean to say that she'll be all
right. Other than a slight concussion from
the fall, she seems unharmed."

Gabe's stare held the weight of a brewing
storm that communicated everything —
she'd been fine before I'd opened up the
door to the truth. I was, after all, supposed

to be on *his* side. He scooped the ghostly pale woman up in his arms and settled her on the red damask settee as she clung to him. "You're all right, Mother?"

"I'm coming 'round. Go on, now." She lifted a spindly white hand and placed it on his cheek. "Dear boy." How weak she looked.

He studied her a moment longer, then gave a nod and rose. "You have the maid find me if you need me for anything. Anything at all."

I followed him to the doorway, my heart thumping against my ribs. "I never intended to stir things up that way, you must believe me. I was merely speaking the truth because no one else would. She may have many talents, but she is not a singer."

"It's not about her being bad or good at it, Willa. It's never been about that."

"False encouragement isn't love. It's wrong to pretend you enjoy her singing when you don't."

"I *do* enjoy it." His face was dark and passionate. "I enjoy every moment of watching her light up, hearing her voice rather than her silence, being in the presence of such passion when I've seen her deflated. There's far more to what a person does than whether or not it impresses other people."

"But her friends . . . they'll all laugh."

"Not the right ones."

I breathed out, my mind spent and my heart depleted. Somehow if this man did not think much of me, I could do naught but share his opinion.

"Singing fills her heart. A filled heart keeps beating, longer than it's supposed to, and that makes it all valuable to me."

Her . . . heart. Her *heart.* Jagged pain tore through my chest. Awareness thrummed. I spun, looking with fresh eyes at the woman wilted onto her fainting couch, seeing the pallid skin, the weak rise and fall of her chest, the swollen feet she'd kept hidden beneath her hem until now.

"You of all people, Willa, should realize how fragile and precious life is. Every life. It's worth preserving, however we can."

I couldn't speak. When Gabe slipped out, I untangled my stethoscope from my bag and settled the diaphragm gently on Golda's rising and falling chest, moving aside the ivory cameo necklace and listening to the erratic heartbeat buried beneath finery. Hard as ice she was, yet just as easily shattered it would seem.

I sat back on my heels with a sigh, and a sick rolling in my belly. "Why didn't you tell me?"

She lifted those ever-elegant blue eyes to me, shifting the cameo back into place. "Why ever would I? No one can fix it."

"I could have helped you differently, worked on other things instead of giving you those . . . those silly singing lessons."

Her gaze met mine, steady and meaningful. "Nothing is truly silly." It was a moment of rare openness, a glimpse into how she grappled with her approaching death, yet it made *me* feel like the vulnerable one.

I swallowed as my heart rose into my throat. "Why do they let you go on this way when they know —"

"They *don't* know. Only Gabe."

Because he noticed. He listened. Words may be powerful, as I'd tried to convince him, but sometimes an absence of them was even more so. "I suppose he assumed I already knew." As my heart began a painful realignment regarding this woman, it melted into compassion. Curiosity. "Why singing, Mrs. Gresham?"

"You mean, why sing when I possess no talent for it?"

"Well, I mean . . . that is —"

"Come now, let's speak plainly with one another. I'm ill, not deaf."

I traced the edges of my stethoscope. "All right then, why?"

She turned to stare at the empty fireplace, the silence stretching long enough to make me wonder if she was going to answer. "Because I am not ready to cease existing." She remained poised, candle glow smoothing the lines of her face into a nearly youthful expression. "When you first learn your end is coming, it becomes obvious just how much of this life does not matter. Why decorate for Christmas? I may not live until then. Why learn something new? I shan't be here to use it." She inhaled, then let out a long sigh. "But then you realize there *are* things that matter, more than you ever thought, because they will last longer than one's body."

I'd seen this before — the desperate scramble to put into place a few things that will mark a person's existence, something besides a stone and a name in the family Bible to show who you were.

"I've learned so much in life, felt so deeply, but it'll all be lost. Everything I know and think and care about will fade away like me . . . unless I leave something behind." She ran one finger along the spine of her red book. "I used to sing like a bird, many years ago." Another caress of the spine, then she tossed the book into the cold hearth. "I suppose I ought to give up that notion."

"We must tell your family of your condition. Perhaps your children would all join together and . . ." My voice faded miserably as I remembered what she'd heard below.

Her sad smile extended past me into the emptiness of the room. "As we both heard tonight, I have surprisingly little influence here."

"You have more than you'd think. Everything you say —"

"Has made them hate me, turned them all into ruined towers of bitterness like me."

"And it can build those same ruins right back up. Make *that* your legacy."

She shot me a look, her gaze taking me in, assessing my meaning.

"There's always hope to repair what's broken. Every breath in your body means there's still a chance."

She frowned and turned away.

"Mrs. Gresham, I need to see exactly how advanced your condition is." When she gave a reluctant nod, I performed a more thorough examination, looking beyond the throat and voice to the deeper issues. The stethoscope told me everything I'd feared, and I wrote it down slowly in my notebook:

Diastolic murmur, frequent irregularity

likely in the aortic chamber, possible regurgitation in the valve.

I looked her over, taking note of the symptoms she'd hidden so masterfully.

Shortness of breath, especially when taxed, fainting spells, swollen feet and ankles.

I lowered my notebook to my lap and exhaled the weight of my failure. I'd lost sight of the patient in treating symptoms. That's what overworked hospital doctors did, and what I vowed I'd never do. No, I'd be different, I always thought. I'd combine the intellect of men like my father with the compassionate, perceptive eye of a woman, yet I'd failed already. When had I ever neglected to dig for the cause of illness?

When I began treatment with passing judgment.

I looked up at the woman whose severe, hostile face suddenly morphed from bitter to hurting — from controlling to one desperately clinging to life.

"I hope you are not set on saving me. Even the daughter of the great Phineas Duvall cannot work miracles."

"I just want to understand. As your nurse,

184

I must be allowed to care for you however I can. To start, I'll need to draw blood so I can learn more."

She gave a regal nod, and I began, removing syringes and test tubes from my bag.

I looked up at her when the needle was established. "How long has it been this way? Your heart, I mean."

"I had rheumatic fever as a girl."

"None of this was in your patient file."

"Because I'm not truly anyone's patient. Your father was my husband's physician, and by default our family's doctor, but not mine. He never examined me, never treated anything. Then came Dr. Tillman, taking over for your father, but I found him distasteful. Burke sent him 'round to talk sense into me a few times, but I never gave him leave to examine me."

"So who . . . ?"

She took a deep breath. "A traveling doctor. Years ago, in my youth. He told me the fever had likely settled into my heart when he heard an abnormal rhythm after a relapse. I grew better and worse throughout the years, but that was the beginning of my end. I didn't care to know the details then, and pretended when I felt well, I'd stay that way, but now it will not be escaped. Nor can it be cured."

"Then all this time, you've merely been preparing to —" I clamped my mouth shut. My foot had fit into it enough times for one day.

She lifted a hard, practiced smile. "Aren't we all?"

I watched the little tube fill with blood, scrambling for something concrete, something factual to say. I tripped over deep, maudlin thoughts. "Inflammation is probably what you were noticing. It might come and go for years, but the problem is actually the scar tissue from the fever that has built up in one of the heart valves. It slows down blood flow and makes you weak, especially in times of distress. Which is what happened tonight, and it will only worsen as this progresses."

"Eventually it'll be blocked completely, I suppose."

Her question hovered in the quiet room as I withdrew the needle and focused on applying pressure to the spot. The ever-present aroma of chamomile and rose water stung my nose with each quick breath.

"Come now, Miss Duvall, this is the time for that truth you claim to peddle, since you've come this far."

I took a long breath and looked at her. It was easier now to see her as Gabe did. She was both stronger and more delicate than I'd ever imagined. "Yes, that is the eventual outcome. But it needn't happen anytime soon. I will do all I can to —"

She laid a clammy hand on mine, lips firm. "Don't bother trying to wrestle my life away from the Almighty if he wants it. There are precious few here who do."

I put my tools away, cleaning and packaging the syringes with my usual precision. What a relief routines could be, procedures one could simply follow without involving the brain. I breathed in and released it as I looked at the cold hearth with the discarded red book. I glanced again at my patient, so lovely and intimidating, who had chased away everyone except the one paid to be here, and I finally understood. I grasped why I was here.

Being alone is a wretched way to live, but an unbearable way to die.

My neck ached hours later as I curled over my microscope, studying the blood samples. My patient slept across the room. I glanced up at the woman's rising and falling chest, willing it to continue.

So much for being a healer.

I jerked up at a noise. Someone stepped in and I blinked, adjusting my eyes.

"How is she?" Aunt Maisie approached with a whisper of taffeta and set her candlestick on the night table.

I rose and moved to the little chair beside my patient's bed. "Recovering. Sleeping, just now."

"And you?"

Better than I deserved to be. "I'm well."

"You look terrible." The statement was warm with compassion. The old woman moved a chair up to the bedside next to mine. "You needn't feel it's your fault. If that's what is flying through that oversized heart of yours, simply tell it to stop. The Almighty's hand is much, much stronger than your nursing hands, and Golda Gresham is cradled in the palm of his sovereignty."

I swallowed my arguments. I could handle all manner of criticism as a female doctor, ridicule for being a spinster, even scorn from rejected suitors. Yet watching a patient suffer, especially if I had a hand in it . . . nothing did my heart in more thoroughly than that.

The old woman perched on the chair and pulled out a tangle of string, expertly arranging her fingers in the mess, and beginning to work. "No one should be alone at such a tumultuous time. I'll stay for company."

"She won't be alone, I can promise you that. I plan to remain through the night."

"Not for her — she wouldn't know if the entire *circus* visited her room, tired as she is. For *you.* I will not let you spend the entire night slandering yourself in your own mind." She settled in and smiled as her fingers moved nimbly in and around the threads, tatting with surprising ease. "I expect we can find something to talk about for a few hours."

I looked up at this blessed little package of energy and couldn't help but feel utter gratitude for her. "Why don't you talk, Aunt Maisie? I believe I've said far too much already."

She rocked back and forth, her body melting into the wooden spindles behind her as she watched me. "You needn't be afraid of your words, Miss Duvall. Only careful. They're as easy to gather as rocks, and just as easy to throw about, but don't underestimate them. I've never happened upon a neutral word." Her rocker creaked against the floor as she rested, eyes closed and head back, and knotted by feel. "What do you think of *charlatan*? I've just discovered it. Isn't it simply ripe with danger?"

"If you aimed it at someone, I suppose."

"One day I'd like to. *Charlatan*. What a lark." A chain of perfectly formed little circles and knots appeared from the tips of her nimble fingers, even as her mind lost itself in a forest of inconsequential thoughts. "Now then, what shall we talk about to keep ourselves awake?"

"I want the rest of the Aberdeen story." I breathed out this answer without hesitation, and felt it again — that gentle undercurrent of love about the house, like wind through silvery little wind chimes. With all the damage I'd caused in this house, I felt the need to restore something, to offer at least one person a happy ending.

She watched me for several silent moments, as if assessing my worthiness to be admitted deeper into the story. "Very well, then. Not the whole thing, mind you. Now where did we end?"

"He'd caught her picking flowers that were not his and she taught him to paint."

"Ah yes, the flowers. As it turns out, they were *his mother's* prize flowers. She was the lady of the estate, the wife of the squire. Which made him —"

"The heir. Grayson Aberdeen was the heir."

"That he was. And his little Rose was not

190

exactly who his flower-growing mother had in mind for her firstborn to marry."

"I assume Rose was poor." My mind grasped all the clues as they came, trying to make sense of them. Why did the letter make it sound as though he was the one undeserving of her, though? Had he committed some horrible deed?

"Her father was a butcher. They had sufficient income, but she was from a small hamlet near here and certainly not of the right pedigree to marry a gentleman."

"I thought they met in the country, not at the coast."

Her pointed look of annoyance silenced me. "Does a body never set foot outside her home? Of course they met in the country. She summered with a relation near Hassocks every year. Stiff old lady, she was, and in need of a bright and sunny companion. She found that in little Rose."

"I could imagine you being such a girl." I threw the bait out and watched her reaction.

The shock was evident, but she recovered quickly and cleared her throat. "Now, then." As if she hadn't heard. "The story. Our hero asked for Rose's hand no less than three times before he was accepted. He hadn't a token to give her, but he brought her as many of his mother's flowers as he could

191

carry each time he proposed."

"Cad."

She blinked.

"He should bring something that's his, rather than flowers belonging to his mother."

"He was the heir. That means he was *about* to have many things, but as of yet he had nothing of his own."

"Is he not capable of making her something? Perhaps a painting."

Her mouth twitched up into a smile. "Perhaps it wouldn't have taken three tries if he'd had a mind like yours. He did, however, make one of those little flowers into a ring for her. Just a little purple weed, twisted into a circle, but she said yes."

I sighed a fluttering, breathy little sound. I couldn't help it.

This earned me a stern look of disapproval. "I told you, the story isn't over. Don't be all twitter-brained over them yet."

"So they married. How did they manage to convince his family?"

The clouds descended over her expression. "They didn't. Therein lies the problem. He knew they'd never agree to the match, so it had to be done in secret. They ran to Gretna Green during a terrible thunderstorm that boded rain but did not come to fruition, and their wedding in a little shop overlooking the River Esk went much the same way. They planned a honeymoon along the Rhine, with stops in Paris and Portugal, but none of it came to pass."

"They disinherited him. Rose and Grayson were destitute after the wedding, weren't they?"

"No, they did not disinherit him. He had been groomed to be the heir, mind you, so they took him back. Only . . . without her."

I gasped. "They couldn't." I ached inside as I tried to fit together how the letter figured in. Oh, how big and terrible and captivating was the story behind that note. I was beginning to understand why he believed himself unworthy of her.

"Unfortunately, they could. Very convincing, his parents, and they were accustomed to having their way. Especially that mother of his. They pounced on them as they emerged from saying vows and forced them to annul it, then sent the girl on her way."

"How terrible. What wretched people."

She sighed and shook her head, gaze staring into nothingness as her fingers resumed their mad dance of strings. "Such things happen every day, I'm afraid."

The story turned my insides, leaving them hollow and aching. "It cannot end that way.

Surely there's more to the tale."

"Oh yes, but later. It'll have to wait for another night." She lowered her voice. "It seems we're disturbing someone."

Footsteps padded down the hall. I nodded, swallowing my disappointment. *"Later,"* she had said, and I clung to that like the last rose of summer. *Later* meant more was coming. The story was not yet over.

I pondered everything until even Aunt Maisie slept, eyelids fluttering. How helpless it seemed, this love story I'd determined to piece back together. Yet I had another purpose here. I hugged my knees to my chest and looked at my sleeping patient, the delicate woman whom I had hurt with my foolish tongue. After all the trouble I'd caused this night, it was time I did something good with my words.

Moving to a little desk, I burned through one quarter of a candle and several pages of perfectly good paper composing a letter. The idea had been blossoming for hours, culminating when Golda had tossed her red book into the hearth — and I'd felt compelled to retrieve it. *Longfellow, is it, Mrs. Gresham?* Now I scribbled like mad, praying that with a few well-placed words the sold-out event was not so terribly sold-out.

Yet the lines all sounded hollow. Weak. I

194

laid my forehead on a blank page, took a breath, and humbled myself before the only one who could help, the one who had harnessed words to create the entire earth. *What would you have me write, Lord? Do what you will with this letter, with this position at Crestwicke. With her life and mine.*

A surge of strength and compassion cooled my skin, urging me on. Rising and dipping the pen, I took a breath and started in, the tip scratching against thick paper.

I'd like to write to you concerning your poetry night to be held on September the 29th. I know the event is now closed, but I also know that the purpose of your work is to inspire life in people's hearts. Now I beg of you to do that for a woman named Golda Gresham. I am her nurse, treating her dire heart condition, yet I'm afraid her problem extends beyond the power of medicine . . .

After a page and a half of writing that bled directly from my overfull heart, I folded it into an envelope and dripped red wax on its flap. *Please, please. Send a reply.*

For a moment I sat back and stared at it, imagining Grayson penning his love letter by candlelight. Had he written it after the annulment — and lost the courage to send it?

When I'd laid my missive on the side table in the foyer for the post, another whish of footfall against tile made me jump, as if the ghost of Grayson Aberdeen walked about every time we dug up a little more of his story. A childish thought, of course, but many times at night those sorts of notions crowded out reason. Chiding my foolishness, I crossed the hall and edged toward the shadows, but the footfall — a man's — came again. "Hello, is someone there?" A few steps forward. A gulp, then a bold attempt. "Mr. Aberdeen? Grayson Aberdeen?"

A deep, growling voice rolled over my senses, and I spun to face it in the dark. "What are you doing here? Who are you?" A grim, fully suited man with silver-streaked hair stepped into my candle glow, scowling like a bear who had been poked. Tall and gaunt, he wore his white skin on hollowed-out cheeks as if it were one size too small. I couldn't determine his age — life had used him hard.

"If you please, sir, I have something that belongs to you. A letter."

Thick eyebrows descended further. "What sort of letter?"

"Well — that is, you *are* Mr. Aberdeen,

are you not? You must be, for you're the only person in this house I've never met and —"

"Why not give me the letter, then?" He held out one long hand and the light sparkled against his cufflinks. Did ghosts wear cufflinks?

"I would, sir, but I don't have it with me this moment, you see. In fact, it seems to be misplaced. It was a silly thing, really —"

He released a long, windy sigh that left his shoulders stooped. "It's just as well, since my name is Gresham."

I blinked. "Oh, Mr. Gresham. Of course. You are Mr. Gresham."

"And who might you be?"

I stuck out my hand, eager for something to do, no matter how improper. "Willa Duvall, sir. Daughter of Phineas Duvall. Nurse to your wife."

A grimace contorted his sallow face. "What connection have you to the Aberdeens?"

"None at all. I've come across a letter he wrote, but no one will tell me where he is so I can return it. He's like a ghost in this house, who no one sees but everyone fears."

"Ghost, indeed. He haunts the very walls of this house, yet I doubt he's even dead yet, the scoundrel." He licked his lips, a flash of stubble showing across his jaw. "What sort of letter?"

"A love letter. But I've no idea who it was intended for."

He shoved his hands deep into his pockets, driving back his jacket. Silence followed with his slow breaths marking the seconds that passed. "If you happen upon it again, burn the thing."

I stared at the candle flame, feeling terribly intrusive even in my silence, as if I'd tread deeply into a family story in which I had no business. Cobwebs was exactly how it felt — thick and repulsive, the type you walk into unawares, praying there was not a spider at home.

"Would you like me to inform your family that you're here?"

"No." The return was swift and final. "I'll be gone by first light, so I've no wish to disturb anyone."

He spun and so did my thoughts. I was beset with the idea that I *must* tell him of his wife's condition. It was imperative that he understand. I'd be breaking my promise of privacy, but a husband should know when his wife was lingering near the exit of this earth. "Sir, there's something you need to hear. It's about your wife."

But he didn't stop. I closed my eyes and

pushed out a breath.

When he disappeared without turning back, I hurried to the sitting room and brandished a paper and pen, pouring out more words in another pointed letter. The man was needed at home, and he should know it. Details would only be given in person. I carried it about with me the next morning, but he'd already left. I asked Parker to post it to Mr. Gresham's London address, praying I hadn't done the wrong thing.

THIRTEEN

When it comes to marriage and all human relationships, the last place we ever search for problems — or hope to find them — is within us.

~A scientist's observations on love

"Dress? Whatever for?" Golda watched me imperiously from her chair at the window on Thursday as I threw open the curtains in her dreary sitting room, releasing glorious streams of sunshine into the room. It had been overcast for the three days since the incident, so I'd allowed her to remain indoors and wallow in her hurt, but now the sun was out. It's time she was too.

She shielded her eyes as if struck. "What is the meaning of this?"

"It's a glorious day, and I'll not let you miss it." I wheeled my own blend of tea to the table, inhaling the magnificent swirl of mint and citrus. She'd recovered well from her fall, and her heart rhythm seemed stable — surprisingly so.

"We did actually speak the other night about what I think we did, correct? You do realize I have a —"

"Dire need for adventure? Without a doubt." I'd poured over graphs of heart function, cardiology studies, clinical data of autopsied hearts that had been thickened by a similar disease. The heart, it seemed, was the source of many ailments and problems all over the body. Too often, only the symptoms were treated while the undetected illness created further damage.

I'd found no evidence of a cure, and after all my research and scientific analysis, it was Gabe's solution that rang truest — filled hearts keep beating. The one time she seemed truly happy was when she spoke of her horses, so when she'd dressed, her hair smoothed back into fine netting, I led her down to the stables and handed her a riding hat.

She blinked at the groom holding a horse by the bridle, ready to help her mount. "What is this?"

"A ride. You do know how, I assume."

She narrowed her eyes. "You are relentless. Is this why you forced me out of my room?"

I held the bridle while the groom went to fetch a second horse. "Are you coming?"

"I should say not. I'm not even wearing a riding habit."

"I've heard you can ride, but I've yet to see it." I lowered my voice. "Most of your grooms say the same."

With a grimace and a glance toward the lone groom about, she dug her foot into the stirrup and pulled up in one smooth, expert move. "There, now. Satisfied, Miss Duvall?"

I grinned, raising my eyebrows. "Are you?"

She looked at home on the back of that regal animal, her posture sensitive to the horse's movements. I'd never known a lady to mount a horse without help, and my estimation of her rose. The groom returned with a second horse and handed me up.

Golda watched me, eyes snapping. "Now, let's see how well *you* ride, Miss Duvall." Then, before I could ease her into a gentle plod over the fields, she clucked to her horse and they were off at a decent canter, sending up a swirl of white cottonwood fluff behind them. With a grumble, I urged my mount on, galloping toward the cliff's edge. The woman's laugh echoed over the open field as the wind swept over it, loosening our hair and billowing our skirts.

I caught up to her near the coast as she

reined in to an easy trot, face lifted to the breeze, hand clasping her hat to her head. "You mustn't go racing off that way. This was meant to be a slow, easy ride. Remember what you have."

"A dire need for adventure, if I remember correctly." She gave me a sardonic look. "What good is having breath left in my body if I don't use it?" Her lips looked a bit pale, but her eyes were bright and shining.

I bit my lip to keep from smiling. "You're an expert horsewoman, Mrs. Gresham."

"You don't live for years on a stallion estate without knowing how to ride." She shook out her silvery locks and fixed her hat back onto her loosened hair.

I looked at my patient, studying her face for signs of fatigue, for a relapse, but I saw only life and full-bodied passion there. Her eyes shone.

"And don't you feel better now?"

We rounded a hill that blocked the wind, and the world quieted around us, the distant waves sounding like the inside of a shell. She studied me with that unyielding gaze. "I do." Our horses paced along the upward-winding path. "You know, I shouldn't have minded if fate had seen fit to give me a daughter like you, Miss Duvall. You are, at least, interesting."

"Thank you." I staggered under the immensity of her compliment, like a small streak of gold in a mine that only gave an ounce for every hundred feet of rock. "The ones you do have are marvelous human beings, Mrs. Gresham. You should be proud."

She frowned. "You say that as if you believe I despise them. Do you agree with them, then? Do you believe I've . . . ruined them, as they said?"

I hesitated. "You're quite direct with them."

"It's a great passion of mine to see them succeed, to help their strengths rise above their weakness. What good am I to them if I do not push them forward and upward every moment they're under my roof? They have such incredible talent, you know, each one of them."

"Why not tell them so?"

"A body only fixes what's broken, Miss Duvall." She sat tall on her horse.

I breathed in the fresh sea air and sensed the weight of conviction upon my heart. "Pardon my forwardness, madam, but there's much more to helping shape a person than lopping off their flaws." I shoved aside thoughts of degrees and arranged marriages, of promises and futures, and continued up my brazen path. "Every

204

word a mother speaks is like a knife — with power to shape or to wound. To guide or merely interfere and compel —"

"Why must you drag this out? I thought you intended to make me feel better, not worse."

"Because things needn't remain the way they are between you all. I can tell you want it to be different, that your heart yearns for it, and I cannot bear to see you lean on a nurse — a *stranger* — when you have an entire family under your roof. There's hope for the Greshams to become a warm and strongly united family, a glorious Crestwicke legacy for you to leave that's far more personal and weighty than mere poetry. But it's up to you to make it so."

She sat straight and silent, and the soft echo of my passionate words felt foolish. I'd let myself go again, spouting every thought that came into my silly head. I couldn't even tell if she'd heard anything I said, until she spoke at last. "Would that I had someone who cared enough to interfere when I was their age — so much might have been different for me."

I said no more.

We had reached the ruins, our horses pacing beside each other as we looked up in respectful silence. Her thoughts shifted almost visibly as she studied the crumbling stones, expression softening. "We almost married here, you know. Mr. Gresham insisted on a church wedding, though."

"What a perfect place for it." The air wet my face and I smiled, sinking into delight. "It's like heaven up here. A taste of God. I've always felt that, even as a visitor."

She looked me over and gave a satisfied nod, as if I'd accurately answered one of her many unspoken tests. "I began coming here to play when I was a girl, and all of Crestwicke was a derelict ruin like this tower. Trees growing through the windows, vines around the railings. Such a crime it seemed, to neglect a place like this."

"You bought it in disrepair, then?"

"Not me, but Mr. Gresham. He knew I loved the place." She looked into the trees beyond, into the pleasant glow of sun streaming toward us through the leaves. "He fell in love with me first, and I merely thought him ridiculous. I laughed, actually, when he first told me. We were but chums."

"But you eventually came to love him too."

She turned, blinking, and the heavy curtain swept back across her face, separating us once again. "Yes, of course."

"It's a beautiful story."

She bestowed a faint smile, as if I'd

206

eavesdropped on everything she'd just said. "Quite." She reached down and smoothed a gloved hand down her horse's neck, running fingers through its mane. "It's time we turned back."

"Yes, I'm sure it's nearly time to dress for dinner." I checked over my horse's bridle. "Do you think you could eat?"

She gave a light smile. "Enough to feed a regiment."

I grinned at this unladylike admission and shifted, settling into the saddle on stiff muscles. Hunger indicated life had been lived thoroughly, and that was just what we needed this day. "No race this time."

She merely raised an eyebrow and turned her horse. I released my pent-up breath and urged my mount to trot alongside hers, hooves whipping the grass. Even at this slower pace she looked wild, but blazing with freedom and delight. What a change — such spirit, even in her illness. A remarkable woman I would never forget, no matter how many patients I had.

We crossed through the trees and approached the stables from the back as a tall figure marched up and grabbed hold of Golda's reins, flashing a look of burning anger toward me.

"What is the meaning of this?" Burke

growled the words. "What sort of nurse are you, Miss Duvall? Other than sacked."

"I still do the sacking in this house, and I'll thank you to remember it." Golda spoke imperiously from atop her mount, where she'd begun to pale.

"You don't rule the medical licensing board, though." He narrowed his eyes at me. "One claim of medical negligence and your career will be over. You think it's hard to gain acceptance in the field as a woman, it's nothing compared to a woman under investigation."

I stared at this man, my gaze hardening. He was the one guilty of neglect, the way he'd wanted to ship his mother off to an institution. He had no idea — *no idea* — what those places were like, yet they were somehow his preferred solution. Odd how his first show of protectiveness appeared when she looked fresher and more alive than ever. Perhaps that threatened his plans.

Burke helped Golda down. "If you won't remove this woman from your employ, you will at least accept Dr. Tillman as your physician. Perhaps he can talk some sense into you." With a firm arm around his mother, who seemed suddenly resigned, Burke moved with her toward the house. "I'll call him now."

I simply stared, visions of the dungeon-like asylums where Golda would die, of my dear friend losing his mother in a most wretched, unnecessary manner. And the contract — my own sort of dungeon.

I watched her rigid back as she allowed herself to be taken to the house, knowing I could do nothing. The truth was, I had all the heart of a doctor, but none of the credentials. I led the horses into the stables to hand them off to a groom, but it was Gabe who met me there, freshly oiled bridles hanging over his shoulder. He watched me as he discarded his load and snapped on our mount's leads. By the look of his face, he'd overheard. "You're all right, then?"

"Oh, Gabe. What can be done now?" I felt strangled.

He ushered the first horse into her stall. "Panic, I suppose."

I blew out my breath and hit his arm.

He turned solemn eyes on me while the other horse stamped and tossed her head. "Let God be God, Willa. He knows a fair bit more than you, believe it or not." He slipped the bridle off, then guided the creature into its stall with a hand along his flanks. "For what it's worth, you've won my mother over. That was plain just now."

I gave him a brokenhearted smile. Did his mother's approval earn back his, as well? "She loves an excuse to stand up to Burke, I believe."

"She wouldn't bother if she didn't want you around. She likes you."

Warmth flooded my chest with a nearly tangible force. How did he always do that? I smiled sadly at him. "She's begun telling me things. Very authentic, surprising things."

He froze, leather bridle dangling over his head as he went to hang it. His back was to me. "Oh?"

"Did you know she wanted to be married at the old ruins? Perhaps she has a touch of romance in her after all."

He frowned. "Did she also tell you that theirs is a marriage of convenience?"

This stopped me cold, jaw slack. "A . . . what?"

"But you eventually came to love him too, right?"

An awkward shift. "Of course."

Another piece to the puzzle, a fuller picture taking shape. The lack of romance in this house, the broken love matches . . . her own discontent had trickled down to the entire household, every love story that came after it, dulling what could be with what made sense. "Everyone has a story, it seems. I've merely scratched the surface of hers."

He turned and his look was intense, waiting to hear what she'd told me.

I did not indulge his curiosity.

Dr. Tillman arrived at the house, and I begrudgingly told him everything I knew, then he asked, per Burke's orders, to meet with the patient alone. I obeyed, but a new protectiveness had settled over my heart toward this patient, for she had no one. She was surrounded by family, but she was truly alone.

I waited in the empty library, helplessly leafing through books and outdated periodicals, and listening for Tillman's departing footsteps. Before I heard them, I looked up, and there he stood in the doorway. "I'd like her to see a specialist."

"Why, so they can tell her she's broken beyond repair? She already knows that."

"New discoveries in cardiology are unfolding. With the innovation of anesthesia, surgery is a safer, more common occurrence. You never know what science can do until you try." He strode into the room. "I'm acquainted with a physician who's devoted his life to understanding heart function, and

211

if anyone can help her, it's him. He operates from a specialist hospital in London, and I'm certain I could convince him to admit our patient."

I stared, unblinking at the casual use of *our*. "You cannot expect me to support this."

He let out a breath. "No, I suppose that's too much to ask, isn't it?" He studied me, making note of something. "I know how you and your father feel about institutions."

"And do you know why? Have you seen the inside of one?"

"Not since university days."

"I've watched surgeons don coats with years' worth of blood and fluids as they go to operate. I've seen them move from a tuberculosis patient to a child with an open gash without washing infected blood off their hands. Did you know the assistant surgeon at St. Thomas's sees over two hundred patients a day? Do you realize they only accept patients who come with burial money in hand?"

"This is not a regular hospital, and it's far better than doing nothing."

"Is it? She's lived this long with the condition, right at home. This would merely ensure her speedy end."

He raked a hand through his hair. "It goes against everything I value to not at least *try*."

I looked directly into his eyes. "And it goes against everything *I* value to turn her over to such a fate." I studied him, debating my next move. "Come." Leading him toward the rows of books, I headed straight for a particular shelf.

"It's no use showing me your propaganda on miasma. Miss Barton's on to something, but —"

"Actually, I was going to show you this." I pulled a heavy Bible from the shelf and paged to the verse that had propelled me on Father's journey with him years ago. "Leviticus says this: 'And he that is to be cleansed shall wash his clothes, and shave off all his hair, and wash himself in water, that he may be clean.' There are plenty more admonitions like this."

"A ritual cleansing — an act of respect."

"Of necessity. Don't you see? God told his people to wash their hands after slaughtering their burnt offerings, after working with open sores, any time they came in contact with blood. That was for a reason."

He frowned, running fingers along his whiskered jaw. "Blood is blood, and in this modern world with too many patients and too few doctors, there's no sense in cleaning what's about to become dirty again. There isn't time for such formality."

"But don't you see, all God's instructions have a layered purpose — letting fields lay fallow every few years — which allows them to replenish. Waiting to circumcise baby boys until the eighth day — which is when blood begins to coagulate. And abstaining from pork — which is deadly if left under-cooked, as the Israelites then certainly would have done. Dr. Tillman, he's a God of order and sense. He doesn't ask us to do things for pomp and show. He's wise to the ways of the world he created, and his instructions are meant to help us navigate it, even if we don't understand them."

He looked down and toyed with the signet ring on his finger. By his silence, I knew I'd lifted the corner of his interest, his intellect.

"Come, now look at this." I selected one of the journals containing Snow's germ theory and opened to the article. "Just look at these photos of what's under his micro-scope — the organisms, the bacteria. Look, here are the types of bacterium that grew from his samples. Vulnerable patients come in direct contact with all of it, and it's seep-ing into open cuts, flourishing into infec-tions and disease that spreads like wildfire. This — *this* — is why Father and I are so passionate about starting a new type of clinic. It's *needed*."

He exhaled, looking around the room. "All right, all right. So what if there is truth behind this? You'll have a hard time convincing overworked surgeons to go to such lengths in their postoperative work — this means cleaning instruments, hands, clothing, linens . . . between every single patient. You also run the risk of losing more patients because the surgeons won't be able to see as many."

"Well, perhaps they shouldn't short staff themselves by keeping half the population from becoming doctors." I raised an eyebrow, and his expression melted into a small smile.

"You're a force, Miss Duvall. It's no wonder you aren't content to remain a nurse." He put the journal back. "What if I promise she'll not be operated on without a clear benefit, and you will be consulted before anything is done? This initial trip will be a mere consultation, and then I'll bring her home for your advice before anything more is done. It's worth a try."

I sighed. "I don't see what good it'll do. Perhaps if she'd gotten help earlier, but now . . ."

"Do not underestimate the power of hope, Miss Duvall. When all seems lost, sometimes that's all we have — and it can mean a lot."

"Prepare, then, to also face the power of crushed hope." I leveled a heavy stare, but he only smiled.

"We're agreed, then. We'll make a go of it and see who is right."

FOURTEEN

People marry based on the scientific assumption that two halves make a whole, but that's false. Only God makes something whole.
~A scientist's observations on love

Dr. Lucas Tillman paused with one arm in his riding coat and listened. Footfall neared the foyer where he stood ready to leave, but it was not a man's heavy step as he'd expected. With a frown, he straightened and turned, shoving the other arm into its sleeve.

"Beg pardon, sir." A uniformed maid appeared under the glowing light, dipping a brief curtsey. "You're wanted in the drawing room before you leave."

With a nod, he shrugged back out of his coat and handed it to her before making his way back through the house. He dared not hope at who had asked him to stay — Willa? Perhaps she'd changed her blessedly obstinate mind. His heart sped and he straightened, adjusting his cravat. Why was he always such a fool with that woman? Her mere presence tangled his tongue and twisted his brain.

But it was a little brown-garbed figure with dark hair and a darker look that stepped from the shadows. "I'd like a bottle of tablets, please." Celeste Gresham, of all people, looked up at him, knitted shawl wrapped around her like a shield. But from what? She looked ready to march into battle, dark eyes wide. What had happened to make this poised and easygoing woman seem so ill at ease?

He attempted to warm the air with a smile as he stepped closer. "You mean *my* tablets, Miss Gresham?"

"Yes, of course." She looked down, smoothing her skirt. "I can pay for them, but this must remain between us."

He'd once coaxed his sister's kitten from a tree, its wide, wary eyes staring down at him. This left him with a similar feeling, making him want to simply hold up his hands and declare his lack of ill intent. "Of course." He tried a few steps forward. "But I'd like to first understand why you wish to take them."

Her shield went up. "You said they cure

most anything. Is it important what they're for?"

"I've never given medicine of any sort without understanding the symptoms." He folded his arms across his chest and lowered his voice. "Pray, Miss Gresham, what is it? I'm a physician, don't forget. I have handled two or three unpleasant illnesses."

She hesitated, something jerking within her squarish jaw. "You'll not tell anyone?"

"Of course not." He stood at the edge of this odd mystery, staring down into the darkness as he anxiously waited for the answer.

She stepped forward, head down as she mumbled her reply behind her hand. "It's for my *tmpr.*"

He blinked, uncrossing his arms. "Beg pardon, what did you say?"

She cleared her throat. "My *tm-pr.*"

He pursed his lips. "You'll have to speak up, Miss Gresham. I cannot —"

"Tem-per!" She spit it out, then moved back, visibly shaken.

"Right, then. That's what I thought you said." He leaned on the desk and folded his arms, studying her. If only she could appreciate the humor in what she was suggesting. "Miss Gresham, why do you believe you have a temper?"

She stared, the whites of her eyes framing the dark centers. She shifted. Colored painfully. "Come to think of it, perhaps I don't need pills. Yes, I rather believe I'll be all right after all. So sorry, Doctor, to take your time. I suppose I need a good night of rest and —"

Her tense posture compelled him to reach out and touch her arm. "Miss Gresham."

She jumped, spinning to look at him.

"Everyone's allowed moments of frustration now and again. Grant yourself the chance to express your thoughts without believing yourself mad."

She just stared.

"You're not wicked." He spooned the simple phrases out to her, watching her melt into an acceptance of their truth. "And I don't believe you have a temper."

Her features eased, fingers unclenching and chin tipping up a little.

"What you do have, however, is a case of nerves. How long has it been since you've left your family and taken a holiday?"

"A . . . holiday? Alone?" She laughed, a tight sound high in her throat. "What a notion, Doctor."

"I'd sell you my tablets if I thought they'd help, but I see nothing wrong. Not truly."

She turned when a noise echoed some-

220

where deep in the house. "Oh, excuse me, Doctor. I must go. Thank you so much for your time, and please do let me know if you need anything." She spun with a swirl of heavy skirts and left.

With a frown, Tillman walked to the desk and looked about. He took the liberty of borrowing a page of stationery from the blotter and scribbled his instructions in light pencil.

Official script for Miss Celeste Gresham, written by Dr. Tillman

One holiday, to be taken for the course of a full week.

Nightly hot baths, with fresh scented soap.

A full cleanse of all worrying thoughts into a notebook or a good friend.

Daily diet of Scripture to replace falsehoods, fear, and worry.

Avoid infectious ailments, such as pessimism and anger, and those who carry them.

He couldn't bear to take the two pounds from her. Much as the healing power of the pills excited him, they were the wrong cure for her ailment, and it didn't take a licensed doctor to see that. He shoved the thick vellum page in his pocket and went in search of his newest patient.

Another figure approached from the stairs, one who stirred his heart with a painful little jolt of out-of-reach. Every time he saw her, the effect was the same. He was struck speechless by that rosy complexion, the little dimples that appeared and vanished playfully.

"You're still here," she said.

"It would seem so." He offered a slight bow, keeping every muscle in check under her bright scrutiny. Sweat beaded on his face. When her eyes beamed their lofty disapproval, the strain on his nerves heightened. "Have you seen Miss Gresham about?"

The delicate frown deepened. "Celeste? You've not agreed to peddle your bottle of nonsense to her, have you?"

The word *nonsense* hit him in the chest, winding him. Years of endless research, digging, prayer, trial and error, failures and epiphanies all stacked up before this pert woman's stunning gaze and suddenly seemed silly and wasted. Infantile.

She lowered her head. "I apologize, Doctor. There was no call to say it that way. But I do hope you've not taken her money."

He cleared his throat and forced a smile

as images of those he'd helped flashed before his weary mind. He mustn't forget them. "Not at all. I have something for her."

"I'll deliver it for you." She held out a hand.

He thought of her reading the impromptu "prescription," as she certainly would, and the idea of her lovely, keen eyes on his scrawled lines made him feel foolish. "I'll simply leave it for her in the study, if you'd be kind enough to tell her."

He excused himself and pushed past his mentor's beautiful daughter. Reaching the room, he felt flushed and cold at the same time from his encounter. He sank into a chair and shoved a hand through his hair, forcing an exhale.

Nonsense.

That's what all his work amounted to. In the end, he rose and shoved the foolish "prescription" into his pocket and slipped out of the house. He knew Willa would read it, and the very idea made him feel like a boy in the schoolyard.

Celeste sank into the stiff little parlor chair and touched both hands to her burning cheeks. What had possessed her to tell him of her temper? Now he knew. Every time he saw her, he'd look at her with new knowledge. Ugly knowledge.

After a moment of berating herself, she made her way through the narrow halls to the study, where he'd apparently left something for her. "He seemed terribly unsettled," Willa had said as she'd given her the message, "but I cannot imagine why."

Now alone in the room that still rang with her confession, she glanced about the bleak, open space for what he'd left. Her frowning gaze finally landed on a folded paper on the floor before the cold hearth, highlighted by a streak of sunshine glowing through the drapes. It must have blown off the mantelpiece when he'd opened the doors. She knelt and fingered the paper's lovely scarlet border. How curious.

When she unfolded the paper and read, her heart erupted in shock and disbelief. She forced herself to slow and read every line carefully.

You inspired in me a passion both bright and deep . . .

This couldn't be what he'd meant to leave her. She'd never inspired passion in anything or anyone.

Yet she remembered what Willa had said

— he'd seemed nervous. Flushed. Could it be?

I marvel at the way you are, those strengths and weaknesses woven so deftly together, driving you through life with such passion . . .

No. This wasn't right. This couldn't be for her. Celeste's brow drew into a natural frown, as it always did when she encountered overt shows of affection, but the words gently probed the walls of her heart and loosened its mortar, finding the hidden softness within that wanted it to be for her. Did someone actually see her detachment, her attempts to heal, as strength?
She read more.

I choose you. Every day, every moment, I choose you.

She'd forgotten what that felt like. Being not just tolerated, but desired. Sought after. The warm, intoxicating notion reached something inside her that she hadn't known still glowed and stoked its coals. Her gaze darted to the window where the doctor was mounting his horse in the drive. He admired her? He thought her lovely and talented and remarkable? He thought her out of reach? A draft from the leaky old window brushed her hot skin as she watched him shake out the reins, straighten on his horse, and glance back at the house before riding away. Had any man ever looked more handsome than when on horseback?

She turned, schooling her thoughts. Yet did she truly need to? He'd declared himself. Probably. She'd heard of gentlemen doing such things through letters, but still, it hardly seemed real. She'd laid out a fine road for herself, a lifetime of being a singular force of good in this world, but it seemed someone had stepped into that path and insisted on interrupting the journey.

Something throbbed in her neck as she read it a third time, trying to wrap the beautiful sentiments around her prim appearance and aloof nature. How could anyone see beyond those things?

I've seen the strength and kindness you believe go unnoticed, watched when you thought no one was looking, and observed what exists below the surface.

An unexpected surge of femininity flooded her veins, and it was not altogether unpleasant. He knew her strengths and weaknesses, he claimed, and yes, even the secret she'd tried to hide. It was true, he knew the worst, now. He'd glimpsed the evil within.

And moments later, he somehow still chose her.

Doubt niggled at her when she realized the ink was far from fresh, so it couldn't have been dashed off this minute, after she'd revealed what she had. What other secret had she? She must have been mistaken — and that knowledge brought a surprising stab of disappointment.

Yet there was a terrible bleakness to her world without this letter in it, so she clung to the glimmer of hope that it was real. The "secret" could be anything. He *had* left something for her, and what else was there in the room? And the tender look in his eyes . . . No, there was simply no other explanation for it — he'd written the letter for her. The dry ink simply meant he'd written it some time ago and carried it around with him, waiting for the right opportunity to give it to her. Perhaps her moment of vulnerability had been that.

A trace of hope invaded her spinsterhood. Could love and family truly be in her future?

Yet she dared not hope, even if the letter was real, that it would last. After all, she'd been hurt before. The familiar jagged ache pierced her gut as if she were still seventeen

227

and smitten with that abominable Frenchman. She'd been placed up on that heady mountaintop of romantic possibilities, only to topple off and go crashing to the ground. The rejection had been so unexpected, so sudden and thorough, that she could do nothing but reject, in turn, all other romantic attachments. It had given her a sense of dignity and safety, which she'd thoroughly appreciated.

Until now. The letter stirred girlish fantasies and hopes, bringing to the surface the undeniable desire to belong to someone.

Tucking the letter away, Celeste went in search of Burke, but instead she found Gabe in the servant's hall, scraping his boots with a blade. "Playing in the mud again, are we?"

Her brother lifted his kindhearted smile, welcoming her without a word. Men like Gabe Gresham were a warm embrace, a solid place to land. Not all men, it would seem, were the forceful, domineering sort the womens' league fought against, and she forgot that at times. "Was that Caroline's horse I heard leaving? Mother's been relentless lately."

"Tillman's." She looked him over. "So why is it you've steered away from marriage, dear brother?"

"Perhaps it's marriage that's steered away

228

from me."

"Do you think . . . is it possible to have something better than they do?" She jerked her head toward the master suite. "Or is a better sort of love the thing of novels?"

He stopped scraping and studied her, seeming to sense the depth of her wondering. "It's real. It's possible. Just not likely, when people approach marriage as medicine for what ails them, as they seem to do around here."

"Hmm." Celeste leaned on a chair back, pondering. What was the ache inside her that she was finally acknowledging? Perhaps that was all she was longing for — a balm for past hurts. Not a true desire for something new. "I suppose Jacques simply left a wound that hasn't been repaired. And sometimes I feel it again."

"Wounds are only useful for reminding us when to duck next time."

A smile tugged at her mouth. "Sometimes I think you're brilliant."

He straightened and gave a small bow. "I do try." Then he took her hand, towering over her with concern. "Don't close yourself off from love — just from the wrong people, yes?"

She gave him a nod, this big brother who absorbed the hurts of those he loved and carried their pain along with them, bearing it all on those broad shoulders of untold strength. Perhaps Tillman, who made his living in healing, would be the same way.

Gabe was right. She had to know for certain what Tillman's intentions were — no more coquetry and witty banter, no more guessing and second-guessing. It was the good doctor's turn for a thorough examination. The very next time his boots crossed the threshold of Crestwicke Manor, she would find out for sure what was truly in his heart concerning her.

FIFTEEN

Don't disregard what a man says to you. If it comes out his lips, it was, in some form, in his heart at some point.
~A scientist's observations on love

"I despise being forced to do anything." Golda's voice cut through the peaceful night. "Almost as much as I despise an unknown destination."

On Saturday evening we rode like two opposing forces of nature trapped in the same carriage — Golda, the storm cloud, and me, the penetrating sunlight attempting to break through. "Give it a chance and perhaps you'll enjoy yourself."

I'd finally received a reply to my audacious letter, and it was better than I had dared hope. We were invited to attend the sold-out event and given most enviable seating — included in the response were notes of admittance for Mrs. Gresham, her "clever nurse," and one relation. Which turned out, thanks to Aunt Maisie's cupid-like maneuvering, to be Gabe. Mr. Gresham had still not responded to my urging to return to Crestwicke, and Celeste wouldn't give up her ladies' meeting.

"If everything in the world was known, what intrigue would be left to us?"

She grimaced and turned away. On the rear-facing seats sat Gabe, and Golda's lady's maid, Jenny.

"A clue, then." I turned toward my patient on the seat. "You'll need your fan."

She glared at me. "I *seldom* have need of my fan. I'm not given to vapors over mere surprises."

The maid piped up from her seat. "You won't keep us in suspense all the way to Brighton, will you, Miss Duvall? I can hardly bear it."

But keep the suspense I did, and soon we were rolling up New Street in Brighton before the expanded Theatre Royal, and the very sight of its lit-up columned entrance against red brick made me gasp. The stately old building had always imposed over Pavilion Gardens with a commanding dignity, but since it had come under the management of imaginative actor Henry John Nye Chart some years ago, the new face of this four-story structure lent it a gleaming magnificence that hinted at the talent displayed inside.

"The theatre?"

I turned to smile at Gabe, but the poor man looked stricken and pale at the notion of entering the social spotlight of Brighton. I'd warned him to dress for the event — what had he expected?

We all climbed from the carriage, and with a gallant bow, Gabe escorted his mother up the torch-lit steps along with the throngs of well-dressed gents with ladies on their arms. Shoes clicked amidst the muffled tones of happy voices and swishing gowns. Soon we were escorted to a box seat near the stage, with red velvet chairs and gold-fringed curtains, the smell of gaslights filling our nostrils. It was a small auditorium compared to the houses in London, seating maybe one hundred fifty in the main level, but it was richly appointed and quite full.

Gabe leaned over to whisper. "You are the oddest nurse I know, with the strangest treatments."

I gave a prim smile. "Why, thank you."

The red curtains parted, a weighty hush fell over the crowd, and a man stepped out onto the dim stage. He spoke his welcome and thanked everyone for coming to a most auspicious presentation. Golda gasped as a bearded gent in a brown tweed suit stepped onto the stage next, his weathered face framed by great clouds of white beard that had become his signature. "That's . . . My heavens, is it . . . ?"

"Henry Wadsworth Longfellow." I drew out the name with delicious pleasure.

She gasped again, and I leaned close with a raised brow. "Fan?"

Grabbing it with a pointed look, she flipped it open and fanned vigorously.

Longfellow bowed deeply, generating hearty applause, then introduced the first poet of the night in his deep American accent. The tall gent read his verses about leaves and grass, and the way the light struck these ordinary things. I'm certain he was famous and ingenious, but it was my patient who held my attention. Every emotion in the rainbow showed on her face through the night.

Gabe noticed too, I could tell even from the shadows, but he said nothing. With the next artist, her fan paused at the emotional crescendo of each poem, then sped up as applause burst across the auditorium.

Longfellow loped back onto the stage after all six poets had read selected pieces of work. The great man held up thick hands to quell the applause. Then he bowed his head and spoke. "I thank you all from the depths of my humble heart for humoring an old man this night." His rumbling voice, though more strained than some of the others, rolled up into the rounded ceiling and carried across the theatre.

Gabe leaned over to whisper to Golda, their heads bent together. I kicked his foot, but he ignored it. Of all the times for the man to begin a conversation.

"It has truly been a much-needed inspiration for me, hearing these honored voices here tonight. I have a treat for you now — the first new material I've presented in years."

He fixed wire spectacles on his face, wrapping them behind his ears, and pulled out a familiar red book, flipping to a marked page. I had to clench my hands to keep from grabbing Golda's arm and forcing her to look at the stage, where her own notebook now lay in the hands of her favorite poet.

That wretched Gabe. *Must* he speak now? Whatever it was, it could wait.

I gripped the arms of my chair and the poem rolled out in the man's deep, weighty voice.

Every pair of footsteps, marks left in the
    sand,
Lovers walking side by side, strolling
    hand in hand.
There but for a moment when the tide of
    everyday
washes over everything, fading love
    away.

Golda's head lifted, eyes steadily ahead as
the man continued. Gabe's hand immediately covered hers. "What is it, Mother?"

"That's . . ." Her mouth hung open in a
most unladylike fashion. "My song."

The man carried the verses to their peak
and let them fall over his eager audience.
For a full three seconds, no one moved or
spoke. Then applause erupted.

After a moment, the man on stage raised
one gloved hand to dim the flow of praise.
His American accent glinted across them.
"These new lines, friends, are not from me."
The applause stopped at the sound of his
voice. "They were written by a promising
new voice in poetry who will share the rest
herself. So if you'll allow, I'd like to ask Mrs.
Golda Gresham to the stage, for a reading
of her work. Mrs. Gresham, are you present
tonight?"

Murmurs lifted into the air as people

turned, craning their necks for the first glimpse of the woman who now sat two seats from me. White-knuckling her chair, Golda looked to Gabe, to the red book she'd thrown away, then to me.

I offered a gentle smile amid the whispers. "You said you wanted your verses heard."

She stared, and I merely shrugged. Golda Gresham rose, for once meek and unbalanced, and applause erupted when they caught sight of her.

As I watched her wobbly smile blossom, this woman once called impossible, victory surged through my chest. She moved past us with Gabe's assistance. I rose to join her, but she waved me back to my seat. She wanted to go alone. As she moved in her unhurried, queenly way across the stage, I turned to Gabe and burrowed deep into his gaze, looking for a spark of the approval I'd once found there without effort. "I'd call the night a success, wouldn't you? A triumph to compensate for my previous missteps."

He stared at me with that frank and open face. "No one's keeping score."

Well then, I was no one. If this bold act didn't convince Gabe I meant well, little else would. "I've managed to hold my tongue for days now. Your lecture was not without impact."

He frowned slightly and lowered his voice when there were dark stares in our direction. "I don't want you to hold back your opinions, Willa. I've never asked you to."

I puffed out my breath and fell back against the seat. Hadn't he? "You are exasperating, Gabe Gresham. There, that's one opinion."

A sharp shushing sound came from the seats just outside our box, and I clamped my mouth shut.

"Well and good. Especially if it means I can take my exasperating company away early." He leaned back with a slight grin. Then he looked to his mother highlighted in gaslights on the stage as applause rippled between her poems. "I'll admit, your odd tonic seems to have worked."

I narrowed my eyes at him and grinned. "I don't intend to stop with her."

He raised dark eyebrows as he joined the applause.

"Oh yes, I have plans for you too, Mr. Gresham."

He paled. "Not dancing."

I gave a prim smile, and he stiffened in his seat. "I'm determined to break through that thick shell of yours and draw you out into daylight."

"I rather like the dark. A cave would suit."

I eyed him from the side. "What do you have against dancing anyway? Have you a lame leg?"

"No."

"Then why not join in?"

He shifted in his seat. "I've never done it before."

"Well, if that isn't the worst reason not to do something. One waltz, at least. I'm not in the habit of leading, but perhaps I can fumble through. I'm certain you'll survive."

The gray pallor to his face expressed his doubts on the matter. He let my assertion hang in the air as silence drew our attention to the stage and a poised, glorious Golda Gresham. Her even voice fell upon a hushed audience, melodic and poignant.

"My love has been smoothed to
   perfection,
A pearl against the sands of adversity;
You take it in hand, merely a bead,
A string about your neck, a tiny seed;
Yet it's all I have to give, so I implore
When you no longer have need
Of this pearl I've given, set it free,
That I may guard it and deliver it again
To one who will be true, always true to
   me."

The surprising delightfulness of the lines was fully felt when stripped of the background noise of her singing. I glanced about the audience, glad that they seemed charmed by her.

After her final poem and the hearty applause, Gabe and I rose to help Golda from the stage. I looked up when she was settled into the seat and Gabe was gone. "Where did he go?"

"Gabe?" She gave a vague smile, still floating on a cloud of delight. "I haven't the slightest idea. You know that boy — likely gone to find us rooms . . . then close himself inside them. See if you can't fetch him back and we'll make him be social for once."

I attempted to check her pulse, but she batted me away. "Miss Duvall, you really needn't be at my elbow all night."

"It's my job."

Her gaze iced. "Your job is doing what you're told. Now, go and find my son."

When Golda's lady's maid approached from her waiting spot just outside the auditorium, I slipped away. Past the thickening crowds, I bolted into the empty atrium, nearly colliding with a stout older gentleman. "Oh, I beg your pardon." I put a hand to my racing heart. "Have you seen a tall man in black come through here?"

240

"I've not seen a soul save the one who nearly toppled me this minute."

I stepped back with a jolt of horrified recognition. "Oh! Mr. Longfellow." I bobbed two curtsies. "My deepest apologies, sir." Another dip. "My name is Willa Duvall, nurse to —"

"Golda Gresham. Ah yes, now I know you, Miss Duvall." His easy voice had a casual, meandering quality that loosened my tension and put me at ease. "It's a pleasure running into you, even in this manner."

I smiled at the light accent to his speech, the plunging "r" sound that marked him as an American. "I'm glad for it too, sir. I've wanted to thank you from the deepest parts of my heart for allowing Mrs. Gresham to attend and even be a part of this wonderful night. I cannot begin to tell you what it means . . ."

My voice faded as he continued to stare at me, that timeless face watching me as if he never had anywhere else to be in his life. "Your letter, Miss Duvall. It resurrected my stale old heart for a moment, and I was compelled to act. You've quite a convincing way about you. Made me feel I still might do something worthwhile, even in my dried-up state."

I saw in him, with an ache, the same sense of resigned despair that had settled over Aunt Maisie. It was a sense of life being over before the body had given out, with one constantly left questioning why they were still bound to earth, and little broke my heart more. "You are anything but dried up, sir."

He turned away with a dismissive nod toward me, the younger woman he felt could not possibly understand. Yet my heart couldn't bear to let the man leave more broken than when I found him. A future physician, I was compelled to restore what I could. I laid a hand on his arm.

"Read from some humbler poet,
Whose songs gushed from his heart.
Such songs have power to quiet
The restless pulse of care,
And come like the benediction
That follows after prayer."

He turned back to me, stricken as I paraphrased lines of his own poetry.

"Your words resurrected my heart once too. In the worst year of my life, in fact. You were that 'humbler poet' whose songs quieted my heart when nothing else would."

He studied me, as if trying to determine

whether or not he believed it.

"It was the one about the reaper and the flowers, how the Lord had need of such beauty, and they would bloom with him. It made me feel that perhaps my mother . . ." I dropped my gaze, feeling foolish. Exposed. "That perhaps God simply had need of her, and she was blooming up there with him. That it wasn't my fault."

When I looked up, the ache in my heart was mirrored in his face, and he shifted, visibly wrestling with what to say. "It's curious to me how a young woman can find relief in the poems of a man writing in vain to find it himself."

"Perhaps because in all those moments of regret, of silent chastisement, of torturing myself with the past, I was not alone."

This simple answer satisfied him, and his beard stretched into a sad smile. "It's an exquisite sort of pain, isn't it? Walking through the important parts of life without them, seeing everything they should have seen, every milestone they would have enjoyed . . ."

"The holidays and highpoints, the parts of their story that should have been but never were, all because . . ."

"Because of you." He frowned and blinked, patting about his pockets, and I immediately produced a clean handkerchief from my reticule. He accepted it and wiped his face, dabbed his forehead, and blew his nose loudly.

"I'm sorry, sir, for your loss too."

He put a hand on my shoulder. "Don't be terribly hard on yourself over the past, Miss Duvall. As Mr. Dickens wrote, no one is useless in this world who lightens the burdens of another. You've done it for me tonight and, I daresay, for many others. Never tire of being such a person."

I smiled at him. "Even in conversation your words are beautiful. Please tell me you'll not abandon your writing. Even with a hurting heart."

He gave a slight shrug. "If my heart is empty, where will the words even come from? They'd be mere shapes on the page."

A man hurried over and spoke in low tones to Longfellow. With a grim look, the poet excused himself, and left me in the atrium alone. I watched him go, then I circled the atrium again without finding a trace of Gabe. Perhaps he'd returned to his mother.

I wove through the crowds back to Golda. "Ah, there you are, Miss Duvall. What have you done with my son?" Her smile froze on her powdered face, dangerous lights coming

244

into her eyes. "Have you been with him all this time — *alone* with him? After I made it quite clear —"

"Perfectly clear. I assure you, I've not seen him. I thought perhaps he returned here."

Her stare relaxed a bit. "Well, then. Why not find him and send him to me? Then you are free to retire for the night."

"I must insist on remaining with you. You've had a great deal of excitement."

"And I plan to have a great deal more." She smiled. "Please, Miss Duvall. I'd like to pretend, at least for one lovely evening, that I am as unfettered and free as anyone else. Do remember that until you arrived, I was carrying on quite nicely on my own. I shall allow you to come and fetch me after nine."

"Very well, my lady."

I backed up the aisle, watching her poised back, then turned and searched in earnest for Gabe. I finally spotted his loping stride out the window, moving deep into the foggy night with his hands in his pockets.

Where was he going? I paused at the window, simply watching him. He was so very *Gabe*. His broad back, the aura of solitude, a lone dark figure outside the glittery social scene — it was all so familiar. With another glance toward my patient, who'd once again become absorbed by the

245

admiring crowds, I hurried toward the arched entryway and down the steps into the crisp autumn evening that smelled of pooling water and fresh rain.

Sixteen

"For of the abundance of the heart his mouth speaketh," it says in Scripture. If a woman wishes to change her words toward a man, she must start with restructuring the place from which they spill.

~A scientist's observations on love

I lifted my skirts and ran to catch him as he headed east toward the Royal Pavilion, disappearing across the foggy street. "Gabe!" The air was wet and chilly, impossibly dense with fog. I called out again but heard no answer. No footfall. I looked up and down New Street, straining to see all the way to the end where something moved, but —

Oof. I collided with a person. I stepped back, staring into the fog, but two hands grabbed my shoulders to steady me.

"And you want to teach *me* to dance?" Gabe's deep voice rumbled against my hands where they rested on his chest. He stepped forward, his face aglow under the lights. "How is she?"

I blew out a breath. "Riding on a cloud of praise."

He smiled, gratified, and held out his arm to escort me. "This was a good idea, you know. Bringing her here. So why have you left?"

"She sent me looking for you. Partly to be rid of me."

"Hmm." He looked out at the distant buildings' outlines rising all around us. "Walk with me first, then. I want to show you something."

The click of our shoes echoed together as we made our way along the sidewalk, nodding at the lamplighter, and we paused under the stone arch to the pavilion grounds. Without a word, he hoisted me gently over the closed gate, then planted his hands on the iron bar and launched his tall frame over. With a giggle, I took his arm and we trotted up the promenade that was ours alone. The pavilion looked down upon us with its Taj Mahal air, towers rising to rounded roofs of bud-shaped beauty.

"It's spectacular." I breathed the words.

"Reminds me of Aunt Maisie's descriptions of India."

I looked up at that palace of a place as we took the path around it. "I used to think she was bold and strong for doing so much without a husband, but do you know, I think she'd rather have had the husband after all."

"Hmm." He pulled me close to pass by thorny shrubs.

"Do you think she's ever been in love?"

"Yes, once. Years ago. I don't know why they didn't marry. Perhaps because he couldn't dance."

I gave him a playful shove.

We crossed St. James and found our way into the Old Steine Gardens, staring at the softly illuminated Victoria Fountain. Flowers had been planted in colorful bunches since I'd been here for the unveiling several years ago, with Victoria's two tiers of cascading water a magnificent, sparkling centerpiece. Pink and blue hues from the setting sun rippled over the water as we walked side by side, our arms nearly touching. "How isolated from the city, yet right in the center of it."

"The perfect spot." He paused beside the fountain and took my hands, turning me to face him as the spray dotted my arms. The earnest lights in his eyes like two soft lanterns melted something within. "Teach me, Willa." He breathed the words out, as if they'd taken all his courage. "Right now."

I blinked. "To dance?"

He nodded.

"I thought you didn't —"

"Not in front of people."

I tipped my head. "What, am I not people, then?"

That rare smile glinted in the setting sun, teeth white against his sun-darkened face. He shrugged. "You, I trust."

With a wry smile, I slid close and fixed his hand on my waist. "Flattery will get you everywhere, Mr. Gresham."

He breathed deep and braced himself, staring intensely at my feet.

"All right, then. Follow along, and count with me." I moved into a slow waltz with fluid steps, pulling him with me, and he came willingly. "One-two-three, one-two-three. Like this." He followed, forcing his solid legs into the delicate paces as sparkling water sprayed over its fountain base beside us.

Every third step he ran into my feet, kicked my toes, or tripped over his own, twisting his face in all manner of bemused expressions that kept me laughing, but I kept my guiding tug through the steps, drawing him along. We fumbled through with much amusement and a little shared

laughter.

Finally he stumbled and pulled back. "Aye, just like the horses — I've two left feet."

I gave a wry grin. "Chin up. Look at me, not at your feet."

"How'll I know what yours are doing?"

"By feel. We are a team, remember? Follow the pressure as my hand guides you."

He remained transfixed on my face, allowing his gaze to settle into mine, and I guided with gentle backward pushes against his hand. We glided through two sets of three-count, his body following my lead with surprising ease and compliance.

"You're doing it, Gabe." I flashed him a full smile. "You're dancing."

He grinned and his boot thunked the fountain wall, making him stumble. I helped him up with an echoing laugh in the empty garden, and he sighed, brushing off h jacket front. "Would you by chance impressed by standing still? I can do quite well."

"Oh, Gabe." I smiled playfully and up to the fountain's rim, spinning as to his hand and splashing the toe c boot into the water with each tw do I love thee, let me count the solemn brow, chock-full of knc

way your waltzing sways." I threw my head back and laughed, stumbling off the ledge and he caught me.

His eyes were glowing down at me, a solemn smile creasing his rugged cheeks, and suddenly my memory faded from the present, the fountain and the gardens, replacing it with the sunlit backdrop of the ruins, with that same face — years younger — looking down upon me with that ocean-deep smile and those soul-rich hazel eyes.

Mum had been freshly buried, the wound of her passing still sharp and fresh. I'd lugged my heavy grief up to a ledge on that ruined tower, not sure how to untangle myself from it. Gabe had scrambled up and settled his lanky frame beside me, resting for a few moments before breaking the silence. "A cold castle you've chosen for yourself. It hasn't even got a roof."

I leaned back against the mossy stones and looked up into that face that would come to mean so much to me. "All the better to see the stars. I rather like the stars."

He turned to look up at them without a word, as if he valued the sight as deeply as he eight-year-old girl beside him. He'd ken me riding every time we'd come, owing me how it was done and turning into a proper horsewoman with patience

252

and good humor. Seconds stretched on and his presence weighted my soul back down into me, making the world feel like something I could handle even if it was messy. "Might I coax the lady to leave her castle for another turn at the horses?"

I smiled a little, dried tears stretching on my skin.

"That spritely little mare won't take to anyone else the way she does you. I need someone to work her out. I don't suppose the princess of the castle could help a lad out, could she?"

"I'm no princess."

"Sure you are." He leaped down, disappearing in the shadows of the old ruin, then reappearing with a thin rope-like thing. "All you need is a proper crown." He grinned like a little elf, ears jutting out from scraggly brown hair, and wove flower stems into a pink-blossom crown. "I dub thee Princess of the ammenomies."

I blinked moist lashes. A giggle escaped. "Ameno-what?"

He scowled playfully and crossed his arms. "You know. Ammeno— anemo—"

"They're anemones. And they don't make me a princess. My father'd have to be a . . ." I glanced down the hill at the giant house that had swallowed him hours ago.

"King. And he is, you know." He looked up into the great open sky. "*That* Father, anyway." He settled beside me and his chest rose and fell for several silent moments. "You come out here and talk to him when the house gets too noisy. It'll hold your soul together when no human hands can manage it."

I breathed in the fresh sea air and smiled, for I could feel it too. I hadn't known what to call it, but it was God, and he was here, no matter where my earthly father was. The notion blew my chest wide open with wonder and eternally flavored thanks and made me love the place.

And miss her. Miss her all over again. She'd have loved this so. Fresh tears leaked out of swollen eyes and slid down my cheeks. I fisted my hand, pretending I was holding hers.

When the weight threatened to crush me, this unusual lad bounded down and held up his hand. "A proper royal must dance in her own castle. Would you do me the honor?"

I giggled through my unwanted tears and climbed down into his spindly arms. "I'm not certain I know how."

"Good. Neither do I."

He spun me about in awkward circles as

we tripped over each other's feet and laughed like the silly children we were, shaking the grief loose for a moment. In those stolen sunlit hours, I remember feeling blessedly whole and hopeful for a normal future. I knew there'd be healing someday, because I'd tasted it.

He now tucked my hand safely into the crook of his arm, and the motion jolted me from my memory and back into the present.

"You've gotten your dance out of me," he said. "Will that do?"

"For what?" We walked through the trimmed shrubbery as crickets began their serenade.

"For my apology. I oughtn't have been so harsh with you when Mother fainted. I had no idea you didn't know about her condition. She's wretchedly closed off about it and, well . . . I hope this'll make up for it."

I looked down at the path, at the shined shoes of this man who had rescued me from pits I hadn't even known how to describe. "Yes, Gabe. It'll do," I said softly.

I had come out here to teach him to dance tonight, but I suddenly struggled to remember why it mattered. We walked along the bridge together, striding through the gaslight muted by drifting fog, our footfall echoing in tandem, when I spotted a smattering of pink flowers in pots near the entrance gate. I stopped to pick one and consider its simple petals so like the anemone. "Gabe?"

"Hmm?"

"You don't *have* to learn to dance, you know." My voice was quiet, and I offered a shy smile up toward him. "You're mostly all right the way you are."

His face grew tender as he looked down at me. "Good to know."

"I wouldn't mind you being right a little less often, though."

"I rather like being right. It's one of the few advantages I have over you."

I laughed, then sobered, squeezing his arm where my hand lay nestled in its crook. "No, I believe you have a few more than that."

He stopped to take the little flower from my hand and twirled it before me, then he tucked it behind my ear with a tilt of his head and a smile.

He paused near the theatre steps, shoulders hunched and stretching his well-cut coat. "Thank you."

"For?"

He shrugged, a boyish grin peeking out. "For enjoying me anyway."

Before I could gather a response, he was

gone, melting into the shadows of Brighton that stretched beyond the garish lights of the theatre. No, Gabe did not fit into this world at all. He did not bear the polished sheen of the people with whom he was raised, but he glowed and flickered like a flame, warm and alive, the glass and crystal people around him merely reflecting his light. There was something so very real, so rich and deep, about Gabe Gresham that I struggled to remember exactly why I'd decided he needed to be improved at all.

"Well done, young lady."

I spun at the gravelly voice behind me. "Mr. Longfellow, sir."

"I came looking for you to beg your address, so I may return your handkerchief."

"Oh, thank you." I handed him my card and tried to shake the odd sensation Gabe had left on me.

He jerked his head toward Gabe's retreating form. "You've chosen well." A wistful smile touched his lips as he tucked it into his breast pocket. "I wish you well, and that you have a long and happy love story."

"Love?" My face heated, and I looked to the theatre as if Golda could overhear. "Oh no, sir. We don't have that sort of acquaintance." How could I put into words what we were to each other?

"A pity." He heaved a sigh. "Well, perhaps there is hope for the future. I take it you are not well acquainted yet?"

"He is Golda Gresham's son, and I've known him since I was a girl, but there's no understanding of that nature between us." I'd had a sense for some time that Gabe nurtured a budding infatuation for me, but it was easy to put it from my mind when nothing changed between us. If it existed, it would fade with time, and our friendship would outlive it — at least I hoped so.

He frowned, and I hurried to explain, even though my argument felt solid as pudding. "I value freedom and independence, and I hope to one day become a doctor."

His mouth slid closed, as if words could not properly convey his thoughts. "Might I be so bold as to suggest you reconsider? You've stumbled upon a rare gentleman. I don't know him, of course, but any man who honors his mother with the devotion and gentleness I witnessed tonight is a gem. Take note of it, Miss Duvall, for he will do the same for his wife one day. You'd be smart to make certain that was you."

I stiffened. If I had feathers, they would be ruffled. Did the man believe me helpless? "Thank you, but I have no need for a caretaker."

"Yet."

"Marriage is not an insurance policy." I studied the man for a moment, weighing my words. "However, I shall consider changing my mind if you change yours."

His eyebrows rose.

"Write poetry again, Mr. Longfellow. Not those plays and translations you've done of late, but the words of your heart. Even if they're dark. Write them down so those of us who are lost from time to time can stumble upon them in a dusty old book and fill the cracks of our hearts."

He sighed. "It's hard to imagine a broken old man has anything to offer the world."

I smiled, hugging my arms around myself and looking boldly up at him.

"Lives of great men all remind us
We can make our lives sublime,
And, departing, leave behind us
Footprints on the sands of time;

Footprints, that perhaps another,
Sailing o'er life's solemn main,
A forlorn and shipwrecked brother,
Seeing, shall take heart again."

The words of his own poetry once again filled the chilly space between us. "Keep leaving your footprints, sir. You have many finding their way through the dark by them."

He stared at me for long moments as he retracted a worn, square envelope from his breast pocket. "It took me seven years to earn this letter, and I cannot part with it. Of all my published works, everything I've ever written, these are the words I deem most important in my life."

I opened and read the strong, angular writing of Frances Appleton, who was agreeing, against her long-held inclinations, to accept the many proposals of Mr. Henry Wordsworth Longfellow.

He shook his head. "Once I had her beside me, I wasted a great deal of time — on writing. I wore myself out one night pouring my stormy, passionate words onto the page, and the next day I was abed by teatime. I slept like one dead, and I never heard the chaos below." He blinked, nostrils flaring. "She was melting wax, sealing up locks of our childrens' hair. She was like that, taking care of the little things, savoring those sweet remembrances. Who ever knew a dress could catch fire from a few drops of wax? Or perhaps the candle fell. I'll never know, because I wasn't there. I had spent myself on poetry and pride, with little left for her." His beard trembled, and I noticed the jagged burn scars beneath. "She was gone the next morning, but I watched my love suffer the torture of my neglect through the night. Because of my selfish need to write."

My hands trembled. Tears burned the backs of my eyes and I blinked them back. "I'm so sorry, sir."

"Don't waste a moment when you find the one you love. I hope my story encourages you to do that, at least."

"In truth, it inspires me to wait until I find a love equal to yours, one that's burned into my heart. I shall not settle for less."

A small smile stretched his voluminous white beard, and his eyes twinkled with sad merriment, if that was a possible combination. "Don't take terribly long to find him, Miss Duvall, for he's already found you." He gave a nod toward the darkness where Gabe had disappeared, then he too was gone.

It was now nearly dark. I stood alone in the encroaching shadows, under the glare of theatre lights, my heart tangled.

As we rode back to Crestwicke the next day, the entire town seemed quiet as most Brighton residents had been tucked neatly into Sunday services. I tried to open my heart to the idea of marrying, for it seemed that would be my eventual end, but none of it seemed right. Thick silk and organdy dress, orange blossoms in my hair, my own name read in the banns . . .

I shivered.

With Golda staring out the window, her lady's maid buried in Colin Fairchild's serial, and Gabe nearly asleep, I mentally wandered back over Grayson Aberdeen's love letter and pondered the missing man who'd written it. What was it about this love story that drew me so? What ingredient did it have that had been missing in all of mine?

Everything. It was courage in the face of denied love, tender hope without demands, a raw expression of total and complete love for someone who was known, seen, and desired. Perhaps if my flaws were more acceptable or my nature more demure, more controlled, and feminine . . .

When we returned to Crestwicke on Sunday afternoon, we brought Golda to her chambers, settled her in, then I turned to face a very pink-cheeked Essie. The cobwebs of my thoughts were sliced through by her news.

"Oh miss, I've had another letter — from *him*."

SEVENTEEN

The secret to finding true love is not in discovering someone who will give it to you but learning how to give it.
~A scientist's observations on love

I dropped my reticule in my adjoining chamber, then hurried back to the maid accepting garments as Jenny slipped them off her mistress. I held Golda's arms to steady her and looked back at Essie. "You're certain it's the same person?" I whispered this.

"Oh, yes, quite." She hugged the stack of linens with joy about to burst as Jenny continued discarding items across Essie's freckled arms. "I hardly know what to think."

I felt the same. "Well, what did it say?"

"He thinks my face is beautiful." She shrugged as her cheeks pinked with pleasure. "He's happy simply being nearby, even

263

if we never speak. Oh, it makes me so curious, doesn't it you?"

"Enormously." My brain spun as Mrs. Gresham donned a burgundy housedress and moved into her sitting room to give orders concerning dinner. I ducked into my own room to change out of traveling garments, eying my patient as I went. She looked tired but poised.

Alone, I stood in the window. Essie was Rose? Aberdeen was *here*? I shivered with the warm awareness of Grayson's presence creeping up around me, that foggy sense of something occurring beyond what I could see.

A distant knock on Golda's sitting room door startled me more than it should. I heard Parker admit Dr. Tillman, and I moved deeper into my room.

"Welcome home, Mrs. Gresham. I trust your trip was uneventful."

A rustle of skirts. "I wouldn't call it that, but it was a success."

"I had a few calls to pay in this district, so I thought I'd stop and see that the trip had no ill effects on you. Also, I wanted to know if you'd given any thought to that specialist I mentioned."

I imagined her watching him with steely eyes.

"I'll accompany you, of course, and you can bring along anyone else you wish."

I held my breath. Would she go?

Her teacup clinked against its saucer. "Won't you stay to dinner, Dr. Tillman?"

"Dinner? I suppose . . . but I wouldn't think of imposing."

"Well now, there's a first." The coy curl to her words delighted me. I leaned back against the wall with a smile. She was returning to herself. She seemed stronger, more alive. "Miss Duvall must join us then, so we have an even number."

So much for a private evening.

When I escorted my patient into the drawing room for the meal at half past, Parker met me at the door with a long white envelope. "This came for you, miss."

I hardly glanced at the thing, intending to slip it in my pocket, but the return address shocked me. I stopped and leaned one hand on the wall as Golda brushed through the doors — *Durham University School of Medicine.*

It was a cruel mistake, this letter from the school that had already barred my application. I tore at the wax seal with trembling fingers. I yanked out the single folded sheet, eagerly reading it all.

265

We are pleased to inform you that your application has been received by the admissions board and we are considering it along with the other submissions. Be advised that, should you be accepted for admission to this university, you will receive a separate letter with the applicable dates for arrival and fee schedule for . . .

My vision blurred, then refocused. I scanned it again. Was this real? Yes, it was. But how? I read the letter again, feeling this moment sinking into the history pages of my life. It was here in black-and-white — they were considering my application, the one that listed a woman's name on the top. They were considering a woman. *This* woman.

My heart pounded and tears formed. It was my very own sort of love letter, one that thrilled my heart with a rapture greater than all four proposals combined. I sank onto a page boy stool in the hall, clutching the letter and wondering what sort of magic had occurred. For them to send this, to know I was here, rather than at home — a miracle, that's how. *God is God,* Mama had always said. *He can do anything he wants.*

How interesting and lovely the world suddenly seemed.

I nearly pounced on poor Aunt Maisie when she rounded the corner and held the letter before her cloudy blue eyes. She blinked through it, then that whiskered chin hung down to her chest, eyes wide and lips quivering.

"Ahahah, you've *done it,* my girl. You've done it!" She cackled with glee and wrapped her arms around me.

I walked into dinner with poise and tried to focus enough to join the conversation.

"I trust things are going well with your patient, Miss Duvall." Dr. Tillman spoke from across the table when we'd been seated.

They'd paired us together at the end, as we had both been included by a technicality of social graces, and Aunt Maisie eyed us with her shrewd monkey-eyes. She'd turned into her usual dinnertime statue, but I felt her gaze. Oddly enough, I seemed to have Celeste's as well. "As well as can be expected, I suppose."

"Glad to hear it." Tillman smiled around his bite and continued to watch me expectantly.

I gave a faltering smile, uncertain exactly what I was supposed to say. "And you? Did you pass a few productive days in town?"

"Quite."

A pleasant hum of voices punctuated by clinking flatware served as the background noise. Golda spoke to Burke about her presentation of verses and meeting Longfellow. Burke and Clara hardly spoke, and Celeste's frequent glances toward our end of the table did not go unnoticed.

Then a door banged open toward the front of the house, echoing through the front entry, and the pleasant chatter dimmed. The dining room door opened, and it was Mr. Gresham, that ghostly shadow of a man filling the doorway behind Parker. The butler bowed and removed himself, leaving the awkward owner of the house to face us all.

He shifted, looking at the faces turned toward him, and fiddled with the buttons of his suitcoat. "Well then, carry on." He seated himself as a footman pulled out a chair at the far end between the doctor and myself, separated from his wife by the massive walnut affair holding our meal.

"Why, Mr. Gresham, what a surprise." Golda's slight frown said it wasn't a welcome one.

"I do live here, after all." He lifted knife and fork, eyeing the meat on his plate.

"So you do."

I flashed a glance toward Golda and suddenly became aware that her husband was here because *I* had goaded him into it.

Which had been less than brilliant, as it turned out.

The diners returned to eating, but the talking had ceased. Footsteps of the staff moving here and there punctuated the hushed moments. Mr. Gresham sat at the head of his own table clearing his throat and keeping his gaze down as if he were a guest at the palace. "You look well, Mrs. Gresham."

Golda gifted him with a tolerant smile. "I'm glad I appear that way, Mr. Gresham."

Celeste and Burke exchanged looks of longsuffering while Gabe studied his mother with keen eyes.

Celeste forced a bright smile. "What sort of adventures have you had lately, Father?"

"Business matters, mostly." He took a bite. "I've been pursuing a lead on a completely new type of stallion. It's an untapped opportunity, and I've arranged to travel there and pursue it before others get wind of it. It'll be a big undertaking, but an even larger reward, if it pays off."

Golda froze, napkin at her lips. "I see."

"I meant to write you about it, but I thought —"

"That it was meaningless, of course, as

269

my opinion often is to you."

He hunched his tall frame over his food and silence reigned again. The web of private tension thickened, all of us finding ourselves caught up in it.

Burke spoke in low tones to Celeste about a garden party, and the attention of the room dissipated. A sense of release spread over us.

"So here I am, Miss Duvall." Mr. Gresham leaned toward me as he sipped his drink and blotted his lips. "Is it what you hoped it would be, having me at Crestwicke?"

"Ah, so *you* are the reason for his return." Dr. Tillman smiled at me, one eyebrow raised. "Very keen powers of persuasion."

Gresham turned to his physician. "Speaking of which, the entire board is still in shock over what you've done."

"Oh?" Tillman stared at his plate, avoiding my gaze.

What *had* the man done now? Perhaps "Tillman's Tablets" turned out to be a hoax, and now he had to answer for them.

Gresham buttered his bread. "On that note, Miss Duvall, I wish you all the best in medical school."

I bit down hard on my tongue, and cried out, blinking back tears. Silence blanketed the room again, but with my small smile of

270

apology, the talk resumed around us. Heat washed over my skin. The letter from the admissions board — that precious letter, in the long envelope. Magic, indeed. The board hadn't changed their minds — Tillman had.

But why?

Mr. Gresham slipped out the tall doors after quickly clearing his plate, and I turned to Dr. Tillman, looking over his scholarly face behind the spectacles. "Whatever you did, thank you. But I hope it wasn't some misguided effort to gain my affections."

"As I had no plans to tell you I'd done it, it's safe to assume that wasn't the reason."

It was impossible to believe. There had to be more. I stared at him unflinchingly, waiting for him to crack, but he didn't. "Then what was it?"

"What?"

"The reason."

"Are you suggesting I recommended a potential student for reasons other than pure talent and suitability for the field? I pride myself in a keen perception of people and their abilities. I happen to believe you'd make a fine doctor. Better than most, actually."

I narrowed my gaze. "Why?"

"Well, your research, for one. It's quite

impressive. But mostly . . . let's just say I've watched you face the flames of a rather sizable dragon and barely flinch at the heat." The edges of his mouth jerked up in the hint of a smile. "If that is any testament to how well you can hold your own with patients, this profession needs at least ten more of you." He paused to wipe his hands with a napkin. "Congratulations, Miss Duvall. I wish you every success."

What in the world was he doing? He flustered and flattered me in the same sentence, his even tone conveying thoughts I could hardly wrap my mind around. I clamped my mouth shut, horrified to realize it had been hanging open.

He sipped his drink. "Is something the matter?"

"I've said nothing."

"Exactly." He winked.

A series of tingles passed over my skin in quick succession, the sensation not altogether unpleasant.

He threw me a terribly playful grin then, and it only made it worse. "Well?"

I blinked, faltered, then returned his charming smile with a shy one of my own. He'd asked how I was. "I'm better than I ever have been, Dr. Tillman. Which I suppose I owe to you."

"It was your skill that earned my recommendation. I only suggested they reconsider you. I'm honored to have you as a colleague in this harrowing world of medicine."

Colleague. My mind fixated on the term he'd so casually dropped into conversation. He saw me as a peer? With all the suitors who had scraped together the words of a poem-worthy proposal, none had ever granted me this level of dignity.

I rather liked it.

Our eyes met for a moment and I straightened. Those uninvited chills continued to climb into my scalp. I couldn't make head or tail of the man before me, or my own heart for that matter, but I knew that the icy air of Crestwicke had been pierced by a small sliver of warmth. He'd done this, knowing I didn't care for him. I studied his familiar features, the once-despised face that now seemed . . . what, exactly? Tolerable? Handsome? He met my stare with unblinking ease, his eyes crinkling at the edges in an endearing way, and I hadn't any idea what I was supposed to do with my arms, my fidgeting hands.

The moment snapped with the shove of a chair. Celeste rose with unusual force and hurried from the room.

I followed her into the hall, wondering if I

should fetch my medical bag. "What is it, Celeste?"

She turned troubled eyes on me when I reached her. "Trying for a fifth proposal now, are we?"

I blinked as hot and cold chased through me. "Who? What?"

"You are considering Dr. Tillman now, are you not?"

Was I? "Well, he isn't completely odious." I lowered my gaze from the accusation in hers. I could only picture the hope in her eyes when she'd first asked if I was "one of us," and I felt now as though I'd betrayed her, even though nothing had occurred. I still wanted, more than anything, to be a doctor — especially now.

She stepped back, her eyes narrowed. "You spoke with more passion about him when you hated him."

"I never *hated* —"

But she was gone, sailing through the door. I exhaled.

"Well, what was that about?" Aunt Maisie moved up behind me.

"I'm not certain, truly. I want to help, but I feel as though I've only stirred the pot." I shifted on my feet. "Why can't I ever seem to say the right thing? My words . . . they're still wrong, Aunt Maisie."

"Because they're yours." She hobbled close and rested a crooked hand on my arm. "Make your heart a deep well of the Almighty by saturating yourself in his presence, and your words will come out drenched in him no matter what you say. I can promise you, no matter how many brilliant things you have to say, he has better ones." With a nod, she hobbled out of the room.

The whole thing left me confused and not a little unsure of myself. I'd stepped into the middle of a novel — no, a chapter — and was attempting to fumble through it.

Yet I wanted the rest of the story.

EIGHTEEN

Love may come unexpectedly by getting
to know someone different, or getting to
know them differently.
    ~A scientist's observations on love

The passageway was starkly quiet as Gabe
Gresham slipped into it from the drawing
room. He needed space, silence, and several
feet of solid wall between himself and the
rest of the family. Ever since the trip to
Brighton, his brain was alive with questions,
what-ifs, and bright, sparkling hope. Willa
Duvall had said she loved him.

Well, in a way. She'd recited a silly poem
while dancing and twirling around him like
a ridiculous little woodland sprite. Un-
quenchable she was, and sort of a mystery.

Which was precisely why he adored her. It
was a truth so ingrained in him he'd wear it
to his grave. She drew out something primal
in him, a visceral magnetism that awakened

life. He was a black-and-white charcoal sketch turned full color when she was here.

Gabe stopped at a window to look up at the distant ruins, inhaling with the sweet aroma brought by memories of their times together. It was a delight having her back here. Perhaps it was time to tell her the truth about himself. She should know, if her feelings for him were changing even in the slightest. But after watching her with the doctor at dinner . . . now he was confused.

He returned to his original mission — Celeste — and the morning room where he heard voices. What could have upset her? Yet when he pushed open the doors, only Dr. Tillman stood there, staring down at a piece of paper with a look of utter bemusement. His gaze jerked up when Gabe stepped in. "Doctor. I trust it is not our family that has left you so unsettled."

He blinked, looking back to the paper then up at Gabe. "I'm not certain what I am, to be honest." He held up the paper. "This is from your sister. Or at least, I think it is. Here, see what you make of it. It doesn't sound like her, but she's just flung it at me with the greatest fit of passion. I've never seen the like."

"She *threw* it?"

"Well, yes, after saying a great long string of nonsensical things. Something about what was between us, and then something about Miss Duvall. It left me feeling like quite a cad, and I'm certain I must be, but I cannot for the life of me understand why."

Gabe accepted the letter and frowned as he read the unusual lines. The handwriting looked familiar, but he wasn't certain if it belonged to Celeste or someone else.

Tillman's face was grim. "Perhaps I should go sort this out. If you'll excuse me . . ."

"Why not give her the night? Let us sort through it here, see if we can't reason with her."

Unguarded relief shone through the man's face. "Perhaps that's best." The doctor slipped the note into a book and set it on the desk. "I'll just . . ." He cleared his throat. "In case she asks for it." Then he darted out as if through an escape hatch.

Gabe stared at the door, his mind plagued with questions and a strong sense of duty toward the hurting sister more delicate than she let on. If only he understood what to do for her. He was as lost concerning love as she was, though.

Perhaps Burke would have an idea. He was far better with people and words. Gabe found him in the study.

"Well, then. Come to help, have you?" Burke shuffled papers into a pile and set them aside. "I cannot seem to make head or tail of Father's new venture, and I could use a second opinion on a few matters."

"I'm more suited to the stables than the desk."

"I've no idea if we're to expect racers or sires or hunting steeds, or perhaps all they'll be good for is renting out to the tenant farmers to pull a plow."

"Labels are about as helpful for horses as they are people. Simply expect them to be horses and let them show you over time what they are."

Burke grimaced. "Can't you at least make a guess? We have some sketches here, and some possible bloodlines." He dropped the messy stack on the desk before Gabe.

He didn't touch them. "It's not for us to know before they're ready to reveal it." How like these wild stallions Willa could be. Untamable, unpredictable, defying labels . . .

"I'm not asking you to read the creatures' minds, Gabe. Simply look at their legs, their bearing. Make a guess as to what they might be."

Oh, how her eyes twinkled. Her words so flippant yet intimate too. She didn't speak of love with every man, of that he was certain. Yet she'd meant it in a friendly manner this time.

Right?

"Gabe."

He shook himself free of his tangled thoughts — but too late.

Burke paused his paper shuffling to stare at him, as if truly noticing him for the first time. Something in his expression made Gabe painfully aware of himself and the tiny glimpses of his thoughts he'd let leak out onto his face. He was used to knowing all about the people around him, but not the reverse.

"Something troubling you?" Burke came around to stand in front of the desk. "Is it Celeste? Women are a confusing lot, I'll grant you that. She'll come around, though."

Gabe stared.

"Something else. Is it woman troubles?"

Gabe's jaw tensed.

"There *is* someone, isn't there? Some woman has worked her way into Gabe Gresham's solid heart and set up home there, at last." His smile was mercifully solemn and brotherly, rather than the mocking expression he so often wore. "And now you are in a muddle about what to do with it all."

"Merely attempting to understand."

He gave a harsh laugh. "Give up now. Take it from a married man — women are as confounding as they are lovely, and the moment you think you've untangled things, you see the knotted mess it truly is."

"Hmm." Uneasy, Gabe let the implications hang in the air and disintegrate. Of all the things people had divulged to him over the years, he didn't care to feel like a bedroom eavesdropper.

"One word of advice — do your own choosing. Never let *her* interfere, no matter how hard she works to insert herself. She's made more than one unhappy match, including her own. So when it comes time, make certain you choose your own person to love."

Gabe looked down. For him, it was never a matter of *who,* but *if.* He had never considered himself, a true loner, fit for marriage. Unless it was to *her.* Willa Duvall had woven herself into his life as thoroughly as a golden thread running through a tapestry, never to be removed without a thorough unraveling.

He remembered the first time her smile had caught him off guard — he'd been following her up a path and she'd flung a bright, dimpled smile back over her shoulder. He stumbled and tried to feign a trip over the rocks. Her melodic laughter followed — never directed at him, but somehow coloring their encounters with joy. It was infectious.

Burke's voice broke through his sweet memory. "I suppose I shouldn't be speaking of her so, especially to you, but she drives you mad at times too, doesn't she?"

Willa? No. Gabe blinked, circling back to their conversation. Mother. He'd been speaking of Mother. "She has my pity. My empathy."

Burke eyed him. "You're not a bad sort, Gabe, even if you don't say much." He returned to his chair behind the desk, blotting his pen and writing. "I suppose I'll merely figure those horses in as sires until we have a look at them and know more. Any horse can be that much, at least. Here, take these bloodline papers with you. Once you've untangled the great mystery of these creatures, you let me know."

"The horses?"

"Well, them too." His smile was coy.

Gabe ignored the insinuation. "It'll take time."

"So be it. And Gabe." He lowered the pen,

his gaze direct. "Go on and ask her, whoever she is. It can't hurt. The worst she can say is no."

He was absolutely right — *nothing* could be worse than her saying no. And she'd had a fair bit of practice at it.

Burke watched Gabe's broad back move through the doorway and disappear into the dark passageway beyond, his mind still simmering with thoughts of his wife. Perhaps Clara should have married someone like Gabe, who was as quiet and reclusive as her.

His gut gave a sickening lurch. Was it *him*? Had Gabe written the letter? He couldn't recall just then what Gabe's handwriting even looked like.

Where was Gabe going, anyway? Where was Clara?

Panic seized him once again, as it had of late, compelling him toward the hall. The stranglehold only released whenever he found his wife involved in some innocent task, without the company of a man, without a new letter. Candle leading the way, he slipped through the long, shadowed passageway until he heard her voice, low and solemn, in Celeste's chamber.

"Perhaps there was a misunderstanding. That Willa Duvall has a habit of accumulating men without the intention of keeping them. Dr. Tillman may find you utterly appealing in her wake."

What was this? He stood at the door, which was slightly ajar, and watched his wife in intimate conversation with a very unsettled Celeste, who was apparently pining over Tillman. All the pieces fitted into place with a gush of relief. Celeste and the good doctor — who knew?

Celeste sniffed. "That Dr. Tillman had to go and ruin everything. Now all I can think of is marriage and children and . . ."

"And now you'll find someone far better, and much more dashing."

What if Tillman *was* interested, though? The man would make his sister a fine match. Perhaps it was time to play a little chess himself — only, he'd unite the forlorn with the one she truly loved.

He let out his breath and turned to go, but something drew him back. They giggled together, then there was another sniff. How uncouth it was to spy this way, yet he was compelled to simply watch. Their conversation hummed in the background, but it was his wife's face that drew him, sweet and charming in the midst of Celeste's turmoil.

I've seen the strength and kindness you believe go unnoticed . . .

The lines of that fool letter had burned themselves into the back of his eyelids, and now they returned as he watched the woman for whom they were written. Kindness. Yes, that described her immensely. And in that kindness, he saw the strength her admirer noticed. Bent near to his bereft sister, her very posture exuded a powerful sisterly empathy for this woman who had once been quick to snub Clara when she entered their household. Clara had, in fact, been more accepting of any person in this entire house than they had been of her.

. . . breathless with wonder and profound respect for who you are.

How much that woman had shifted the atmosphere of that room, even in her quiet — from dinner to now, Celeste was completely changed. He'd never thought of Clara as especially accomplished or mature, but there was a settled look in her eyes, a look of patient intelligence. How utterly appealing.

You inspired in me a passion both bright and deep . . .

He blinked, unable to tear his gaze away from the lithe figure perched on the settee like a little gem of sweetness in this stale old house.

Burke pulled back and shook his head.

What nonsense. It was only some primal territorial instinct brought out by this admirer that made him see her so. The unknown letter writer had nothing on him, anyway. Nothing. Burke was her husband. He gave her everything she had, including a family name and home. Even those paints she loved so much had come from him. What had this letter writer given her in comparison?

As if on cue, another sentence from the letter surfaced in his brain. *Dearest, if only you could see yourself from where I stand — how brave and unstoppable you would become.*

And now she did. Through that wretched letter, Clara had the benefit of seeing herself through the rosy, dewy-eyed lens he handed her, with all the pent-up passion and admiration a woman could want.

Yet that was foolish. Foolish! How could mere words outweigh everything he'd given her? This man was simply spouting off flattering turns of phrase to catch her attention.

Quite suddenly, pieces of the letter interrupted his little rant, thumping through his head with every pulse of his heart. *Let me remind you that I've known you long enough to see it all . . . I've watched when you thought no one was looking, and observed what exists below the surface . . . I even know that secret you hoped to keep from everyone.*

He stretched his neck and forced a swallow as fear and anger wrestled in his gut. Somehow that stranger knew something he did not. Burke stared with new intensity at the woman on the settee with one thought burning in his skull — he simply *had* to know that secret. If it took his whole life, his entire marriage, he would know that one part of his wife that she had not shared with him.

NINETEEN

If I should happen to fall in love, the outcome of such a plight depends, like any big fall, on who is there to catch me.
    ~A scientist's observations on love

My words . . . they're still wrong, Aunt Maisie. Because they're yours.

I clambered up the crumbling rock slope as the sun crested the next morning, the household behind me still abed, and braced myself against the wind. It was time to have one more private conversation about that letter, before I said another regrettable word.

I should have realized what had upset Celeste. Or at least, I should have kept quiet until I did. That letter had been shaking up the household ever since it had been unleashed here, and now it seemed to have somehow landed with her.

When Celeste had finally told me about

her secret admirer, quoting lines I recognized from the letter, I'd forced myself to swallow the truth that was ripe and ready on the edge of my tongue. "It likely isn't what it seems, Celeste," was all I'd said in the moment. After our last conversation, I would not say more until I'd first talked it over with the One of infinite wisdom.

Now, stepping into the center of the ruins, those massive old stone walls became a barrier from the wind, creating a small square of quiet in the big loud world. There I knelt and rested my soul before God. I sank into his presence, offering up my raw worries and hope as the sun warmed the back of my neck.

The air of Crestwicke had felt even thicker lately with the longing for authentic love, the silent pain of disappointment in dashed hopes. I'd come to uncover a single broken love story and encountered a house full of brokenness and unsettled hearts longing for a safe place to land.

Time elapsed with the muffled crash of waves below. Finally my legs grew stiff, my skin chilled with moisture. With a sigh I rose, filling my lungs with fresh air and looking over the bracken-laden cliffs that all spoke in vivid color of their Creator. Flowers gave a fresh powdery scent to the air.

Drenched in God Almighty was exactly how my heart felt then, seeing traces of him everywhere, beating a steady rhythm of strength for whatever came next.

I made my way down the path and across the misty yard, but the sound of my name from a familiar voice arrested me.

Gabe stood framed in the stable doorway. "I have something for you." Something in his demeanor had changed, but I couldn't place what it was. He was more watchful of me, his gaze burrowing through all the layers, and I looked away, neck warm. Perhaps the aura of Crestwicke had invaded me too.

The aroma of horses and fresh hay greeted me, drawing me in, inviting me to stay. Just as Gabe's smiling eyes did while he guided me, enticing me to follow him, and I was glad I did. Around a corner I caught a glimpse of the most majestic, wild-eyed creature I'd ever seen, circling the square enclosure and tossing her head. Around she paced, as if she'd find an exit and dart to safety. The wild white-gray horse stopped to stare back at us from the far end of her enclosure, eyes wide and glassy with fear, then spun into her circle again, tossing her wavy mane. Even disheveled and jittery from head to flanks, she was magnificent.

"Oh, Gabe."

When the horse stopped again, Gabe entered the enclosure, arm out, and approached with steady steps. His gaze was fixed and gentle, his very aura permeating the space and calming the beast's frayed edges. Thawing my heart. It was beautiful to witness their interaction. Gabe was tall and steady as granite, his nature just as solid.

He looked my way. "Give her any name you like, Willa. She isn't broken yet, but she's yours."

My heart lurched. "You . . . bought me a horse?"

He gave the slightest shake of his head, and the horse flinched, ears back and head high. "Brought her in last night from the beach. She has a nasty gash on her hind leg that'll be infected if she's left on her own." One more step and she jerked back, prancing in a circle again. "I patched her up, and she's here to heal." Gabe exited and came to stand beside me.

"How, pray, did you *patch her up*?"

Another shrug, arms folded on the fence as he leaned over to watch her. "A few stitches. They should hold."

The horse stepped closer, neck out toward Gabe as if she couldn't keep away, despite her fear. Looking at this rock of a man who exuded a magnetic gentleness, I couldn't help but understand. What was this enchantment he wielded over all wild creatures?

The horse inched close to Gabe again, ears back, and I held my breath for their contact. She sniffed in a few times and huffed out, jerking away and circling again. Our eyes met and I recognized myself once again in the creature. My heart pounded as I took in the flared gray nostrils, quivering flesh, mane still wild with the wind and freedom she'd so recently had, and something within me trembled. "I can't do it, Gabe. I cannot keep her. Beautiful as she is, she's a wild animal. She'd be miserable. She'd make you miserable."

"Right, then." He eyed me, and I wondered if he glimpsed the deeper thoughts on my face. "Just until she's healed. Would that suit?"

I glanced his way with a smile. "I suppose that'll do."

"While she's here, you might as well come and spend time with her, get her used to the idea that humans aren't terrible. It'll make it easier for me to treat her wounds." More time here? More of these stables and this man, working his charm on all things wild?

"You've never had trouble earning the

trust of a horse."

He considered me. "Thought she'd be good for you too. Give you something to do besides caring for a rather demanding patient." I blinked, and he shrugged. "No harm in admitting the truth now and again."

"I'm beginning to think your mother isn't so terrible."

Something beautiful swelled in his expression, glowing from every plane of his face. "After winning her over, a mere horse should be no trouble."

I turned back to the creature still hovering in the corner. "I shall make it my special mission to love the fear right out of this horse. You see if I don't."

"I have no doubt. Your impact is felt wherever you go."

I sighed as the horse skittered about the stall. "For better or worse."

Just like his horses. "Be patient with her, no? It'll take time, but she'll be worth it. I promise." A hint of a smile tugged his lips. "The best ones always are."

I dropped my gaze. "The horse or the patient?"

"Have your pick."

"I thought we were freeing this horse once she healed." I turned and placed a hand on the gate, watching the caged thing.

"Perhaps." He stepped up behind me, placing his hand beside mine. "Don't be surprised if she decides to stay. Funny thing about scars is that when they heal, they rebuild around whatever they're touching. You very well might be stuck with her."

I smiled. "I suppose I could live with that."

We stared at one another, that horse and I, her breath puffing quick and short through those flared nostrils. How I longed to smooth my hand along that velvety gray muzzle and up into her mane. I laid my cheek on my folded arms. "There, now. We're to be friends, you and I. Perhaps someday you'll let me ride you. What if I promise to go bareback? Yes, I think that would suit you. Besides, you're far too pretty to be covered up with a saddle. What do you say, shall we make a go of it?"

She jerked her head, then danced back and forth across the farthest part of the stall, neck arching and tangled mane feathering out behind her. Keeping my eyes on her, I stepped up onto the bottom rail of the gate and held out my hand, palm up. What lovely, wild eyes she had, and I could see the fear sparkling in their depths. Back and forth she went, trying to make sense of me.

Then she darted forward and nipped. I

jolted back with a cry and laughed, stumbling off the gate. I turned to Gabe to share the moment with him and found him watching me with deliberate interest, as if he were evaluating something. His look sobered me, and I stood in the quiet stable staring back at him, trying desperately to read what I saw there. He did not let me. Long lashes dropped and guarded his secrets.

I forced a smile into the heavy silence. "Thank you, Gabe. She's perfect. For however long she lets me keep her."

"I'm betting on forever." His voice rumbled from his chest as he lifted his gaze again.

I looked down, unsure what to say.

"I was thinking Luna for her name. After the French word for —"

"Moon." I lifted a smile to him. "Yes, it's perfect. She's like a lovely moonbeam, lighting up this dark stable as she shoots across the sky." I faced the skittish horse. "All right then . . . Luna."

"You'll be perfect for each other."

"Yes, perfect." I turned to him as he tossed a bridle over his shoulder, my heart still full of letters and broken hearts and solemn vows. "Gabe, why does your mother separate so many couples?"

He didn't flinch at the randomness of my

question, but instead lifted an armload of leather bridles and things from a chair, continuing his work. "She has a keen eye, and she isn't blinded by a cloud of feelings. She can see things better than the people in the midst of their infatuation. She practically saved Celeste's life years ago."

Poor Celeste. "That's all it was with her Frenchman — infatuation? She still bears the scars of that break, you know."

"She might bear a lot more if she'd gone forward with him. The truth is, he enjoyed the company of ladies a great deal. Or rather, the company of a great deal of ladies. Maybe he'd have settled on Celeste for life, maybe not."

"So she was protecting her."

"Burke has a good woman because of her, even if they've managed to muck it up a bit, and me . . ." His jaw jutted to the side. "Well, Caroline would mean the fulfillment of a great many dreams for me, and she's kind and beautiful. My mother may be prickly as a pincushion, but she knows the desires of her children and seeks to fill them in whatever way seems logical."

Yet from where I sat, she'd done nothing but form business alliances and tie everyone into knots. No one ever knew how it would be until a person was in it, it seemed, all freedom signed away.

Soon afterward, I walked back to the house, staring up at it with a deep gratitude for my spinsterhood. There existed in me a dull, general ache for the love story I didn't have, for a lasting home for my heart, but that discomfort seemed far better than giving up my future and living through a marriage like those at Crestwicke. Not a single pairing outside of my sainted parents' marriage was better than flying across the beach, mane fluttering and an ocean of possibilities before me.

Days later, a storm rattled the very bones of Crestwicke Manor, slicing the sky with light followed by ominous rolling thunder that vibrated through the timbers. I sat curled into Golda's sitting room window to study, drawn there in spite of the moist air stealing through the casement. Golda sat at her desk, writing. Rain swelled the clouds, threatening to fall but not making good as of yet. Just like the night Rose and Grayson were married.

I hadn't been able to get that story from my head, for the sadness of it remained heavy in my heart. Had she felt clammy, standing there in the rain-pregnant air with her best gown, praying she could wed

Grayson before they were caught?

I forced my attention onto the text on my lap, an abstract from Dr. Henry Currey on his "pavilion principle," which is what I'd finally decided on for Father's new clinic design. Basic and logical, it allowed for ventilation of every part of the building and kept contagions from becoming cooped up with the patients. It had proved wildly successful in France already.

Each strike of lightning jerked my attention back to the window, every rumble sent a shiver through me. Then one sharp crack split the peace, and I dropped my book with a cry. Below a stable door banged. A horse's frantic neigh echoed. Wood splintered, and I strained to see the stables.

Golda's voice made me jump. "Go and see what that's about, will you?"

"Oh yes, of course." I flung aside my wrap and hurried down the hall, planting my face in the leaded glass window at the end of the hall. Then I saw her — that familiar white-gray creature bucking wildly, tangling her legs in the broken corral fence. Another pop and the animal tore into the open field, stumbling on her lame leg.

I spun to bolt outside, but a gentle hand on my arm stopped me. I nearly fell backward in my shock, as if touched by a specter.

"No need to panic." Another flash of lightning illuminated Aunt Maisie, who must have come down the hall for the same reason. "Just wait here."

"But that horse is horribly injured." As thunder rumbled in the background, images of that sleek body tumbling over jagged cliffs ripped through my mind. "I've got to find her. I need a lantern, and rope. And a groom, and —"

Her gnarled hand clamped onto my shoulder. "You need nothing but to stay right here, out of the way."

"But —"

"Look." Her raspy voice arrested my attention as she lifted one crooked finger to the window. Another horse tore out of the stables, a cloaked rider clinging to its neck.

"Gabe." I breathed his name in relief and touched the rippled glass.

I waited for their return, watching my breath steam the window, counting endless seconds. Then they crested the far hill, both horses side by side with Gabe tall and able on his. Lightning crackled as they came down the hill, the white horse favoring her injured leg but no longer fighting. In fact, she seemed eager for the shelter as they reached the stable, head bowed as they stopped under the eaves.

She'd begun to make her peace with us lately, to hesitantly take an apple from me, a calming stroke from Gabe, and it had solidified my heart toward her, filled it with protectiveness. Gabe loosened the rope around her neck and smoothed his hand down to her shoulder. She threw her head back when thunder rumbled, giving little bucks, then she visibly eased under Gabe's soothing touch.

"Belonging to Gabe Gresham is not the worst thing that's happened to that wild horse." Aunt Maisie's voice was faint and thoughtful.

My heart squeezed, watching Gabe coax the horses back to the stable. She'd given up her freedom, but she had someone to go after her in a storm. My heart stretched in many directions, tainted with longing.

Yet not everyone's story ended that way. Few did, in fact. Images of Rose and Grayson in that Gretna Green stable flashed before me with each lightning bolt. "Oh, Aunt Maisie, how can you possibly want me to fan those desires into flames when they only consume a person and leave her so broken and alone."

"If that's how it leaves her, then she hasn't finished the search."

"But if a person is already married . . ." I

lowered my voice to a whisper. "Aunt Maisie, why did Grayson abandon her?"

She straightened. "We haven't finished the story yet, have we? Besides, it was his *family* who forced the annulment."

"That means he still had to stand before the church and claim the marriage was never valid, retract his vows as if they were nothing more than a mistake. What good is it to belong to someone if they can suddenly decide you no longer do?" I pushed the words out, and my heart retracted, as if it had just released something important from its very core. I stared at the cold fear exposed in me. Everyone left, whether they meant to or not. So many married couples remained present in body, but their heart had long since departed the union. Even Mother had left Father, in a way, and a gaping hole had grown in her absence. How could I bear it? How could anyone?

"It's far more complicated than that, lass. You see, poor Grayson was forbidden from seeing his Rose. They even planned to have her arrested and sent to America. They didn't want their son wasted on a little butcher shop girl, and their wishes had a nasty habit of becoming reality. They arranged for a servant to plant an heirloom necklace on the girl, but Grayson found out

301

and bargained with them. Rather than having Rose forced to go overseas, where she'd be destitute, he would go himself. He'd join his father's regiment if they promised to leave the girl alone. They agreed, and he was shipped out to the West Indies."

"Did Rose follow him?"

She shook her head sadly. "She didn't know what had become of him for a long time."

"Didn't she try to win him back?"

"Of course she did." The old woman grimaced. "What kind of spineless heroine do you think she was? Every week for several months, Rose appeared at their doorstep, asking for Grayson. Every time, they sent her away. Then she came one last time and confessed, in all irony, that she actually *was* in possession of a priceless family heirloom from Grayson, but they didn't believe her."

"What did she do?"

"There was nothing for it but to return home, ruined and abandoned. No one would marry her after that, and truth be told, she didn't wish to wed. Those years broke her. When her father found out what had happened, he kicked poor Rose out, calling her a disgrace and a great deal of other names not repeated by decent folk.

The only man who thought well of her was Grayson, and he was off fighting for his queen."

"Did he ever come home? Surely his parents would not stand between them forever, if they were truly in love."

She offered a weak shrug, her faded eyes wandering into some unseen attic room of her mind. "I looked for him for a while, but no one knew where he was, or wouldn't say. He'd been known all over Upton Currey for his charm and wealth, but suddenly no one spoke of him. It was as if he hadn't existed, and there was nothing to be done about it."

Emotion shimmered in me, absorbing the immensity of this story . . . and the shift in her narrative, that single word giving it all away: *I.* It wasn't Clara's story, or Gabe's betrothed, but the bright-eyed sharp-witted grown-up young woman before me. She *had* been telling me her own story. Another listener might have missed the subtle slip, but my medical mind sorted through emotion daily to thread out facts.

Despair and hope mingled in my heart, swirling into a chaotic desperation to find that love note. I had to deliver it to her, even if she never saw its writer again. She had to know how he felt. If only I knew where it was! I fisted my hands, wishing they still held that elusive letter.

Aunt Maisie ran her crippled old hands along my arm and grabbed at my hand. Her skin was loose but smooth. "Don't let this story cause you to give up, child. Keep looking, keep chasing that deep desire for real love. Cast aside every wrong one, and eventually . . . eventually you'll find the real thing."

I looked her full in the face, heart pounding. "Tell Rose, if you should see her, that it isn't time for her to give up just yet either."

Her gaze locked onto my face, searching for something of vital importance. "You've found her letter."

"No, but it's turned up again. It's still here."

She stilled. "Who?"

"Celeste."

"Truly?"

"She believes she has an admirer now too. I've no idea how to break the truth to her — or to Essie. And somehow Clara Gresham is part of this." What had Aunt Maisie said about Burke keeping tabs on his wife? A mess is what I'd created. Not a reunion, but a volatile mess. "Perhaps we should tell —"

"No." She squeezed my hand with a strangle-

hold. "Whatever comes, you must not tell them anything. Not yet, anyway. Promise me you won't."

"Why ever not? They can't go on believing —"

"What, that someone, somewhere truly loves them? Don't you see? These words have a life beyond the page. They've taken flight in this house, moving where they will, seeping into the cracks of hearts. It's woken something up in them, opened them to the possibility that love exists and they are the worthy recipients. And that is *vital.*"

Truth and compassion, always at war within my outspoken self. This time my strangled heart chose compassion . . . and silence. Not a lie, just silence. "How long?"

"Find that letter, and we'll discuss what comes next."

I couldn't stop thinking about the path that missive seemed to be carving through the hard rock of Crestwicke's walls. Even I had been captivated by the thing.

What makes the past so intriguing, anyway? Perhaps because understanding those stories that so enchant us, those ghostly echoes of long-ago mistakes and passions, means untangling the present and changing the future.

Which is what I intended to do. Armed

now with the name of a town, I would find Grayson Aberdeen and see if, by some chance, he was unattached.

TWENTY

There's power in simply listening to the one you love, because it gives weight and value to your beloved's thoughts before they are even spoken.
~A scientist's observations on love

Upton Currey. There was nothing magical about that hamlet, but in order to sew the whole mystery together, I needed a story thread that wove through that little place — Grayson Aberdeen's whereabouts. An opportunity to chase the lead came a mere three days after Aunt Maisie had let the name slip.

By Tuesday of the following week, exactly three weeks into my stay, Golda had agreed to see the specialist, and she planned to leave with Dr. Tillman in two days' time. I forced myself not to think of the looming contract deadline — one week away. Unless Father forgot — but he never did.

"Why not give your nurse the day off, and let her have a little holiday?" Burke sipped his water that evening and pointed his glass in my direction. Suspicion arose, but I thrilled at the idea of sneaking off to pursue Grayson. I could do it — there and back within the day. But what would it cost? I watched Burke through slitted eyes, waiting for him to reveal his angle. "She hasn't taken any of her half days, and I'm certain Celeste could accompany you and Dr. Tillman to town." He gave a wink toward his sister.

Celeste reddened, and my mind watched the puzzle take shape. So, it was Dr. Tillman she suspected of being her secret letter writer, and somehow Burke had found out. How on earth had all that come about? And which of them had the letter now?

Golda fidgeted. "I suppose I do owe you a day."

"If you could spare me, ma'am, I have an errand to do that's several towns over."

Mrs. Gresham turned her imperial gaze on me. "I wouldn't pay you for the day off."

"Naturally."

"Very well, then." Golda Gresham looked me over. "I suppose I'll oblige you. I assume you'll have a traveling companion, yes? I'll not have a member of my staff act-

308

ing in an unbecoming manner."

I struggled to find my voice. "I hadn't given it a thought. I don't imagine I could find anyone to accompany me at this late hour."

She raised an eyebrow, silently berating the unseemly individuals who had raised me this way. "I suppose if you have no one, you shall simply come with Dr. Tillman and me."

Celeste's fingers struck a dissonant chord on the piano and she spun on the bench. "I'll do it."

We all turned to Celeste as she rose, closing the lid over the keys. "A trip sounds delightful, and I'll take any excuse to see something new." She came to stand beside me and impulsively slipped her hand into the crook of my arm. "Come, it'll be nice for the both of us. Poor Miss Duvall should have her holiday, and Dr. Tillman mentioned earlier that he'd rather take his own nurses. I'd merely be in the way."

Golda gave a queenly nod. "Very well, then. On Thursday we shall go our separate ways."

We rode on horseback toward the burning orb of a sun that Thursday morning, bright enough to blind me from the road. My mind spun. The *clop-clop* of our mounts was the only sound until Celeste finally spoke. "How do you do it, exactly?"

The sound of her voice startled me after a quarter mile or so of silence. I turned to blink at my longtime friend and recall the threads of some conversation we'd dropped. "Do what?"

"Draw men to you like honey and have them pining after you?"

I blew out a breath. "I only wish I knew — so I could stop doing it."

She blinked in shock, then the tension faded from her face. A chortling giggle came out, ending in a small snort.

A smile pulled at my lips and my stress lightened. "What, you don't believe me? It isn't purposeful, you know. I'd rather enchant no one than break hearts and sully friendships. Everywhere I go, there's a trail of misread feelings and dashed hopes. Believe me, it's nothing to be jealous of." I turned in my saddle to look at plain, spinsterly Celeste, who was made much prettier by a genuine smile. *Please help me form the right words, God. There is more than I even understand happening in her heart.* "About that letter . . ."

Her gaze snapped to me.

"Have you gone and changed your mind

310

about men?"

Her smile faded and our horses plodded on in quiet. She stared at the road ahead. "I thought I was completely happy. The women's league is important work, after all, and I'm proud to be part of it. But perhaps . . . perhaps *someone* changed my mind." She sighed. "I've had another letter. It was left in my chambers, and it was even more memorable."

"Another." This was becoming a pattern. An odd one.

A brilliant array of possibilities spun, then narrowed to one. Maisie. *When words are all you have, it suddenly makes you want to keep as many as you can and do something with them.*

She had imitated Grayson's handwriting to stir the pot. An attempt to help or wreak havoc? Either way, she was making an impact.

I sighed in my utter helplessness and looked at Celeste. I couldn't tell her. Not yet, at least. The new lift of her chin, the easy manner of her movements, the dewy hope in her eyes — I couldn't crush that until I knew for certain.

Besides, I'd promised Aunt Maisie my silence. Now I knew why she'd asked it of me. Quiet closed back over the conversation once again and remained until we neared the village.

"So tell me more about this errand, Miss Duvall. Is it to do with your relations?"

"Not at all. I'm tracking down half of an age-old love story, and I hope to find closure for someone." I'd only promised silence concerning the letter, right? Not the story. "A man named Grayson Aberdeen once married a girl for love, but his parents forced an annulment. They never spoke again."

She looked at me. "Well, that's a fine thing to do, toss me crumbs that way and not finish the story. Who are these people? What's become of them?"

I shifted on the creaky leather sidesaddle and ushered her into the magnificent old love story of Aunt Maisie and Grayson Aberdeen. I called the girl Rose, of course, to keep her secret, and left out the part about the letter. The tale spilled out of my overfull heart in an easy, flowing tempo, and my companion listened intently. "You find it remarkable too, don't you?"

"I admit, I'm intrigued. Perhaps we can work together on it."

I smiled at this woman who was surprisingly as receptive to authentic love as I was and sensed a reemerging kinship. "I'd like that."

We rode into the small town of Upton Currey before I realized I had no destination more specific than the town itself. How did one go about inquiring after an individual to whom she'd never been formally introduced? Perhaps this entire trip was rather uncouth of me. I admitted my lack of plans to Celeste, but she merely smiled and said, "Why, we begin with the church, of course. The parish vicar will know everyone."

We slowed our mounts and steered them toward the distant clang of a bell, aiming for the steeple that rose above cresting green hills. We reined in at a black iron fence and dismounted.

After securing our horses, we approached the weathered wooden doors and pulled on the iron ring.

Celeste stepped in first. "Hello there!"

A young face popped out from behind a curtain, eyeing us with hesitant welcome.

"I was hoping you might direct us, sir. Where might we find the vicar?"

He shrugged. "No telling, this time of day. Out winning souls, I expect."

"Perhaps you can help us. You are his . . . ?"

"Curate. I don't hear confessions, mind you."

"What can you tell us about the Aberdeen family? Do they live around here?"

I braced myself for a look of confusion, an apologetic no, but instead his face lit with interest. "Of course. They have for generations."

"Generations." I breathed this out, my heart suddenly pummeling my ribs. It was real — Maisie's story was real. "What do you know of them?"

He smoothed his oiled hair parted in the center. "The Aberdeens haven't been to church in some time. He isn't well — rather delicate of mind, you see. He was once a force about this village, old Grayson Aberdeen, but now he's an old man locked up in his tower."

I could barely breathe. "Is that so? I suspect he's grieving some deep sorrow."

"Certainly he is." The man waved for us to follow him out the door and into the churchyard with crooked grave markers stuck into rocky soil. He led us to a large crypt in the rear and pointed at the sign. "Most of the family lies here, and those still living have a place reserved."

I scanned the engraved plates, pulse pounding, until I saw his name.

314

"His wife is still living?"

"That she is, and it's a good thing too. There's no one else to see to his care."

I closed my eyes as my heart sank to the floor with utter disappointment. This was not the ending I was hoping for. "I thought you said he was grieving . . ."

"That's right, their children. All died many years ago." He pointed to the engraved plates of three more Aberdeens, all with dates of death in the '30s. "Were you acquainted with the family, then?"

"A little." Just the contents of one of their hearts.

"There are a great many legends about them. They're the oldest family in these parts, going nigh on four hundred years. That house up on the hill there, it's been theirs for many generations." He pointed with a long finger to the fog-drenched hill in the distance that balanced a crooked old mansion on its peak. Slender towers flanked long stucco and timber walls, providing a charm that came from age rather than beauty.

"What sort of stories?"

"Oh, dealings with pirates, embezzlement,

an illegitimate duke."

"Anything about a Gretna-Green marriage?"

"You'd have to ask up at the house. I seem to remember something, but it may have only been rumors. People in Upton Currey, they do love to tell stories. It's all they have to be excited over."

It was only after the curate walked away that I noticed the inscription on several name plates also bore the name *G. Aberdeen,* and they all had a date after the *d.* I pointed them out to Celeste. "A lifetime of waiting, and it all ends like this. Either he's dead, or he's mad and married to someone else up in that old tower."

I smiled at my companion, but she was pensive. "Well now, it seems there's only one thing to do, if we wish to know for sure."

The crooked castle looked almost eerie as we climbed the winding bramble-covered road, its walls designed to separate the family within from the rest of the world. With a breath, I leaned into my mount and urged her up the steep incline. A pair of stone gargoyles greeted us at the massive timber doorway, and I nearly didn't dismount. It was Celeste who urged me on.

"Come now, we won't find any answers

from the backs of our horses."

I slipped down and braved the steps. The knocker stuck to the door with a layer of grime, but I banged it a few times and stepped back.

An ancient maid opened the door, blinking as if she hadn't seen sunlight in a decade. "Miss?"

I asked to speak to Mr. Aberdeen, and we were led hesitantly into a dark drawing room that was curtained with old threadbare velvet and limp gold tassels and promptly abandoned there. Dust collected along my moist skin while we waited. The place seemed more like a neglected curiosity shop than a home. Finally the owners appeared together, oddly similar to their furniture with outdated garments and haggard faces. The lady of the house wheeled in her slender husband, who sat arched forward in his chair, reminding me of a grasshopper with his bowed legs and round, dark eyes.

Deep pain and age had drawn their faces down like melted candle wax, and it struck me how wrong it was to come. I was asking them to dredge up pain that still obviously haunted them, poking their hearts into remembering little details that might feed into my foolish search.

We exchanged awkward pleasantries with

Lady Aberdeen while his cautious face silently asked the purpose of our visit. Finally I sat forward on the horsehair sofa, breathing in dust with each shift upon its surface. "I have something that belonged to a Grayson Aberdeen, and I'd like to return it."

"I am Grayson Aberdeen," the man said with a wobbling voice. I looked over the once-tall frame now folded into a chair, drained of all the passion Maisie's stories had painted him with. "What do you have that belongs to me?"

My heart swelled with sorrow. "Just a small memento from the past. It may not be important anymore. Perhaps there are . . . that is, are there other Grayson Aberdeens in your family?"

"My father, my grandfather, my uncle . . . ."

"Do any of them live near here?" I tried not to let hope blossom.

He wilted and shook his head. "None are living . . . anywhere. I'm the last one left."

Heavy with disappointment, I rose and thanked them for allowing us to call.

"You could send it to us," Lady Aberdeen said softly as we stepped toward the door. "Whatever you have, that is. We do treasure all those family remembrances."

I watched this pair that wore the air of

spent life, of simply waiting for death to sweep over them. "I don't have it with me, but I'll see what can be done, now that I know where to send it. Thank you for seeing us. It was so good of you to let us call unannounced."

She gave a weak nod to my curtsey and asked the housekeeper, who seemed to be the only remaining servant, to show us out.

As we followed the frazzle-haired woman, Celeste leaned close. "Why did you not mention Rose? They might want to know."

I merely pursed my lips and gave a slight shake of my head. It would do no good now. No good at all.

We turned a corner into the great hall, and the maid pulled open the front doors, eyeing us as we passed through. I flashed her a smile, but it didn't loosen her frown. She watched our descent, as if to make sure we fully left.

"Another sad ending." Celeste murmured this as we made our way back to our horses. "Makes one rather relieved, at times, to be a spinster after all."

We were halfway down the steps, staring at dead ends ahead, when the maid called out to us in her gravelly voice. "Just a moment, there." She worked her way down to us, her elbows bowed as she held up the hem of her uniform. "I can't do it, can't let you leave without knowing. I overheard you mention Rose." How anxious was that haggard face. "I cannot go to my grave without word of her. I've always wondered if her claims were true, if she truly was . . ." She gulped as a nervous tick twitched her hand.

"A thief?" I hurried back to the steps, my heart pounding double-time. "No, I don't believe she was." Yet what did I believe anymore?

"Oh no, not that. I knew she weren't no thief. I was to be the one what helped them frame her, before I knew better. Just a girl I was, a scullery maid. Rotten foolish keeping them apart, but the Aberdeens were that afraid."

"Of her poverty?"

"No, miss. Her disease. They couldn't abide her passing it onto their son's children, the Aberdeen heirs. Terrible superstitious they were in those days, a-feared of everything they didn't understand. Look where it left 'em — no heirs a'tall and no one to care about them."

I could hardly breathe. "What sickness did she have?"

She shoved the cloth back over her hair. "Rheumatic fever, miss. Childhood ailment, but doctors say it settled in her heart. They simply couldn't abide their son bringing such a blight as her into their family."

TWENTY-ONE

It is said you cannot change your spouse, but that's a lie. Few others have daily access to a person's heart, where every word and reaction is another stroke painted on the canvas of one's reality.
~A scientist's observations on love

A little round face appeared at the door, and Clara Gresham smiled, beckoning the maid in. "Come, Essie. Has there been word on Mrs. Gresham?"

"Nothing yet."

"You don't think there's truly anything the matter with her, do you?"

The maid shrugged, her brow pinched. "I'm no doctor, miss. She's complained something fierce as long as I've worked here, though."

"That's simply her way. Come, see what I've made." Clara pushed back from the little desk and admired her handiwork.

She'd painted a tiny forget-me-not on each invitation, her brushstrokes so minute that they blended into one iridescent blue flower.

"Why, Miss Clara, they look like real pressed flowers."

She giggled. "Quite a lark, don't you think? Like sending out a small piece of Crestwicke." She'd been doing her best to convince her family to visit, but so far they'd given nothing but excuses. They were terrified of Crestwicke, she knew, and all its finery. Perhaps these invitations, complete with a specific time and date, would encourage them to come. Loneliness had begun to slice deeper into her soul, demanding a fill for the ever-widening crevice. Nothing repaired that quite as well as one's own family.

Burke strode into the room, throwing Essie into a sudden fit of polishing as if she were scrubbing the life out of the poor silver spoon. Clara straightened in her chair and dropped a blank paper over the invitations. He would not be happy that her relations were coming, for they were a blemish worse than paint on a new sleeve. He wouldn't dare forbid it, but she had no desire to suffer through his reaction either. She'd picked a date that coincided with the horse show in Bristol, the one event guaranteed to take her husband away from Crestwicke, and he never had to know they'd been.

"Good day, my dear." He dropped the nicety in her direction and bent over a pile of letters on the far desk, leafing through each one. At least he wasn't hovering, but even across the room he made her uncomfortable.

With a glance his direction, Essie leaned near. "Miss Clara, I was wondering if there had been any news. You know. Anything about a certain . . . letter. Because . . . well, there's been another one."

Burke stopped paging.

Clara stole sidelong glances at the man, well aware that her husband's hearing was impeccable. "It's proven more difficult than I thought to learn anything about it." She lowered her voice, hoping he was absorbed in whatever he was doing. "Are you certain it's from the same man?"

Essie nodded with a glittering smile. "He said so many nice things in this one, and the handwriting is the same. It was left on the washbasin. Oh Miss Clara, it's so very romantic!"

Clara grabbed the girl's hand and squeezed a warning, stealing covert glances at Burke. They definitely had the man's attention now, and she could hear the lecture forming: *You're too familiar with the staff, Clara. Why do you chatter away with a maid as if you're both kitchen wenches?*

He watched her with a heavy-lidded gaze. Perhaps he only looked absently their way as some business matter consumed his mind. He might not have heard a thing at all.

Clara lifted her stiff shoulders and forced them back. "It would seem to be an ill-advised affection, after all. Let us remember that. This isn't a romance novel."

"No, it's not." She grinned with irrepressible joy. "It's quite real, and that makes it even lovelier. I've been able to think of little else for days. Do you suppose they truly are from Mr. Gabe, miss? Or was he merely delivering that first one?"

Clara dug her fingertips into the maid's arm until she cried out. Clara shushed her with a sharp look.

Essie lifted a glance of apology and lowered her voice to the softest whisper. "I suppose I'm simply anxious. I've never had a secret admirer before. Heavens, I've never had an *admirer* before, and it feels quite nice. I suppose I've let my romantic notions run away with me."

"Quite all right, Essie. But let's keep this between ourselves."

"Yes, ma'am."

She glanced back up to check Burke's face and see if he heard, but he'd vanished. Her stomach clenched. Having him in the room had rattled her nerves but having him suddenly disappear left her uneasy. Shaken.

"We'll continue to work on it, Essie. Your admirer will be found before a fortnight has passed, I'm certain of it. Just leave it to me."

A silly, lopsided grin stretched her freckled face. "I thank my lucky stars for the day you came to Crestwicke, Miss Clara."

She rose, shifting uncomfortably. "You must call me Mrs. Gresham. See if you can remember. At least when Burke is about."

"Oh yes, of course, *Mrs. Gresham.*" She bobbed a curtsey. "Oh, and Miss Clara."

She steeled herself against correcting the maid. "Yes?"

"Might I have it back sometime? I do miss reading it."

Clara squeezed the maid's hand. "Of course. Let me simply find something with Gabe's handwriting on it to compare. The man doesn't write much, apparently, for I've found no trace of his hand yet."

With a small smile of approval, Clara excused herself and slipped out of the room with the invitation clutched tightly to her. There was only one place in this house she might go to evade her husband, and to hide the invitation until it could be posted. She climbed the grand staircase, strode down the long hall, then ascended the steep attic stairs where the light seemed softer and the air easier. She took a breath and nudged open the door to her haven but jolted back. There before the window, blocking the light with his large frame, was Burke.

Her breath caught. He didn't seem to be aware she was there, or aware of anything at all, really. What was he doing? She edged the door open a little more.

Horror of horrors! There on the easel was her very private work in progress, the cathartic painting dredged from the depths of her pained heart. The one no one was meant to see. Especially the man now staring at it with rapt fascination. Every nuance and brushstroke was exposed to the intensity of his glare.

Dread pulsed over her. How terrible it looked from this distance, like the work of a mad mind. Dark and bleak with sweeping, angry lines and angular features, the portrait exposed every minute detail of her husband's profile, from the hard set of his jaw to the narrowed eyes glowing with irritation. Lately she had superimposed the matching face of his mother over half of his, both glowing with ire toward the tiny image of herself she'd penciled in the corner. That part hadn't been painted yet, but she wished with painful intensity that none of it had.

She spun away and closed the door, leaning her back against the wall. She might die. Yes, that must be what happened next, because she simply couldn't imagine anything less occurring once she left this attic. Fear tingled. What on earth would become of her marriage after this?

Breathless, she hurried down the stairs and tucked herself into the little window seat in her bedchamber, trembling hands over her face. What haven was left to her now that her dear little attic space had been invaded too? And what would he do to her out here?

TWENTY-TWO

I've always been a proponent of real, authentic, heart-aching love. But not when it interferes with a marriage.

~A scientist's observations on love

I saw myself in them. Like a prism of possibilities, each fractured relationship in Crestwicke was an image of what I might become. I stood at the shadows and felt the dark emotions vibrate through the house the next afternoon as Burke Gresham stormed down the hall and slammed a door at the end. I shuddered.

Golda is Rose. Those three words resounded through my thoughts in ghostly whispers, even while I talked with Celeste and wandered about the house. All the bitterness that had twisted up Golda's brittle soul now had a name — regret. Lost love. Abandonment, and then a marriage of necessity. One thought lingered above the

329

rest — she hadn't always been this way.

"What will you do about Grayson Aberdeen?" Celeste stood at the desk behind me and sliced through her mail with a silver letter opener. "Will you tell his lost love what we found?"

"I've no idea." Sooner or later I'd find that letter, and then I'd have to make a decision. "What good could possibly come of it?"

She sighed. "I suppose you're right. It didn't end happily, did it? Perhaps we should keep the end of the story to ourselves."

According to the maid, the elderly couple's only son and heir, Grayson Aberdeen, had annulled his marriage to Rose Ellis, then died overseas in honorable duty to the queen — and had remained unmarried. How desperately I wished to hand Rose — no, Golda — that letter from her long-dead love, to let those words impact her deeply as she realized he'd died loving her. Yet he was gone and she was married to someone else.

I closed my eyes and saw the passionate strokes of pen on that vellum page, felt the warmth of the lost letter's tender words. They'd never had a chance to touch Golda's heart, to soften her with the truth, but they'd carved their way neatly through

Crestwicke, disrupting lives and hearts, stirring desires and awakening hope. The letter's original story may be over, dropped like a rock in the water, but its ripples were just beginning to cascade over the house.

"It almost makes one glad to be a spinster after all. Almost." Celeste gave a weak smile. "I'd rather that than to be in Rose's position, at least."

I studied my friend. "Yet suddenly you've released your determined grip on spinsterhood. Was it the letter?"

She shrugged, giving a half smile. "It'd be silly of me, wouldn't it, to admit such a thing? I can't even be certain who he is."

I pressed my lips together, pondering everything Maisie had said about this magical letter and its impact on the house. Awakening a desire for love — was it truly a good thing?

"Well, I don't suppose I can be truly in love, but I'm open to it." She looked toward the window, a faint smile about her lips. "For the first time in years, my heart is fertile soil ready for someone's love to be cast onto it."

My stomach knotted at the faraway look on her face, and I began to doubt Maisie. Celeste would be crushed — *crushed* — to learn the truth. "Perhaps you shouldn't take

that letter to heart, though. You've no idea
—"

"Would you have me end up like Gabe,
then? With love right before me, ever afraid
to leap?"

This stopped me cold. "You mean Caroline?" I forced the name past my lips, and
she nodded.

"She's smitten with him, in spite of everything, and refusing all other suitors in hopes
that Gabe will eventually have the courage
to propose."

"She's in love with him."

"Yet here we all sit, gathering dust and
wrinkles, waiting for courage to find us."

I stared at the woman who'd just weeks
ago tried to talk me out of ever marrying.
Oh, how that letter sliced through this house
like a knife, changing and shaping as it
went. "Truly, you think Gabe, who prefers
solitude, should be married?"

Her smile softened. "Nothing softens a
person's hard defensive shell more than
someone who loves him immensely."

When dusk cloaked the world around the
manor, I was looking in vain for an apple in
the larder to give Luna. Essie the lonely
parlor maid now danced around the
otherwise-empty servant's hall with a laun-

dry tub paddle, and Burke Gresham banged out the side door and stalked away. Somewhere Celeste was dreaming and longing again for what did not exist.

What a mess I'd made of everything with that letter. A wretched mess. I grabbed a lantern and trekked out toward the stables. How would it ever be set to rights when the scaffolding of secrets came tumbling down? I knew it would, eventually. My thoughts intensified on my solitary trek across the yard, and I reached the stables in quite a state. Poor Luna would get an earful.

Yet it was Gabe who looked up when I entered, bent over a horse's upturned hoof with a knife to pry something loose. One casual look from him and the tip of a smile, and my soul calmed, the way those horses did around him. Yes, the man needed a wife — he was the sort of blessing who should not be wasted on a life of seclusion.

"She's missed you." He jerked his head toward the back.

Of all the people I'd invested in within this house, it was the horse who missed me. "You've asked her this, I assume?"

"Didn't have to. She's been standing at the gate, watching for you. She's in there dancing back and forth in her stall because she knows you're here."

The distant shuffle of hooves made me grin. "It's nice to be missed."

He straightened with a pat to his horse's neck, then led me back toward the creature to whom I had grown far too attached. At the sight of me, she bucked her head and danced, hesitantly approaching for her usual treat. "Sorry, girl. All I have to offer tonight is me. Little old me." I reached my hand over the gate. She jerked away, tossing her head, but kept near the entry. "What a change in you, old girl. We're nearly chums now, aren't we?"

I felt Gabe's eyes on me as I hummed softly and let myself into her enclosure. One lap about the fence, then she slowed, dancing in the corner. I moved toward her injured leg and inspected it with my fingertips. The flesh felt strong and healthy around the stitches, and they'd soon be ready to come out. She bobbed her head and trotted away.

"She certainly knows who helped her."

I rose. "She's still afraid, but she's more grateful than most human patients I've had."

Gabe opened the gate to let me back out, planting one boot on the lower rung. "What do you say to another ride?" His grin held a sparkle of challenge as he leaned near, once again my old chum. "The beach is wide open and the horses are itching for a good run."

I felt the weight of all the trouble I'd caused slipping from my shoulders for a moment, and I smiled. "I think it's *you* who is." I raised an eyebrow, arms folded, and strode back into the main barn. A light glowed from an upper room in Crestwicke and a figure slid across it. "Perhaps away from the house, though, yes?"

Within minutes we were tearing along the beach, our mounts neck and neck, their hooves skimming the shallows. "You've met your match, Gabe Gresham." I threw him a smile and laughed, the wind whipping my voice up into the dusky sky.

He watched me from his roan with sparks in his knowing eyes. "That I have."

When we reined in at the curve in the cliffs, my heart kept pounding.

Gabe rode beside me, his tanned skin flushed with adventure. "Enough?" How different he looked out here atop that fine horse, how bold and regal. The confidence he lacked around other people saved itself for the moments he was out here, becoming one with a barely subdued wild animal.

"Never." I gave a wide smile. "This beach tastes like freedom and feels like bliss."

His eyes danced. "You paint the world a lovely color when you talk. You know that?"

I glanced at his profile, the rugged yet familiar lines of his face. "It seems you don't find *all* my words objectionable, then."

"You are sorely needed here, a candle in the shadows. Tapestry on a gray wall. The best remedy you've ever given . . . is yourself."

His declaration burrowed deep into cracks forming that night and filled them with warm liquid gold. He was constantly doing that, just when I needed it most, and I began to wonder how I had gone the last five years without this friend. "All this, from the man who barely speaks."

"I always speak up when I've something worth saying."

I watched his face that was calm yet full of unspoken thoughts that numbered more than the stars. "You should speak up more. Especially to me."

She must know all your stories. I could hear Caroline Tremaine's melodic voice. *No,* Gabe had returned. *Not the big ones.* "You talk to Miss Tremaine, don't you?" Our horses plodded over the hard-packed sand with the sparkling waves stretching clear fingers up the shore beside us. "Gabe, are you in love with her?" It was brash of me, but it was *Gabe.*

He stared at his hands clutching those poor reins like a lifeline, then looked out across the foamy water where it met in that distant line with the bright orange sky.

"Come now, it's only me." Our horses paused by the water and the silence congealed, weighted with many unspoken things. "Gabe?"

Then, without warning he lifted that vibrant gaze full of his entire soul, and I glimpsed the startling truth in all its raw power, shining out on me like the sun. It wasn't Caroline he loved — not at all. His tender heart was full to overflowing with unbridled affection — for *me.*

I looked away, but his gaze remained on me, steady and solid. I could feel it. Gabe, dear Gabe — like a brother, a soft soul so easily punctured, the friend of my heart and childhood. He'd fallen for me, much more deeply than the mere infatuation I'd suspected, and I hardly knew what to do with it. I only wanted to handle this affection delicately until I could place it back in its box and hand it to its rightful owner.

He shifted, boots creaking in the stirrups, and cleared his throat. My skin tingled with the familiar cliff-like sensation of a coming declaration, the feeling of impending loss, the ache of the inevitable end that came to so many friendships.

"Willa . . ."

Gabe's sleek profile feathered at the edges in my hazy vision. The cliff edge was near, and I was going over.

I said the only two words a lady could say when facing a fifth declaration. "Race you!" I jabbed my poor horse in the sides, shocking her into motion, pivoting with a spray of sand and water. I wished I could pivot this slowly unfolding reality in the same way and turn everything back to what it was.

I leaned into the wind, feeling the power of the creature beneath me and the intensity of the race. I dreaded its end. I'd lost so many friends this way, but I couldn't stand — couldn't *bear* to lose Gabe. The very idea of devastating him, of losing the sweetness of our friendship, ripped my heart from my chest.

Yet I couldn't bear to say yes. Not to anyone except the admissions board of Durham University, to the patients dying in hospitals, and to a lifetime of freedom.

Yes. Yes, I'm coming for you, just as fast as I can.

Together we tore across the sloping countryside, my horse and I, daring anyone to cage our free spirits. My heart thundered in time to the pounding hooves and I threw a glance over my shoulder. Gabe followed in the near-dark, broad chest bent low over his horse. We climbed the winding incline, rounded the fence, and reined our mounts to a dancing stop at the stables.

Pulsing with nerves, I dismounted and turned to meet my pursuer with what I hoped was a chummy smile, even in the descending dark. "I suppose I'll have to concede that race since I didn't give you fair warning."

"Do you ever?"

"Come now, I've granted —"

A bolt of movement flashed before us, and Gabe's horse startled, dancing and throwing back his head. "Woah, woah." Gabe climbed down but a shadow whipped before us. The horse bucked, whinnying and kicking.

I clutched my reins. "A person. It's a person."

A sickening thunk of hooves on flesh, and the figure flew left and hit the side of the barn with a guttural groan. With a terrible, wrenching cry, the horse reared and bolted into the dark. I ran to the poor wretch who lay on his side, writhing and panting with pain. It was a stranger — a mere boy — and he rolled in agony, clutching his abdomen.

"Only meant to look. Just look."

"Shhh. Lie still." I smoothed clumps of wavy hair from a half-starved lad's forehead and ran practiced fingertips over his torso, along the ribs.

He hit my hands away and rolled onto his side with a wretched groaning noise. I touched his ribs on the right and his body spasmed.

"Where do you come from? Where are your parents, child?" I reached toward him again and he growled like an animal, slapping me away.

Gabe scooped the lad into his arms and strode toward the stables while the boy fought in vain. "Willa, bring your horse. I'll go for mine later." To the boy, his voice was firm but gentle around the edges. "It's no use. You're not fit to run." He loped across the yard, holding the boy close as his flailing slowed. "We'll help you."

The boy eventually went limp, the spell of Gabe Gresham falling upon him with those few rumbling words. I tugged my mount into her stall, grateful she wasn't as skittish as Gabe's, and yanked a lantern off the wall to inspect the boy's injuries. His ribs flexed easily under the pressure of my fingers, and the grimy skin was moist and desperately in need of a wash.

When I pried his hand off his side, I glimpsed a jagged laceration across deeply red, swollen skin that would become a terrible mess by morning. I poked the flesh gently, and the boy recoiled. I squeezed the raw skin together and wrapped it when Gabe brought me clean scraps, but I could do nothing for the possible damage inside.

"Shh, shh." I smoothed hair off his forehead, watched his eyes slide closed. Those scrawny shoulders relaxed beneath my grip, and I looked this pitiful child over — he couldn't be more than eight or nine years of age. How would I get him clean enough to avoid infection? It seemed the dirt had become part of his skin, rubbed into his very pores, but at least he was calmer now, his breathing more even. I turned to Gabe. "Can you help me lift him if I have to move him?"

He gave a single nod.

I looked over the boy's sorry clothing, the rope belt holding up frayed trousers several sizes too big. "What are you doing all the way out here? Have you family nearby?"

"Come from just outside Crawley." He took several hard breaths, as if willing the pain away. "No one's left, though. Come here to find work." The talking seemed to distract him from pain.

"And what is it you plan to do?" Those scrawny arms could be broken with two fingers.

"Anything that needs doing, miss. Came here when I saw the stables." He looked past me, eyes bright and breath still heavy. "Never seen such a fine set of horses. Like someone took a wild animal and . . . and made friends with it. Let it keep being wild."

That thought played about my heart, tugging at some question festering in the background, but I shoved it all aside, my focus on saving a life. Nothing was more important.

I waved Gabe out to the fringe of the lantern's glow and stood close. "We need to bring him to the house tonight. Your mother is away and I must watch him."

"He's that bad, is he?"

I hugged my middle against the chilly evening. "Definitely some damage to his ribs. It's hard to tell more without seeing inside, which is why I must keep careful watch tonight. I don't want him out of my sight."

"Can you give him anything?"

"Perhaps a little laudanum to dull the pain, but that's all. I don't want to ignore whatever his body needs to tell us, because it could quickly become too late."

We returned and I explained to the lad where we'd be taking him. I stood back to watch Gabe scoop the boy into his arms again, oblivious of the blood and grime smudging his white shirt. Gabe looked down at him with gentle concern. Solidness. How quickly Gabe's protectiveness flared out, blanketing any creature who came near. It wasn't pity in the man's face, but a sort of empathy — of knowing what it meant to be beat down and wanting to do whatever he could to ease this little soul.

He crossed the yard with long, silent strides while the boy's worn boots thudded against Gabe's thigh. We brought him in through the back entrance and snuck him up the narrow rear stairway to my little room, where I settled him on some blankets and gave him a touch of laudanum.

His eyelids soon drooped with the effects of it. "I don't need nothing fancy, miss. Truly."

"Food is the next order of business. You stay here and we'll return with something."

The heavy lids fluttered. "Won't say no."

Together Gabe and I slipped down the service stairs to the kitchen.

"I'll see to his food, and you go take care of the horses." I handed him my lantern. "Thank you, Gabe, for everything. Now pray no one finds out he's here . . . and that he lasts the night."

As he slipped into the darkness, the distant rumble of an approaching carriage made me freeze. The glow of four swinging lanterns highlighted the sleek black vehicle carrying Golda Gresham and her attendants up the long drive. All I could think when I looked out and pictured the woman's austere face framed behind the glass was, *That is Rose.*

I brought a little food upstairs, but I was soon swept along with the other servants to bring the lady of the house to her chambers and settle her in the sitting room. The boy remained on my mind with aching clarity, but with one glimpse at Golda's pale face, eyes glassy with resignation, I knew I couldn't leave her. I'd seen that look often — just before the hallucinations began and death descended.

I checked her for signs of worsening and pulled out my stethoscope, placing the wooden horn on her chest. "You are all right, Mrs. Gresham?" Her pulse seemed weak, her heart about the same.

She merely turned her gaze on me and didn't honor my question with the obvious answer. Red lined her eyes and a grimace pulled her features into an odd contortion.

Her head angled toward my room and a frown flitted briefly over her face.

I stiffened, not daring to glance at the door separating this woman from the little stable waif we'd tucked inside. *Stay silent, boy. Don't open that door. Not for anything.* Why hadn't I warned him?

"Aside from sneaking about the kitchen with my son, have you also brought the contents of my stables up here? It reeks of horses."

My heart stretched in every direction. Her statement, though sharp, was utterly drained of all force. She'd been gone a day and aged a decade. I had never wished harder for the staccato of her retorts.

When the maids left, the patient was abed, and we were alone, I knelt by her side. "What did they do to you?" I clutched her cold hand and felt for her pulse again.

"Exactly what they could do for a woman in my condition — absolutely nothing."

Only then did I recognize the change in this magnificent woman. She had given up. She'd known all along what ailed her, but the truth had finally been handed down like a judgment, her fate determined, outcome unavoidable. A few cold words of truth had given actual shape to her grim reality, demolishing my petty attempts at restoring life to her soul.

She stared at me with those slitted feline eyes that still shone brightly under dark lashes. "Promise me something, Miss Duvall."

"Anything." In that hasty promise, I realized how dear this woman had become to me.

"If something should happen to me before . . . promise me you won't marry Gabe."

Her words hit me like ice down my back, but I forced a smile. "You've nothing to fear, Mrs. Gresham. Gabe is a dear and trusted friend. Nothing more, and certainly not less." Gabe's own words. "But I'll not hear you speak this way, as if the end has come."

"I've nothing left to do here, no reason to linger in a place that has shown me more than my share of pain."

I sat forward, alive with one specific thought — *the letter!* She still didn't know what had happened to Grayson, and that he died loving her. Yet what sort of ending might it bring to her story? There had to be a way to bring her joy from it, to bring resolution to so many broken pieces of her story. "You cannot allow yourself to slip away just yet. I simply won't let you."

She raised her eyebrows. "I wasn't aware

my time of death was up to you."

"You never know what's around the corner." When I looked into her eyes that seemed to dim like a neglected hearth, desperation eclipsed all fear. "Mrs. Gresham, I know about all the pain in your past, and I can't bear to let it end there. There are more chances, more love, to be had."

She trained those pallid blue eyes on me as if waiting for proof of my claims, not even flinching that I knew some of her secrets.

"If there's one thing I learned in this house, it's that medical people — myself included — have no control over these bodies compared to the God who created them. That means there's so much hope for new and beautiful chapters, because God's the one writing them and he isn't done yet. You never know what's coming — unexpected tender moments, closure and healing, delightful surprises, a chance to fix what's broken."

She narrowed her eyes. "With words, right? Isn't that what you told me before? What I say has the power to cut or shape, wound or heal. Well, I took your advice. I've done what you suggested."

Under her steady gaze, awareness flashed over me. *I've had another letter, miss.* I heard

Essie's voice, then Celeste's.

"You. It was *you* who left those new letters. But how . . ." Another realization struck, the full puzzle coming together. It wasn't just the new letters she'd written, was it? I lifted the sacred volume of verses from the table and opened it for the first time, and there it was — those spiraling letters that looped and swirled, creating the same beautiful artwork contained in the lost letter from my desk. It was *her.*

I thought back to the very first clue that had set me chasing after the name Aberdeen — the inscription in those books in the library: *G. Aberdeen.* Not Grayson, but *Golda* Aberdeen. She must have insisted on thinking of herself so, even after the annulment. She'd written her reckless feelings in a letter and hid it in the old desk where no one found it — until me. I looked back at the wilted woman on the bed who'd somehow produced the most beautiful, passionate words I'd ever read. Life had broken her. It could break any of us, with enough weight. "You wrote the unsigned love letter from years ago, didn't you? And the ones that came after it."

Her steady gaze was the only affirmation.

"How did you know . . . ?"

"I sat in that very chair over there and

348

listened to you telling Aunt Maisie about my letter, about everyone who'd stumbled upon the thing, and it seemed that you were right — words can change so much. *My* words, even. So I merely extended that impact, handing each person the . . . *positive* words you so strongly believed they needed — through the mouth of a secret admirer. They'd never have believed them coming from me." She ended with a weakly wry grin.

I took her hand. "Which is the perfect reason to keep living. They should hear them from you. Believe me, you are not yet ready to die."

She frowned, her gaze holding mine. "I'm not afraid of being dead, Miss Duvall. Only of getting there." She shifted. "Will you stay with me for a while?"

My heart swelled with sadness and despair. Dread. "Of course."

I watched her fall asleep, my head bowed over her, heart squeezing with earnest pleas. *God, please leave her here. Her story cannot end this way, so steeped in bitterness and pain. I see myself in her, full of sharp words coming from a critical spirit, and I long for her to have the release I have only begun to feel. Please grant her that before taking her, Lord. Grant it to her and to this household.*

My gift was in saving lives, yet I was helpless on so many levels that night. How desperately I wanted to tell her that change was possible, that life could be beautiful, and also what I'd learned of Grayson — that he'd sacrificed himself for her. It might utterly destroy the last remnants of her peace, or perhaps releasing that part of the past would allow her to heal, and to repair the family that had become infected with her pain. Yet as I watched her sallow face in sleep, I feared it might already be too late for either one.

Life was so wretchedly unfair.

I tore myself from her side and snuck in to check on the boy. His face was contorted in pain, even in sleep, and he jerked about on the makeshift bedroll. His chest rose and fell in quick bursts, as if he strained for breath, and I put my hand on his ribs. I half expected the rhythm to stall out.

I prayed over him too, giving the entire house into God's care as I released all control, thread by thread, from my tight grip. At times my abilities seemed so minuscule, but there was a lovely, crucial peace in that realization. It was a daily wrestling match to let trust win out, one I'd been bringing to the ruined tower every morning. *It's up to you, God. But it's always been that way, hasn't it?* With that prayer filling my soul, I hurried down to the kitchen for the boy's bread and found Gabe in the shadows. He looked at me with a probing question in his eyes.

"He's asleep, but miserable. I'm afraid we'll have to take further action come morning."

"And Mother?" His voice held a raw edge.

I chose the merciful path of truth. Better to know while there was time than to be surprised. "Resting, but she has a new weakness — a deeper one." No medical equipment could reach this ailment.

He gave a grim nod. How many years had he lived with the knowledge of his mother's impending death?

"I'm afraid the specialist did nothing but steal her cushion of hope."

"I'm glad she has you, Willa." I trembled at the raw depth of his masculine voice. "You've given her more than any specialist, and I don't want you to leave. I couldn't bear it."

"Where would I go?" I gave a wan smile. "Besides, I now find myself with two patients. I cannot very well abandon them, can I?"

A hint of smile flickered in return, gratifying me in this night so heavy with dread. I gave a nod and turned, but something made me look back. Perhaps it was the budding doctor in me needing to know he was all right, or perhaps it was the tender moments we'd spent together knitting my heart to his, aching when he ached.

I regretted that last look the minute I glimpsed the brokenness streaked across the face of the man who had always been so strong. His broad shoulders sagged. I simply reached out and squeezed his arm, for I couldn't bear to ruin the moment with words.

Then he did something so very un-Gabe-like — he moved closer as if compelled by need, by force, and wrapped those massive arms around me to pull me close. His chest jerked in and out against the side of my face and his heart fluttered near my ear. He clung as if I was holding him up, and he shared, without words, his deepest hurts.

I made small circles on his back with my fingertips, as I so often did for hurting patients, assuring him of my presence without intruding.

With one shuddering exhale, he pulled back and lingered in the doorway, the night sky highlighting his haggard face. "We do seem to find the adventures, don't we?"

"Or they find us if we're too long about

it." I offered a warm smile. "It'll be all right, Gabe. You'll be all right. Maybe not this moment . . ."

"I know. And Willa — thank you."

I squeezed his hand, the same one that had pulled me up out of the depths when my own mother had died. "It's what friends do."

Frogs and birds chorused behind him, creating a lovely symphony of night noises. His jaw twitched against the force of bottled-up thoughts. "Willa, what you said about . . . about me speaking up." His features tensed, as though he were wrestling with some mighty unseen thing. "I need to tell you something." His voice was husky.

I put a hand on his arm to stop him as my stomach knotted. "Let's not take this night any deeper. Perhaps another time."

He relaxed, his mouth returning to its natural pleasant curves.

"I'll see you tomorrow."

"Tomorrow."

Yet there was a great deal of night to be lived through first, and death hovered over Crestwicke. I sensed that before another night passed, it would descend. That familiar panicky helplessness tightened around me — strangling, suffocating.

I can't do it, God. I can't save them. I need you.

TWENTY-THREE

Love is not limited to romance, nor is happiness reserved for marriage.
    ~A scientist's observations on love

I stared down the wretched surgeon the next morning with his top hat covering fiery red hair and dared him to push past me. We'd survived the night without death, and he seemed terribly uninterested in helping to preserve that delicate state. "He's a patient like any other, sir, and you must treat him. I've paid you what I could."

The boy's thrashing had awakened me in the predawn hours, and he'd emptied his stomach onto the floor. He'd then looked up at me with terror as a groan was wrenched from somewhere inside.

I'd shushed him as panic rose. The damage was internal, and he required an operation if he was to see the next dawn. I'd snuck him down to the unused back parlor where the furniture lay covered in dust sheets, and sent Gabe tearing into Brighton for a surgeon when Dr. Tillman was nowhere to be found.

Now that very surgeon was here, checking his pocket watch more thoroughly than his patient. He'd taken one look at the boy, assessed the worth of his life, and acted accordingly. "I must be off. I've a train to catch, and it's the last one this morning."

"You've a more important patient expecting you?"

He stiffened. "I'll be on holiday, actually, and my family has already gone ahead."

"A *holiday*?"

"That's right." He snapped his bag shut. "It'll be my first in years, and I'll not be made to feel guilty over it. An unsettled stomach is nothing to worry over. Happens all the time to boys who can't stay out of trouble."

"Surely you can see it's more than that." The boy shifted and looked at me, his eyes dull with pain. After all he'd endured, would this be the last thing the poor lad remembered about this life — horrible agony? His body quaked, and I shuddered with him. "Please, help him."

"Stable boys are kicked every day. With a

356

little rest and good care, he'll be perfectly fine."

I spun around, but Gabe, who'd been standing in the doorway, was gone. Planting myself before the surgeon, arms crossed, I met Dr. Axel's gaze with boldness. Solid conviction. I wouldn't be bullied. "I'm telling you, he's *not* fine, and he needs your help."

He wore that passive smile of tolerance only bestowed on nurses, then the man was fitting his top hat onto his head and slipping his arms into his traveling jacket. "It's good of you to worry, but he'll come 'round. I'll check him when I return."

I grabbed his arm. "Please. I know it's inconvenient, but you *must* operate on this boy or he'll die."

"I'm leaving a tonic for the pain. That should help considerably." The man turned his back on me. "Good day." The doctor tipped his hat and moved quickly out of the room, taking all hope for the lad's survival with him.

Panic bloomed. There I stood, stranded without tools or experience to operate, asking for a miracle. I closed my eyes, touching his small chest and willing the blood leaking through his body to stop. *Please, Father. Give this boy a chance.*

Boot clomps startled me, and the door burst open. The surgeon's anger exploded into the room. "Where's my horse?"

I blinked. "Your horse, sir?"

"My horse. My horse is *gone* from the stables. Where in heaven's name is he?"

Then I caught sight of Gabe, dear Gabe, who had somehow reappeared in the doorway. We all looked at him as the barest trace of smile dented his cheeks. "On holiday, sir."

Our eyes met for a brief moment, a look of utter kinship passing in a flicker. We were alike, he and I.

In a fluster of anger, the surgeon marched up to Gabe, his nose stopping at Gabe's chest. "Tell me where you've put my horse or I'll have you thrown in prison for theft."

Gabe shrugged. "Do what you like, but you won't be leaving here until you do your job."

The surgeon's look held enough venom to kill an elephant. He dropped his bag and threw off his jacket. "Boil the instruments."

"Of course, Doctor." I kept my voice level despite the waves of relief that swept over me, loosening the knots inside and leaving a fresh peace.

And that was how the lofty surgeon came to operate on an orphan boy at Crestwicke in the early morning hours. It was a tedious and nerve-wracking procedure that seemed tentatively successful — but left us with a surprising revelation. A true shock, really. When I slipped out of the room to tell Gabe, the household had begun to stir. The discreet footfall of servants sounded on tile and wood, and quiet voices carried through the halls.

Gabe lifted his head. "How is the boy? Did you manage to save him?"

A sharp cry jarred the moment. Celeste stood in the shadows behind Gabe, pale as rice powder.

"What? What is it, Celeste? Please, tell — oh." I looked down at my hands, stained with blood that the brief toweling had not cleaned away.

She stumbled through words. "What — what — *Oh!*"

"Oh no, please don't panic. There's been no murder. Quite the opposite, actually."

Her horrified gaze shot from me to the back parlor doors.

"There was an accident — a stranger — and we had to perform an emergency surgery."

"Surgery?" She trembled. "You would turn our home into your operating theatre, Miss Duvall? How could you —"

"I must ask you to keep your voice down.

We cannot afford to alarm your mother."

She glanced at Gabe with disbelief, then back at me, pushing past us to make her way into the little parlor.

"Please, don't go in there. Celeste!" I hurried in after her.

Yet she simply stood there, back erect, staring down at our sodden little patient still groggy from chloroform. The surgeon was cleaning his tools with linen strips, his entire bearing sobered by the effort we'd just undertaken. The intensity of the close call, the shocking revelation, had replaced the urgency to begin his holiday.

Celeste ignored his presence. "What sort of beggar have you allowed into our home, Miss Duvall? I shall blame you if we are robbed."

I looked down at the pale face that just now showed signs of stirring. I exhaled in relief as my patient's eyes blinked open.

"You can't possibly plan to keep this boy here, can you?"

Gabe entered with a frown. "Will he be all right?"

"No." I met Gabe's gaze and lowered my voice. "That is, it's not a boy."

This shocked the room into silence.

Within an hour, we'd cleaned up the worst

of our mess. The morning had drained me, and I wondered why on earth I continued to put myself through this.

Then I glanced at my patient's long eyelashes feathered over grimy cheeks, the gentle stirring of gangly limbs that would have been dumped in a pauper's grave by now if I hadn't forced the operation, and I remembered why. *Yes,* I breathed. I needed to insert myself in the medical world. People were dying in stuffy, dirty hospitals who might have lived, and I could help them. Every time I thought of it, of Father's research and the clinic so badly needed, my brain spiraled with thoughts of what could be.

When the patient was actively stirring, I peeked in on Golda and found her still sleeping off the effects of travel, her breathing even and steady. It seemed we had escaped death after all.

Exhaling the morning's tension, I returned to my newer patient and found Celeste hovering about the sagging cot, attacking the child's grime with a rag and bucket and much gusto. "You certainly don't *look* like a girl, layered in all this filth. How could you allow yourself to become this way?"

The child grimaced at the scrubbing. I hesitated, wondering if I should intrude.

"Are you a heathen?"

"Not that I know, miss." Her voice had begun to gain a little strength.

"Then who on earth has forced you to pretend you were a boy?"

"No one, miss. I done it meself after me mum up and died."

The rag slowed. "You mean you *want* to dress as a boy?"

"No, I *had* to. Girls have the deck stacked against 'em the minute they're born, especially if they're alone." Her chin jutted. "Can't do nothing in this world. Can't even protect their own selves, if someone bigger than 'em sees something he wants."

A muscle jerked in Celeste's neck as she absorbed the large statement from so small a person. "Then the world sorely needs to change. And you know who will change it? Women. Because God gave us our own type of strength. We must never let it go to waste by wishing we were something different. What's your name?"

"Frankie."

"That's your true Christian name?"

The child grimaced. "Phoebe."

"You'll stay here for a while, Phoebe, until we see what can be done about you. In the meantime, I will show you what it means to be a woman."

"Right, then." The girl glared. "I suppose you and your pretty ideas will pay my way, then, and buy the headstones for the entire family, fill me belly every day, protect me from every man who —" She looked down, dirty hair falling over her face.

Celeste slowed her work to consider the girl, her shoulders stiff beneath her cotton day gown as she wrung out the rag. She lifted the girl's other arm and smoothed the rag over it. "Why yes, I believe I will. I have need of an assistant. Are you clever?"

"Compared to some." Phoebe shifted awkwardly.

"When you're well, you can come with me to commission the headstones. We may have to do simple limestone. Have you many to bury?"

Phoebe stared at her, looking even more pitiful as cleanliness streaked through the grime on her face. "Six of us, if I make it. Seven if I don't."

"Six, then." Celeste helped the girl sit and reached for a towel. "Here, dry off. We'll have to soak some of this filth off, but this will do for now. At least a body can tell you're human."

Phoebe eyed the woman now unexpectedly mothering her, and I couldn't be sure if she enjoyed it or wanted to dash off in utter panic. When Celeste began to comb Phoebe's hair down her slender back, smoothing her hand over the wet strands, the girl's eyes fluttered closed.

"We'll have to keep this quiet until I figure out how on earth to break the news to the lady of the house. I'll have the maids put a cot in one of the spare servant's rooms until I decide what's to be done. Will that suit?"

"I don't know what I can do around a place like this. I'm not sure what good —"

"You leave that to me."

The girl turned and frowned at Celeste, scrunching up her brow as if her calculations weren't adding up. "I don't have dresses anymore."

"That can be remedied."

"I can't pay for dresses, for headstones, for food without work, and I ain't fit for much yet, and I'm so . . . so tired . . ." Her sagging shoulders trembled, the lavender circles under her eyes making her appear so much older.

"Phoebe." Celeste put a hand on the girl's shoulder. "You cannot possibly earn enough to pay for all that. So stop trying and accept it."

Phoebe stared for long moments, then wilted onto Celeste's lap in sheer exhaustion and began to weep.

Stiff with shock, Celeste shifted and gave a few awkward pats to the girl's back, as if uncertain exactly where to touch her — or if she wanted to. Yet the longer the girl clung, tucking her face into the inexperienced woman's skirts, Celeste's body softened and she laid her hand on the girl's head like a solemn benediction. A promise.

My heart is fertile soil ready for someone's love to be cast onto it . . .

The passing moments melted Celeste's pinched features into something akin to affection. With a sigh, that modern, independent woman leaned down and smoothed her fingers over the girl's hair. "There, now." Then she began to rock her, saying something in a low, quiet voice. It was an instinct I'd seen in mothers across all walks of life as they chatted or worked, even when their arms cradled nothing more than a basket of bread. I'd never expected it from Celeste.

As the moment crystalized into sacredness, I slipped out with a tired smile and pulled off my stained apron, balling it up.

Celeste exited soon after and froze at the sight of me. "Miss Duvall."

I smiled. "A very fine heart beats in that chest, Celeste. You're changing her life and demonstrating what truly sets women apart."

She straightened. "Every girl deserves a little looking after." With a nod, she moved past me down the hall.

Breakfast sat on the sideboard yet, and already I'd witnessed two miracles and completed what felt like a full day of work. *Thank you, Father.* My soft heart gushed with praise. *Thank you for bringing me to a helpless state so I might witness what you wanted to do.*

I jumped when I felt a tap on my arm.

"You get more mail here than I do." Gabe stood just behind, towering over me with a squarish envelope in one hand.

Looking up into his dear face, squeezing the hand that held my letter, I silently expressed my gratitude that was too great for words for what he'd done that day. He gave an answering nod with the barest trace of a smile. With a tender touch to my cheek, he moved into the room.

I leaned against a pillar and opened the letter, surprised to see Longfellow's name at the bottom. It was a pleasure, he said, to serve Golda Gresham and to hear a fresh poet as yet unspoiled by fame. He made several remarks about our conversation, then spoke of romance. *Allow yourself to be caught by a man, Miss Duvall. The right one is worth the risk.*

I read those words several times, but my spirit was freshly alive with the victory of rescuing a life, my mind awakened to my vital role in the medical world.

Don't concern yourself so much with the great search for passion and sparks — those can be cultivated as well as found, often with greater reward. We are both like flags, you and I — erratic and passionate, colors on display, blowing wherever the wind takes us. Do not be afraid to marry a man who's firmly planted to earth, for he is the flagpole to your flag — not restricting, but anchoring, so that you may be free to fly. In return, you shall decorate the dull gray metal of his life forevermore.

I lifted my gaze to the triangle of Gabe's back. He worked quietly, piling used rags and sheets onto the drape cloth and bundling them all for the burn pile, then placing my medical instruments back in their bag with all the precision I used when working with them. The sight of his dear profile stirred a smile that came from deep within. Every time I was near Gabe, I felt something solid and quiet in my chest, and I delighted in it. Why ever would I change the precious thing we had? At times, there were friends who were better than suitors, finer even than husbands. I crossed the room and laid my small hand on his back, and he turned with that heartfelt smile that always calmed my soul.

"Don't you have work to do, Gabe? I can handle this."

He hefted the bundle of rags in one arm. "You see to your patients. Let me do this." His gaze caressed me as he walked by, bearing the load.

I watched him go. Two deep breaths were all I allowed myself before I moved up the stairs to see to my patient. Golda still lay cocooned in her bed, but her languid eyes had opened to look about.

They angled toward me when I entered. "I suppose you have your wish, Miss Duvall, for here I am, still weighted down to this earth."

I smiled. "I'm glad, my lady. We have plenty more work to do. God isn't finished with you and neither am I."

Her lashes lowered, but she said nothing.

As I moved toward my room to soak my balled-up apron and change into a fresh dress, a terrible, strangled shriek rang throughout the house. I turned and ran, others joining me as we rushed to find the source.

It seemed we might not have escaped death after all.

TWENTY-FOUR

No human's story truly ends. Even the sad
ones, the empty ones, trickle down and
soften or harden those who stood near.
   ~A scientist's observations on love

By evening, the front-facing windows and
doorknobs were draped in crepe, the parish
minister summoned, and death notices sent.
A pallor of gloom descended upon Crestwicke Manor, wrapping us all in the sudden
awareness of our frail existence on earth.

"You will, of course, lay out the body."
Celeste spoke to me with a lowered gaze.
"You are the nurse among us."

"Of course."

For the entire three days in which we
observed her death, the term *Crazy Maisie*
was never once uttered. Perhaps this was, in
part, because the outspoken Burke Gresham
was still absent, with no one seeming to
know where to send word to him. Even

Golda, in all her sharpness, did not speak ill of Maisie. The departed was painted as a dear, confused old woman, one to be remembered fondly, as most often are when viewed in hindsight.

I missed her with wretched, arresting pain. Her passing created an ache of longing and deep regret. All I could see when I closed my eyes was her desperate face begging me to return and hear her story — any story, for all she cared — and rescue her for a moment from the suffocation of insignificance. I felt as though I had failed her.

Questions piled up, too, that I could no longer ask her. Questions about words, about the search for real love, about her extraordinary life. It hadn't been her tale she'd been telling me — I knew that now. Hers would take much longer, and it would have been an adventure story.

I dreamed of her sprinting through heaven with a belly laugh and a twirl, her immensely beautiful soul freed from the earthly shell that had failed her toward the end. That image, the sweet, sweet hope of it, kept me afloat.

Aunt Maisie was buried at the rise of a grassy hill in the family cemetery, where an iron fence guarded the sleeping inhabitants. Golda leaned on me and her lady's maid all the way up the hill and throughout the service. We huddled together beside the willow tree as the minister uttered his sermon over the fresh hole in the ground, directing each of us to afterward throw a handful of dirt. The others eventually peeled off and strode back to the house, but Golda remained. Therefore, so did I.

I glanced at her face and saw there the orphaned look of one who'd just lost the one person who always loved her completely, the same look I'd worn after Mama died. Had they been close once? I braved a gentle touch to her taffeta-covered shoulder, and it remained stiff and jutted.

A small shudder passed through her, but she didn't cry. "I rather expected her to live forever." Golda stared straight ahead, her eyes red-rimmed but tearless. "She's simply always been here, never truly aging on the inside . . . It seems so sudden."

"Maybe to us, but she lived a long life. Not everyone is blessed with that."

Wind played with the crepe strings holding the black hat to her head as she gave a single nod, her gaze wandering across the other stones in the family plot. Then she rose and crossed to kneel before a lovely stone covered in lichen, a female figure carrying a small lamb etched into its base. A lump bobbed in my throat and I dared not approach. It seemed a sacred moment between her and whatever absent life the stone recorded, so I remained in place, watching with fascination as the layers of poise trembled around her like petals in a breeze. She stooped to pick a wildflower and place it on the grave, tracing the etching with her fingertips.

I glanced at the stone when Golda turned from it.

George Charles Gresham 1841
Josephine Louise Gresham 1841
Eloise Margaret Gresham 1843
Unnamed infant Gresham 1844
Beloved ones

Infants, every one of them, with only one date each on the stone. Another gaping wound in Golda's life came uncovered, rendering a starkly clearer picture than I'd had the day I'd come. It was true — everyone had a story, some with cracks deeper than anyone could imagine.

A solicitor arrived at the house, bearing the last will and testament of the deceased, and my name was mentioned among those he called. My heart thudded as I followed the black-garbed Greshams into the library, which I found a delightfully fitting setting. No one dared look about at the others as the solicitor began with the usual language. To Golda, she left her meager heirloom pieces. Clara received a lovely ivory and pink shell comb, Gabe a stack of books, and a handful of ancient foreign coins of untold value from all her travels were distributed to "the *charlatan* family members who never knew a thing about me."

I smiled. She'd finally used the word.

Celeste blinked. "That's truly what it says?"

"I can read it again if you'd like."

"That's quite all right. Is there more?"

He cleared his throat. "To Miss Duvall, the lovely little nurse who attended my Golda, I entrust the greatest of all my possessions." Silence tightened the air, but then he finished with, "My book of words."

A nearly giddy relief passed around the listeners, and I lowered my face to hide a smile. Of all the ways that sentence could have ended, nothing delighted me more.

Yet it was the final lines of the will that intrigued me most, made my imagination run wild. "The one possession that I insist on taking with me to my grave is the secrets I've been asked to keep. They are bequeathed to no one and will not be let to leak from this old soul who's kept them well for years. May they all rest in peace as I now surely do."

Golda disappeared and I found her sitting alone in the drawing room with marble-like poise, arrayed in Maisie's modest jewelry, fingers wrapped around the end of the chair arms. "Leave me." She whispered the words, but they were clear.

I obeyed but remained close.

I checked on little Phoebe often during those days of mourning, looking over her neatly stitched incision, and I had the privilege of watching Celeste cut the girl's wild mass of hair as she prattled on about her meetings and the powerful women there. They were a pair, each with their own strength that was magnified in the presence of the other. Celeste spoke long and often about the women's league and everything they accomplished, and Phoebe, sweet wide-eyed Phoebe, looked up at her with all the adoration stored up in her neglected little heart.

That they had found each other was a miracle. The affection between them was evident, and watching them together balmed my grief a little.

I lay like a dull rock on my bed at night,

sadness and shock and regret all fighting within me for release. Tears built up behind my eyelids, hot and pressurized. When I could not find sleep, I comforted myself by leafing tenderly through her book. She'd inserted a note at the beginning — *For the future doctor, who will wield her powerful words along with bandages and stethoscope.*

And the final notation that nearly broke me — *Never stop searching for authentic love. You'll find it.*

Yet she hadn't. *She hadn't.*

I clutched my chest with a wave of loss and turned the pages.

Sequacious — A splendid, most delicious word on the tongue, until one learns its meaning and promptly spits it out. "A blind and submissive following of another." I follow, but never blindly. I submit, but not without cause. Marriage has not come upon me because I've not found a one that would allow me to enter it unsequaciously, so unmarried and unsequacious I remain. I follow God, 'tis true, but that is done in full possession of my thoughts and will. It is an active pursuit, with nothing sequacious about it.

Sovereignty — The sovereignty of God is a thing of utter beauty. But like any good piece of art, to fully appreciate its magnitude, one must step back and drink it in as a whole, seeing how the brushstrokes of little everyday occurrences all combine to create a larger picture. Blessed are those who have the opportunity to do so this side of heaven.

Golda woke in a sullen state three mornings after the burial, her shell of bitter hurt having solidified overnight. I remained on the fringes of wherever she was in those days, leaving her to herself but always nearby to help when needed. I became enraptured in Maisie's writings, forgetting the rest of the world existed.

Until it intruded.

The door opened downstairs, footsteps were on the landing, then Dr. Tillman strode in behind Parker with a long envelope that he held out to me. "This came to my residence. I couldn't wait."

Durham University Admissions was stamped boldly across the top, their red seal on the flap. I grabbed it and looked up into the face of the man who was unwittingly handing me the very axe that would sever any chance of romance with him or anyone else. Would he still bring it if he knew?

Golda straightened in her parlor chair,

lowering her stitching project. "Whatever is the matter over there? I detest secrets."

I shot him a warning look, my pulse vibrating through the hand that held that letter. The balance had been delicate since Aunt Maisie's passing, and I dared not upset it. He gave a grim nod and backed away, expression burning with nearly as much fervor as my heart. "Just a letter."

Shoving the envelope in my apron pocket, as if it were any old correspondence from any old place, I went through the motions of my duties — locating vials, urging my patient to rest, propping her swelled feet. In a quiet moment, I reached down and touched the letter in my pocket. *You did it, God. Giving me a miracle, going beyond my abilities.* I walked about in a cloud of gratitude, but kept my lips pressed firmly together to guard my secret.

When I could bear it no longer, I slipped out into the hall on the pretext of visiting the water closet — which I'd make time to do as well, if only to validate my excuse — and tore open the envelope. My vision blurred, but there were words. What did they say? It wasn't long. Why wasn't it long?

We regret to inform you . . .

I blinked, clearing my vision. The heat of shock pulsed through my whole frame. No, this couldn't be! It wasn't what it seemed. Not a refusal, not after everything.

Our schoolboard has made the joint decision not to admit a female student at this time. We feel the field of medicine is best led by men, as it has been for centuries, and trust you will understand our decision . . .

I barely saw the other words. The floor beneath me shifted, reality spinning until I was nearly ill. How could this be? How could they take this away from me with a few half-hearted sentences? I shoved the paper back in my pocket and backed against the wall. The path before me had moved — no, it had gone missing — and I had no direction. This school was my one hope, the only one professing liberal policies. Now my future narrowed to nothing. Everything melted like snow against my clutched fingers — the respect of a degree, a future in medicine, the legacy of Father's research. I would not be a doctor after all. Just regular Miss Duvall, the insignificant spinster who could always be pushed aside to make room for a man.

I slipped into my chamber to compose myself, but the inscription in the front of Maisie's book jarred my tender heart. *For the future doctor.* I closed my eyes and choked back sobs. It all felt so very wrong — the letter, that contract with Father, Maisie's death. The thread of her life had been cut, and it felt like mine had too, in a way. The grief I'd so carefully stitched up these last days swelled, threatening to burst. Maisie had died feeling useless, which was wretched and unforgiveable.

Because I had once again failed to stop and truly see what someone needed.

I hurried into the hall to find Golda again, but a sudden weakness stopped me. White dots swirled in my vision. I leaned on the wall and willed myself back to normalcy.

"Willa."

I flinched. It was Gabe. I straightened my expression and lifted a benign look. "Yes?"

He was not fooled. "What is it, Willa? Is it your father? My mother?" He took my shoulders. "Pray, what's wrong?"

Chin trembling, I pulled the shameful rejection from my pocket and held it out, letting it reveal the truth. He expelled a single laugh, dropping his head. "That's all?"

All? I snatched back the letter, every

380

muscle stiff. All the hurt, the crushed hope, the immense grief, swirled together and boiled out. "What do you mean, 'all'? How dare you! You've no idea about anything."

"I merely thought —" He gestured toward the closed door behind me.

"No, you *don't* think, Gabe. You've never even left home, and you couldn't possibly know what it means to have dreams crushed because you haven't *got* any." My heart wrenched at my spiteful tirade, but I couldn't unspill those words. I couldn't bear to humble myself just now, either.

I spun on my heel, thrusting open the doors, and moved away with a thudding heart. Thankfully the room was dim with a coming storm, but I still turned my face away when Mrs. Gresham looked up at me.

"Bad news, I take it?"

"Yes, ma'am."

A pained look of longsuffering stretched across her porcelain face. Yes, she'd have to endure a little bit of cloudiness inside the house as well today. I simply could not produce sunshine when my heart was storming.

"Your father is well? And your step-mother?"

"Yes, everyone is well."

"Then what is the matter?"

"I'd rather not speak of it."

"I see."

For a tedious three-quarters of an hour, I watched the unfolding events of the household with a measure of disconnect. None of it seemed quite as important, no task truly worth doing. Vials were refilled, tea poured, heartbeat monitored, but it was merely my hands performing the work. The rest of me was somewhere else.

When the rain poured in earnest, a deluge down the rippled window glass, a carriage rode up and delivered a man to the front door. He entered below with a squeak of boots on tile, then a quick march up the stairs to us.

Moments later, Mr. Gresham appeared in the doorway, his face pale. "Has Burke returned?"

Golda straightened. "Hello, yourself."

"Burke — is he here?"

"We've not heard from him lately. I assume he wasn't at the London flat?"

"He was. Left this morning. Something's happened that I think you should know about."

A grave look passed between them and Golda Gresham turned to me. "Go on, get along with you. We must speak in private."

I hesitated, evaluating her pale face. "You

don't need me?"

"Take care of your little secret problems. I'll be here with all my usual infirmities and demands when you return." A glimmer of a smile appeared. "Have a good cry into a cup of tea and come back in an hour."

But it wasn't a cup of tea I needed.

Desperate for the weighty peace I always found in the ruined tower, desperate for God, I sprinted out the side door without lantern or cape, tearing across the yard and up the winding path. Cold rain pricked my back through my cotton uniform. *Please, God,* I begged, even as I came in sight of the ruins. The heavens opened and the rain poured down, and I reached the ruins breathless and soaked. A sensible girl would take cover, but I had no sense then. Only deep grief over unexpected loss and jagged endings.

I closed my eyes and lifted my upturned face to the sky, to the God who had loved me enough to bless me in spite of myself. *Was all that for naught, Lord? Have you no more use for me?* The sting of becoming useless — of watching Maisie end her days in that state — tore at my heart. God would of course know of the contract with Father — that I'd be headed into marriage with Dr. Tillman after all these years of pouring myself into medical training.

A rumble of thunder was the only reply, and I shivered. Cold rain poured down my face, trailing down my back and soaking into my stays, my chemise, my very skin, cooling and cleansing my hurt. I waited there for my answer as the storm raged on around me, willing God to give me some direction that made sense of all this. I shuddered with the immensity of the world spread out below me, the magnificent impact of the storm and crashing waves, my own small self atop that muddy hill.

Soon my entire body trembled with cold, and I had nothing from above. *Please, God.* One final whispered prayer, then I sank to my knees and convulsed with uncontrollable chills. I stood on trembling limbs and tried to climb down the cliff face toward the beach without muddying my skirts, but the second rock gave way, dropping me down the embankment. Rocks and grit tore at my skin, until I landed on a rocky ledge with a thud and hit my head. With a groan I rolled over and looked up. It was a long, rocky path back. I was stuck here. Just me and the Almighty.

Breathe. I closed my eyes as pain swam.

A warm hand rested on my drenched

back, gentle and weighty. *God? Have you come?*

TWENTY-FIVE

Studies have tried to prove there's nothing special about fresh spring water, and thirsty people seem eager to settle for the public variety — unless they've tasted the alternative. It is the same in love.
~A scientist's observations on love

Another convulsion of chills, then I felt myself swept up in strong arms, my body lolling against a chest that was stone-wall thick as he climbed back up the cliff face on a narrow rock path. "Gabe." Of course it was Gabe. Who else would come out here after a mere nurse? To him, I'd never be "merely" anything.

"You're all right, I'll help you."

I blinked against the rain to look up at him to argue, but my cloudy mind had no words. I'd cracked my head and all the words had fallen out. I couldn't speak. So for once, I didn't. I simply stared up into that fathomless face with eyes so rich in kindness, a gaze that wrapped itself so thoroughly around me that my shivering relaxed. His steady eyes looked into mine, drenching me in reassurance.

I'd been mad at him. My stomach soured over the memory. My brain wouldn't let me recall the details.

Oh, how I adored this man. Gabe — dear, wonderful Gabe — whose heart was so big that, like any good home, everyone had a place there. Even a friend who'd scorned him.

I studied every inch of his familiar face, noticing a long scar on his temple, a slightly crooked bend to his nose, a cleft in his masculine chin. I looked him over with the eyes of my heart that had been softening in every direction, seeing things and people with new clarity.

That small warmth of familiarity and friendship I always felt around him glowed again in my chest as I watched him. Yet the longer I looked up at him, wrapped in that gaze, with no words to interrupt what existed between us, that feeling of warm ash in the hearth slowly swelled as if someone had blown gently on the embers. They glowed with pleasant intensity through my whole body, pulsing through every inch in powerful waves that left me tingling with an inescapable, heady delight. I had no power to stop it, but neither did I want to. I shivered at its immensity.

What was this?

Warmth poured through my veins and magnificently eclipsed the tingles of romance I'd been waiting for, plunging far deeper into my soul. My tired brain struggled to understand it. He'd always been like a brother to me, hadn't he? A *brother.* Yet as I looked into his precious face, I couldn't remember why. I tried to piece together a single reason I should feel that way about him when he was so wretchedly handsome, so rugged and magnificent, both inside and out.

I felt dizzy. There was a reason I never thought of Gabe this way — I *knew* there was. I simply couldn't think straight. Why was reason escaping me? Questions stalled out. Thoughts fizzled. I blinked, staring up at him, and sank into the relaxed posture of trust.

"Stay awake, Willa."

I groaned. Contrary man, never letting me do what I wished. I desired nothing more than sleep this minute.

He never took his eyes off me, sloshing through mud and rain. Why hadn't he taken me through the tunnel? It was shorter. Drier. Perhaps because he hadn't thought to bring a light. Or it was too wet for one. You couldn't go through a dark place without light.

Yet darkness edged my vision, framing the world in a soft haze. How desperately I wanted to sleep, and Gabe's chest was so comfortable, so strong. The smell of him, the feel of his movements against me as if we rode his horse together. All so wonderful and inviting. So very safe. Warm.

Fuzzy light seeped into my vision as I stirred. My eyes were closed.

"Willa?" It was a familiar voice, calling to me through the thickness. A man.

Everything was still. Heavy. I ached.

As I surfaced from the murky darkness of a headache-induced slumber, my mind slogged along, slowly righting itself with each fragmented memory. Dr. Tillman had prodded me with questions at some point, giving me something to drink. The servants had looked on. Further back — there had been a letter from the university, a muddy climb to the ruins . . . and Gabe.

Gabe.

The memory of his gentle smile pulsed through my hazy thoughts. The stronger my mind became, the larger Gabe loomed in it, eclipsing everything else and filling my head with an abundance of colorful memories, heady words, and powerful sentiments. Where was he? I parted my dry lips to ask, but nothing came out.

"There she is. Keen to sleep the rest of your life now, are you, girl?" Father's voice was gruff yet gentle as he put a hand to my forehead, then my wrist. I turned my head and he hoisted me from behind my shoulder blades, folding me into a warm embrace. "There we are."

"Mrs. Gresham." I croaked the words out.

He leaned back with a sigh, resting me on the headboard and propping my pillows behind me. "She's doing well. Tillman has been seeing to her."

"Gabe?"

"I assume he's about."

He handed me a glass of liquid, which I downed with haste and cleared my cottony throat. "He came for me — out in the rain."

He grew solemn. "I know."

I looked down, fingering the edge of my sheet, an ocean of feelings surfacing within. "Papa, there's something I need to tell you about Gabe . . ."

"Don't."

I blinked, wondering at the tightness in

his face, and a memory flashed. Then another. Father frowning at the sight of me standing with Gabe Gresham, pulling me away, Father laughing off my suggestion that Gabe and I write to each other, Father knocking Gabe's flowers out of my girlish hand. "He's like a brother to you, Willa. A *brother.*" The tone of that single word, the look of aversion on his face, had pivoted my thoughts for years to come, settling firmly in my head the utter inappropriateness of anything blossoming between Gabe and me. Father had almost been angry when he'd said, "He'll have the wrong idea about you. You mustn't let him think of you as a match."

I looked up into his worried face now, years later, as he held the same firm opinion. "Why not, Father?"

"Because you deserve more. You always have." He sat on the edge of my bed with a sigh. "Do you remember how it was between your beloved mother and me? How intense the air felt, how dark and teasing her eyes were, the deep, deep adoration that went on forever . . . I cannot have that anymore, lass." He lifted a strand of my unruly hair with one finger. "But my precious daughter can take it as her legacy, and find for herself the very same happiness."

"Gabe is —"

"A kind person, but not the one for you. I've always thought there was something amiss with him, quiet as he is. It isn't natural."

"I thought you were so eager for me to marry — anyone."

"Heavens, girl. Not *anyone.* Not a single man came to our home with a bid for your affection that I did not first allow in. I approved each one, knowing the chemical makeup of my daughter and what compound might bring about the most fantastic reaction."

Ah yes, Father the medical professional, who had a scientific equation for all things — and a deep distrust of anything that didn't neatly fit into his calculations.

"And you chose Dr. Tillman?"

"He's your equal, Willa. Intelligent, accomplished, innovative. Now think of Gabe — what future would you have with a recluse?"

I bowed my head, hands wilted in my lap.

"You'd putter away in some lonely cottage still tied and indebted to his parents, tinkering with your microscope while he chased his horses about. He's not a match for you, Willa. He's merely a man you've known your whole life who makes you feel at ease.

But is that all you want? Is that what my girl's worth?"

My mind spun. "I felt something, Father. Something deep."

"Many a man in search of gold has been fooled into thinking he's found the real thing, only because he wants to have found it. Learn to sift through the rocks and cast aside the shiny fool's gold, or you'll miss out on the real thing. So will he."

I'd never thought of that. Gabe's "gold," it would seem, was the horse trainer's daughter — Caroline Tremaine. What a life they'd have together, and his dreams would multiply as far as he could see. I couldn't give him that, nor could he give me my dreams. "Perhaps you're right."

"Don't feel bad, daughter. You often lead with your heart, that headstrong heart that sees value in everyone, and your misguided feminine instincts. Neither are to be trusted, though."

I nodded.

But when he left to have food sent up, closing the door behind him, something in me rose up and rebelled. With my eyes closed against earthly sights, I felt traces of God's presence that had remained from my time with him at the ruins. I sank back onto the pillow and let the past unfold from first meeting to hilltop rescue like the pages of an illustrated book, savoring each image as truth swelled from somewhere inside me.

I finally pushed the truth to the surface — *Father is wrong.* It was a thought I'd never dared entertain before, but there was no escaping it — Gabe was something precious and beautiful buried in rock that no one had bothered to chip away.

Reaching for a wrap, I struggled from the bed and looked at the little secretary against the wall. I blinked a few times to make the world stop tilting. It was nearly dusk. My head ached, so I sipped from the cup on the bedside table, which cooled the pain and let me think.

Sometimes it helps to put it on paper, you know, Aunt Maisie had said once. *Taking the time to put it in black and white solidifies your thoughts and pulls out the truth of the matter.*

Truth was exactly what I needed. With my head pounding, emotions swirling, and Father's truths threatening to crowd out God's, I had to carve reality out of the thing Father's words had made of this situation.

Massaging my temples, I fetched Aunt Maisie's giant book of words and leafed through to the blank pages at the end, running my hand along the empty paper. I thought again of the honest, heartfelt letter that had brought me here, of the visceral feelings loosed, and the release Golda must have felt in writing it — even though Grayson Aberdeen would not read it in his lifetime. Yet perhaps this one would be sent.

I dipped the pen and summoned courage. A drop of ink fell, marring the perfect page, but then I wrote. Swift and certain my pen moved across the page, leaving behind traces of my raw heart like a trail of flower petals to the truth.

Dearest Father,

With the greatest respect a young woman can feel for her father, I wish to now write out the truth concerning the matter we discussed.

Since childhood, you've sent me on a search for a love equal to yours, but that simply doesn't exist. Every love, you see, is quite unique. Gabe is a different sort than you imagined for me, and different from myself, but perhaps that's an unexpected blessing. In the words of a great poet, "Every flag needs a flagpole if it will be truly free to fly," and Gabe is the flagpole to my flag. He not only anchors me to solid ground, he anchors me to God, ever driving me toward him. No firmer foundation exists, and there is no stronger, steadier flagpole for this flag. I clung to him in childhood, and my life was never restricted for it — only richer, freer, and with a far better view, for his strength is greater than mine, his wisdom beyond the scope of my understanding.

For so long I allowed the labels you gave him to shape my view of things, but I fear you did not know truth well enough to give it to me. Gabe is not "quiet" except for his voice. His thoughts and his heart are vibrant as my own, maybe more. Neither is he chasing about his horses, as you said. He is skillfully training wild stallions that no other human being has been able to approach, drawing them to himself with a rare charm rather than forcing submission, as most resort to doing.

Lastly, Gabe is not "tied to home" because he's dependent on his parents and sucking from them resources he hasn't the innovation to find himself, but rather he chooses to stay out of deep loyalty to his ailing mother, propping up his broken family in a way no other man would care to do. Take heed of this last one, for a wise man once told me, as a man treats his mother, so will he treat his wife.

Yes, his wife. That is what I envision myself becoming, if I am asked. It's bold of me to write this to you when he hasn't made any claim on my affections, but I see no other man for me on this earth, and I believe he feels the same. Our story may be different than yours with Mother, but it's no less sacred in my heart, no less real.

He waits only because he believes I wish it so, and up to now, I admit that I did. I thought perhaps my feelings for him would change in some drastic way if we were meant to wed, and that hasn't happened. I realize now that it's because I've always loved Gabe Gresham — there was no beginning to it, and I foresee no end. I only had to pause in my day long enough to let it be fully felt, and to hear God's voice above the human ones, gently explaining what love truly is.

On and on they poured, those words that came from the unchecked recesses of myself, and they brought tears of understanding to my eyes, realization to my heart. For better or worse, nothing was more real than the deep, permanent, genuine love I felt for

Gabe Gresham. It was not the pleasant little spark on my skin I'd expected, but it was a far deeper, more consuming fire that had always burned, gaining strength over the years even when it wasn't tended, powerfully warming my soul from the inside out.

I dropped my pen and sat back when I'd filled the page, imagining this paper being sealed, lost, then found again in the cracks of this desk forty years later when I was married to Dr. Tillman. I fingered the letter, knowing I'd never have the courage to hand it to Father — at least, not yet. When it came down to it, I was as fearful as that original letter writer. For all my unfiltered speech and bold words, I hardly knew how to speak the secret things of my heart that mattered most.

I laid down the pen, closed Maisie's book, and climbed back into bed as another headache eclipsed wakefulness.

TWENTY-SIX

What you notice in the person you love,
whether or not you mention it out loud,
magnifies that trait a little more every day.
~A scientist's observations on love

"You are all right, then?" Clara Gresham
approached a waterlogged Gabe as he
rubbed a towel through his hair in the
empty servant's hall.

"Yes, thank you kindly."

How very different this man was from
Burke, the brother she'd made her husband,
and how more suited to marriage — yet
somehow Gabe was the one who remained
unwed. The towel flipped off and his hair
frizzed out in all directions.

Clara tried not to laugh at this man who
looked like a wet dog shaking off after a
jump in the pond.

"You braved the rain a second time, I see."

"Wouldn't let up all day. Had to see to

the horses."

"Where did you find her?"

He pressed his lips together. "Up at the ruins."

"And she's well?"

He exhaled and leaned his forehead onto the window before him. "Let's hope so."

The gruff brokenness of his voice resonated through Clara's hollowed-out heart. How fortunate Willa Duvall was. "She does have one thing in her favor — *you.*"

He stared out at the waning storm. "At least while she's here."

"Or forever, if you'll only have the courage to ask her for it." She tensed at her forwardness, but Gabe didn't blink. They walked into the morning room together where the servants had started a fire for him. "Your affection for her is clear to anyone with eyes."

"Did those eyes also tell you she isn't looking at me the same way?"

"Only because Golda Gresham has forbidden it, most likely. She's inserted herself into every life in this household." She clutched her hands before her as the familiar bitterness hardened. *I speak as a victim of her work. A lonely, wretchedly unhappy victim.* "She's a terrible matchmaker, and I truly wish the people of Crestwicke would stop letting her direct their lives."

He turned to her, and she was suddenly aware of her unusual rush of words. She hardly ever spoke anymore, except to the maid. A door slammed outside somewhere and Clara jolted. Across the lawn she spotted the starkly pale face of her husband, staring at them framed in the window from astride his horse, riding whip against his thigh. He'd returned. Pure white anger smoothed his features as he looked at her. Whatever had she done now? Perhaps he was still cross about the painting.

She straightened her back, chin up. "Burke's returned. I suppose I should ready myself."

Gabe nodded and Clara climbed the long staircase to her bedchamber. All she could do was huddle under her wrap in the window seat and wait.

Eventually her husband's boots sounded on the stairs, slow and heavy. He'd been inside at least a quarter of an hour, and the dread had nearly eaten her alive. Images of that terrible painting he'd discovered, now secreted away, burned in her skull. She suddenly hated the fact that this was his room too, and she could not shut her door against him. That's what it meant to be married. It was nothing like her girlish fancies.

Then he appeared in the doorway, blinking in the candlelight as if stunned by the sight of her. She curled back into the pillows, wishing to disappear. He strode directly to his wardrobe and threw it open, tugging at his cravat and shedding his jacket.

She shivered at the ripple of muscle beneath his white linen sleeves.

"You've been well, I trust?" His voice was surprisingly steady.

"Yes, well. And you?" She dared not ask where he'd been — or anything, really.

He faced her, evaluating her in a glance. Now is when he'd mention that painting in the attic. She felt it. "You've not invited that aunt and uncle of yours to Crestwicke yet. Perhaps we should have them."

She blinked and tried to clear the odd gunk gathering in her throat. "If you wish it." Guilt tugged at her, and she straightened in her window seat. "Actually I've sent them an invitation to dine on November the seventh." She shouldn't have kept it from him.

He peered out from behind the wardrobe door, his shirt unbuttoned. "That won't suit."

She braced for the lecture, but his face seemed open. Thoughtful. "Why?"

"Well, because I'll be in Bristol for the

trading show."

"You . . . you wish to be here too?"

He threw her a darkly shadowed smirk that pleasantly curled something deep inside her. "Trying to be rid of me, are you?"

But then he sobered. He glanced down and pulled at his waistcoat. "I should like to speak with them. It occurs to me how little I know of your childhood, of who you are outside of Crestwicke and the Greshams. Who better to tell me than the people who raised you?"

Clara was speechless. And bemused.

The wardrobe door shut, and she flinched, struck with the sudden realization that it was not even seven in the evening and Burke was undressing. "Is something the matter with your work?"

"What makes you ask such a thing?"

She hesitated, gathering the words. "Well, only that you're not still doing it. Especially after a long absence." She wished to swallow those last words that sounded like an accusation.

He gave a long sigh, after which he settled himself on the window seat beside her, cravat still hanging over his unbuttoned shirt as he stared at the floor. "No, I suppose I'm not."

The memory of that terrible painting

hung between them, a massive, pulsing thing sucking all the air from the room.

"Are you happy here, Clara?"

"Of course." The words snapped out like a reflex.

He waited, continuing to stare ahead, and the silence magnified the actual truth that lay buried inside her. Happy? Hardly. She tried again. "It is a little different than I expected, I suppose. The days can be rather empty."

He fidgeted, as if deciding something. "I've a favor to ask, then. If you would."

She nodded, mind fraying at the hem.

"I'd like to commission you to make a portrait."

She blinked. "A portrait? Of who?"

"You." More fidgeting. "I want . . . that is, I very much desire a likeness of you to hang in my office."

She tensed. What an odd request. What could it mean?

He took her hand. "Will you do it?" It felt as though he were courting her, stepping through that delicate dance toward a possible future together.

"I suppose I could." She couldn't see a reason not to, yet there had to be a catch. Burke and her paintings never mixed willingly.

He studied her as if trying to glimpse something more than she'd meant to allow, sorting all the pieces of her and arranging them into place. "I've also been wanting an oil of that black stallion, if you have the chance. It doesn't make sense to bring in a stranger to do it when my wife is an artist."

Mouth slack, she rolled that word around in her mind, tasting the fresh loveliness of it. *Artist.* She was an artist. Not merely Burke's childish wife who dabbled in paints now and again, but an artist.

He tore his gaze from her, shoulders hunched to his jaw. What was this new awkwardness that cloaked him? He laced his fingers, unlaced them, pulled at his trousers around the knee. "Right, then. I suppose I could . . . pay you for it. Like commissioned work. A little extra spending money, at least."

Heat climbed into her face. "Don't be silly." What man handed his wife money? He'd already lavished on her every material thing she could want and paid every note she brought home. And resented her childish mistreatment of those things.

"Right, then." He turned his gaze back on her then, all dark-eyed and passionate and bare of annoyance, and her poise buckled in the face of it. Why did he have to be so handsome?

He rebuttoned his shirt and left her then, disappearing through the door without another word. She remained exactly where she'd been when he'd entered, but everything inside her had turned upside down and spun around, leaving her pulse pounding. She forced her breath in and out. What was happening? This surprising side of him scared her in a different way than his anger. With that, at least she knew what to expect.

Burke Gresham didn't tell his wife where he'd been. How could he explain the odd impulse he'd had to go into town, lock himself into the London flat, and simply stare at the scattered boxes of her paintings left in the rafters? First, he'd stumbled upon a small square piece that was a man's face in close range — mostly his right eye. Upon closer inspection, one could see the entire ocean painted in great detail within that blue-green iris, as if it filled his vision.

He dug through boxes and stacks of her childhood pieces stored there, seeing the world through his wife's eyes, reading her thoughts. They were more than mere replications of reality — they were her view of it. He found, to his surprise, that her reflections captivated him. She had a lovely spin on the world, unique insights and a knack for capturing them in an image.

Then there was one single painting that rocked him to his core. He gaped at the portrait where it languished in the corner of the dusty attic, discarded on its side. He propped it upright and stared at it as if into a mirror that regressed time. A bold and gallant man, the hero of a great story, stared back at him, a face that sparked with such life, with expectation and adventure.

It was the same man that was now overlaid by the face of Golda Gresham, twin lines of anger hardening their features, yet how vastly different the two depictions were.

And the truth broke him.

He'd wrapped the piece up and had it sent to Crestwicke where he could stare at it more intently. This painting had embellished his masculine features and softened his faults, giving him a distinctly heroic glow, and he desperately wanted his wife to see him that way again.

Now he stared into the gilded mirror at Crestwicke, smoothing fingers along his two-day stubble and wondering how Clara had ever seen him as the man in that first painting. Hitching up his shoulders, he continued on to the morning room where he'd seen his wife through the window speaking with that wretch who called himself Burke's brother. He'd been right in his hunch about Gabe, it seemed, and if Burke were to ever right this mess, he had to remove his competition.

"Parker, assemble the family, if you would. I have an announcement."

"Of course, sir."

He felt no anger toward Clara over the matter. There'd been no evidence that she'd entertained his advances or even written back. No, the seething wrath was all channeled now toward the only person who was to blame for the havoc in his life. As he entered, a tall figure hovered near the fire, hands stretched before it, and Burke bent his lips into a smile. "Gabe."

The man in question turned. "Welcome home. I suppose you've been to London."

"I've investigated the wild stallion opportunity and decided that Gresham Stables will be fully taking part, with one change. You, lucky man, will be at the helm. I've called the family together to make the announcement of your departure."

Gabe simply stared.

"You've never met a horse you couldn't best, and you're the only one with nothing tying you to Crestwicke. I've already purchased your passage while I was in London."

"Passage? Where are these horses?"

"Mongolia. It's a newly discovered species — the only truly feral horses left — that are said to be both untamable and stunning. Not even the Gypsies could break them. That is, until Gabe Gresham attempts it."

Gabe's face was hesitant, but his silent zeal for this project shone through, as Burke knew it would. The man couldn't resist an untamable horse — or an unavailable woman, it would seem.

"The grooms will take over here while you're away, and it'll be a whole new chapter for the Greshams. It's said the wealthiest men in Europe are looking to purchase these creatures, if someone could be found to break them and bring them across."

Indecision played over his features. "From where, again?"

"Mongolia."

"Is that past London?"

Burke smirked. "It's past Russia. You leave tomorrow."

"That soon?"

"Word has gotten out in the equestrian circles, and there will be other businessmen scouting soon. There's a vast fortune to be made from this, if it's handled right. I've already spoken to someone about purchasing land out there, and you'll find it stunning."

"Yes, but . . . tomorrow?"

"Would you rather it be today?"

Gabe ran fingers through his hair. "I'll go, of course, but I cannot leave Crestwicke so soon. I have people here depending on me. People I care about."

Burke forced his practiced smile. "One in particular, if I remember correctly. Have you made any forward progress with this mystery woman?" He tapped the table edge with his thumb, forcing that hard smile to remain on his face.

Gabe dropped his gaze, staring down into a steaming cup that sat on an end table. "Only a little. But it's an inch in a mile-long path."

An inch he never should have taken — not with someone else's wife. "Perhaps you should go to your cottage and pack your things. I'll make your excuses with everyone here."

Gabe crossed his arms over that solid work-toughened chest. "I'm not ready to leave. I have certain unfinished business here, people I cannot leave just yet."

Insolent bloke. *I know too much about you to make this easy on you, Gabe Gresham. I'll use your secrets against you if I have to.*

410

"The passage is booked, and there's no other ship departing for several more months." Burke narrowed his eyes. "Be on it, or you're out of Gresham Stallions, and Crestwicke."

That steady look of Gabe's that had unsettled Burke for years remained. "I'll need to say goodbye, leave a small note of explanation for someone."

"For who?"

"That's none of your concern."

"I believe it is, and you've no business writing to her. You may not care for the customs of society, but a certain level of decorum is expected of everyone here."

Gabe's nostrils flared. "I care not for decorum or expectations, I care for *her.*"

Rage blared through every pore, consuming him. A deep growl tore out of his chest and he grabbed a book from the desk, hurling it. It whacked a vase off a little table, shattering it against the wall.

A pause, a flinch deep in his jaw, but Gabe remained silent. Coward. That's why he'd written Clara a note instead of speaking up — he hadn't the courage to say things to people's faces. Anger throbbed through his limbs, spidered up his scalp. What a fool he'd been, thinking Gabe harmless all these years simply because he kept quiet.

411

Then, in that moment he saw it — lying open on the plush burgundy carpet, where it had fallen from the book he'd hurtled, that horrible, cursed letter with the scarlet border.

The door inched open and Celeste appeared. "What was the crash?" She stepped further into the room when he didn't answer and spotted the letter, her gaze locking on it. She froze. Soon his father appeared, and Clara close behind. In minutes the room had clogged with servants and family, answering his summons.

He could tell when Clara spotted it, but she remained rooted to the rug by the door. Was that shame in her posture? Perhaps she wasn't as innocent as she seemed. That silly little upstairs maid with the red hair whimpered, she and Clara exchanging secret glances. Clara gestured for her to be quiet. Ah yes, that's right. The little imp had been in on it with her.

"It seems someone's misplaced a letter." Burke eyed his wife out of his peripheral vision as he said this, daring her to disgrace both of them.

Twenty-Seven

The quickest way to repair a broken heart
is to use it.

~A scientist's observations on love

Who knows what would have happened if
I'd simply remained upstairs? Yet when I
found Golda's chambers empty, my instincts
drew me to investigate the crash downstairs.
I hadn't seen my patient since Gabe had
brought me back from the ruins, nor had I
heard stirring there, and worry seeped into
my thoughts. I made my way toward the
center of the house, where the noise had
come from. Hurrying down the hall, I
peeked into the cracked-open morning
room door. I only saw Burke, his face pale
and drawn. I nudged the door open further
to look for Golda, but the door squeaked
with a terrible dying-mouse noise.

Several pairs of eyes turned to me, and
my gaze locked onto a heart-stopping sight.

It was there, on the floor — *the letter.* I took one step toward it but stopped at the sight of both Celeste and Essie. No one looked at each other. The tension was palpable.

Burke strode forward and stooped to collect the letter, then held it out to Clara. "I believe you dropped this."

She paled, then frowned, backing away from the letter and folding her arms. "So that's what all this has been about lately, has it? You think —"

He stepped near and spoke low, private words that left her even paler.

Her gaze radiated heat. "How dare you." The words were low and succinct. After delivering them, she spun and walked toward the door with one last glance, and slipped out.

I opened my mouth to say something — anything — but Essie stumbled forward, head bowed and hands clasped over her apron. "It's mine, sir. Don't blame her. I'd no idea it would cause trouble. I meant no harm."

Burke spun on the girl and I launched forward, diving between them. "No, it isn't hers, either. I promise you, it isn't. Please, it's not what you think. This letter simply needs to be thrown away — it was all a misunderstanding." How could I confess the truth now — after keeping it veiled for so long? My silence sickened me as much as my rash words usually did.

He glared at me. "Did you write it?"

"No, I —"

Burke faced the room with a growl, waving the letter. "Will someone please claim this letter before I go mad?"

"Very well then, *I will.*"

A hush draped us. Golda Gresham's aura preceded her into the room, spreading the cluster of people as if parting the Red Sea when she approached Burke. Mr. Gresham shot her a look of challenge, daring her to claim this love letter written for another man. Shadows had etched themselves into his long face, making it even more somber. *How could you?* he mouthed and stalked from the room when she did not back down.

With one black-gloved hand and all the quiet elegance in the world, Golda plucked that letter from her son's fingers. No one moved.

"*You?*" Celeste was pale, her fingers clutching the back of a chair. "You wrote . . ." A storm of emotions played over her face. Hurt, betrayal, fury. It was as if Golda had once again stripped her of the hope of love.

Golda turned those icy blue eyes on her

in answer. She paused before her son and turned to glare at the lot of them. "What is the meaning of this? Can you all not handle a civilized conversation?" Silence reigned. "How wretched that a mere letter can create such a ripple simply because no one knows how to talk to one another about it." She looked once more over those gathered, pocketed the letter, and turned to me. "If you please, Miss Duvall, I'd like a word with you."

With one last glance at the stricken watchers, I followed her down the hall to the drawing room. My head throbbed terribly against the warmth of two popping fires, and I massaged my temples after settling Golda in a high-backed chair. I stared at my patient's profile leaning against ivory fabric as she opened the letter and began to read, poring over the lines within, and all I could do was wait and observe. Wind howled outside. Drops splattered the windows. I quaked. She lost herself in that letter for endless minutes, her face a mask.

"Miss Duvall, you never told me when we spoke before. How did you even come to know about this letter?"

"I'm the one who found it. The letter was in a desk that was given to our family years ago. I brought it to this house to find out who it was meant for . . . and give it to them."

Finally she lifted her gaze from that lovely page to my face, those stunning blue slits looking me over. "Yet just now you said it was best discarded. You weren't going to give it to me."

I straightened. "Because I believe in the sanctity of marriage, no matter its state. How could I, in good conscience, bring before you a relic of a past love when you were struggling so to leave it behind?"

She merely stared. Surely she did not mean to keep up the pretense that Grayson Aberdeen was a former servant.

I dove back in. "Aunt Maisie told me of the Aberdeens and the forced annulment, the rumors of you stealing a family heirloom and being kept away from the man you loved. It's a tragic story, but I cannot aid in allowing it to haunt this house forever. I simply saw no good coming of the letter, or in bringing it to light again, once I knew . . ."

She lowered the letter to her lap, her pale face white against the glowing lights around us. "Aunt Maisie told you all that?"

"She called you Rose, but I'm certain it was you. It has to be." I shivered at the memory of that lonely tomb of a house where I'd met the once-great Aberdeens.

"It seems Aunt Maisie hasn't told you the entire story. I *was* that girl and I *did* take a family heirloom, but it was given to me. And what's more, this letter wasn't written by some lovesick peasant girl begging for her wealthy lover to return to her — not at all. Since you seem to be so misinformed as to my loves and dalliances, I suppose I should give you the entire story."

Anticipation flitted up my spine.

"You, in particular, need to hear it, and one day you'll understand why. Lock the door and sit down."

TWENTY-EIGHT

Over the course of a marriage, a man may go from a celebrated hero to the villain without ever changing a thing.
~A scientist's observations on love

"Falling" was the perfect way to describe the way Rose happened upon love. She fought it at first, but soon it was a heady, headlong plummet that had her struggling for balance. Intensity lined their every interaction, even a simple brush of hands. She was hungry for Grayson Aberdeen but also irrepressibly happy, even when she returned home in the fall to her bear of a father.

"What's wrong with you, girl?" Her father grabbed her shoulder and swung her around. He'd just demanded that she take the baked goods to Widow Frasier in a way that assumed she'd refuse, and in truth she might have — before Grayson lit up her world. She'd just returned home from her annual summer stay with Auntie Maisie in Upton Currey, which she'd spent largely with Grayson, and she hadn't yet descended to earth.

"Why, Father, all I've done is agree to take the basket as you asked."

Being in love afforded Rose a surprising affection for her father and a lavish amount of patience for all the tedious tasks he gave her, because now everything mattered, and the whole world was much more hopeful and colorful than it had been before. Even her surly, Bible-quoting father.

The man grimaced like a bulldog. "Since when do you do as I ask?"

"Everyone grows up sometime." She flashed a smile and vanished out the door with the basket on her arm before he could ask anything else. She'd have to tread carefully, keep her feet on solid ground. If he even suspected she'd fallen in love with a man of wealth, he'd never forgive her. Her father looked down his crooked nose at all squires and landed gentry, for they lacked everything the man esteemed — long days, humility, and calloused hands that provided for one's own family.

Rose's walk was filled with bold and shiny daydreams of a future with Grayson. They were interrupted by her childhood chums calling a friendly "halloo" up the path. She slightly resented the intrusion, but she greeted Dinah and Peter with politeness. "I didn't notice you there on the path."

Dinah put a hand on her hip. "Someone's finished that little romance novel she was writing, it would seem. There now, she's even blushing. In love with your own words, are you? Too full of them to see your own two friends 'afore your face?"

Rose grimaced. How dear these friends were — dear, yet provincial and so easily satisfied. They'd likely both marry someone within the hamlet — maybe even each other — and live out their days without ever realizing the immensity of what lay beyond these hills and stone fences.

That story had been her only way of processing what was occurring between her and Grayson Aberdeen, and she'd agonized over it even as the true story delighted her heart. "I've not yet figured out the ending."

Dinah laughed. Peter did not. His somber gaze lifted to hers as if Dinah was not even there. "Has the girl at least realized she loves the hero yet?" Peter took Rose's basket and fell into stride beside her. "In your last letter, you said she still didn't know."

A grin overtook Rose's face. She could

not help it. "The truth finally caught up with her and she is basking in the knowledge of it." She sighed. "The big, bright, glorious truth."

"Sounds as if the story's finished then."

"Oh no, not at all. There's more to happy endings than merely being in love. Why, that takes no effort at all. It's everything that comes after that matters — fires and storms, dragons that need to be slain — before the hero can have his lady."

"Ah." Peter glanced at Dinah, who'd grown sullen. "Have you any plan for how they will defeat these dragons?"

A knot formed in Rose's stomach, and she thought of *them.* Grayson's formidable parents, the most powerful people in ten shires. Although the elder Aberdeens did not have their son's respect, they did hold his future and his inheritance. That knowledge made Rose tremble.

Letters flew between Rose and Grayson throughout the long winter months, warming her in his absence. The following summer she returned with such eagerness that it seemed no reality could possibly live up to her grand daydreams, but it did. In some ways, being there with him in person, feeling the warmth of his hand around hers, experiencing the energy of his kisses, exceeded her expectations. The days passed in lovely silken moments. All the world's wisdom told her this would eventually lessen, that the heady passion that daily threatened to drown her would not — *could* not — last.

But it did. Only, it turned a distinct corner. The change began one day in June when she inquired when he might tell his parents about them. Truly, the whole world should know of their affection for one another in the same way it needed more flowers and lovely art.

His dismissive answer planted the first seed of fear, and his evasive behavior when she tried to speak of their future only watered it. Loss was inevitable, she could sense it. Just as her old nursemaid had been able to predict a coming storm, Rose knew in some unexplainable way what would happen.

Her patience wore thin one day. "When should we tell them, on the first anniversary of our wedding? They'll have to know sometime, if we will truly be together."

Silence heightened on the heels of her words, and her casually spoken "if" hovered like a menacing shadow.

She stilled as realization settled on her, breath thin and fluttery. "You never did intend for us to marry, did you?" A tremble started deep within. "Kiss me one minute, dismiss me the next. Is that how every man of nobility treats a woman? What a weak-minded —"

He turned on her, the passion that had fueled his kisses now breathing fire over her tender heart. "You've no idea what it means to have this burden on me, being an heir. I'm reminded every day of their expectations, their hopes. None of them include friendship with a mere butcher's daughter, much less marriage to her."

Stunned, she'd wilted backward, his words blows to her chest. She couldn't speak. How did one respond to such atrocities from the man whose love had fueled her for months?

His apology was swift and sincere, setting her rocking world back upon its axis. Yet the words could not be unsaid, for even though the barbs were removed, they left holes in her heart.

She sobbed into her pillow that night, and the next day he met her in the orchard as always, legs dangling off the rock outcropping as if he hadn't just smashed her heart the day before. Afraid yet desperate to regain wholeness, she latched onto hope and climbed back into the romance that had brought such soaring heights of delight before.

But that very afternoon there came another explosion between them about something else entirely. The pattern continued through the summer, these bouts of passion that pivoted so quickly between ardor and animosity.

Heartbroken and much grown up, Rose returned to her small hamlet without any certainty about her future, or her feelings for Grayson. She had come awake to the fact that she hadn't truly known him all this time. It was a crushing blow to realize her love — and the man who'd inspired it — might be a farce. Her friends tried to revive her spirits, and her father attempted to exorcise from her whatever sin had beset his wayward daughter.

When she'd grown horribly pale and thin, she finally sat at her little desk to pen the letter that needed to be written. It was a clarifying and thorough missive stating her heart on matters and leaving him to make the decision. She never envisioned carrying out her romance this way, with a reversal of the roles, but it could not be helped. If he still refused to tell his parents and wed her, she would tell him the honest truth of everything, the terrible state he'd brought her to.

I sank onto a divan nearby. "So that's where the letter came in. You wrote to tell him how you felt and straighten out what had happened between you. But it never reached him."

"No, the letter I wrote Grayson that day was an entirely different one, and it was delivered as intended." She eyed the closed door and leaned close to whisper the truth of what she'd put in that letter.

I stifled a gasp and sat back, looking over this woman and trying to understand all the myriad pieces of her story.

"My heart still didn't know what to think, but he gave me a flower ring and we were married in Gretna Green at a blacksmith's shop, with a Bible laid open on the man's anvil. Instead of organs in the background, we had cows lowing. Rather than flower petals at our feet . . . straw. We booked a room at the King's Head in Springfield, but we never made it there. While we supped downstairs, Lady Aberdeen stormed into the inn and snatched Grayson away, leaving me penniless and alone. I was ruined." Her chin lifted as she relayed this low moment.

"How *could* they?"

"The Aberdeens were a law unto themselves. They ruled everything and never forgot it. No one dared stand against them to help us."

"So it was *after* all this that you sent the letter I found, then."

"Yes, but not to Grayson. There was someone else." She gave a watery smile and closed her eyes. "*Thank heavens,* there was someone else."

"What became of this someone else?"

She shrugged, a smile flickering over her lips. "I'd imagine he's still sulking in his smoking room down the hall."

The disgrace set in soon after Rose returned home. After an especially impassioned sermon on secret sin three Sundays in a row, she shattered into a million delicate pieces before her father and told him everything.

He kicked her out without a second thought, wholly unwilling to besmirch the house of Ellis with his daughter's foolishness. Slipping out of town without a word, she used her last bit of change for the train. She finally arrived at the doorstep of her faithful Aunt Maisie, who saw naught but her dear girl at the door and welcomed her in.

"A sinner, you say? Well then, we'll be two of a kind, won't we?"

A wink punctuated the end of her pert response, flooding Rose with relief and a sense of safety she hadn't felt in weeks. Besides that, she was near the Aberdeens again, and that meant there was a possibility for reconciliation.

Once a week for several weeks, Rose climbed that steep hill to the castle, as she called it, and asked for her husband. Despite the annulment, she still thought of him so, but they turned her away. Finally they accused her of theft, just to be rid of her, and Rose fled with her aunt — who refused to leave her alone — to London. She reverted to calling herself Golda, her middle name, and went into hiding from the Aberdeens. For eight years they toiled over laundering fine clothing, mending, and tatting, bringing in money however they could and staying in an old root cellar. They survived until a cholera epidemic shut their part of the city down, and customers weren't willing to use their services anymore. Death hung at every doorstep. Things were bleak, and she was in despair.

At the lowest point, Golda and Maisie found themselves homeless and hungry, sneaking into a rat-infested cellar to stay warm on cold nights, but at least the Aberdeens had not found her. Finally, several years after the ruined wedding, she jumped a coal car and rode back to the coastal hamlet where she grew up, hoping to find her father softened, but nothing was the same. Her father was dead, her friends gone. More desperate than ever, she flew to her place of solace, the haunt of her childhood adventures, the one place she never failed to find peace — the ruins of an old abandoned estate near her hamlet, Crestwicke Manor. How she loved the crumbling old structure inhabited only by wildlife, its windows invaded by trees growing through it and its grand stair railing wrapped in vines that twisted eager fingers around every spindle. In her entire life, no owner had appeared at the place.

Yet that too had changed. It was no longer a ruins, open for all to come and climb about, but had been put to use as someone's summer estate. Walls had been cleared of all overgrown wildlife, window glass replaced, the yard tamed into neat gardens. Heartbroken, she climbed to the tower on the rise, the last remaining ruined thing at Crestwicke, and collapsed in the grass. She cried out to God, but he did not answer.

At least, not for five or six minutes.

A carriage came rumbling up the drive, a black-and-gold affair with four matched horses. Small children hung out the window, but they were yanked back by a woman's arm. A family — it wasn't just a wealthy fop who owned this place, but a family with children who lived and loved here. Bittersweet longing swept through her heart.

Just then footsteps sounded on the stones behind her — it was a fine-looking gent with polished riding boots and a pack of yelping hounds on his heels. The man was fresh and alive, strikingly handsome with an easy gait and broad shoulders. He nearly tripped over her in the grass, and he cried out in surprise.

She cowered, but he merely blinked at the woman sprawled in his yard. "I say, are you all right, miss?"

She lifted her tired eyes to him and beheld a most marvelous sight — not only a kind face, but a familiar one. It was her dear childhood friend, Peter!

He dropped to the ground and gathered her in his arms the minute he saw her face and let her weep years' worth of tears onto his shoulder. Everything else fell away, and it was only two close friends, clinging to each other in their childhood hideaway.

He told her it was he who bought the house when he inherited his uncle's holdings and made good as a horse breeder. "I finally had money enough to buy any home in England, and Crestwicke was the only place I wanted." He smoothed her hair. "It was the capsule of all my favorite memories."

With a kiss to her hand, he sat back and plucked a forget-me-not, twirling it before her face with a crooked smile. They'd scattered seeds as children, delighted to see these wildflowers taking over the forgotten fields, and the memory sweetened in her heart. "They're still here. And now you are too." He tucked it behind her ear. "A forget-me-not for the girl I never forgot." He smoothed her mussed hair and rubbed the strands between his fingers with wonder on his face. There was deep hunger in his dark eyes as he looked her over — a craving.

She read then in his look what she'd missed for many, many years. He was in love with her. Somewhere along the line, between the playful romps and childish arguments, adventures and trials, he'd begun to see her as a woman — a desirable one. But now . . . what had she become?

She scrambled back, a hand to her dirty face. She'd not looked in a mirror in days, and her gown was mussed, torn, and far too big.

He put a hand on her shoulder to stop her crab-like scramble. "Where is your husband?"

She lowered her face, allowing her hair to curtain its heated contours. He'd heard about the elopement, of course, but not what had come of it.

Her heart pounded. Yes, her husband. Where was her husband? The answer swelled up in her breast, suffocating the air from her lungs and constricting her chest. She couldn't voice it. With a weary look, she merely shook her head.

His look softened and he sighed, dropping his head to hers, his arms coming around her possessively. Protectively. He tipped her back to look at her face again, one hand smoothing hair away. "Perhaps you'd be willing to help me, then. I'm in need of a governess for my children, and no one seems to fit the bill. Would you be interested?"

Surprise and hope burst in her heart as she looked up at the friend who'd always been there for her, and who now rescued her again. Truly, could it be that she'd been saved? Fingers over her mouth, she nodded. Tears budded in her dried-out eyes. "I — I must bring someone —"

"Whoever you like. This house is so big,

we rattle around as it is."

"There's more I must tell you."

He shrugged with an easy smile. "If you must."

In the end, Golda was instated as governess to his small children, and she soon discovered Peter Gresham was a widower. His wife had fallen victim to typhoid fever after delivering their youngest child, leaving Peter alone.

It felt so backward, being a servant to her old friend from the hamlet, and she never knew quite where she fit or how to act. He made it easy on her with his usual gracious manner, quiet voice, and lighthearted disposition. Aunt Maisie got on well with Peter, and hinted that they'd make a fine match, but Golda insisted they were merely friends.

Yet the colorless petals of friendship peeled back to reveal layers of deep, sweet-smelling love that had never been explored. It had taken the heartache of Grayson Aberdeen to awaken such feelings, for she realized how different her old friend was — and how rare.

Golda fell headlong in love with Peter in a matter of weeks, for exactly two reasons. The first was the way he ambled about his big mansion with the same humble, playful nature she'd so enjoyed in childhood.

What truly sent her tumbling over the edge was watching him delight in his children. He didn't simply tolerate or discipline them — he *delighted* in them, from their messes to their questions and childish noise. Nothing they did ruffled him, and she never tired of watching them romp about together. They climbed on him as if he were a giant toy and squealed with delight as he dropped them playfully onto the horsehair sofa and chased them about.

It was during one of these evening tussles before the fire that she collected all her feelings in that battered old heart of hers, and let them burst out all over a page of his late wife's elegant stationery with scarlet edging. He never noticed her writing it, and she didn't want him to. It would take courage to reveal all she felt, and she couldn't bear to hurt again. Every man she'd ever known had broken her heart eventually, leaving her with a sense of impermanence and cynicism, of deep and constant disappointment.

Before she could decide what to do with it, the letter became unnecessary. Golda only served as governess in that house for a few months before it became obvious to all that she would better fit the vacant role of lady of Crestwicke. "I never know which name I should use," she'd told him once, when signing her name in his staff logbook to accept her pay. Sometimes she used Ellis, other times she wrote *Aberdeen* with careful, swooping letters. She hadn't heard from them in years, but what if they still searched for her? "I'm not certain either one is . . . quite right."

He'd looked up, so unassuming and familiar, and blinked. "Well then, perhaps you should change it. Why not take mine?"

After the shock, she agreed with a quiet smile, never giving voice to the true feelings that had blossomed. Little affections soon became common between them, and they enjoyed their new roles. The banns were read in church and the couple married.

"I don't know what I would have done if you hadn't bought this old place. I never would have found you," she whispered to her groom as they shared their wedding breakfast.

He merely smiled down at his beloved bride. "Matched souls always find their way back to one another, for they seek refuge in the same place."

Her head jerked up and she stared at him. "You've read my book."

"Of course." Years of hopeful love bloomed in his expression. "It's another reason I bought Crestwicke." He looked about the

435

grand manor whose ruins had once been their childhood sanctuary. "I knew if I did, I would see you again." Then he leaned down, his expression melting with affection, and kissed her thoroughly.

Matched souls always find their way back to one another, for they seek refuge in the same place.

Golda sighed. "It was Aunt Maisie who convinced me to keep looking for love when I cried into her lap over Grayson. She made me believe that I would find someone, but I suppose I had to discover the great secret . . . that I already had, and it was Peter Gresham."

Lovely. I put my hand over my chest, my heart barely able to hold all the beauty. I felt it all the more deeply after what had occurred concerning my own childhood chum. It was like holding a mirror up to the past and seeing one's self — and needing to know how the reflective story ended.

Yet something wasn't right. It hardly matched what I knew of their reality. It was as if there were pieces missing or put in backward. "So when you married Peter . . ."

"I thought I'd eventually tell him what had happened with Grayson and the Aberdeens, but he never asked and I never offered the details. Those years were simply a shadow that we never explored. Soon there was no need."

"Surely you weren't still afraid of the Aberdeens."

She raised her eyebrows. "And why shouldn't I have been? They were still the squire and lady." She clutched the arms of her chair, eyes shining like two gems. "And I am still in possession of their most precious family heirloom. I have it here at Crestwicke and they'll never find it." She sat back and sipped her tea with satisfaction, that feline look lifting the edges of her lovely blue eyes.

"And what of Peter Gresham? Have you let them drive a wedge between two best friends?"

Her poise wilted. "We've come to have a quiet marriage."

Indeed. "One your family believes is merely a business arrangement. Why didn't you ever give him the letter?"

"He was willing to marry me, wasn't he? And we were always the best of friends, even after we wed. Words were not necessary between us. He knew I cared for him, and we shared a happy marriage for several years."

"But something changed."

I could see by looking at her shadowed face that the years of torment had altered something deep within, shaking loose a delicate piece of her youth. She gave the barest shake of her head, her expression crumpling just as it did before that angel headstone. "I expected too much of our love. Of him. Life broke us." Suddenly the final twisting path of this story reached its conclusion, and I understood. Of all the grief I'd encountered in patients, none tore a jagged path between two people more than the loss of a child. Or in this case, several. Death after suffocating death, a helpless grasp on another perfectly formed yet breathless little body . . .

I looked into her watery eyes. "After all this time, neither of you have recovered, have you?" Not in the elastic way one returns to who she used to be, at least. Despair had settled this woman into a comfortable new shape and she'd continued surviving. I saw that head-above-water look that had settled into powdered lines on her aging face.

"Grief has a funny way of sending two best friends in different directions in search of relief and leaving them very far apart in the end."

"Perhaps it's time they came back to-gether."

She simply stared, seconds ticking by on the clock. "One day after the last baby came early and died, I woke from a nap to see a bonfire out in the yard. I wondered what was burning, and why it was so large. Such a wretched smell it was, that awful smoke." Tears appeared on the glassy surface of her eyes. "Then I walked by the nursery, that sanctuary full of beautiful furniture and toys all set up, where I always went to remember . . ."

Everything inside me twisted.

"I practically *flew* out that door and across the yard, but he just stood there, watching it all burn like he was glad to be rid of the rubbish. It felt so familiar, rushing headlong into the stone wall of a man who's made up his mind, who'd taken the choice from my hands, and I couldn't bear it happening again.

"I hurled the most wretched insults, anything to make him feel a sliver of the pain I felt every day, even that I'd never loved him. That I married him only because I had to. That he'd never measure up to Grayson."

I stifled a gasp.

"It felt *good* to say it — ripe and delicious

— but even then, he was so wretchedly unmovable. He said only two hateful words — *no more.* There would be no more babies. I loathed having no say in the matter. Something snapped in me, and I determined to speak out always, about everything."

A small shudder passed over her. "Those days seemed so long, but years went by without a blink. Bitterness grew up like briars between us, all those little jabs like thorns, and I was hardly aware until it was too vast to climb through. He left for London one day and rarely came back." She gave a weak shrug, as if to say it was the end. "As I said, I simply expected too much of him. Every man eventually disappoints, somehow."

Yet my mind wouldn't release the heart-rending words from her novel, the words Peter had spoken on the morning of their wedding — *Matched souls always find their way back to one another, for they seek refuge in the same place.* "It *cannot* end that way. He rescued you, over and over again, loving you before you ever loved him. There's something incredible in that — something nearly divine. Please, you have to try." I thought of Gabe. Dear, precious, overlooked Gabe who had gently pulled me from many pits — including the pit of self.

"No one can write the letter I read without fully meaning it, and that doesn't simply vanish. You think it's too late, the wall between you too thick, but look what your letters did to this entire household. Imagine if such words came directly from your mouth, and he heard you saying everything you've put off telling him. He has always been your hero, your rescuer, even if he isn't perfect, and you've been his love. Please, Mrs. Gresham, won't you give him another chance?"

She looked at me steadily, chin trembling. A horse clopped outside and the clock behind her tick-ticked. "Will you fetch a tincture, please? I have a headache."

"But —"

"Please."

So I left.

But not without the letter.

TWENTY-NINE

When all you have left is words, it's more than enough.
~A scientist's observations on love

He was your hero.

Golda Gresham stared into the cold hearth for long moments after her nurse left, those words nagging at her worn-out heart. That was exactly what Maisie had told her to search for years ago — a true hero. It rattled her a little to hear Miss Duvall utter the same phrase about Peter, because as the waning years and approaching death began to muffle so many past hurts, she knew it was true.

She couldn't bear to let that little nurse see how much she always affected her, pushing and prodding at the calcified shelter of hurt she'd allowed to grow up around her. Holding onto that anger came easier, felt safer, than exposing her raw and battered heart. Yet that heart had an end date, and ever since the doctor had given his prognosis — three to six months — she'd been able to loosen her protective grip on it. Not that much longer and she'd be free of it, and everything that hurt it.

Her mind journeyed up to the attic, where a certain self-bound romantic novel created in her youth lay in an old hatbox. A dashing hero had swept through the city and charmed the sense right out of the heroine. It had been deeply thrilling and romantic to write it, and living it out with Grayson had been even more intense.

Yet it was the story she'd written next that gripped her heart now. It was an illustrated children's story about an unlikely hero, a quiet blacksmith, who fashioned his own armor from scraps in his shop when his maiden was in trouble and charged off to rescue her. She'd wept as she'd sketched Peter, her beloved and gallant friend, and thought about how to explain to a young mind how she was being rescued as she wed him. She hardly dared breathe in those days for fear it would all vanish, after all she'd climbed through already, all she'd escaped. It couldn't be so easy — so right.

Peter had always been the constant in her life, the safe rock outcropping on which to land. Yet somehow, just like everyone else, he had slipped from the hero pedestal.

She had changed too, though. That letter had been the most convicting peek into who she used to be, like the aroma of chestnuts on the fire that reminded one of cozy childhood Christmases. She looked now into the mirror at the sharp-featured old woman with purple moons under her eyes and was repulsed. Bitterness had made her ugly. Staring at her reflection over the little glass bottles of perfume lining her vanity table, she decided a little kindness was due her childhood hero.

Leaning to the left, she pulled the bell, and soon the little redheaded maid Essie was scurrying down the hall. When her nervous face appeared in the doorway, Golda beckoned her in. "You may ask Cook to prepare a roast pheasant — exactly the way Mr. Gresham likes it. And have her make a lemon truffle with raisins for dessert."

A quick bob. "Will there be anything else, my lady?"

With an eye to her reflection, Golda gentled her features and smiled at the young woman, working hard to overlook the loose strand of hair and drooping apron. "You've such an eagerness about you, Essie."

"I'm sorry, Mrs. Gresham. I'll try to be more composed."

"No, no. It's . . . commendable." Her smile wobbled.

Essie's hands stilled from smoothing her apron. "Pardon, my lady?"

Heavens, she was horrible at this anymore. Like a squeaky gear forced into action after many years of neglect. She straightened. "You've become a fine maid, Essie. So many in service are apathetic, idle even, but you're so keen to our whims and needs, and you've an air of modesty about you that's quite pleasing."

She blinked like a fox cornered by hounds. "Oh." She fidgeted with her apron again. "Thank you, my lady." She backed out with another bow to relay the message to Cook, but a moment later she reappeared, her fingers worrying the edge of her apron even harder. "You must have found out about the teacup. I'm so sorry, my lady, and I'd gladly replace it from my wages. Truly, I would. It was only an accident."

Golda Gresham pushed aside the news about her teacup and let her gaze wander over the slender maid. "That won't be necessary." The letter had also provided a keen insight into the large cracks that existed in the hearts of those around her as well, as they clung to those rare words of affection like the last crumbs on the luncheon table.

They deserved more than crumbs — all of them.

She tilted her head. "Have you a young man, Essie?"

She dropped her gaze with a powerful flush. "No, ma'am. I don't break your rules."

Only my cups, it would seem. She looked over that plain face and saw the appealing sweetness that might catch a man's eye. She'd make a fine wife, modest and kind-hearted. "Perhaps I'll lift that rule. It is a bit harsh, don't you think?"

The girl merely blinked.

"In the meantime, Essie, it's perfectly acceptable to remain as you are. You've been a faithful servant, and you'll have a place here as long as you want it." She fidgeted. "Marriage isn't always a fitting solution, mind you. It's often merely exchanging one set of problems for another. But if you happen to find one who's suited to you . . ."

The girl nodded awkwardly and backed toward the door.

"Oh, and Essie." Golda smiled. "I've heard you're learning to read. Parker would make an excellent teacher, don't you think?"

She gave a prim smile, and the flustered girl turned and hurried out to the hall.

A fine start, even if a little rocky.

The word *more* echoed through Golda Gresham's brain as she left her room, along with all the other things Willa Duvall had said to her. More chances, more love, were all possible. Despite her narrowing future, what she did have right now was more. More time, more words, more choices to make. A little bit, at least. As the final grains of sand neared the hourglass spout, she would make use of them.

After a moment alone, her cupid's heart compelled her toward the servant's hall to see if Essie had the courage to follow through. It was Celeste she encountered in the narrow hall, though, pale and dumbstruck at the sight of her. She hid a *child,* of all things, behind her skirts, shielding her from Golda as a mother bear might defend her young.

Celeste tipped her chin. "It's my house too, you know. More than yours, I think. We were here first, and we have every right to invite guests."

Golda took in the defensive posture, braced against the "you're not my real mother" glare Celeste hadn't used since her youth, and found her heart was no longer capable of hardening to this tenacious stepdaughter. In fact, the arrogant tilt of her head reminded Golda how marvelously strong Celeste was, and also how vulnerable. It seemed she was still upset about the little game she'd played, leaving those additional letters. Everything she'd written to Celeste had been true, even if there had been no secret admirer writing them.

Golda steeled herself against voicing the smart remarks that came naturally and knelt before the spindly creature behind Celeste's skirt. Her knees slipped and popped. "Who might you be? Are you visiting Celeste?"

"She's taken me in, ma'am, and she's going to teach me things. I'm going to university someday, even though my mam and pap couldn't read. Miss Celeste says so."

Golda swallowed her surprise, keeping her gaze steadily on the somewhat uncouth girl with wide-set eyes and wildly crooked lower teeth. Freckles covered her face with the same disorder. "Does she, now?"

"She has no one." Celeste spoke with an edge of defensiveness, her hand tightening on the girl's shoulders. How long had this been going on? Golda supposed she deserved to not be consulted. Celeste's eyes still snapped with the same fire she'd heard in her voice that awful day in the parlor, when the truth had come out. What could she do now? Was it all too far gone to be mended?

The words need to come from you. Drat that little nurse, with the voice that echoed through her skull.

Golda looked back to the girl. "What's your name, child?"

"Phoebe, ma'am."

With a weak smile, Golda touched the girl's arm and looked directly into her gold-green eyes. "Well, Phoebe, you've found yourself the finest advocate a girl could ever have. Celeste is a fierce champion, and a wise teacher. You'd do well to model yourself after such a woman. Very few have strength to match hers."

She pulled herself up, praying her knees wouldn't give out.

"You might as well give her the green room. I assume there's no one else from whom you're hiding her." Golda leaned on the back of a chair, her gaze level with an astonished Celeste. She considered her stepdaughter. "You know, perhaps you should start a girls' school someday. If you're planning to empower and embolden one young foundling, you might as well save some time and do it to a whole roomful at once."

Celeste's nostrils flared, eyes wide. All well and good — it'd take time to adjust to change, and even Golda wasn't convinced of its permanence. Speaking this way hardly felt natural, even if the words were quite true.

"It would be a daring and colorful future for Crestwicke, don't you think? A refuge for girls who've given up." She paused and smiled, caught up in the fragrant sweetness of it. "I believe they need to hear what you're advocating even more than anyone."

Celeste stared, every emotion flickering over her face, but no words came.

With a nod to them both, Golda moved to sweep down the hall, but paused, considering this strong-willed stepdaughter who'd grown into a woman in so short a time. "By the way, Celeste, it was I who was here first. Crestwicke was my haven long before you were even born. But that's a story for another day."

Golda turned and paced down the narrow passageway, smiling at the way Celeste's mouth had hung open. That plucky little nurse was right — there were second chances to be had. Even for her. Overwhelming despair threatened to steal over her again as her lonely footsteps clicked on wood, but she lifted her head and moved forward, not giving it a chance to settle. Time was short, and she had some living to do yet.

Burke was next, but he wasn't in the study anymore, or his chambers. In fact, Clara seemed absent as well. How quiet this old house seemed.

Finally her maid located Burke in the attic, and Golda forced her stiff body up the narrow stairs and into the stuffy old rafters. Light burst upon her senses when she entered, with no curtains blocking the light, but there sat Burke, straddling a paint-stained stool and staring out the dormered window. Golda grimaced, shielded her eyes, then forced her uncooperative body forward. Her problematic heart pumped hard to keep up with the strain, but she was determined. Burke turned at the sound of her huffing, his grimace solidifying at the sight of her.

"I've never known you to hide yourself away up here, Burke."

His eyes narrowed.

Golda steadied her breathing, her racing heart, and felt the latter pop a little before settling into a regular rhythm. She straightened, taking in a breath. "I owe you an apology for that whole letter business. It was never meant to cause trouble."

"Ha! You, not mean to cause trouble?"

She cringed. "From boyhood you possessed such potential, and I couldn't bear to see you settle — ever." She adjusted her weight, plagued with that awful tightening in her chest that reminded her of her own mortality. "When a person lives long enough, they gain experience. It's no good unless you pass it on to those depending on you to teach them."

"Teach or command? First it was what to study, which university to attend. Then it was a leading share of the family business, but only if I signed my life away to the little shop girl. She doesn't even love me, did you know that? Doesn't care a fig about me."

"Surely you're not blind to the way she looks at you — adores you."

"It's you who is blind, dear stepmother." He spat out the last words. "She's left. Gone home to her decrepit shanty by the river with her no-account relations. It seems if she can't control me, she doesn't want any part of me." With that, he swiveled away on the stool, offering Golda a view of his hunched back. "I've tried, and it's all come to nothing."

Golda straightened and stared down the beast that so resembled the one inside her. Anger was always coupled with fear —

insecurity. She could hear it, smell it on his voice like drink. "Don't you dare curl into that shell of yours and harden yourself against the truth simply because you're hurt. I know better than anyone what a person can become in such a shell, and I won't let any son of mine spend his life that way." She trembled as the raw words sank into the air between them. "I want you to go downstairs, climb on that horse, and go after her. And for pity's sake, sheathe your temper while you're at it."

He gave a harsh laugh. "*You* are going to advise me in matters of the heart?"

"Who better than one who's had a lifetime of failing at it?" She forced her stiff fingers to unclamp, letting her hands fall at her sides. "I chose her because I hoped she'd draw out the protective side of you — the fierce and loyal warrior who was ready, at the age of eight, to defend his father from my advances, to protect anyone who happened to find themselves under his care."

His shoulders tensed.

"And I chose her because she adored you. That sort of open admiration will balm even the most ravaged heart, such as the one who lost his mother at too tender an age. I thought you'd draw out the best in each other, but instead it seems you've managed

453

to drown it."

He was silent for long breaths of time, his back to her, and she studied that golden hair, the fine set of his shoulders. How striking he was — much like his mother must have been.

Life was wretchedly unfair at times. The waters that had parted to provide her the husband she needed had also swept his mother away and left him with an uptight stepmother, too laden with her own burdens to properly mother him. Guilt stabbed her.

"I'm afraid you're too late."

"You both have a lifetime ahead of you. Children, adventures, horses bought and sold, new homes and acquaintances . . . and you've a powerful talent in persuasion that could come in handy this very minute."

"Did you hear me? She's *gone*."

"There's still time to fix it."

"How?" The word rang with a mix of bitter cynicism and shards of hope.

She filled her lungs. "The same way you broke it — *with your words*." She left him and eased her trembling limbs back down those narrow attic stairs, one hand to her chest. And once again, she was alone.

Willa's question to Maisie, heard through the hearth, settled over her mind and rang true with her heart: *Oh, Aunt Maisie, how can you possibly want me to fan those desires into flames when they only consume a person and leave her so broken and alone?*

It's what this quest for love eventually did to people. Her, at least. Even solid and dependable Peter had abandoned her, and although she was partly to blame, she couldn't stop the resentment from climbing. A true hero should always be there, no matter what a woman did. She'd forgiven plenty of his mistakes. Yet here she was, broken . . . and quite alone.

But then Aunt Maisie's response came on the next wave. *If that's how it leaves her, then she hasn't finished the search.*

Yet she was legally wed, and nearing the end of her story. What else was there for her to find?

THIRTY

Do away with petty criticisms and subtle corrections, and leave the fixing of your spouse to God. It frees you up to simply love and enjoy them, which will prove a greater influence in the end.

~A scientist's observations on love

There would be no more bowing and scraping, no more biding time with polite words. The time had come to deliver the letter that had brought me to Crestwicke, and God was behind me like the wind at my back. Boldness rippled through me as I moved along the corridor and down the stairs and heard the click-click of boots on tile.

Peter Gresham looked up from the shadowed entry, blinking in the dimness. Hat and coat were already in hand. "Miss Duvall. I trust everything is well."

"Mr. Gresham, if you please, it's time we speak plainly." I approached, breathless, stood before him. "If you'll only give me a moment, I'll speak in haste."

His eyes dropped to the pocket watch in his hand. "I haven't the time. I'm sorry, Miss Duvall." He turned, shoulders hunching as he donned his coat.

I expelled a breath and invited God into the conversation. Strength descended like armor. "Mr. Gresham, your wife is in love with you."

He froze at the door, hand on the knob, and I knew my arrow had hit the mark. "I beg your pardon?" His voice was sharp.

"I thought you should know." My legs trembled a little as the enormity of my impudence struck me, yet a greater strength inside seemed to hold me up.

He turned, grimacing with shock. "How dare you shove your nose into this family's affairs in such an indecent —"

"Someone needs to do it." With a deep breath, I approached and held out the single folded page, my gaze daring him to skitter away. "This is for you." And in that simple moment, I delivered the letter at long last, the time capsule of true feelings, preserved like a relic at the museum for this moment when people had forgotten what used to be.

He glowered and did not take it. "Aberdeen's letter?"

"Yours." He turned to go, and I stepped before him. "Unless Aberdeen has a long-standing connection to forget-me-nots . . . and Crestwicke."

He scowled. "This is no business of yours."

"Isn't it?" I stepped around again so he had to look at me. "Have you any idea why she hired me, sir? It's because she was terrified of walking alone through something terrible, and I'm merely trying to ensure she doesn't."

"There's only one thing that woman has *ever* feared, and that's —" He paled, his hand leaving the doorknob. It shook a little. Then he lifted his agonized gaze to mine, a question in his eyes.

"She needs you, sir." My voice was quiet. "As I've been saying all along."

Anger melted from his face, leaving his features haggard and bright with worry.

I held out the letter one more time. "At least read it, sir. Despite everyone who has stumbled upon it, this letter was actually meant for you."

"And if you're mistaken, like the rest?"

"I've had the truth from her own mouth, sir. Please, just read it and you'll see."

He stared down at the thing. "You are a most unusual nurse."

458

"An advocate of healing, as any nurse should be." I shoved it forward. "And quite stubborn."

The glare hardened, but he snatched it from my hand and turned, flipping it open to skim in haste. His grimace released as he neared the end of the page, though, and as he read it again from the top, I realized something had happened to those words with time — they'd strengthened. They had a greater impact now than they would have if they'd been read fresh, all those years ago when everyone languished in a state of contentment.

"She wrote all this . . . when?"

"While she was your governess. Just before your engagement."

His gaze shot to mine. "What of Aberdeen? Did she not tell you of her affection for him? She may have been fond of me, but it was him who truly owned her love. She never got over him. Even when he was a brute to her, she married him because she was —"

"Expecting." I eyed him directly. "His child, that is."

Shock struck his angular features, drawing out his age even more. Understanding dawned. Yes, there had been a baby, and it had happened *before* the marriage — had compelled the union to happen.

"She's been hurting alone all these years. I believe she was embarrassed to tell you much of this, how she fell out of love with Grayson, how awful he was. Since you'd rescued her from so much, she wanted you to see her as strong, capable. You know how she is." I took a breath, watched the words sink in. "I realize she's hurt you, but —"

"So, my wife." He cleared his throat, frowned at the floor. "How long . . . ?"

I shook my head. "Maybe months, if there are no complications — apoplexy, infection, things of that nature. She must not be allowed to worry."

He nodded, staring down at that page from the past, blinking, trying to take it all in. His voice sobered. "It's so strange, seeing this. It's in her hand, with pieces of *our* story, but she never spoke this way."

"Every man in her life has broken her heart. Including . . ." I pinched my lips shut.

"Including *me.* Isn't that what you mean, Miss Duvall?"

"It was a terrible time for both of you."

He raked his long fingers through his hair. "She was . . . *miserable.* Every one of them came early, and we never knew why. I thought she'd die and soak right into the ground with them. I couldn't bear her suffering that way." The hand holding the letter trembled. "I had . . . to end it. Somehow." His face wore every inch of his strained heart, every fiber of love still stitched into his soul for the woman he'd married.

"She believes all is lost between you, but I don't. Do you?"

He blinked tired eyes. "You . . . you — why is that?"

I smiled. "Because matched souls seek refuge in the same place." I nodded at the interior of the house, the grand estate he'd spent years and fortunes rebuilding — for her. Their childhood refuge, her adult sanctuary when everyone had abandoned her.

His full lips parted, emitting a gasping groan as he sank onto a bench, head in his hands.

A rustle, a gasp, then there she was at the top of the stairs, horrified. Stiff. "Miss Duvall, *what have you done?*" Golda Gresham clung to the bannister on the landing, watching us with wide eyes set in a pale face.

Peter's gaze shot up, his expression raw and vulnerable.

I hurried up to her, helping her lean on me as I whispered. "This has gone on long enough, and I won't allow it to continue, promise or not."

She straightened. "I can see what you're doing and I do not approve."

"Very well." I pulled her forward anyway. "You were wrong before, you know. About expecting too much of your marriage. The problem is that you didn't expect nearly enough. It's far more than a business arrangement, and he is your ally, Mrs. Gresham. It's time you started treating him that way."

Peter Gresham climbed the steps, and I pulled back, prepared to slip away. "I'll just leave you to —"

"No." Her voice was direct, her grip firm as she leaned on me. She leaned near to hiss in my ear. *"You caused this."*

I placed her hand on the smooth railing. "I'll sit just below, in case you need me." With an affirming smile, I backed down the steps and curled onto a bench in the shadows.

He took his time climbing the remaining stairs and stood before her on the landing, tall and gallant and full of hope.

"Mr. Gresham." She met his gaze with weary eyes. "You'll miss your train."

He reached out and touched her cheek. "So I will." His solemn voice echoed softly through the entryway.

"I suppose Miss Duvall's been telling you all sorts of fanciful stories."

He continued tracing the line of her jaw, her ear, tucking loose silver strands behind it. Her posture began to soften.

"She has a fanciful imagination, you know."

He held up the letter with his free hand. "You never wrote a thing that wasn't true, even in your novels." He stepped closer, looking down at her as her long white fingers gripped the bannister. "To read what you wrote, things you never said about . . . about loving me . . ." He studied her as if he couldn't believe it.

"Well, I couldn't very well stop it, now could I? It's almost as though you *tried* to make it so. What was I supposed to do? Grown-up Peter Gresham, with his wild long hair and dashing suits, romping about with his children, all masculinity and kindness and —"

He swept her up in a desperate kiss, shushing her stumbling words with long-bridled affection and pulling her close. Her arms floundered, then relaxed, hesitatingly slipping around him as he continued to kiss the girl he'd loved since childhood. That blessed page with the scarlet border fluttered down toward me from his hand and I smiled at it, lying there on the floor of their home, their sanctuary, its mission finally complete.

I slipped out, basking in the warmth that still existed between them, the years of deep friendship and heartache. I stopped in the servant's hall to tell Parker that Mr. Gresham wouldn't need his carriage just yet, then I snuck up to my room. For once, I was not needed. She had someone else to care for her.

Hours later, my heart ached with bittersweet longing as I watched from my window. Peter Gresham's tall frame bore his wife across the front yard, her dress hem billowing out like flower petals, and up the path to the hill where their past was buried. After grieving separately for years, the pair was finally going together to visit that little grave containing the lives that had broken both of their hearts — and their bond to each other.

When they'd gone, my heart was full of love stories, and aching for my own. How similar it was to Gabe and me, and how beautiful. I opened Maisie's book to tear out my letter to Father, to see if there was anything there I dared voice to Gabe.

Yet only Aunt Maisie's feminine writing filled the pages. I blinked, mind tilting and

shifting as I realized *I had never written it* —
except in my head. Had Father even visited?
Plagued with uncertainty, with fear of what
was reality and what I'd imagined after my
head injury, I hurried to the window. Gabe
was not even about the grounds today.

With a frown, I spread my research out
before me, those black-and-white studies
that were dependable and true, and lost
myself in Kryschinsky's theory of sanitation
and ventilation, but Gabe remained ever in
the back of my mind.

Tomorrow. I'd find him tomorrow, when I
made certain my mind was righted again.

THIRTY-ONE

When one sets out to tame a wild stallion,
the most important part is letting it go —
it's only yours if it has a choice.
~A scientist's observations on love

The horses were quiet the next morning as
the moist haze lay over the corral, and a
young stable hand was the one to open the
doors and release the animals. As I neared,
my skirt sweeping up sparkling dew, I held
my breath. "Where's Gabe Gresham this
morning, Luke?"

He turned with a cascade of hay falling
from his pitchfork. "Mr. Gabe? He's already
gone, I expect. His boat leaves today."

"Boat?" I nearly choked on the word.

"Mr. Burke is sending him off on some
horse chase in Asia. Asked me to look after
things while he was gone."

I clutched a beam. "Luke, how do I get to
his cottage?"

"Out along the coastline, over the field, and through the little gate at the end of the path."

A lot of ground to cover.

The young groom gave a half smile. "Best take one of the horses, miss. Here, this one's saddled and —"

"Thank you, Luke." I leaped astride the creature, bracing myself in sidesaddle position, and shot out of the stables like an arrow. *Please don't be too late.* By the time a letter reached him, Father would have me married off and settled in a little cottage in Brighton, forever preventing any hope of a future with the one man I wanted. Wet sea air washed my hot skin, the golden field laid out before me. This place had always felt like home, and perhaps Gabe was the reason — he was the dear, overlooked home for my soul.

I reined in before the frame house on the rise and sprang down while my mount danced in place. I flung myself up onto the porch and knocked. Banged, really, for all the nervous energy I poured into it. My heart thudded in the terrible, wretched silence, and waves crested in a glittering display below. I knocked again and the door squeaked open. In the shadows stood Gabe, tall in his boots and brown serge suit, with suitcases on the floor beside him.

He frowned, looking me up and down. "Willa?"

I gasped for breath. "You were going to leave. Without a goodbye. Without telling me . . . without . . . whatever you wanted to say."

He shoved his hands into his pockets, scuffing the floor with the heel of his boot. "I'd have left you a note."

"A *note*!" But then I remembered the treasured letter. Perhaps that would have made a fitting end to this visit. Yet I cringed at the word *end*. With a breath, I looked up into his rugged face. "I'm here now, Gabe."

"I have to leave."

I grabbed his arm. "Say it. Please. Just tell me what you wanted to say. Aren't you the one who said the important things should be spoken in person?"

He glanced at my hand resting on his arm, his gaze caressing and tender as always. Then he looked to my face and it gentled even more. I imagined what it would feel like for him to touch me in a few short seconds, how our first kiss would taste.

"I was afraid you'd say no."

"I won't." I swallowed, my throat suddenly tight.

"All right, then." His gaze burrowed into

isn't fit to
you, Willa
modify his
of the line,
y. He was
told him,

open like
seem to

d pay for
xpenses,
d to save
a whole
rs, Willa.
r you to
. . ."

out the
I felt it
a lock.
ll along
he isn't
from a

ng out.
in your

m.
it. It'll
etting

Villa, I've watched
I first met you."

affection intense
y on its crest. "I'm

d?"

r you to go."
n. "Go where?"
back and disappeared
s of his home. He
ed letter bearing some
orner and held it out.

then. "What on earth
a?"
was sailing to Asia.
es you talk about." He
n. "There's a hospital
quaintance of mine, Dr.
danger of being shut
r of preventable deaths
a matter just begging for
father already know. He
ke changes or he'll lose
life work will melt away,
the countless lives that
ld him a little about your

469

research, and since your father
make the trip at his age, he wants
Duvall, to go there and help him
Boston hospital. He's at the end
and willing to do anything you sa
ecstatic about your ideas — what
anyway."

I could feel my mouth hanging
a regular monkey, but I couldn'
get it closed. "Pardon?"

"It'll take at least a year, and he'
everything. Your passage, living
even a small stipend. If you manage
the hospital together, it would mean
new life for his dreams — and you
I could see him paving the way fo
study medicine, and you'd become

"A doctor." I could barely breathe
sacred title. It fit — all of it fit, and
slipping into my heart like a key into
This was what God had in mind a
— I sensed it immediately. "And
bothered that all this help is coming
woman?"

He shrugged, an impish grin peeki
"I may have underemphasized the *a*
name."

"Gabe Gresham!" I smacked his ar

"He's desperate, and you're brillian
be fine. You're not in the habit of

refusals stand in your way, as I remember."

I pinched my lips together.

He gripped my shoulders, squeezing with a gentle strength that nearly undid me. "You can do this, Willa. You're no longer just a voice shooting out opinions, but one that brings beauty and life. Truth."

Tears pricked my eyes. Both rejected and magnificently accepted in this moment, I hardly knew what to feel or — in this rare instance — what to say. "You're certain he wants me?"

"After what I said of you, he believes you are his miracle. I told him how brilliant you are, how capable and intelligent, how you had the ability to turn everything around."

I tipped my head. "You said all that?"

A tender smile spread over his face. "I told you, I always speak up when it counts."

A lump in my throat threatened to strangle me, bobbing up and down and refusing to go away, but that was all right. Speaking my feelings for him would somehow desecrate this splendid act of love. Instead I leaned near, this great man with a heart the size of a continent, and stood toe to toe with him. Grabbing hold of his lapels, I pulled him down and kissed him with abandon, and I felt the heat of those embers flare into a blaze when he answered back with great fervor and warmth.

I breathed in the fresh scent of his wild nature, that faint aroma of cinnamon, bottling it up to store in my most precious memories. Where words failed, my lips expressed years of gratitude, respect, and deep affection for the man who now folded his arms and his whole heart around me, embracing me as he'd done all these years in so many ways. I tasted the rugged sweetness of him in those lips, the strength and softness combined into one striking man, and I couldn't get enough.

Finally I pulled back, looking up at him, and found my voice again. "There are horses in America, you know."

"Not the sort waiting in Asia."

"Where is it you're going again?"

"Mongolia." He drew out the syllables. "Has a nicer ring to it than Ammenemonie."

I burst out laughing, which was a blessed relief. "Oh, Gabe." I took his hand, looking down at our hands clutched together. The feelings in my heart billowed with even more intensity and ached for release, but I couldn't form them into words. They were simply too big, stretched too wide over my life.

He ran his thumb over my knuckles. "Come." He dropped my hand and strode out the door. When we reached a small lean-to behind his cottage, he threw open the doors, and there, in all her wild glory, was my white horse. She tossed her head when she saw me, pacing.

I ran my hand along her gray snout, laid my face against it. "Hello, old girl."

"It's time." Gabe looked at me, assessing something in my face, and I knew what came next. "I figured it would be the last thing I did before I left."

"I'm not ready."

"I know. But that's what makes it loving."

With a deep breath, I gave a single nod and stepped back. He opened the gate, one hand on her nose to steady her, and threw it wide. "Go on, *git*!" She froze, glancing over at me as if also deciding between two things. For a fleeting, heart-pounding moment I wondered if she'd stay. But she danced out, paused to get her bearings, and broke into a sprint toward freedom. I clutched Gabe's arm as Luna tore across the field, sand flying under her hooves and tale rippling like a flag. How glorious she looked, nose to the wind and muscled legs pounding.

Tears budded and began to leak. "What's in Mongolia, Gabe?" It was on the tip of my tongue to beg him outright to join me in America. Maybe I could have both love *and* my career.

He inhaled and released it over top of my head, scattering stray wisps of hair. "You think she's beautiful, your Luna, but it's nothing compared to the creatures in Mongolia. Here the so-called wild horses are merely feral creatures, the abandoned descendants of horses in captivity, but in Mongolia they're truly wild. It would be incredible to be near them, uncover their true magnificence, and see what they're capable of."

The brilliant glow of his face touched my heart, warming it to the truth. This was his dream just as medicine was mine, and I needed to release him to this the same way he had for me. The raw love in my heart would let me do no less. I gulped back my pronouncement. How selfish my view of him had been, as if his only role in my life was that of my flagpole. He had color of his own, and now was the time for it to fly.

His voice was low when he spoke again. Solemn and deep. "Burke insisted on this trip, but I find it's calling to me, Willa." He rested his hand on my shoulder. "Those horses, all that wild open land . . ."

I stared up at his dear, dear face, memorizing the lines of it, the scar along his jaw, the exact color of his gold-flecked eyes, the jagged indents along his cheeks. "Yes, I understand." Too well. I reached out and touched his rugged cheek. "Goodbye, Gabe."

Those indents on his cheeks creased under my fingers as he smiled. "There's no such thing as goodbye between us."

I took his hands in mine, cherishing the feel of them. Their strength. "Gabe?"

"Hmm?"

"Will you write?" It was a window cracked open, a door left ajar.

He flung it wide open with a glorious smile. "Count on it, Doc."

THIRTY-TWO

In marriage, there is a great deal of power
in saying no — to yourself.
　　　　~A scientist's observations on love

I felt the old cynicism toward romance
creeping over me as I rode back to the
house, the settling awareness that it never
truly seemed to last, but also a bittersweet
gratitude for the authentic love, in whatever
form, from Gabe. I paused at the stables
and looked up to the ruins, knowing what
must come next. Leaving my horse with the
groom, I climbed that path once more to
speak with God, but even before I reached
the top, the truth settled solidly upon my
soul. God had given me this position as the
answer to my heart's desire. This huge step,
this unknown position, was God's blessing.

So was the man who had brought it to
me.

My heart broke as I knelt at the ruins. *Why*

did you draw me toward the truth of my feel-
ings for Gabe, then take him away? Love had
broken us all, and led to so many dead ends.
I thought over all the fractured love stories
— Celeste, Tillman, Essie, the Greshams,
Grayson and Rose, Burke and Clara, even
Father. Was it fair to add myself and Gabe
to that list? I knelt atop that hill and turned
to look across to the iron fence on another
hill, where the Greshams of the past lay —
including Aunt Maisie. Even she had died
alone and unwed, still longing for love. *For-*
give me if I cast off your advice, beautiful
woman, but not everyone is meant to fulfill
that hunger for love. I cannot keep searching
for what I wasn't meant to find.

My love story was about dreams pursued,
with the happy ending being the day I
finally reached them. I bowed and thanked
my Father for bestowing on me a most glittering and fitting future — the culmination
of all I'd asked for — and the love of a dear
friend besides.

I slipped inside to find Mrs. Gresham in the
music room, perched at the piano. She
looked up as I entered. "So, you are still at
Crestwicke after all. I was beginning to
think you'd left us."

"No, my lady."

"Good, because your father is here to collect you."

I froze. "Here?"

"He's made some rounds since his visit and returned for you. He believes it best that you return home, after your . . ." She waved vaguely toward my head. "He's been posted near the front door, awaiting your return."

My skin chilled. *The contract.* No. No, it couldn't end this way. My selfish heart longed to chase Gabe down and . . . what, make him marry me to keep Tillman away? Take away his dreams? I sank to the ottoman, trembling hands bracing my head. I hadn't even failed, had I? Well, I hadn't succeeded either.

"Are you unwell, Miss Duvall?"

"No, it's just . . ." Puffing out a quick breath, I sat up and told her of my contract with Father.

"*Tillman?* Oh heavens no, you cannot marry Tillman."

"I must keep my word."

She closed the lid over the piano keys and stood, one hand on the polished wood. "What you were required to do, if I understand, is successfully complete one nursing job, no?"

"*This* nursing job."

"Which, if you remember, was created because of my fear of passing from this world alone. And in my estimation, though I'm yet alive, that job is now complete."

I smiled, taking her hand in mine. "Does this mean you're not afraid anymore?"

She raised her eyebrows and smiled that feline smile, eyes sparkling. She looked past me to her husband who was standing in the open window to watch the horses, hands clasped behind his back. "No. But I'm not alone."

My heart swelled. I leaned forward and kissed her brow, which seemed to please her immensely. The letter had done more than I could have ever imagined — it *had* brought the couple together, helped them recognize their end of the rainbow in each other.

"Now, I hope you have a man in mind you'd rather marry."

I flinched and worked hard to push Gabe from my thoughts. "Not at the moment." What would she say if I gave her the name currently on my heart? "However, a medical position in America has come up."

"One you would like?"

"One I believe is a heaven-sent gift from God."

"Then by all means, do take it."

I dropped my gaze to her gold ring with

the pink stone. "Father will never agree with your assessment, though. I did not cure you. He'll hold me to that contract the moment I near your front door."

She offered a pert smile, hands folded neatly in her lap. "Then I suggest you use the *back* door. Oh and Miss Duvall." She studied me as if memorizing my face. "Let us both heed Aunt Maisie's advice — don't stop searching for love until you've tasted it, yes? The Almighty won't create a hole he doesn't intend to fill."

It was the first time I'd defied Father outright. The Greshams' carriage crunched up the drive with me and my luggage the following morning, leaving Crestwicke and all its broken love stories behind — as well as my very angry father. I'd told him of my decision, of my fulfillment of the contract, and new veins appeared along his scalp and neck as his anger boiled that I'd never seen before. I reasoned and pleaded, but in the end Golda's advice won out — I took the back door.

I wept every night for a week over Father and wrote him two letters, which received no response. I'd never envisioned a future without him, for a girl never outgrows her father, but my heavenly Father had carved out this path for me, and now that I'd tasted such connection with him, I dared not go anywhere without him.

As painful as my departure was, my arrival in America resulted in a fresh batch of insecurity as I was met with shock and disdain — by all except the physician who had sent for me. He merely blinked his blue eyes behind thick spectacles, stumbled over a few words in his delicate accent, then invited me to outline my ideas. Once I had unleashed the knowledge built up through years of study, his keen face relaxed and his posture became remarkably welcoming.

Boston was alive every minute, with steam engines and crowded streets, vendors on street corners and crowds of people going about their lives in one concentrated space. The hospital astonished me at every turn, including the man who ran it. The charity run by Franciscan-order nuns had almost no money to stretch over its one-hundred-twenty-bed wards, for it served the poor and the immigrants, and it couldn't compare to the well-constructed hospitals the man was used to in his home country of Sweden. He was a consummate professional, a healer of the highest quality, and he hadn't any idea how to repair the mess of a hospital America had constructed for its poor.

The soft-spoken Dr. Sjöberg was a smart, energetic leader no older than two and forty years who came to be a dear friend and only sometimes a partner in verbal sparring. We had ideas as different as our accents, but that seemed to amuse him more than anything, and we got on well.

Journal after journal of my research blossomed into the open, turning into reality as all my ideas for Father's clinic took shape on a grander scale around us. Ventilation changed the entire atmosphere of the structure that had once induced claustrophobia at the front door, opening it up into a refreshing place of healing. Dr. Sjöberg latched onto all my notions regarding sanitation, as he was nothing if not precise. Cleanliness suited his sensibilities.

I came alive with the opportunities and sheer amount of work begging to be done. I even began an unofficial clinic for those turned away from the hospital for moral reasons, serving a reluctant community of thieves and prostitutes who needed even more help than those admitted to the main hospital. Rough seamen and young pickpockets regularly walked in my doors, and I treated them all. I saved as many lives as I could and sobbed heartily over those I could not.

I requested supplies as part compensation for my efforts, and Dr. Sjöberg ensured that the hospital complied. Life was hard, but the good sort of hard. It reminded me of pushing a carriage out of the mud and watching it move, inch by inch. Victory came as I toiled alongside God, meeting often with him in the haven of my heart, and words — the right words — appeared in my quiver whenever I had need of them.

We were invited to speak to various hospital boards, and I always brought along my sketches and notes. When they were accompanied by my impassioned explanations, lights began to flicker in those stale old faces and the wheel of change groaned into motion. The first to accept our ideas, outside of the Boston hospital, was the Dulmuth Hospital in New York — which had rejected me for a training program years ago.

After more than two years of toiling in America, I passed the clinic on to new hands, and we returned to "my island," as he called the UK, and set to work on a hospital in Scotland run by his protégé, a Dr. Johannson, who was far less receptive to working with a woman. I visited Father by train for whole weekends at a time, and he met me reluctantly in the parlor before escaping into his office. News of my work seemed to dishearten him, as if he were watching me progress on a track that he wasn't guiding. He'd aged, but he still worked long hours for his patients and had a foundation laid for his clinic.

Life flew by in blinding, vivid color until I received a letter from Crestwicke — by then it had been three years since I'd left. I hurried through the narrow streets of Glasgow with grates that puffed steam, dodging bicycles and pedestrians, settling into the stoop of my rooming house to tear the thing open. The vellum smelled of seaside air, or perhaps that was my imagination, but I devoured the news from that old manor, my chest constricting.

Golda Gresham has departed this life. The Gresham family invites you to Crestwicke Manor on August the sixth at two in the afternoon for remembrances.

With kind regard,
Peter Gresham

I glanced up from the page to situate myself back into my new reality, dragging myself out of the one I'd left behind. Yet it pulled at my heart. Three years she'd lived

— three years the lovers in that letter had spent together. I inhaled and released a long, shuddering sigh.

In the morning, I marched right into Dr. Sjöberg's office and told him I would have to miss the final meeting with the hospital board in Edinburgh. "It's a matter of great importance."

He blinked through his spectacles in that endearing way. "It cannot be put off?"

I pictured Crestwicke, and instantly my soul settled, my memory recalling the crash of waves and scent of the fresh air. I remembered Golda, poised yet fragile. "I'm afraid not. I'll leave you copies of all my drawings and research."

"And your keen mind?" His soft voice calmed me. "May I have a copy of that too?"

I smiled. "It's a pleasure to have it in demand. I'll be in contact as soon as I've seen to a few personal matters."

At last I was returning to Crestwicke — not only for the dead, but for the living. It seemed Aunt Maisie's dearest wish for me would come true. My longing for real, authentic love had only swelled since being gone, but there was no one in America or Scotland to fill it. No one outside of Crestwicke, actually.

Gabe and I had written on occasion, his

short missives in reply to my long and rambling ones, but I never had a sense of what he actually felt concerning me, or what he intended. Every time he spoke of his horses, I sensed an undercurrent of energy that I couldn't bear to interrupt. I simply assumed I'd read the truth in his face if I saw him again. Much as I adored the love letter that had drawn me to Crestwicke, some things were meant to be said in person.

Which I dearly hoped was about to happen.

THIRTY-THREE

Final diagnosis of my condition: I have
come to appreciate my ailment, this aversion to marriage, for it has helped me
bypass many false cures for my heart until
I discovered the real one, and my hungry
soul was satisfied at last.
~A scientist's observations on love

Crestwicke, August 1862
When my hired carriage rode up the lane at
Crestwicke, so much had changed. Another
corral had been added, the garden extended,
and Gabe's cozy house by the water taken
over by a family with children playing in the
yard. His? Or was he still in Mongolia? He'd
also given me an address in Cornwall to
write. Part of me hoped he'd found the happiness he'd given me — the other part
hoped he was still looking for it.

Had it truly been three years? I walked up
those steps as if in a dream and knocked on

the door. It was answered by the same tall butler who had admitted me years ago, and I flashed him a warm smile. "Hello, Parker. I've come for the services."

His face melted into a smile of welcome. "It's good to have you back at Crestwicke, Miss Duvall, but I'm afraid you're too late. The services were a few weeks ago. Today is merely a gathering for close friends and family — you included."

"A gathering?"

"By her request, miss. Come, they're just preparing in the morning room." He led me through the great house, each turn striking me with memories of the woman I'd never see again. Things were different, though. The house had a faint freshness to it, with windows thrown open to the sea air all along the main floor, a new lightness among the people who scurried about.

"Is Gabe here, Parker?"

"Mr. Gabe?" He blinked. "No, miss. I haven't seen him. I heard he was living in Cornwall with his own stallion farm. Does well for himself but doesn't mix with the other Greshams much. Especially since she's gone. He used to come for long weekends on the train now and again, but he's all but vanished in the weeks since her death. He thinks of it as Burke's house, and they've never seen eye to eye. He sent his regrets to this afternoon's gathering. He was here for the funeral, but he left the moment he placed a bouquet on her grave."

My heart fell. It was so like him, to focus on the living rather than the departed.

Burke received me in the morning room, and he seemed older, but in a good way. The lines of anger had settled into maturity, and his smile came more easily — especially when Clara glided by. They still seemed hesitant around each other, but the hard tension had faded. Seated in a straight-back chair along with the others, I glanced around at the family in mourning, plus a handful of strangers who must be the Greshams' acquaintances.

Burke stood at the front of the room, holding up a thick package. "Well now, at last we can see what all the mystery's about." He broke the seal and opened it. "Golda Gresham has requested that we all be here to receive her final words." He opened a single sheet and cleared his throat.

To those gathered at Crestwicke, my lifelong haven —

You are likely expecting an explanation behind the letter that so upset the household, an apology perhaps, but none of those are within this package. I vowed to myself I'd limit this to a single page of words, which makes me consider more heavily what those words should be, and the aroma they'll leave behind. This is my one last chance to impact the atmosphere of this house, which I've done a great deal over the years — for better or worse — so I will only say this.

I have many regrets concerning all of you, but I do not regret the letter that has unsettled so many of your hearts. It has yawned wide the great chasm we all secretly feel for a true and lasting love, drawing it to the surface where we cannot ignore it, and I'm glad. After all, a person cannot find that for which he has not sufficiently longed. Only the restless will leave the familiar behind in search of deep satisfaction. Such a desire has been sewn into the fabric of our humanity, and we cannot — and should not — be rid of it.

Beyond that, I am not content to leave you with a sentimental blanket message that applies to everyone and touches no one, so I've written something specific to each of you. Burke will pass them out now. Accept them, and my final meddling, with my blessing and affection.

Warmly,

Rosalind Golda

Ellis Gresham

The folded notes were handed to each guest by Burke and Clara, and when mine was in my hand, I could not bring myself to open it. I laid it on my lap and watched the others. There were nods and sniffles, a fumbling for handkerchiefs. It was a sacred moment, and time seemed suspended.

Finally I tore open the seal on my own and took a breath.

Dearest Miss Duvall,

You offered me the chance to remember what I had once with my Peter, because I watched it lived out once again — right under my own roof. Two dear friends, two opposites who fit perfectly, reuniting on Crestwicke's shores and realizing their friendship had turned to love of the deepest sort.

I hereby retract the promise you made to me, and bequeath and release to you the much coveted, long-lost, "stolen" Aberdeen family heirloom — the last remaining Aberdeen heir and the only surviving child I have borne. You are his

Rose, and he your Peter.

Go to him, with my blessing. Live the long and happy love story I should have had, if I'd had half as much sense as you possess.

My eyes stung and I blinked rapidly, reading those words over and over again. I moved between the chairs, the clusters of guests, to find Clara, dark braid over her shoulder. "Have you seen Gabe?"

She offered a sad smile. "Gabe sends his warmest regards, Miss Duvall, but he isn't here. He was delighted to hear you'd accepted the invitation, though."

"He knew I'd be coming?"

She nodded. "When he came for the burial, he talked to Burke about it. We were all hoping he'd stay."

I gave a small nod and slipped away with my twisting, winding thoughts, my churning insides, to the ultimate place of untangling. I carried my broken heart there and stood on the grassy landing halfway up the hill, looking up at the ancient stone tower that waited for me.

The climb winded me, but once I reached the ruins, fresh new life filled my soul, and I stepped into God's presence. There on the same sod that had accepted my little-girl

492

tears when Mama died, I knelt and poured my heart out once again to God and felt him drenching my parched spirit that grieved for Golda Aberdeen — and the love of her son.

That authentic love Golda spoke of had eluded me again, and I was at the foot of the ruins, broken and alone once more. Two men had left me this way, Father and now Gabe, and I still had not found a love that would remain. Aunt Maisie's words drifted into the middle of my grief. *If that's how it leaves her, then she hasn't finished the search.*

Yet no matter what shifted in or out of my life, all that truly remained dependable in the end were those stones that had been here for hundreds of years, ready to comfort heartbreak, overlooking countless generations, always waiting for someone to come enjoy them.

They alone were permanent.

And in that moment, truth dawned in glorious, vibrant color. That longing I'd finally given in to now swelled in my heart, and it was saturated with a love I'd known my whole life — one I'd only recently pursued in earnest. Yet it had always pursued me.

I know you have the hunger in you — I can

see it glowing in those eyes of yours. I felt it. Oh, how I felt it. *Let me tell you, Miss Duvall, that the most important advice I can ever give to a young woman is lean into that hunger — allow yourself to feel it fully and let it consume you and drive you until you find that perfect love.*

Yes. My heart breathed the single word.

I thought then of the love letter that said all the things every one of our hearts had longed to hear, and the lines came back to me in a different voice.

Dear one, I love you more than you know.

I've seen everything you believe goes unnoticed, I've watched when you thought no one was looking, observed what exists below the surface.

I know your strengths, and I know your weaknesses too.

I even know that secret you hoped to keep from everyone. Yes, I know all of it, and I choose you in spite of — maybe because of — all those things.

I choose those unbelievable strengths, those weaknesses you try to hide — every bit of it because it's all you, my creation, and I choose you. Every day, every moment, I choose you.

Dearest, if only you could see yourself from where I stand — how brave and unstoppable you would become.

Yet this one would be signed. Signed by the love that Aunt Maisie, in all her unmarried life, had attained and found peace in after the long search and many, many dead ends. *Yahweh.*

I bowed again, releasing my tears into the soil. *I entrust my heart to you, Father. And my future. No matter what else enters it, may it be full of you.* Then I rested in the knowledge of God's immensity that could be felt here better than anywhere else and basked in who he was. This was my love. He was my sanctuary. Just as Golda had said, we'd all been created with this deep desire for love woven into our being, but what all of us at Crestwicke had failed to understand was that depth of longing was simply too much to be filled by any human.

I rose when my heart felt anchored and looked over the wide ribbon of sea. Crestwicke and its ruined tower had been Rose and Peter's sanctuary, and it was mine too, in a way. No, God . . . God was my sanctuary, and I'd merely rediscovered him here in these ruins.

How much heartache had come to this

house in the search for authentic love and all its disappointments. I looked over Golda's letter to me again, feeling the weight of her dramatic love story that was now at an end. I folded it to tuck it away, and that's when I saw it on the back — one final sentence that stole my breath and plummeted my heart into my stomach.

P.S. You delivered my love letter . . . so I delivered yours.

I looked up, shock warming my flesh. Partial thoughts crowded and spun in my mind. *My* love letter? When had I ever . . .

Then I became aware that the rhythmic thudding I'd heard was horse hooves somewhere below. I straightened, looking about for the wild horses, but it was only one — and she was bright and glorious and familiar. So was the man astride her. I caught my breath at the sight of Gabe, tall and proud on his horse, countenance fresh and alive. They crested the distant hill and cantered down, heading straight for me. I scrambled up the outcropping and hid behind a crumbling wall as they neared, and he reined in at the center of the ruins.

He swung down into our little sanctuary with a solid thump of boots, removed his hat, and bowed his great shoulders before God. *Matched souls always find their way back to one another, for they seek refuge in the same place.* Looking over his painfully familiar profile, the masculine man who could tame wild stallions and utterly enchant my finicky heart, his gentle face, the humble reverence cast over it all, no one had seemed more beautiful or more powerful.

Or more perfect for me.

He knelt among the little white flowers, a sparkling ocean beyond him, and prayed. When his massive shoulders trembled, I approached, drawn to help as I witnessed his grief, and placed my open palm on his back. He hadn't let me walk through this part alone years ago, and I would do no less.

He flinched and turned, rising to tower over me and washing me in a look of such enduring affection that I felt it climb through my chest. I went to him, tucking myself against him, and he swept me up close, weeping into my hair with long silent sobs. It was the first I'd ever seen him cry. I laid a solemn kiss on his thick hair and smoothed my hand through it.

Then he pulled back and looked at me with new awareness, tears still glimmering in his eyes. I saw a trace of Golda in him, a quiet self-assurance and poise, and wondered why I'd never noticed how alike they were. How curious was this story of Aberdeens and Greshams, two families with a bevy of misplaced and unspoken things.

"You, in particular, need to hear it, and one day you'll understand why."

There in the sacred silence, barely daring to breathe, the truth crystalized in magnificent sparkling revelation. This was why Golda Gresham had cracked open her tragic past to me that day long ago, sharing what she hadn't dared to tell anyone else — *we* were the happy ending to her love story, the culmination of deep and abiding love formed among the enchantment of Crestwicke Manor.

You are his Rose, and he your Peter.

I stood now in the blissful, climactic end to her epic love story that had come full circle with the letter she'd once written so long ago. I smiled up at Gabe against the backdrop of our ruins and reached out to touch my wild horse's soft gray nose. "She came back. Our wild horse."

His face melted into an endless smile. "I always hoped she would." His voice rumbled through my heart, and I swallowed in earnest. He was so much more vivid, more stunning, in person, and I could barely hold myself together. I understood how those horses felt. Not subdued or trained but charmed. Drawn. How did he do it? Perhaps it was the magic of Crestwicke in him, tinting the air with romance.

I ran my fingers along the horse's face until they reached Gabe's hand holding the bridle and curled them into the hollow of his palm. He tugged me closer until we stood heart-poundingly close, and I tipped my head up to see him. He pulled a folded paper from his pocket, extending it without a word.

I opened it and there was my heart splashed onto the page, the letter I'd written to Father about Gabe, cut neatly from Maisie's book. *"Oh my."*

"My thoughts too." He tucked it back into his breast pocket as if keeping my love safe there and brushed my wind-swept curls off my face with tender strokes, allowing his fingers to linger bravely along my cheek, down my neck.

I shivered in delight. It was a bold step, one that he'd never taken in all the years of our friendship.

"Did you mean it? About the flagpole, about needing . . . wanting . . ."

I looked up into his face and released a brilliant smile. "Every word."

His arms came around me then, folding me into the warmth of his embrace and kissing my face, my hair, like a long-lost gem. That wonderful sweep of emotions surfaced again from the deep, strengthening and pulsing with each moment until I thought I'd drown. I closed my eyes and he finally gave in to years of hunger, kissing me fully on the lips that had spoken so many things to him, both good and bad. He stroked my loose hair, following the trail of his fingers with eager, warm kisses. Here it was, the sweetly human reflection of the larger, more epic story unfurling in my life. Together they'd both walked me through the hard parts, Gabe and God, patiently waiting for me to realize the true value and the depth of love they had for me, waiting for me to stop chasing all the other things and come home to them.

The deep-seated desire in all of us for authentic love is a miracle. Not because of the bliss of a fulfilled ending, but because of the relentless pursuit it awakens in us — and the treasure we eventually find if we search long enough.

I found it, Maisie. Thanks to you.

Now years after the dear woman's death, I find she's not truly dead. Her body has left us, to be sure, but her words linger well after her voice lay silent. They echoed across Golda's heart and now mine, a legacy and a gift. Because that's what words do, when you choose ones with eternal impact. They are remembered, repeated, embraced. They burrow deep and remain, outliving short human lives and becoming a legacy.

"I don't know how we'll do this." Gabe spoke into my hair.

I giggled. "We'll manage." When you have real gold, you hold on to it.

"Would it be possible — well, someday might we — that is, if you would — I was hoping you'd consider —"

"Finishing your sentence before we're eighty?"

He smiled, looking down, the tension diffusing from his face.

My voice softened. "I'll marry you, Gabe. Yes, I'll marry you. Only, let's do it right here." I looked up at the ruins where Golda had once wished to marry her Peter.

With a shout that startled me, for I'd never heard Gabe shout, he swung me around as his voice echoed down to the waves below. I laughed, throwing my head back. When he set me on my feet, his face was tender. Bright with wonder. "Truly?"

"Most definitely."

My love story took longer than most to

fully show itself, but it was worth it. Worth the wait for my matched soul, worth the journey it took me on toward a deeper, greater, more eternal love than I could have ever imagined.

And I would always be grateful for what I found.

To fall in love with God is the greatest
    romance;
to seek him the greatest adventure;
to find him, the greatest human
    achievement.
                    Saint Augustine of Hippo

DISCUSSION QUESTIONS

1. As the story unfolded, which characters did you believe might be the letter writer or the intended recipient? How did your theories change throughout the novel?
2. Each person who receives the love letter quickly talks themselves into believing it's actually for them — partly because they want it to be. Why do you think this is? What deeper things might they be longing for?
3. How did the letter impact each person? How might it have affected you?
4. How would you say Golda's heart disease is symbolic to her character? How does it go deeper than a physical ailment?
5. How is this line from the injured orphan symbolic of Gabe's attitude toward everyone — especially Willa: "Never seen such a fine set of horses. Like someone took a wild animal and . . . and made friends with it. Let it keep being wild"?

6. What surprised you most throughout the plot? Which scene or line resonated with you most as you read?
7. How did the setting — the coast, the house, the horses — play into the story?
8. Do you think Golda truly had her children's best interest at heart when she meddled in their romances? Did her meddling do more good or harm in the end?
9. How has your perception of Gabe changed throughout the novel? Do you think he's a fitting hero for Willa? What do you think their life together looked like?

enerating
ity going
text gets
he finest

y writing
lent and
vers that
n up the
help me
do this
forever
s on my
rleaders.
fans of
ank you!
my heart
ry. I felt
e people
omplete
and the
. These
nd so is
of fans

ratitude
what I
e never

DGMENTS

wouldn't have hap-
ndless creative bril-
it, and feedback of
e partner extraordi-
y her friendship, and
iy books. She helped
apter after frustrating
n't see the big picture
d went back and forth
tangled it. I'm also
for the wisdom and
Arnold, who helped
ry and see clearly the
taken every story I've
irther, and he's taught
a writer. Crystal Cau-
partner, thank you for
pinions, and even the
me always.
of those brilliant minds
t. Whenever I'm stuck,

a simple conversation with him g
all these wild ideas gets my creati
again, and his help throughout the
me thinking and polishing. He's
first reader.

My team at Revell has shaped m
career and my books with much t
artistry. They provide gorgeous co
become the face of each story, clea
plots and polish the prose, then
send it into the world. I couldn'
without them behind me, and I'n
grateful for each person who work
stories. No girl ever had better chee

To the producers, actors, and
Signed, Sealed, and Delivered — th
This show was wonderful food for
as I wrote my own "lost letter" sto
over and over again the passion thes
had for repairing the story of c
strangers through their letters,
importance of the written word
shows are a gold mine of beauty, a
the tight-knit, kindhearted group
who enjoy them.

Mostly, I am overwhelmed with g
to God for reshaping this book fror
originally thought it should be. F
fails to impress and surprise me.

ABOUT THE AUTHOR

Joanna Davidson Politano is the award-winning author of *Lady Jayne Disappears, A Rumored Fortune,* and *Finding Lady Enderly.* She loves tales that capture the colorful, exquisite details in ordinary lives and is eager to hear anyone's story. She lives with her husband and their two kids in a house in the woods near Lake Michigan. You can find her at www.jdpstories.com.

The employees of Thorndike Press hope you have enjoyed this Large Print book. All our Thorndike, Wheeler, and Kennebec Large Print titles are designed for easy reading, and all our books are made to last. Other Thorndike Press Large Print books are available at your library, through selected bookstores, or directly from us.

For information about titles, please call:
(800) 223-1244

or visit our website at:
gale.com/thorndike

To share your comments, please write:
Publisher
Thorndike Press
10 Water St., Suite 310
Waterville, ME 04901